DJ

The Sarnian
Dead in the Water

For complete character guides and photos of locations that feature in the Sarnian series, check out:

www.thesarnian.com

Published by Ovingo Limited in 2016

Designed and typeset by Nik Rawlinson at Ovingo Limited // www.ovingo.com

The author greatly appreciates you taking the time to read this work. Please consider leaving a review wherever you bought the book, or telling your friends or blog readers about The Sarnian.

DAY ONE

St Peter Port, 7.15am

States of Guernsey Police Headquarters

Christine Le Page opened the door with her shoulder. She carried two beakers; the paper packets of sugar and sweeteners were clamped between her teeth.

She placed a beaker before him and let the packets fall from her mouth. Dixon slid back in his chair as they skittered across the table. Did he think they might be infected?

She closed the door with her hip, curled a foot round the leg of her chair and let herself fall on its over-stuffed cushion, which issued a flatulent sigh.

Christine smiled.

Dixon refused to smile back. He held her stare until she uncapped her pen and directed towards him the tiniest shake of her head.

'Now,' she said, looking down. 'Dick-sun, Dick--sun, Dick---sun.'

She opened a folder and took out a form and wrote his name on the top. 'George, yes?'

'Look.' He pulled up his cuff and checked his

watch, ignoring the question. She knew what his name was. He couldn't imagine anyone wouldn't. 'Is this going to take long? I've been here half an hour.'

It wasn't his first time in an interview room, nor his first time sitting across the desk from a plain-clothed officer. The last had been on a soundstage at Pinewood and this, the real thing, hadn't turned out to be nearly so bad as the set dressers seemed to believe.

There was even a window – a small one. They hadn't had that on the set, just clean enough to let through some light and a hint of blue from beyond. The morning looked clear; the mail plane would have got in without problems, the papers unloaded and stacked... He silently cursed for not having come in much later, after some tea and toast and marmalade, thick-cut, with broadsheets fresh from the mainland.

'Age?'

He stared at her, tight-lipped. She raised her eyebrows, assessed the wrinkles, the expanding waistline, the bristle that tufted his nostrils, and ticked the box marked '55–64'. He saw her do it and didn't object.

'Ethnicity?'

'Is this relevant?'

'Just demographics.'

He wondered about her own demographics.

Her hips were wide, her breasts were heavy – like two sandy seal pups trapped beneath a tarpaulin. She'd bounced down the stairs and gripped his hand far too tightly for a woman, let alone one who was clearly five years younger than himself. She shook it, spouted some French-sounding name – DI Le-something-or-other – and taken to calling him George.

'Mr Dixon, if you don't mind.'

'Of course not, Mr Dixon,' she'd said, and so it had begun. Dick-sun, Dick-sun, Dick-SUN. Tock-tock, tick-tock, like a faulty metronome.

'So, your wife...' She turned the page.

'My partner.'

'Partner...' She circled the word on her form. 'Rachel?'

'Richelle. Richelle Ibbott.'

'How are you spelling that, Mr Dick-sun?'

He spelled it out. Both words.

'When did you last see her?'

'Friday night. Five, five thirty.'

'Closer to one than the other?'

He thought for a moment. 'Five. I was leaving for work. She was going to Forest Stores, I'd imagine. We didn't have much food and –'

'You eat separately, Mr Dick-sun?'

'I'm sorry?'

'You were heading for work.'

'Oh, I see. Well, no, I mean... obviously.' He slid

back his seat an inch or two so she could see him more clearly. He cocked his head to one side and widened his eyes. He was waiting for her to recognise him. She was waiting for him to realise she wasn't playing along.

Christine shook her head. 'I'm sorry, I...'

'Dear girl,' he said, smiling as though forgiving some oversight, bringing her into the conspiracy, revealing a secret. He leaned forward and gently took her hand, the pen now protruding from both of their curled fists. 'I'm George Dixon.'

'So you said.' She extracted her hand and tapped the pen on the top of the form. 'But you haven't told me what you –'

'I'm the skipper...' He paused, giving her time to make the connection. 'In The Fleet?'

'Forgive me, Mr Dick-sun.' She licked the end of her pen and turned her attention back to the form. 'Fisshrrmann,' she drawled as she wrote it down. 'Night fishing?'

Dixon sighed.

'Only, if you were heading down to your boat at five,' she continued, 'I presume you'd have been casting off shortly before the tide –'

He shook his head, and Christine noticed how his hair lifted slightly, revealing itself as an otherwise convincing wig. 'I'm an actor. A radio actor.' Each time he said it he stressed the 'ac' and left the closing 'tor' to float free. 'Surely you know The Fleet?'

She shook her head - a non-verbal lie. She knew very well what it was; her husband tuned in every night. But she also knew from years of taking statements that leading the witness would get her nowhere. If there were inconsistencies to uncover, the only way to expose them would be to let Dixon talk himself into a corner.

'Heavens to blazes,' he said, not quite under his breath. 'What kind of a cultural wasteland do you inhabit on this godforsaken island?' He picked up a sachet of sweetener and threw it down in disgust. The single tablet was too light to fall with any great force, and instead its oversized packet drifted down on a gentle arc that entirely spoiled the effect.

'Oh come, now, Mr Dick-sun, I listen to –'

'Music?'

'And the news. The weather, of course, and the airport arrivals, and on Thursday...'

'The Fleet, as it's clear you lack the slightest idea, is a long-running, award-winning –'

'Soap?'

'A continuing radio drama.' He stressed the words in such a way that it almost seemed a waste not to have held up his fingers and drawn out speech marks either side of his head. 'It's testament to the effort the BBC puts into regional programming at the expense of –'

'Ah.' Christine clapped her hand on the table. 'A local drama.'

'It has won an award.' Dixon was struggling to keep himself calm.

'Yes.' Christine drew out the word and tapped her teeth with the end of her pen. She stared at him for thirty seconds to press home the point that his growing excitement would have no effect on the way she conducted the interview. 'I'm sorry,' she said at last. 'I might be missing something, but I can't see what this... Award... has to do with the disappearance of your wife.'

'Nothing,' Dixon snapped. 'Nothing at all, except that the last time I saw my partner - not my wife, my partner - was Friday night.'

'When you left for work.'

'When I left for work.'

'On the boat?'

'No.' At last, she'd provoked him to snap at her.

'Where do you work, Mr Dick-sun?'

'The BBC.'

'Which is where?'

He slid back down in his seat. 'Is there someone else I could speak to?'

Christine looked at her watch. 'DCI Pawsey should be in around nine. I can get you some more coffee if you want to wait...'

'I don't drink coffee.'

'You should have said.'

'I did.' He pursed his lips and blinked, very slowly. 'Now, if you don't mind, I shall be signing books in Town this morning. If you happen to find my partner, would you be good enough to let me know?'

'We certainly shall, Mr Dick-sun.'

'Perhaps this would help.' He reached into his pocket and took out a small, creased photograph. 'She can't have gone far. Now if you'll excuse me...' He stood, allowing the chair to scrape on the floor, expecting Christine to look up. She didn't. Instead, she reached across the table and picked up the picture. Dixon shook his head.

'If you wouldn't mind.' She tapped the form with the nib of her pen. 'Your signature, please. Just here.'

He took the pen and bent down to sign, planting his scrawl beside her own: Christine Le Page. He tossed down the pen and headed for the door.

'Before you go, Mr Dick-sun...'

He stood, with the handle cupped in his palm.

'Why did you leave it so long to report your wife's disappearance?'

'This is a small island, Miss Le Page.' He spoke each word slowly, splitting them up carefully.

'My partner can hardly have gone very far, can she.'

At last Christine met his eyes, and she smiled. 'We can but hope, Mr Dick-sun. We can but hope.'

Marble Bay, 8.15am

When Oliver Carey replayed the moment later that day in the newsroom, it was always the ring he saw first. A small clear stone set in a thin band of gold, just enough to catch the light as it gently softened the bay. What he'd read as a pebble or rock - or a twist of rope washed up by the tide - was an outstretched hand on a slender white arm, thrown wide on the pebbly sand.

He swam there three times a week, and this was the first time he'd ever had to share the bay with anyone else. That was why he swam there.

He could have swum in Town, up on the hill at Beau Sejour, or outside by the castle at La Vallette, but in both of those places he'd have to wear shorts, and he father wouldn't have liked that.

So instead, he'd ride across the island, from his boat to the car park at Jerbourg Point, and he'd run along the soft bed of needles as far as the steps to the bay. If he was on the late shift, he'd turn there and clamber down them, stripping off at the bottom and cooling himself in the sea.

It was still three days until May when he found her. Still a little too cool for comfort. He'd been swimming around the rock, then turned on his back and lay with his arms outstretched, naked but for the salty tracks that the trickling water sketched on his chest.

He wasn't afraid he'd be seen - not down there. Walkers were rare at that time of day, and most would be focused on keeping their dogs on the track. Few would come down, and even those that looked out to the sea would find their eyes caught by the ferry en route from the mainland, or maybe the cut of the crumbling cliff as it turned the corner and carried the path to Fermain.

So he'd tipped back his head and blown through his nose to stop the sea from flooding his nostrils - and then, swinging his hips, he'd thrown his legs over himself and turned a full circle. He'd swept through the waves, brushing the sand with the tip of his nose and planting his feet on the bed.

Only then did he open his eyes, and that's when he'd seen that he wasn't alone.

That's when he'd seen the hand.

He sank to his knees and crabbed to the

right to find a more favourable viewpoint, then lifted his feet and trod water while scanning the beach for a story.

There were no signs of life: no empty bottles or tins, no black ring of a long-spent fire or hint of an overnight party. He supposed that the arm might have belonged to a tourist, but why would she be here alone? She couldn't have slipped from a liner anchored in sight of Town. A missing passenger would have been noticed; the police would have sent a release to each of the papers and radio stations. The newsroom would have received a copy, yet it hadn't come up at the daily conference at which the contents of each day's paper were settled.

She didn't seem to be moving.

He kicked out his feet and swam to the beach. His mind was made up: he'd leave her to sleep off the drink, but first he'd gather his clothes and his phone and take a quick picture. There was always the chance that she wasn't a tourist, but someone of note on the island.

Detective Chief Inspector Marc Renouf settled the phone on its cradle. He looked at the desolate office. The early shift was heading home, the day shift was just coming on. The office was empty except for himself and his newest recruit, a transfer from Jersey who'd just settled down at her desk: middle-aged, read-headed, Christine Le Page. She was reading a handwritten form and warming her hand on a half-drunk beaker of coffee.

He gathered his thoughts for a moment, then stood up and walked across.

'Sir.' She nodded without looking up.

He knelt on the floor and rested his arms on the edge of her desk. He read the form sideways on: a witness statement signed by George Dixon.

'I've just had a rather unusual call.'

'Unusual?' She put down the form and looked at him. They were about the same age: he perhaps a few years younger, with lightly receding hair and a stomach that pulled at his shirt when he squatted like that.

'Said he was a journalist,' Renouf said. 'Guy by the name of Carey. Oliver Carey. Claims he works for The Sarnian. Ring any bells?'

'Not really. We used to get it in Jersey, but I can't say I read it. Too much of a Guernsey bias.'

Renouf chuckled.

'Guernsey Police does have a press office?' Le Page asked.

'Ah, no. Well, yes, but he wasn't chasing a story,' Renouf corrected her. 'He had something for me. Us.'

Christine Le Page raised her eyebrows. 'A no-notice chance to be quoted? No time to come up with a tactful statement.'

'Not at all.'

'Because it's entirely self-serving, you know.' Christine distrusted the press. She tried to steer whenever she could, and knew that the option to comment was almost always a losing hand. If you played along, you were quoted on the paper's own terms. If you declined, they ran the story anyway.

'It's a bit more important than that. Maybe. He says he's found a body.'

'A dead body?'

'Is there any other kind?'

'Where?' She set down her beaker - the one she'd brought through from the interview room, having poured Dixon's drink down the sink.

'Marble Bay.'

Christine shook her head. 'You'll have to forgive me -'

'East coast. A mile or so south of Fermain. I thought you might like to accompany me?'

'Now?'

'The tide's turning, so unless you want to get your feet wet...'

She tidied the statement into a drawer and locked it, tucking the keys in her pocket. 'Two minutes. I'll get my coat.'

Renouf reached across for her desk phone and then, pulling his mobile out of his pocket, he looked up the number for Charlie Dubois, the island's forensics officer.

Oliver Carey stepped over the splatter of vomit, the passage of which still burned in his throat. He picked up the rest of his clothes and pulled on his shirt. In the time it had taken to call the police and empty his stomach onto the beach, the gentle breeze had more or less dried him off. His shorts were clammy but his shirt, which he'd anchored beneath a small rock as he swam, was still wet with sweat, and he shivered as he pulled it over his arms and his chest.

He climbed the steps to the line of the trees and sat on a carved granite block that marked the way to the bay. He looked out to sea and tried to ignore the body.

8.52am

Marc Renouf stood back from the corpse, a handkerchief pressed to his nose and mouth. 'Richelle Ibbott,' he said in a muffled voice, confirming what they'd read on the cards in her purse. 'Friend of my wife.'

'George Dixon's partner?' Christine asked.

'You know her?'

She shook her head. 'No, but Dixon came in this morning. Reported her missing.'

'Now there's a thing.' Renouf scanned the cliff for walkers. He'd posted Constable Falla at the point where the track led down to the bay, but the path was a tortuous route, twisting around the headland, and he knew that without more time and more help someone would happen upon them sooner or later. He was grateful, for once, that the second way down to the bay was roped off, awaiting repairs.

'You know he's an incomer.' Renouf said absentmindedly, still thinking of Dixon.

'Yes,' said Christine. 'Though Lord knows why. Do you know what he calls this place?'

Renouf pursed his lips.

'Godforsaken,' she said.

'Does he now? Does he indeed?' He shaded his eyes as he peered at the point where the path showed itself through the trees, high on the steep ochre slopes that hugged the back of the bay. In the summer they'd be thick with wild flowers, the trees to their right weighed down by damson and sloe. But not this morning. The trees were just budding, the leaves still small and light, and not yet dense enough to properly shield the bay.

On the cliffs that faced them, to Renouf's left and behind Le Page, was the fringe of the pine forest that sheltered the path as it curved to the south. The branches on those trees started too high to offer any protection, whatever the time of year.

It wasn't the most attractive beach Christine had seen in her short time on the island. She could see why Renouf had described it as one of Guernsey's less visited spots. To get there from any direction required a long and uneven walk. There was no close parking, no kiosk or toilets, and not that much sand when you discounted the pebbles and rocks. The water was clear, though, and she could see why Oliver Carey would choose to swim there. To the back of the bay lay a series of caves, and she made a mental note to explore them before she returned to Jersey.

'Do you know Dixon yourself?' she asked, turning back to face Renouf.

He shook his head. 'Barely. My wife introduced us once. Struck me as rather naive on the whole. Not the sharpest tool, but a fairly high self regard, from what I could tell.'

'And a low one of everyone else.' She paused. 'It didn't take much to convince him my senses were on sabbatical.'

Renouf raised his eyebrows. 'To any avail?'

'None. No slips, nothing to say, no explanation for why he'd left it so long to report her missing.'

'How long?'

'Four days.'

Renouf curled his top lip. 'Perhaps she had a habit of wandering off,' he said, apparently unconcerned. 'Did you ask if she'd ever disappeared before?'

'Don't tell me you'd have left it that long,' Christine said.

Renouf was about to reply when someone stepped onto the stones behind them. They turned to see Charlie Dubois jump from the final step. 'Charlie,' Renouf called out, waving a hand at the forensics officer. 'What's the verdict?'

Dubois had already seen the body. Renouf's call had caught him in his car, and he'd diverted down to meet them, parking at Jerbourg and walking the coast path to the bay. Renouf and Christine had passed him on their way down the steps as he jogged back up in search of a better signal on his phone.

He shook his head and handed some tape to Constable Falla, who'd trailed down the steps behind him. He pointed at two large rocks either side of the steps and told him to tie it between them, then started to walk towards Renouf and Le Page.

'There's no sign of trauma. Nothing conspicuous, anyway,' Charlie called as he stumbled over the pebbles towards them. 'No obvious weapon.'

Renouf took the cloth from his nose. 'Can you

tell how long she's been dead?'

Charlie had reached them now, and he dropped his bag on the pebbles. 'Not right away,' he said, inhaling the sour aroma as though it might deliver an answer. 'Two or three days, I'd say. Not much more. Four at the most.'

'She's been here since Friday?' Christine asked.

'Maybe,' Charlie said. 'Looks that way, anyway. There was a high tide that night, would have pushed her this far up the beach. If she was killed any later she'd still be a couple of metres down there at the most.' He pointed towards the shore and away from the line of pebbles and seaweed on which she'd come to rest. 'I'll need to get her back to the lab before I can say for sure, though. How many bodies can you spare?'

'Four, five.' Renouf ignored his poor choice of words.

Charlie ran his hand through his hair. 'Could you stretch to ten?' he asked, tugging back his blond fringe to reveal a fine line of untanned skin where the roots met his scalp. His hair was thick and curly, and far too long for someone of his position. He had about him the air of a man who spent much of his life on the beach, surfing from Vazon when time and tides allowed.

'Well, if you ignore the nine-fifteen ferry, the farmer's market at Castel,' said Renouf, 'the cliff walk to Pleinmont, two follow-ups at St Sampson, one officer on leave, another sick…'

'And I've got a tide heading inshore and two acres of beach to comb before it disappears.'

'I can give you seven. Absolute tops, but I'd need Falla back at base by two. And Clarke by noon – I need him to call in a media briefing.'

'I'll stay,' Christine said. 'That would make eight.'

'No,' Renouf cut in before Charlie could commandeer her. 'You can find our friend Dixon and tell him the news. I'll let you decide how best to approach him.'

The Sarnian, St Peter Port, 9.34am

Ollie ran back up the hill. He'd given his name and number to Christine Le Page – gave her his card, too, to make sure she knew who he was – and Renouf had told him to stay by the phone.

'We'll call you later,' Christine said.

'And in the meantime,' Renouf chipped in, 'be discreet, eh?'

At least he hadn't asked him not to talk or write at all. Discretion was subjective – Renouf knew that just as well as Ollie did – and he knew, too, that trying to forbid a write up would spoon-feed The Sarnian an even tastier story. Freya Carlisle would relish the chance to spin it into a tale of state censorship with a side of inferred corruption.

Ollie promised he'd do all he could, knowing full well that was nothing, and then sprinted away from the bay, along the cliff path and up the uneven steps to the car park. He kept his head down, the sweat dripping from the end of his nose and spotting each tread as he climbed. Eighty, seventy, sixty steps to go. Herm rose up behind him, then Sark came into view, and across the horizon the faint grey strip of Jersey appeared through the haze. Forty, thirty, twenty, ten. At last he reached his bike. He unchained it and threw himself over the saddle, then kicked away and up the hill towards Town. By the time he crested the Val des Terres and could cruise the rest of the way, his legs were shaking, his thighs were burning and his calves felt as though they might split.

He cruised down the hill and through the front door of the Sarnian office, braking just short of an open lift door. He wheeled the bike inside, then looked at himself in the mirrored walls as it climbed the three floors to the newsroom.

His shirt was wet through, and it clung to his back like a stranded barnacle sticks to the rocks at low tide. His hair was crispy with salt - the same salt he could taste on his lips and which dusted the hair on his arms. He looked directly into his own eyes and murmured the first few lines of his story. Freya wouldn't give him long to explain himself.

I was down on the beach and...

I was running, and went down to...

Do you know the beach at Marble Bay? Well, I was down there this morning when...

I've got a story...

Too soon, the lift slowed and stopped, its doors opened on the busy newsroom floor and he looked straight ahead at the clear glass box that sectioned off Freya Carlisle from the rest of the open plan office.

The queen bee was holding court in her hive.

She wasn't alone.

He walked to his desk and leaned his bike against it, then knocked on the glass. She called him in with a curl of her finger.

'This had better be good.'

She was sitting at a round wooden table with three other drones from research, sales and marketing.

'Body on the beach,' he said, catching his breath. 'Dead.' So much for planning his story.

He gripped the glass door for support.

'You, you and you.' Freya pointed across the table. 'We'll finish this later.' She turned to Ollie.

'Sit.'

He slipped into one of the seats as the admin people stood to gather their papers. Freya said nothing until they'd left the room.

'Where?' she asked as they closed the door behind them.

'Marble Bay,' Ollie said, regaining control of his breathing.

Freya stood up and walked to the cooler behind her desk. She poured him a beaker of water. 'Start from the beginning,' she said, passing it over.

Ollie drank half of it down, then sketched out the details from the moment he'd spotted the ring to the point he'd handed his card to Christine. The longer he talked, the more Freya's face seemed to harden. When he came to the end of the story she lifted her eyebrows and opened her hands, inviting him to continue.

'Who was she?' she said after a few silent seconds.

Ollie pinched his lip. He didn't know.

'Cause of death?' she asked. 'Quotes...?'

He shook his head, and Freya slowly closed and then opened her eyes. 'Never, ever leave the scene of a crime until you've got the full story.' Her voice was quiet and calm, and all the more threatening for it. Ollie wished he had bypassed her office and taken the story to Alfie instead, not the paper's overall editor, but his own line manager, and editor of the news pages.

'Technically, we don't know if it was a crime,' he said, feeling the ground slipping away, dragging behind it an urgent need for an explanation. 'It looked to me like an accident.'

'And technically,' she mimicked, 'I decide what's a crime on this paper and where I'm concerned it's always a crime unless and until I'm proved wrong. Whatever the story.' Her voice rose a little. 'I mean, bloody hell, Carey, how long have you been here?'

'Eighteen months.'

'Eighteen months.' She took a deep breath and calmed herself. 'And what have you learned? Do you want to go back to laying out the sports results?'

He shook his head. He had no interest in sport, but there were reasons more pressing than that for wanting to stay on the news desk. A seat on the news desk meant he could access the files that might answer his questions - the questions that had brought him back to the island two years before.

'That's why I came straight here,' he said.

'More's the pity.'

'I do have these.' Reaching into his pocket, he pulled out his phone and pushed it across the desk.

Freya picked it up and looked at the screen, swiping her finger two or three times. She sat in silence and tipped her head on one side, then, throwing her glasses down on the desk, she fixed her eyes on his own.

'Consider this your reprieve,' she said.

St Peter Port, 9.40am

The queue for a copy of George Dixon's book might only have been five deep, but on a working day, so soon after opening, it hinted at good things to come. Good for his publisher, at least.

He was sitting at a table, close to the front of the bookshop. Someone had draped a white cloth over it and stacked two piles of his overwritten autobiography either side of him. As Christine entered the store, he was signing the flyleaf of one of the books, smiling and laughing with the middle-aged woman who had handed it over.

'I said as much to the Governor,' he said, closing the cover and handing it back with great care, as though it was precious or fragile. 'But would he listen?' He shook his head and shrugged, then caught sight of the red-headed woman who'd interviewed him at the police station. Le Pepe? Le Pope? He couldn't remember.

He snatched his eyes away from her, and fixed

them back on the pensioner. 'You be careful out there,' he said, signalling that their meeting was over. He smiled at the next in the queue.

Christine stepped forward, around the next customer, and leant in close to his ear. 'Mr Dixon,' she said. He noticed she'd dropped the gap from his name.

He looked at her. 'I'm awfully sorry, Mrs...'

'Le Page.'

'Aah, yes. Well, you see, there's a queue, Mrs Le Page. Perhaps you'd like to wait your turn.'

'Mr Dixon, we've found –'

'Queue,' he said, flapping his hand as though she was an ivy bee buzzing about his ears. He twitched his eyebrows at the customer behind her – a tick that passed silent judgement on 'the cheek of this woman, pushing in before you'.

Christine stood up and looked down on him. He must have known why she was there, so why had he not asked the obvious question. Had she been found? Or had they at least had word she was safe? Was he really so wrapped up in his book, in this handful of fans, that their meeting was now so distant, so irrelevant, so removed from his mind?

'Mr Dixon,' she said, louder now, loud enough for the other customers to hear. If he wanted to play it that way, then she would play too. 'We've found –'

Her professional integrity got the better of her. She should manage the flow of information. She should keep it between them - for the moment, at least. 'Very well.' She took a book from the top of the pile and slipped it under her arm. 'If you want to do it that way...'

She joined the back of the queue and read the blurb on the cover. It was trite and improperly punctuated, and had two erroneous apostrophes in the first four lines. It read as though Dixon had put it together himself and she wondered whether the whole production was anything more than a vanity project - something he'd paid for, or maybe talked Richelle into financing for him?

Another two people joined the back of the queue as Dixon gave a forced laugh to the one remaining customer lined up in front of Christine. She would rather not have told him what they'd found with others around them. From the way that he'd dealt with her, though, he'd made it quite clear that the signing was more important to him than anything else at that moment. The chances of getting him to leave - even briefly - were slim to non-existent.

She reached into her bag and pulled out a pen, then flipping open the cover she wrote her own inscription on the flyleaf. She had finally reached the front of the queue, so she slipped the pen back into her bag and stepped forward for her audience with George Dixon.

'Christine Le Page,' he said, taking the book from her. 'I hadn't expected to see you so soon.'

He opened it and read her inscription.

'We've found a body,' it began. He looked up and she nodded. 'Cards and other items suggest it to be your partner. We need you to make a formal identification.'

He paused for a moment, running his fingers up and down the book, pressing the pages flat.

He sniffed, but he didn't cry.

He wasn't one for crying.

He hadn't cried when his mother had died. He'd done his dry-eyed mourning already, five years before, when they'd loaded her into an ambulance. He'd waved her off to a home and that - to him - was the day she had died. Her actual passing, half a decade, four months and eight days later, had been a mere formality.

A tidying up of loose ends.

He was used to the idea by then.

He hadn't cried when his father had died after tripping and falling a length of the stairs at his home. The man had lived a long, indulgent and largely successful life and Dixon could see no reason to mourn it. It had ended without any pain, without the dreaded forewarning of cancer or the awkward lame years that might follow a stroke. He'd cracked his neck and died in an instant, the moment he hit the half landing. Dixon had instructed an agent that same afternoon to put the house on the market, but put him off coming to take the photos until they'd removed the body.

But here he was, in front of his public. Three real readers and Christine Le Page, and Dixon knew he had little choice but to do what they'd all expect. He picked a point in the middle distance, somewhere between the two of them, and shifted his eyes to the left. He fixed them there and let them glaze over, and forced himself to hold them open until they started to water.

The gullible woman read it to be some kind of emotion, resting her hand on his cuff. He pretended her touch had brought him out of his daze, back to the present moment, and turned his dewy eyes back towards her. He pulled a weak smile.

'What would you like me to write?' he asked, clicking out the nib of his pen. 'Is it for you or a gift?'

The Sarnian, 9.45am

Freya Carlisle threw open the door and addressed the newsroom en masse. 'News, lifestyle and local, editorial conference in ten minutes. Sport, you can stay where you are. Art...' – she turned to look at the two-man art team – 'I want you there too. Bin the lead, I don't care what it is, and set yourselves up with a projector, head of the table, with a blank template. Empty your bladders and fill the kettle, people.' She clapped her hands. 'This could take some time.'

She turned and pointed at Ollie. 'You. Get downstairs and shower. Quickly. You're agenda points one to AOB. Don't let me get there before you.'

Ollie ran back to his desk and kicked off his trainers without untying the laces. He kept some smart clothes in a drawer, which rarely saw light unless to attend an unannounced briefing. Either way, they'd have to suffice. He pulled out his trousers and shirt and kicked the drawer closed as his desk phone started to ring.

'Carey,' he said, snatching it up.

'Oliver!' It was a female voice: familiar, but not one he could place right away.

'Speaking.'

'Oliver, Oliver, Oliver Carey.' She tumbled his name as though it were flotsam caught on a tide. 'I hear you're a bit of a hero.'

The voice was sweet. A little sharper than the feminine mean, but the way it was used to sugar his name... he could only assume it was someone he knew.

'Can I help you?' he asked, hoping she might reveal herself.

'I certainly hope so, my dear. Tell me. Who was she?'

Ollie looked up. 'Who is this?' He stood on tiptoe and turned around, trying to work out who might have leaked the story... then he realised nobody had. He and Freya Carlisle were the only two who knew what had happened that morning. Certainly as far as The Sarnian was concerned.

A short, mocking gasp from the furthest end of the line. 'Do you know how that hurts me, Oliver?'

Ollie chose not to reply.

'That you must ask such a question...'

Still he kept quiet.

'Your silence speaks volumes, my darling. You cannot speak. I know. You feel ashamed of yourself. Very well, I shall forgive you. But on one condition.' A pause, no more than a beat, and then: 'I need a quick description. Something personal. I don't care about her clothes or her hair. I want to know about you. What it was like to find her. Human interest.'

'Amy Sloane,' he said, working it out from the way she said 'darling'.

'My love...'

'How naïve do you think I am?'

'Darling, that stings. It hurts me right here.' Ollie could hear her beating her breast. 'I simply couldn't call you naïve. Unsophisticated, perhaps. A touch too trusting. Maybe a little, dare I say it, jejune...? No. I just want some colour, that's all. Everything else, we can negotiate.'

'Wouldn't negotiation rely on you having something to give in return?'

'Oh, but I do.'

'Yes?'

'Contacts, my dear. Lots of lovely contacts, and lots of favours as ripe as a lemon that's ready to fall from the tree. Could be awfully zesty, couldn't they... if we pooled our resources.'

'Amy,' he said, kicking his chair back under his desk. 'What use are your zesty contacts if they weren't there? Whoever gave you this tip-off has left you half informed, or you wouldn't be calling me.'

'Well that's as maybe, my dear, but this reticence of yours would make me suspect that they've tasted no less of the meat than yourself. All you have is your own experience. You are the story, my dear. What you saw, what you felt, how it made you feel. Sick, I hear... The rest of it is just facts. Stats and incontrovertible facts on which, you know as well as I do, there's no such thing as copyright.'

Ollie said nothing.

'Am I right?'

'The answer's no, Amy. No to all you could ask and no to the little you might have to offer.'

'My darling...'

'No. My own employer would be mighty interested in getting this story itself, don't you think? Even if it wasn't, the chances I'd share anything with a gossipy rag mag like yours are slimmer than your dwindling page count.'

'Now Oliver –' Amy Sloane began, business-like this time, but that was as far as she got. Freya Carlisle had stood up from her desk and looked through the glass of the hive. She gave an attention-grabbing cough and caught his eye. Ollie threw down the phone as though it had just burned his fingers.

The Sarnian, 10am
Editorial Conference

They were sitting around the long wooden table. Harry Ozanne - art - had plugged his notebook into a whirring projector. It cast an empty front page on the conference room wall. That morning's lead, a flabby story about a BBC team investigating shipwrecks off Sark, had been swiftly wiped from the page.

Ollie was sitting beside him, Freya Carlisle on the other side, and all eyes were turned towards them as Ollie brought his story to its climax: the arrival of Marc Renouf and his stand-in deputy, Christine Le Page.

'It took about twenty minutes, I'd guess. I'd gone back up and sat on a bench. They said not to let anyone down to the beach, but I didn't see anyone anyhow.'

'Harry, can you get their pictures?' Freya turned to the art editor. 'Check the States Police website.'

Harry minimised the empty front page and clicked on his browser while Ollie went on.

'I don't know whether they believed me or not.'

'Did you show them the photos?' Freya asked.

Ollie shook his head.

'Good,' she said.

'They asked what I did, why I was down there. She took notes while he asked questions. They were a bit... cagey, I guess, when they heard I worked for the paper. Asked if it was the Press, of course, but I said no. They didn't want to ask many questions after that – took my details and sent me away. I think they wanted to get to the beach without me seeing what they were up to.'

'Which was?'

'Not much. He stuck a hankie over his nose and bent down for a closer look. She kept back. I think she was drawing how it was all laid out, but I guess they'd have a photographer on the way. He made some calls. Probably calling for backup. There was only them and some other guy they left on the path blocking the way. Oh, and a blond guy on his mobile a bit further up the hill.'

'Marc Renouf,' Harry said, enlarging a file photo. 'Fifteen years on the force. Made DCI three years ago.'

'That's him,' Ollie said.

'Yes, we know him.' Freya spoke in a way that suggested there had been a story behind their encounter – a rocky one. 'The woman?'

'Still looking,' Harry said. 'Nothing yet.'

Freya nodded. 'See if you can identify this blond guy, too.' She cleared her throat. 'Right then. Who, when, what, how, and most importantly why? Let's start from the top.' She pulled her own laptop towards her and, logging into her account, opened a folder of pictures. 'Mr Carey here showed uncharacteristic initiative this morning...' – she spun the laptop around as the pictures of the bloated grey woman cascaded onto the screen – 'and took these on his mobile phone. The lighting and framing could be better, but they're useable. Just. Harry, these are your front-page assets. Run them full bleed. Strap the headline across them. "BEACH BODY: FOUL PLAY SUSPECTED".'

Harry switched back to his template and started typing the headline, adjusting the text size to fit. His brother, Tony, who worked the lifestyle pages, raised his hand to speak. 'Shouldn't we find out how she died first?'

'Why would we do that?' Freya asked.

'Well, I mean, we don't really know what the police think yet.'

Freya twitched. 'I see no mention of the police.' She nodded towards the screen.

'Foul play suspected,' he quoted back.

'Yes,' said Freya. 'I suspect foul play. I doubt I'd have much trouble convincing half this island the same thing. Ergo, foul play suspected. What I want to know, though, is who she is. Don't you?'

'Yes, but...' Tony trailed off as Freya turned back towards Harry, who was placing the best of the pictures onto the page.

'Go closer on her face,' she told him.

Harry tapped a couple of keys and enlarged the distended face until it filled the projected page. The pictures were better than Ollie had thought, and they showed the gruesome state of a body that had spent some days on the beach. Her blue lips were starting to bloat and there were black marks on her teeth. Her eyes were open and lifeless; a streak of hair from her fringe rested on one of the eyeballs with nothing to blink it away. Her skin was unbroken but had lost its colour, and now looked a yellowing grey.

The gruesome pictures brought back to his nostrils the foetid smell that had caused him to retch on the beach. Two of the others sitting around the table dropped their eyes to the desk.

'Anyone?' Freya asked. 'Nobody?'

Ella Brouard, who worked with Tony on lifestyle and entertainment, pulled herself up to the front of her seat. She put her head on one side and squinted. 'It's hard to make out. She's so bloated, but it looks...'

Freya raised her eyebrows. 'Yes?'

'Does anyone here know Richelle Ibbott?'

The two sets of downcast eyes looked back towards the projection.

'You know, I think you're right,' said Alfie Erne, the paper's news editor, and Ollie's immediate boss. They'd poached him from the Press two days before their own launch. 'I met her last year at the air display. I'm pretty sure she was at the reception that evening on behalf of some charity or other.'

'Good,' said Freya, jotting down Richelle's first and last name, a slash between them, 'charity' in tidy, cursive script, and a question mark. 'Was anyone else at that reception?'

The twelve staff sitting around the table shook their heads in unison.

'Alfie's right, though,' Ella said. 'She does stuff

for Ormers, the orphan charity. They organise trips and pay for essentials. School stuff and sports kit. I'm sure it's her.'

Harry Ozanne had pulled up a browser and tapped in her name. 'Ormer Orphans works to... blah blah... here we go. Co-founders: Richelle Ibbott and some other guy.' He dragged his pointer across the words: 'Patron - George Dixon.'

'Her husband,' Ella explained.

'She's single,' Alfie said.

'Partner, then.'

'Rather incestuous, isn't it?' Freya asked. 'Partners in arms, partners in alms.' She pointed at Alfie. 'I like that. Run that as a cross-head somewhere in the main copy.'

'Actually,' Ollie chipped in, 'I think I know who he is. He's an actor.' He looked around the table at a row of blank faces. 'The Fleet?' There was no sign of recognition. 'Well, he's pretty well known. It's only logical they should want to have someone there who could stand up and speak on their behalf.'

'And why not her partner?' Tony asked. 'I suppose he'd do it for free.'

'George Dixon, actor, sixty-two,' Harry read out. 'Born and raised in Southampton. It looks like he's had a few bit-parts in some soaps but nothing major. Came to Guernsey eight years ago to take the lead in a radio drama called The Fleet...' He nodded across at Ollie. 'Seems his character had some kind of accident a couple of months back. Typical audience bait for the tenth anniversary... yada yada. Want me to go on?'

'I think we've got the gist,' Freya said. 'I'm more interested in this Ibbott woman. Alfie, what do you know about her?'

'Met her a few times. Nice enough sort. Wealthy, I think. No kids, never married, so no one to leave it to, which probably explains the orphans.'

'Could it be a motive, do you think? The money, I mean.'

Alfie shrugged. 'Don't see why not. Depends how much she carried on her, how much jewellery she wore. That kind of thing.'

'She had a ring,' Ollie said. 'That's the first thing I saw when I –'

'Assuming it wasn't an accident,' Ella interrupted.

'I'm sorry?' Freya said.

'Assuming it wasn't an accident. You're still presuming she was murdered – looking for some kind of motive. She could have fallen from the cliff is all I'm saying. Doesn't the fact she was still wearing a ring suggest it was an accident? If she'd been murdered for money, the ring would be gone, too. Wouldn't it?'

'Your objection is noted,' Freya said. 'For the sake of selling some papers, though, let's assume it was something more dramatic. At least until we know any different.'

Ella lifted her eyes to the ceiling and took a deep breath through her nose. Freya clocked her frustration but chose to ignore it.

'So, contacts,' she said, turning her laptop back towards her and pulling up the shared address book. She scrolled through to the Ds and Is, but neither section listed Dixon or Ibbott's numbers. 'Alfie,' she called down the table. 'You seem to know Miss Ibbott better than the rest of us. Find out whatever you can. No – find out all you can. Who she had lunch with, what she ate, what she spent her money on. Talk to her friends and work colleagues. Dig up some long-lost aunt and see if you can get her blubbing. I want quotes and gossip and a motive on my desk by lunch. This one goes to bed at half two.'

Alfie pulled a crooked smile and nodded his assent. He tapped his forehead as though in salute.

'Carey,' Freya said, turning to Ollie. 'You found the body. Now find me Dixon. Better yet, find me a murderer, if they aren't one and the same.' She slapped down the lid of the laptop. 'Class dismissed.'

Rousse Kiosk, 11.20am

Dixon dialled a familiar number. The line was picked up on the second ring.

'Good,' he said. 'You're there. Stay where you are. I'm coming in.'

Kira Spooner looked around the production office to see if she was alone. 'George,' she said, recognising his voice. She turned her back to the room and dropped her voice to a whisper. They had an intern in that day, and she was sitting close enough to Kira's desk that she might easily have heard him leaking out of the earpiece.

'Of course it's me.'

'I don't think that would be a good idea, do you?'

'Why ever not?'

'You know why.'

'But you're my employer, Kira.'

She could almost believe that he knew she was shielding the phone, perhaps from the way she was hissing at him, and so was booming every word for the sake of her discomfort.

'It's working hours,' he said. 'I still have my BBC pass. I should think it's perfectly reasonable.'

'No. No, it's not. Don't you remember the trouble I went to?'

'Personally, no.'

'Don't play games, George.'

She heard him sigh at the other end of the line. 'Fine. Then where do you suggest?'

'Rousse,' she said, and the word had barely left her mouth before she wished she could claw it back.

Of all the kiosks that dotted the coast, Rousse was the one she held dear. Her mother had taken the lease there and had run it for close to two decades, from the year that Kira turned four, to the month she returned from three years on the mainland with an honours degree to her name.

It was fifteen years since she'd handed back the lease, but Kira's childhood memories still centred on that kiosk – its pebble-dashed beach and the narrow granite jetty that tiptoed into the shallows – and she didn't want them sullied by a fractious meeting with Dixon.

He agreed far too quickly and rang off before she could change her mind. She almost called him back. She could refuse to meet him at all, or at least to change the venue – but hadn't his opening gambit been worse?

If she pulled out now, he'd arrive at the studio, pass in hand, making noise... allowing himself to be seen.

People would think he still worked there.

So there they were. It was late morning, still less than two hours after his second talk with Christine Le Page: George Dixon and Kira

Spooner, facing each other with two mugs of tea, Dixon's already half drunk.

Kira had wondered, on taking the helm at The Fleet, whether they'd brought her in to shake things up - behind the scenes, at least, if not on the air. Ratings were up, the reviews were consistently good, but certain elements - that had been Rosalynd's word, not hers - certain elements were proving to be disruptive.

And here was one of those elements: the only one, as far as Kira could see, for she had no trouble with the rest of the cast. George Dixon, with his plucked eyebrows and false hair and a corset under his shirt that he thought nobody knew about. She was pretty sure it was George's behaviour that had forced Rosalynd Holdbrook into early retirement ten years after she'd devised The Fleet.

It had taken her less than half an hour to get from the studios north of Town to the kiosk she knew so well. Yet there he was already, grinding the stub of a cigarette into the grain of the table.

And why - of all the tables - why had he chosen that one?

To give him his due, he couldn't have sat any further away from the kiosk, but hadn't he noticed the wind? It was coming across from St Sampson that morning, and Kira knew far too well from summers spent working behind the counter that even the lightest of breezes would carry hushed words as far as the kiosk.

The whispered accusations she'd overheard each June and July of her teens would have filled The Sarnian's lifestyle pages week after week after week. And now here she was, and so was he, and she cringed as he outlined his simple demand and leaned back to await her response.

'You want what?' She wasn't sure that she'd heard him right - or if she had, that she'd quite understood what he'd said. The words were English, the sentences perfect, but the request...

'A raise,' George repeated, the way that someone might ask to borrow a book.

'More money?'

'Mmm-hmmm,' he nodded. 'My circumstances have... changed, so I need to review our arrangement.'

'Our arrangement?' She leaned closer and dropped her voice to a loud whisper. 'George, who do you think is in charge here?'

'You tell me, Kira,' he said, making no effort to match her muted tone. 'I rather thought we'd agreed that your nudging and budging of the schedules was to our mutual benefit.'

'Well, yes, George, but you can't just demand a raise. I have a budget. A very small budget.'

'Stretch it.'

'How would it seem if I... I don't even know how I'd do it, but to find some way to pay you more in light of what's happened to your character...'

Dixon shrugged. 'You edit the scripts. You're the creative force. Think of something.'

'Can you imagine what questions might be asked? It could – no, would – it would put all we've done at risk.'

'Call it compensation, then.'

'I can't, George. It can't be done.'

Dixon sat back and pulled a packet of cigarettes out of his jacket pocket. 'Now that's a shame,' he said, flipping open the lid. 'Because I've been doing some thinking. I have an awful lot of time for that these days. You not needing me in, and all.' He paused while he tapped out two cigarettes, letting the implication sink in. He tucked one behind his ear and pinched the second between his lips. 'An awful lot more time, which is why it occurred to me that one of us...' – he pointed across the table – 'one of us has far more to lose than the other.' He lit the cigarette. 'However mutually beneficial our arrangement might be.'

Kira narrowed her eyes. 'What are you saying?'

'Nothing much,' he shrugged. 'Only, what's in it for me, really?'

'Don't you dare, George. Don't you dare go back on our agreement.'

'Why not? What would happen to me if the truth came out? And what might happen to you?'

'You'd lose –'

'My stipend? Because that's all it is.'

'Your respect.'

He laughed. 'I lost that two months ago when you threw Thomas Thoumine into Little Russell and left him mentally crippled.'

'It's fiction, George. Do you really think people believe you're one and the same? Thomas Thoumine isn't real. Thomas Thoumine is a character.'

'That's right, Kira. My character, my life on this island,' he hissed. 'My public face.'

'Oh, grow up, George.' She turned and saw the new kiosk tenant watching them.

George took a long drag from his cigarette and exhaled as slowly as he could. 'Do you know what I discovered this morning?' he asked, flicking ash towards her.

'Your lack of integrity?'

'Richelle,' Dixon said. 'She's dead. I haven't seen her since Friday night.' He held out his cigarette and examined the glowing end. He reached towards it and plucked at the air, as though whipping away a hair from the ash that only he could see. 'They found her body this morning.'

'George,' she stammered. She felt her breath catch. Was it trite to tell him she was sorry? To ask if there was anything she could do. 'That's –'

'Laid out on the beach,' he interrupted. 'Like she was sunbathing.'

'How did she...'

'Die?' He shrugged. 'I suppose they'll find out soon enough.'

He waited for a moment, watching her. It was clear that she didn't know how to reply. He enjoyed her discomfort.

'So you see,' he said at length. 'I'd rather not have been compelled to tell you this, but my circumstances are somewhat refocused. Until her estate is settled my resources might be rather restricted, and you know how long probate can take.'

Kira looked at him, raising her eyebrows. 'That's rather presumptive, don't you think?'

'What?'

'Assuming you'll get anything.'

He shook his head. 'Not really.' He dragged on the cigarette.

'You've read her will?'

'She gave it to me for safekeeping.'

Now it was Kira who shook her head, slowly this time, with a look of disgust on her face.

'So if you could stretch your budget just... Well...' Dixon thought for a moment. 'Shall we say a couple of hundred a week?'

'A couple of hundred? Is that all she was worth to you? Two hundred pounds?'

'Oh, no,' he said, leaning across the table. 'Not at all, Kira. But I'm not the one who's fretting about the BBC budget, am I? I'm not the one who can't afford to make proper reparations.'

'I'm sorry?'

'Reparations, Kira. If it wasn't for you, we wouldn't be here, would we?'

'If it wasn't for me?' she said, loudly enough to be heard. She looked across at the kiosk hatch and saw the tenant duck down below the counter. They used to keep the condiments there and Kira knew quite well that though he was out of sight he would still be able to hear them clearly unless they quietened down.

'Well, as you say, you did spend all those weeks nudging my hours,' Dixon said. 'Isn't that what you called it? – so no one suspected? And all the while I did...' He paused, as though he was thinking, trying to recall what it was he had done. 'Ah, yes. Nothing. Nothing but make your life that little bit easier. So don't talk to me about who has the most to lose, because I assure you, it's you.'

Kira stood up. She didn't care now whether

the tenant could hear them. The revulsion she felt for Dixon was stronger than any desire for privacy. She almost wanted to make a spectacle - to draw attention to him, let everyone see him for what he was: heartless, cold, entirely self-serving.

And right.

She had more to lose than he did. Had he not lost all he could already? There was nothing more she could take from him without losing far more herself.

She picked up the tea she had still barely touched.

'You make me sick,' she said. 'You disgust me.'

She plucked the cigarette from his lips and set it afloat in the tepid drink, then tossed it into his face. She took the mug back to the counter and marched to her car without turning.

She was angry with Dixon and angry, too, with herself, and she wondered whether she'd ever be able to take herself back to Rousse kiosk.

Route de Jerbourg, above Marble Bay, 11.45am

Ollie took his bike back down in the lift, then headed south-west out of Town, back through the trees on the Val des Terres. Uphill, this time.

Ella Brouard had dug out Richelle's address, which the map in the newsroom put on the cliffs above Marble Bay. If the body was hers, as seemed increasingly likely, heading straight there would give him the best chance of finding George Dixon alone.

His calves were starting to burn with the effort of cresting the steep, wooded hill, but all around him the world felt alive and renewed. The sun was shining, summer was on the horizon. It meant Town would be buzzing with visitors, of course, but even this gave him a curious pleasure, for while they would head home – eventually – it reminded him that he was home already, after more than five years on the mainland.

Were they wasted years? He'd prefer to think not, but in truth it was too soon to say. He couldn't rule out heading back there for a while, perhaps to finish his course, perhaps to pick up where things had left off with Kirsty – if she'd have him back.

When that might be, he couldn't say, but one thing he knew for sure: he wouldn't be leaving before he'd applied Freya's five questions to his father's unexplained fate: who, when, what, how, and most importantly, why.

He passed by the end of the road to Fermain and took the next turn on the left. The Ibbott house was halfway down, just set back from the kerb – exactly as Ella had said. The end of a run of terraces, settled among the trees, the small granite home was attached to the dwelling next door, the boundary between them marked out by a neat row of crocus.

The curtains were closed, and although the front door was half glass it was etched with a pattern of gerberas that stopped him seeing through. He put up his hands to shade his eyes and pressed his nose against it, and inside he made out an open door, and somewhere beyond it a table. An open staircase led to the upper floor. There was no sign of movement, no shape of a body passing through, so he propped his bike against the porch and stepped back to look at the upstairs windows.

'There's nobody home.'

Ollie spun round as though he'd been caught doing wrong, and saw a man standing there, watching. Dixon's neighbour, apparently. Mid-seventies, portly, a stomach. Ollie clapped his hand to his own chest, as though calming his heart from the shock. 'Do you know when they might be back?' he asked.

'Give it to me if you want.'

'I'm sorry?'

The man nodded towards Ollie's messenger bag. 'The parcel. I'll make sure they get it.'

Ollie smiled. 'Oliver Carey,' he said, retrieving a card from his wallet and holding it out for the man to take. 'Do they often go out at this time?'

The man narrowed his eyes. 'Now why might that be of interest to you?'

Ollie nodded towards his card, but the man ignored it. Ollie put it back in his pocket.

'I couldn't rightly say,' the man said. 'Sometimes it's quiet at this time of day, but whether that means they're out...' He shrugged.

'They make a lot of noise, do they? Other times?'

The man stared at him, and Ollie looked back at the house. 'We don't all live in granite houses is all, Mr...?' The man didn't tell him his name. 'To hear them through those walls they must be making –'

'You ask an awful lot of questions,' the man interrupted.

'It goes with the job, I'm afraid. I work for the paper.' Ollie retrieved his card and held it out again. He'd learned not to mention The Sarnian by name. 'I was hoping I might find...' He paused, and changing his mind at the last moment he said, 'Miss Ibbott.'

He watched the man as he said her name, hoping to see a twitch or a flinch. There was nothing. No dilating pupils – the outward expression that Ollie had learned was almost impossible to suppress at will. No intake of breath or uncomfortable swallow – just a passive, impartial, unflinching appraisal without a hint that he might have had something to hide.

Finally the man took the card, and casting an eye across it he promised to pass it on.

'Could I take your name?' Ollie asked.

'Ray.'

'Ray...?'

'Just Ray.'

'And quote you?'

Ray shook his head. 'I think not,' he said, nodding towards the card. 'I read the Press, you see. Have done all my life.'

He tucked the card into his pocket. Then, nodding goodbye and lifting his foot from the wall, he turned around and strode towards a rough bush that Ollie now saw was half pruned at the base. He bent down to pick up his secateurs and was hidden once more from the road. That, at least, explained how Ollie had missed him.

Ollie looked at his watch. It was close to noon, but he felt as if he'd already worked a full day. He took a reporter's pad from his bag, tore out a page and wrote a note, asking Dixon to call him. Pushing it through the letterbox, he picked up his bike and cycled some way down the road. When he was sure he was out of earshot, he pulled out his phone and called Simon.

BBC Radio Guernsey, 11.57am

Simon Langlois was almost relieved when his desk phone sprang to life. He quickly agreed to meet for an early lunch.

'I'm working on this Pleinmont path story,' he said. 'Dull as Hull. Can we meet at the Puffin and then I can head straight up?'

'Are you bringing a minder?'

'Are you my mother?'

'You know what I mean. It's a cliff. It's high.'

Simon sighed. 'And I'm not totally blind. Not yet.'

'Listen,' Ollie said, changing the subject. 'I'm down by Marble Bay. I've got my bike. When can you get there?'

Simon flipped open the face of his watch and felt the position of the hands. 'Twelve now... There's a bus in five minutes. Be with you by half past?'

'Perfect,' Ollie told him. 'I'll buy you a sandwich.'

Portelet Harbour, 12.30pm

Ollie rang off and rode west, on a route that took him past hedgerows and fields that all but obscured the sea. He turned at the airport and rode through the lower parishes, past the round tower of Torteval church to the bend at Pleinmont that pitched him back down to the coast. The hill there was steep and fast, and he hunkered down on the handlebars, using his weight to throw the bike around the chicanes that took him right down to the bay.

The tide was still out, but about to turn and Ollie imagined Charlie Dubois at the opposite end of the island, focusing meagre resources on fingertip-searching the pebbles downstream of the corpse. He'd have used up half of his time by now, and soon he'd be wanting to pick up the body and move it. Ollie gave an involuntary shiver and put the image out of his mind, then pulled on the brakes and paused at the wall that marked the western coast of the island. The beach opened up before him: acres of sand, empty but for two riders walking their horses down to the water to paddle about in the shallows.

The lazy sweep of Rocquaine Bay carried his view to Fort Grey - the Cup and Saucer, the locals called it, in a nod to the barrel-like keep and the circular wall running round it. To the left it curled back on itself, taking the road to Portelet and the small granite harbour that Ollie called home. His boat was moored there, just as it had been before he'd returned to the island and the Huffin' Puffin had still belonged to his father.

For as long as Ollie could remember, Remus Carey had spent his summers running visitors about in that boat. Private rides to the outlying islands, or fishing trips for keen anglers, until... who knew? His disappearance, the hole in the side of the boat, and the questions, so many questions, that had brought Ollie back in search of some answers...

The story of Remus Carey remained an unsolved mystery, but Ollie had sworn to himself - and promised his mother, Odette - that with some digging, and access to The Sarnian's shared resources, he'd find out what had happened.

He wheeled his bike to the kiosk and into the garden behind it, and as he gave his order he heard a bus pull up at the stop. He put his head round the corner to watch it disgorge its passengers.

A couple of tourists bundled their kids out before them, and then came the tip of the stick. Tap-tap. Tap-tap. Twice on the edge of each step, then the kerb and the grass, and then Simon appeared, hopping off the bottom step and slapping the side of the bus to thank the driver for waiting.

Ollie knew that Simon wouldn't be able to see him - not from that distance with his marble-white eyes - but he stepped back nonetheless, behind the shelves of buckets and beach toys, and leaned on the counter, pretending not to have noticed the bus or his friend's unsteady approach.

He handed over his money as Simon rounded the corner, then pressed the sandwiches into his free hand and gripped his shoulder. 'You carry these,' he said. 'I'll take your tea.'

Simon hooked the stick in the crook of his arm and they carried their lunch down the slipway. The distant tide had left the harbour dry and the Huffin' Puffin was perched on the stilts of its triple-keeled hull, two stout engines exposed to the elements. It looked for all the world as though it was craning to see beyond the harbour wall. Sampson, Remus Carey's adopted cat, watched them approach and gave a short 'pripp' of welcome as Ollie helped Simon onto the deck. Sampson could smell the crab in their sandwiches and tangled himself about their feet until they sat down on the tarred felt roof of the wheelhouse.

They made some small talk while Simon ate half of his sandwich and waited for Ollie to tell him why he had wanted to meet.

'Nice though this is...' he said at last when nothing seemed forthcoming.

'What's it all about?'

Simon made an affirmative sound, biting into the corner of his second half sandwich.

Ollie took a sip of his tea, and wondered whether Simon knew already what he'd found that morning. Amy Sloane had heard the news soon enough - almost before he'd managed to get it back to the office himself. Might it by now have been general knowledge throughout the island's media?

'Marble Bay,' he said.

'What of it?'

Simon clearly knew nothing.

Ollie took a second sip of tea and put down the cardboard cup. 'I know this cliff path story isn't exactly your thing...'

Simon rolled his eyes.

'...and I know you'd jump on this if you got the chance.' Ollie paused. 'But you have to promise me - absolutely promise - that it goes no further.'

'Is this an actual story, or just an idea?' Simon asked.

'Actual story.'

'Ollie, you know you can -'

Ollie put up his hand. 'Yes. I know. I trust you. That's why I'm telling you. But this is a big one. The biggest, and I'm not the news hound, you are. I know you'd kill for a story like this so it's probably wasted on me, but even so -'

Simon swallowed, and touched Ollie's knee. 'I promise. It's your story. Just - if it's as big as you say, at least give me a head start. Let me go second, before everyone else.'

Ollie looked at him for a moment, as though gauging what his promise was worth. The two of them were as close as brothers. They could sit on the wheelhouse for hours, barely saying a word, each of them lost in the beauty around them. For Ollie, it was all in the gentle rock of the waves as they played with the float of the boat, their white, gambolling crests, the spray on the headland at Lihou, or the playful wink of the sun on the wet, weedy rocks at the edge of the bay. For Simon, the soft hollow beat of the hull on the wall; the tin-tin-tink of close rigging, strummed by the wind on a tall metal mast; or the sound of his friend, Oliver Carey, shifting beside him, moving his feet or twitching his legs on the felt.

Six inches out from the end of his nose, Simon's world was a blur that did little more than hint at the visual beauty around him. Ollie had tried to work out how far he could see. He supposed it might stretch as far as the green of the verge as he stepped off the bus, but certainly not to the shifting seam where the sand met the sea at low tide.

Ollie took out his phone, unlocked it and

scrolled through the pictures. He passed it over face down.

'This is pretty gruesome,' he said. 'Are you sure you –'

'Give it here.' Simon took the phone and held it a couple of inches from his cloudy left eye. It was clear that he couldn't work out for a moment what he was seeing until he said, 'What the –' and left the rest of the sentence unspoken.

Ollie told him to look at the others, and Simon swiped left and right, scrolling in turn through each shot.

'Who sent you these?'

'I took them.'

'You?'

Ollie nodded.

'Here?'

He nodded again. 'Marble Bay, on my run this morning.'

'And you called the police?'

'Of course.'

'And?'

'Nothing. Well, nothing yet. They asked me some questions –'

'What? In-for-questioning questions?'

'No. Just – questions. There's probably nothing in it. She's probably some drunk, fell off the cliff. They took my details and told me to go. I think they wanted me out of the way so they could see to her before the tide came in.'

'Oh, man.' Simon stretched out the words as he lifted the phone for a second look. 'You have got to let me call in on this.'

'No. I told you this on the strict condition –'

'There's no way I'd've agreed to that if I'd known you had something like this.'

'Then I wouldn't have told you. Or shown you. Come on, Simon, it's just for half a day. Freya would kill me if you got this out before we published.'

'Ollie –'

'I mean it, Simon. There's only one reason I came back to Guernsey, and it wasn't to work on the paper. You know that, but that's where I need to be if I'm going to find out what happened. This might actually convince Freya I'm reporter material after all. If you run it first I might as well get straight on the next plane back to the mainland.'

Simon sighed and passed back the phone. 'You kill me. The biggest story this year falls into your lap, without you even trying, and all it means is a shaky reprieve at the office.' Ollie tried to interrupt, but this time it was Simon who put up his hand to stop him. 'I know,' he said softly. 'I know how much that means to you, and you know I'll help however I can, however long it takes, but you drop this on me and then expect me to go up to Pleinmont as though I know nothing and make some crappy report on a cliff walk.'

Ollie knew that Simon was right. He hadn't brought him there to gloat or show off; he had a question - a favour - he needed to ask. He didn't doubt for a moment that Simon would help him, but it still felt a little unfair.

Sampson mewed, and Ollie reached down to pick him up, using him as an excuse to look away.

'The thing is, mate,' he said, settling the cat on his lap and leaning forward so they could bump noses, 'I need to ask you a favour.'

'It better not be anything to do with this story.'

'Actually... it is. But listen - help me out and I'll be your point man on this. I found that body. I've already had Amy Sloane on the phone digging for quotes.'

'You didn't -'

'No, of course I didn't, but I'll tell you everything I know after we hit the streets. Quotes, an interview, whatever. As far as Freya's concerned you'll just be doing your job, following up. She doesn't need to know I told you first.'

Simon thought for a moment, but couldn't see any way in which he could wrangle a better deal. Neither would he want to, if he was honest. Ollie was his friend, and although

Simon's dominant feeling right then was one of professional jealousy, he wouldn't deny Ollie the honour of running the story first. He knew that given a day or two his feelings would change and he'd more than likely be pleased for Ollie. 'Go on...' he said.

'I need to find George Dixon,' Ollie said.

'The actor?'

'Apparently. The guys in the office reckon that this is his partner. Richelle Ibbott...?'

Simon shrugged. The name was new to him.

'Well, anyway, I've been to his house - they lived together - but there's nobody home, just some neighbour who claims to not take much notice of whether they're there or not. I have my doubts on that, though.'

'Nosey?'

'Neighbourhood watch type. Precisely the kind to know who was where and when they were there, neighbours included. Swore he only ever knew they were there because of the noise, though.'

'Do you think they were rowing?'

Ollie held out his hand and wobbled it side to side in a way that suggested he couldn't decide. The gesture was lost on Simon. 'That's what I'd like to ask Dixon,' he said, slipping his fingers beneath the cat's collar to scratch it. 'Only, I don't know where he is right now.'

'Which is why you bought me lunch.'

'No. I wanted to have lunch because... well, yes, in part. But... I'm guessing he must have come to your building once a week to record his parts. Maybe more often. What would really help would be if you could find out when he's next in. Or where he might be right now.'

Simon crumpled his sandwich bag. 'Our paths don't cross very often. They record in a different part of the building, so I'm not sure when he's in. I could look in the visitors' book, but I won't be back there for a couple of hours.'

'That might be cutting it fine,' Ollie said, turning back his cuff to check his watch. 'Who's running the show?'

'The Fleet? Kira Spooner. Took over...' - he thought for a moment — 'a year ago, maybe, something like that. Absolute hermit, even at work, so you won't get much out of her. She spends most of her time locked in an edit suite.' He picked at a bit of crab meat stuck in his teeth. 'You might have more luck with Rosalynd.'

'Who's she?'

'Rosalynd Holdbrook. Kira's predecessor. The Fleet was her idea. Bit of a pet project, I think, as her father fished out of St Sampson between the wars. Kira took over when she retired.'

'Does she know Dixon?'

'Oh, she knows Dixon. She brought him over

from some play on the mainland. Regretted it soon enough.'

'He wasn't very good?'

'I wouldn't know about that, but word on the newsroom floor is that Dixon drove her to early retirement.'

'They didn't get on?'

'No one gets on with George Dixon.'

'Interesting.' Ollie thought back to the portly neighbour and what he hadn't quite said about the noises he'd heard from their cottage. 'Where might I find her?'

'Rosalynd? She comes to the station now and then, but mostly she just does freelance now. From home. I was round there a couple of months ago reading a load of numbers.'

'Phone numbers. No. Just... numbers. They had to be in a monotone. She was very particular. Still, ten minutes work, five hundred quid in the bank.'

Ollie whistled. 'Some of us don't earn much more than that in a week.'

'Believe me; that's not normal. I don't know who she was working for, but at that price I'm happy not to ask many questions.'

'So where is home?'

'For Rosalynd? Vale. Try the phone book. She's listed. That or Facebook; she isn't shy of technology.'

'I'll call her.'

'You do.' Simon slid down from the wheelhouse roof. 'In the meantime, Cecil's probably waiting for me.' He picked up his stick.

'Cecil?'

'Cecil Digard. My chaperone.'

'Be careful,' Ollie said.

Simon paused and raised an eyebrow. 'Yes, Mother.'

'Go!'

He saluted. 'And for goodness sake,' he said, stepping backwards onto the first step, 'if you're not going to eat that crab sandwich, at least give it to poor Sampson. Put him out of his misery.'

Vale Parish, 2.15pm

Ollie called the office and asked Ella Brouard to look up a number for Rosalynd Holdbrook. She was the only Holdbrook listed.

'Looks like she lives in the Vale,' Ella told him. 'Not far from the church, I think. Have you got a pen?'

'Can you text it?' Ollie asked. 'Her number, too.' He was riding the west coast, away from the Huffin' Puffin, and his phone was tucked under the strap of his helmet.

He called ahead, but Rosalynd's phone was engaged, and twenty minutes later he found her house, his arrival unannounced. From the end of her path he could see the spire of the church where it capped the trees behind her roofline.

It was all very compact. Neat, well-maintained: Ollie put it down to her being retired and having spare time on her hands. And money, too, if she could fix a workplace feud by quitting her job and spending her days at home.

He could smell the sea on the wind as he propped his bike on her porch, the odour of weed on the sand as he knocked on the wooden front door. He had more luck this time than he'd had at Dixon's house. She answered a moment later, a phone pressed to her ear. She beckoned him in and left him standing in the hallway as she went to the kitchen to finish her call.

The house was well looked after. It smelled of bread and fresh flowers, and when Rosalynd returned, profuse with her apologies, he noticed the apron tied about her waist. The phone was weighing down its pocket.

In the notes he wrote later that night he described her as fifty to fifty-five - perhaps a youthful sixty. She dusted her hands and gave his own a firm shake. 'Excuse the mess. Baking day.' She nodded back towards the kitchen. 'How can I help?'

'I hope you don't think I'm rude,' Ollie said. 'Turning up unannounced. I called ahead but you were engaged.'

She tapped her apron pocket. 'My daughter. We often lose track of the time.' She looked at her watch and then gestured over her shoulder. 'Do you mind coming through?'

She led the way, taking him through to a sparse, modern kitchen with granite worktops and a deep butler sink.

'I'm a friend of Simon Langlois,' he said, deciding to start with something that might suggest they had a connection. 'I work for The Sarnian.' He pulled out a card and put it down on the worktop, keeping it clear of the settling cloud of flour.

'I see,' she said. 'I read the Press myself.'

'As did my parents. Me, too, until I went away.'

'Not any longer?'

'Well...' Ollie pursed his lips. 'I find... inspiration, shall we say, in its stories.'

'Which you re-word as appropriate?'

'You know how it is.' Ollie smiled, and she smiled back. 'I understand you used to work for the BBC.'

'Did, do. Who can afford to retire any more?'

'But you did. Retire.'

'More or less. I gave up my boss and I changed my place of work, but they call me up now and then.' She turned out a bowl of airy dough and started to knead it.

'Do you still work on The Fleet?'

'Heavens, no. I'm not sure I could. Not now.'

'Why not?'

She pursed her lips and gently shook her head. 'It was time to move on. Bring in some fresh ideas. Hand it over to someone else.'

'To Kira Spooner?'

'Yes.'

'It had nothing to do with George Dixon? Your retirement, I mean?'

She paused for a moment, then carried on kneading as though she hadn't heard him.

'I hear you weren't best friends,' Ollie said.

'From your friend Simon?'

Ollie shrugged.

'It would surprise me if that man had any best friends,' Rosalynd said.

'Yet he found someone to love him.'

Rosalynd laughed. 'Oh, no, no.' She knocked the air out of the dough by dropping it down on the worktop, then hit it twice with the heel of her hand. 'He found someone to tolerate him,' then added, under her breath, 'more's the pity.'

'Why do you say that?'

'Because she's my friend. I introduced them. By the time I knew what he was like it was too late to warn her off.'

'That would be Richelle Ibbott?'

Rosalynd looked up and narrowed her eyes.

'What is this all about?'

'George Dixon.'

'You're writing a story about him?'

'Well, I'm writing a story. How big a part he plays, I don't know. Not yet.'

'I see.' Rosalynd was starting to sound a bit breathy. The kneading was tiring her. 'So what's it about, this story? Has he got a new role?' She shot Ollie a quick look. 'Has he signed up for panto? Oh, Lord, let it be that. We'll be rid of him for the winter at least.'

Ollie smiled and shook his head. 'Did he beat her?'

'Did he?'

'Does he?'

'Has she left him? Is that what this is about?'

Ollie shook his head.

'Did he beat Richelle?' Rosalynd asked herself, and she chuckled. 'Not if he valued his looks. Do you know her?'

'I know of her.'

'But you've met her?'

Ollie thought of her body prostrate on the beach. What defined a meeting? Did both parties need to be aware of it to call it a meeting?

Both awake?

Both alive?

'Once,' he said.

'Then you'll know she's –'

Ollie shook his head. 'We didn't speak.'

He worried now that the story was focusing too much on Richelle Ibbott. She may have been the hook from which it all hung, but she was Alfie Erne's assignment, not his. Ollie had been sent out to chase Dixon - do the police's job, in effect - and turn up the evidence that might allow Freya Carlisle to finger him for murder. A murder he might not have committed. A murder that might not be a murder at all.

He looked over Rosalynd's shoulder at the clock on the kitchen wall. It was already after two. They would be looking to put the paper to bed in half an hour so they could get the first copies onto the street in time for the offices turning out. He knew Alfie would do all he could to hold things back for a few more minutes, but it still meant he'd have to call through his contribution and trust Alfie to edit it on the page.

'Did they argue?' he asked. 'Did they fight?'

'George Dixon is not a nice man. George Dixon only cares about one person, and the only reason...' She caught herself saying something she shouldn't, and stopped. She turned back to her dough and tore it in two, shaping one half and dropping it into a bread tin.

'The only reason...?' Ollie asked.

'You'll have to ask Richelle,' she said, suddenly

businesslike. 'It's not my place to discuss her affairs.'

Ollie reached out and slid the two loaf tins towards him. 'Miss Holdbrook...'

He paused, waiting for her to look back towards him. She reached forward for the tins, but he held them firm until he had her attention.

'I need to get these in the oven,' she said, giving them a gentle tug.

'And I'm going to have to be blunt. I'm sorry about that.' His mouth was dry; he could feel his tongue getting tacky, sticking to the roof of his mouth. 'Would you mind if I got myself some water?'

Rosalynd loosened her grip on the tins, seeing now that his questions might have been more focused than she'd realised. 'Tell me what you were going to say.'

He closed his eyes. 'I think your friend... I found a body this morning –'

'And you're going to tell me it was Richelle?'

Ollie nodded.

Now it was he who had loosened his grip on the tins. Rosalynd felt them slacken and she snatched them away. 'Don't be so silly,' she said, slicing along each rise of dough with the point of a paring knife. 'You don't even know who she is. Not really.'

'I'm fairly sure it was. Three people have

positively identified her from –' He reached for his phone, then thought better of showing her the photos. She'd see them soon enough when the paper came out. 'She was well known in the office.'

'Who?'

'I'm sorry?'

'Who knew her?'

'Well, there was Alfie Erne, for one. He's our –'

She nodded. 'Yes... yes, I know Alfie.'

They both fell silent. Ollie was after some answers, and he knew that the only way to get them now would be to ease off on the questions and let Rosalynd speak for herself. Her mind would be busy processing what she had learned. The less he said, the better chance there was that some of those thoughts would spill out.

Rosalynd picked up the loaf tins and walked them to the sink. She dipped her fingers in a bowl of water and sprinkled droplets over each loaf.

'Where did you find...' She seemed to be searching for the right word, apparently not wanting to mention Richelle's name and give credence to what Ollie had said. She put the loaves into the oven. 'Where did you find this body?'

'Marble Bay. Just above the high water mark'

'She lived above Marble Bay,' Rosalynd

said quietly. It sounded as if she was already reminiscing.

'I know,' said Ollie. 'I went there this morning, looking for George Dixon. I –'

'I should imagine he already knows,' she said, jumping to the wrong conclusion. 'If it really was who you think.'

'Miss Holdbrook, I know this must be a shock. But you see I want to know more about George Dixon. I want to understand whether – perhaps – he was... Involved... in some way.'

'Involved?' Rosalynd frowned. 'In her death?'

Ollie nodded.

'Are you saying she was murdered?'

'No,' Ollie said quickly. 'Absolutely not. I don't know how she died. Or when. I'm just...' He shook his head. 'Pursuing avenues. You know what it's like. I have to find out all that I can. Be absolutely sure I'm right before we publish anything.'

He was lying, of course. He knew that Freya Carlisle wasn't beyond publishing rumour and speculation if it meant she could beat the Press to a story. She'd trail her headlines with question marks, wrap them up in single quotes, as though they excused her misjudgement. They turned the story into speculation, entirely justifiable, and gave opinion pieces greater weight and authority. They encouraged the reader to answer 'yes', even if the correct response was almost always 'no'.

Rosalynd Holdbrook seemed lost in thought. Ollie stood still and kept quiet, watching her from the opposite side of her worktop. It seemed to him she had something to say, but wasn't entirely convinced she should say it. Whoever spoke next, he knew, would be having the final word. He couldn't afford for that to be him.

She looked at his card on the counter, and at last she broke the silence. 'George Dixon didn't love Richelle. I'm sure of it.' Her voice was stronger than Ollie had thought it would be. He'd expected a whisper when she finally spoke, but this was bold and confident. It was almost as though she knew that by saying what she did she was dropping some hints about Dixon himself, directing Ollie's lines of enquiry.

'There were only two things that kept them together,' she said. 'Her dependence on his income, and his...' She shook her head and wiped her dusty hands on her apron. 'He didn't have a residence permit, and wasn't inclined to rent. I tried to set him up with somewhere to stay when he first came over but nowhere was good enough. Nowhere was ever good enough...'

'Thank you,' Ollie said, after a moment's silence told him she'd finished. He gave her a tense smile that he hoped looked sympathetic.

'Thank you so much for your time and your help. If you think of anything else, feel free to...'

He tapped the card on the worktop. Rosalynd nodded and sniffed. She slipped her hand into the apron pocket and half lifted out the phone, to show that she understood.

The Sarnian, 7.28pm

Ollie rolled back his seat as he finished reading the story. He barely recognised what he had phoned through while riding back from Rosalynd's house - not now that he saw it printed. Alfie Erne had translated it into tabloid speak as he'd flowed it onto the page. The result was a mess in Ollie's eyes, and one he was glad he could easily disown. His byline had been swapped out in favour of unnamed 'staff reporters', perhaps because only half of the legwork was his. Alfie himself had attended a briefing at police headquarters and used his notes to pad out the copy. Someone else on the team had clearly managed to track down Dixon at the Ibbott house, too, some time after Ollie's departure.

He didn't notice Ella Brouard until she leaned forward and planted a fresh mug of tea on his desk. She set it down in such a way that it covered the picture of Richelle on the beach and her colourless, bloated face.

'I see you've been reading the style guide,' she said, casting her eye over the first few paragraphs. 'At last. Freya will be pleased.'

Ollie looked up. 'Won't she just. So long as Alfie keeps quiet.'

'Aah,' she said, sitting down beside him. 'Not your work, then?'

'My work. My research, some of it. Just not my words. Except perhaps for that one.' He pointed at the word police. 'And that one.' He moved his finger to murder.

Ella laughed. 'Disappointed?'

'Not at all. Freya will be happy, Alfie seems to be satisfied with this mess, and none of the blame will fall at my feet. Win, win, win.'

Ella smiled and held his gaze for a moment. 'Fancy a celebratory drink?'

'What are we celebrating?'

She thought for a moment. 'Let's say... the preservation of your integrity.'

Now it was Ollie's turn to smile. 'That sounds like a wonderful idea.'

'I'm ready to go now if you...'

He shook his head. 'I'd love to. Really, I would, but this story...' He indicated the paper spread out on his desk and the half-written copy on his screen. 'Maybe some other time?'

'I might hold you to that.'

'Do.'

She flicked one of his ears and picked up her own drink. 'Best you get on, then, boy reporter.'

He watched her walking away. Was he making a stupid mistake? He hadn't dated since he'd returned to the island, and he wasn't unaware of the way Ella seemed to feel. Those feelings might not yet be entirely mutual, but he could think of few others - certainly none within his reach - with whom he would rather spend an evening celebrating the preservation of his integrity.

Behind the half-written story on his screen, though, was a smaller browser window, and inside it a list of results from the Sarnian archive. Each was returned by a search for the term 'lost boat'. He wanted to work his way through them before he went home, at least to eliminate those that were too old or unlikely to help.

He nodded at her as she tidied her desk and picked up her bag, and he made an act of re-reading the paper until she left the newsroom floor.

BEACH BODY: FOUL PLAY SUSPECTED!

by Sarnian Staff Reporters

STATES OF GUERNSEY POLICE TODAY suggested that they are treating as murder the discovery of a female body in Marble Bay.

One-time socialite turned charity patron Richelle Ibbott, 62, was found on the secluded beach by Sarnian reporter Oliver Carey. Eagle-eyed Carey, 32, had been swimming in the bay at the time, cooling down in the tepid waters as part of a vigorous cardio workout.

Alerting authorities, Carey later told Sarnian news editor Alfie Erne that he was shocked to discover that the putrefying pensioner – said once to have accounted for up to ten percent of the island's annual tax revenues – may have been overlooked by island authorities for as long as three days. This, despite the fact that States Police had received reports of her disappearance earlier this morning and chosen not to issue an immediate island-wide alert.

LEGGY LE PAGE

Busty police deputy, Christine Le Page, currently on secondment from the force on the neighbouring island of Jersey, had taken a statement from wannabe celebutard George Dixon a full sixty minutes before Carey phoned through with news of his shocking discovery.

Dixon's statement has been withheld from the public on 'operational grounds', which The Sarnian takes to mean that the force wishes to forestall charges of negligence on its own part.

Island cops remained tight-lipped when quizzed at the end of a brief and hastily convened briefing, leading to speculation that tragic Miss Ibbott, who was wearing size sixteen jeans at the time of her death, along with a halterneck top that did little to preserve her modesty, may have been the victim of a bizarre death plunge from the nearby cliffs during a sex game gone catastrophically wrong.

Orphaned at the age of sixteen, the slaughtered heiress gave up a sizeable fortune in her late forties – along with the family's ancestral home close to Saumerez Park – and used the proceeds to fund Ormer Orphans, the charity for bereaved children she set up in memory of her slain parents.

She had lived since then in a modest Napoleonic terrace close to the bay where her decaying remains were discovered. She invited Dixon to move in shortly after his arrival on the island. Vendor details obtained as a result of diligent inquiries by Sarnian reporters revealed the house to be a single-bedroomed property. She and Dixon were unmarried at the time of her death.

LOVE RAT IN A LOVE NEST

Dixon, who came to prominence in his native Southampton following a one-in-a-bed sex scandal in the salad days of his less than impressive career, currently plays crippled love rat Thomas Thoumine in the BBC's long-running regional radio soap, The Fleet.

He remained holed up in the couple's former love nest for much of the day, refusing to answer questions put to him by tireless Sarnian reporters. After three hours of intense through-the-curtains interrogation, he lifted the flap of his letterbox to reveal a sliver of the house's over-decorated interior. He then subjected our fearless staff – and those of rival publications who had been tipped off on this Sarnian scoop by the irresponsible open-house nature of the police briefing – to an unwarranted verbal assault.

The move sparked outrage from long-suffering neighbours, who slammed the island incomer for his ill-mannered behaviour, claiming they were frequently disturbed by raised voices passing through the walls of their local-market granite houses, which have enjoyed an average uplift of five percent year-on-year thanks to the rising property market.

The BBC declined to comment on Dixon's troubling behaviour, or the likely public backlash as today's edition of your favourite news-and-views-paper hit the streets.

BRIEF BRIEFINGS

Having convened an invite-only briefing at police HQ, curvy Le Page, 55, remained cagey, dodging incoming questions from the assembled press, other than to outline the basics of a case that has seen scant resources consumed at a reckless rate in its first few hours of operation. Aside from Le Page and man of the people Inspector Marc Renouf, famed for his gallant rescue of a family of four in last year's horror smash on the Val Des Terres, Constables Falla and Clarke – relative unknowns who joined the force in the last two years on transfers from Sark and the mainland respectively – have been assigned to head up research and analysis.

Le Page refused to speculate on claims made by sources close to the island's high-tech forensics lab that boffins working there may already have isolated a narrow window during which the voluptuous Miss Ibbott met her untimely end. Nonetheless, motive, suspect and modus operandi remain elusive in the face of what must be growing public clamour for swift action.

Turn to page 3 for The Sarnian's comment.

Police Headquarters, 8.10pm

Renouf and Le Page had given the briefing together. He knew the press had never considered him particularly amenable when it came to answering questions. Taking a back seat to his temporary deputy – on this case at least – might do his image some good. By the time she left at the end of her placement, they'd be happy to live within his slightly more generous limits. Well, that was his theory, anyway.

He spent the rest of the afternoon filing resource chits for a potential incident room. Richelle's death hadn't yet been classed as a murder, whatever The Sarnian might suggest. They'd need the results of Charlie's tests to prove that, but he had a hunch, and was doing all he could to get things in order well in advance of any inquiry proper kicking off.

He'd requisitioned boards, desks and computers, and assigned them to a room set aside for major investigations. He'd also gained preliminary approval to pull together a small team: himself, Christine Le Page, and Constables Falla and Clarke. He'd have liked a couple of extra staff, but agreement on that – even provisional agreement – would be hard to come by until they were sure that this was anything other than an accident.

Charlie Dubois had only authorised the removal of the body within the last hour, by which point the incoming tide was getting uncomfortably close. It would be the following day, at least, before they would know any more. As eight o'clock rolled around, Renouf decided he'd done all he could.

He switched off his monitor and turned to Christine. 'Pub,' he said, nodding towards the door. 'Care to join us?'

She looked at her watch. 'Yes, but no. Thank you.'

'Which means?'

'Which means yes, I would, but Dan's – my husband's – his brothers and sister are having a meal. I think they not so secretly hope we might be staying long-term. It's a bit of a welcome home for him.'

'And a getting-to-know-you-better for you?' Renouf rolled his eyes. 'Fair enough, but drinks are on you come Friday.'

He rapped his knuckles on the edge of her desk, then whistled across to Falla and Clarke. 'Pub,' he called. They stuck up their thumbs and followed him out of the office, leaving Christine alone at her desk.

She listened as their footsteps receded and she heard them come out in the car park below. She walked to the window and watched them go, then picked up a phone and called an internal number.

'Bichard's office,' said the voice at the opposite end of the line. It was male, but high and slightly breathy. Whoever it was – a PA, she imagined – could have done with clearing his throat.

'Is he there?' she asked.

'Who is this?'

'Christine Le Page.'

'The Chief Constable isn't taking calls. Can I take a message?'

'Then he is there?'

'As I say, he's –'

'Could you try him all the same?'

The man paused, then asked her to wait, perhaps deciding not to press matters when he didn't know who she was. He came back on a couple of seconds later, sounding slightly surprised.

‘He says he can see you,’ he said, then remembering himself, he added ‘right away,’ as though to berate her for dithering.

Christine threw her things in her bag and made her way to a south-facing office one floor above her own desk.

She found the man who had answered the phone at a desk in an outer office. ‘Henri,’ he said, as he shook her hand - no surname, she noticed, but he spelled out the ‘i’ at the end - then he knocked on a door marked ‘Bichard’. He didn’t wait for an answer, sweeping it open and steering her in as though she was already wasting the Chief Constable’s time.

The Chief kept his eyes on his papers. ‘Sit,’ he said, pointing at a black leather chair on the opposite side of his desk. He was jotting some notes on a case file, the fat black fountain pen lost in his oversized fingers.

Henri turned, and Bichard continued his writing, waiting for his PA to leave and close the door behind him. Christine watched him working. He had just passed fifty and marked his thirtieth year on the force, yet his face was scored by only the lightest of lines and there was no sign yet of a paunch spilling over his belt. His shirt sleeves were tight over well-worked biceps, the tailored front only just containing his chest.

Christine could see a dark patch of hair pressed against and inside it. Everything about the man seemed coiled, taut and ready for action, and he looked as though his journey home would not require a bus or a car, but a run or a ride or a row round the coast.

At last the door clicked to, and he looked up through dark bushy eyebrows.

'Christine,' he said, standing up and walking around the desk. He threw his arms around her. 'Why did you leave it so long?'

'I've been here less than a week.' She kissed his cheek.

'Even so, even so.' He released her and pulled out the chair to a more casual position, sideways on to the desk. 'You know, you've already made quite an impression.'

'I have?'

'Mmm-hmmm,' he said, smiling. He reached back and moved the file to one side so he could pick up a newspaper. 'Have you seen this evening's Sarnian?'

'Not yet.'

'They're calling you Leggy Le Page.'

She felt herself redden as he pointed at the paragraph and stood over her as she read it.

'I don't know whether I ought to be honoured or offended.'

'Take it as a compliment,' Bichard said.

'Especially coming from that rag. They're few and far between.'

She watched as he walked back and threw himself down in his seat. She'd known him for twenty-five years – half of her lifetime and most of his career – yet he'd barely changed since the day they'd met. His hair was thinner, perhaps a little grey, though she knew for a fact that he patched over much of that steely corrosion with dye.

Chouet, she remembered. That was the beach where they'd first met, when she'd been helping her father keep time at the races as Bichard had crossed the line first. His souped-up Capri had lead the field from the start, swallowing up the rippled beach while the others wobbled about in his wake.

'Do you still race?' she asked.

'Mm-hmm,' he nodded. 'Every fourth Sunday, much to Marlise's dismay. I promise her tea at Icart in lieu of amends. We park up at Jerbourg and walk the cliff path.' He folded closed the report he'd been reading. 'They're making you feel at home, I trust.'

'Yes, yes. A little tricky remembering names, but I think I'm doing alright.'

'Pfft.' He batted the notion, his brawny hand uselessly swiping the air. He looked at her for a moment, the way he might admire a portrait, then pulled himself up in his seat. 'Tell me. How's Dan?'

'Glad to be home, I think. He took to Jersey – in spirit, at least, but I'm not sure his heart ever left Guernsey.'

'Marvellous.'

'In truth, this couldn't have come at a more appropriate time. His sister's due to give birth in three weeks, so he's about to turn uncle again... and of course there's his parents' house to sort out.'

'Ah, yes.' Bichard sighed. 'You know, I miss them still. Dan's parents. Were it not for them...' He smiled. 'Well, we wouldn't be sitting here now, if nothing else.'

'Quite.'

'How's he holding up?'

'Fairly well, all things considered. It wasn't unexpected. Jane had been ill for some time. To lose them both in quick succession was never going to be easy, but I think with his father... I think he just couldn't go on without her, however much of their lives they spent fighting.'

'I'm sorry.'

'Don't be. Life goes on. Dan's out tonight at the Bridge. He's putting it all behind him, best he can.'

'Catching up with old friends?'

'Rest of the family. I told him I'd probably end

up working late. First week files and orientation.'

'If only that were all it was.'

Christine nodded.

'So tell me,' Bichard said, his voice now sober. 'What might I find in those first week files?'

'The public files, or...'

'No. I can read them whenever I want.'

She nodded.

'What have you discovered of our Inspector Marc Renouf?'

Christine thought for a moment, then drew up a list of adjectives. 'Smart - in every sense: common sense and dress sense. A do-er. Organised. Confident. He isn't shy to give orders.'

Bichard grumbled. 'You're practically writing the job description. What of the man?'

She shrugged. 'Not much. Not yet. I've known him a week.'

'Your instincts, then.'

'He seems likeable. I don't think he's cagey. Or if he is I haven't hit on a sensitive subject yet. He isn't evasive. He doesn't seem to be hiding anything, as far as I can tell, but the sum of my time alone with him amounts to a ride between here and Marble Bay.'

'Did you chat?'

'Only small talk. Airport expansion, and which is the better coffee: flat white or latte.'

'What did you decide?'

'He drinks his black. We agreed to disagree.'

'Well, you're gaining his trust. That's a good thing, but it might take some time to work it around to the Carey affair.'

'Assuming Renouf is involved.'

'Do you think he may be?' Bichard asked.

'It's too soon to say,' Christine said. 'Although...'

'Yes?'

'An interesting coincidence. Something we may be able to use to nudge him one way or other.'

Bichard sat forward and folded his arms on the desk. 'Go on...'

'This morning. That body on the beach. You've read the report?'

Bichard nodded. 'In brief.' He tapped the closed folder before him - the one on which he'd been writing his notes.

'The guy who found her and rang it in was an Oliver Carey.'

'Any relation?'

'Quite possibly. I ran a check while Renouf was taking his lunch. It seems he's the registered keeper of a boat moored at Portelet.'

'Not...?'

Christine nodded. 'The Huffin' Puffin.'

'Remus Carey's old boat.' Bichard jotted the letters HP on one corner of the folder. 'Does Renouf know?'

'I don't think so. I haven't told him yet.'

Bichard nodded. 'Let's keep it that way. Don't let him know you've been nosing around.'

'I won't. Beyond the body I've got no interest in Carey as far as he's concerned.'

'Good. Keep an eye on him. Whatever else he might be, he's a first-class investigative officer. He'll turn up the connection himself soon enough.'

'Want me to do some coincidental investigations? Drop an innocent line in the case file?'

Bichard thought for a moment. 'No,' he said at last. 'Let's let Renouf work it out for himself. If he isn't there in a couple of days we'll rethink.'

Christine looked around at the sound of a knock on the door.

'Come,' Bichard called, uncapping his pen and pulling a jotter towards him. From the speed that he did it, it was obvious this was a practiced manoeuvre, and Christine wondered whether he'd done the same just before she'd entered.

Henri pushed open the door and looked in. 'I'll be going, if there's nothing else.'

'Yes, yes, you go,' Bichard said. 'See you tomorrow.' He turned to Christine. 'Do you fancy a drink?'

'Perhaps not tonight,' she said. She waited a

moment for Henri to close the door before going on. 'I told Renouf I was dining with Dan's family tonight. Might be tricky if we bumped into each other in Town.'

'Then come back to mine. I have a view of Fort Grey, and Marlise would love to see you.'

'No, really,' she said, standing up. 'I've joined the gym and I have some notes to write up. Another time.' She leaned across the desk and pecked him on the cheek.

'Before you go...' Bichard turned and unlocked a drawer, then fingered his way through some scarlet folders until he found the one that he needed: Carey, Remus J. 'You'll be needing this.'

He passed it across the desk and she opened the cover to read the first page.

'Is this...' She frowned.

Bichard nodded. 'Guernesiais.'

'But I don't speak it.'

'Neither do I, but I do recall a weekend in Paris.' He sat back and smiled as he rewound the years – to a time when they were both far younger, and free to do whatever they chose. And whoever, it turned out. 'If it wasn't for you, and your French, we'd have ended up on the street. Nothing to eat, and no way of getting around. Guernesiais isn't so different.'

She ran her eye over the first few lines. 'Is this what I think it is?'

'It's a transcript of Remus Carey's logs,' Bichard said, confirming what she suspected. 'There are duplicate folders in Lyon and London. Rather verbose, I'm afraid. He dictated them. Probably the quickest way to bring you up to speed, though.'

Christine flipped over the cover and tucked the folder under her arm. 'So much for the gym.'

'You don't need it.'

Christine raised her eyebrows.

'Seriously, though,' Bichard said. 'These logs are our most important resource. I need you to decode them, and I need you in there with Renouf. He's our target, remember, not whoever or whatever did for Miss Ibbott. She's just a convenient distraction.'

DAY TWO

The Sarnian, 8.10am

Ollie didn't run the next morning. The cliff path was still roped off, the beach out of bounds, and every time he thought of the body - the look and the smell of it - he found himself close to gagging.

Besides, his time was no longer his own.

He was rostered for the late shift but Freya had dropped some heavy hints that until the story had been put to bed the rota no longer applied. The Ibbott case had priority over everything, private lives included.

So he set an alarm and woke as the mail plane banked above the harbour. Peeling himself from the lower bunk he brewed some coffee on the small gas stove and fed Sampson his breakfast on the Puffin's aft deck. He was wheeling his bike through the Sarnian foyer forty minutes later, confident he'd be one of the first, and planning already how he would use the quiet time to mine the newspaper archive.

His hopes were dashed as the lift doors opened onto a swarm of newspaper drones. The writers from lifestyle and news were in place, the art team working on mocked-up front pages, and Freya had taken her place in the hive and was making calls to goodness knew where. Only the sports team was absent, and unless they discovered Richelle had owned shares in the local team it was likely to stay that way until the story ran dry.

Ella smiled and waved at him as he propped his bike at the end of the desk. 'Here he is,' she announced, to nobody in particular. 'Man of the moment.'

Ollie frowned as he took his seat.

'On the telly,' she said, thumbing across to one of the ceiling-slung panels. Each was tuned to Sky News, and they'd been like that for long enough to burn the logo into the screen. 'They keep showing your picture, side by side with Richelle.'

'Which one?'

'Your byline photo.'

Ollie cringed. It wasn't a bad one per se, but the night before it was shot he'd been drinking and only a careful concoction of paracetamol and Photoshop had saved him from bleary-bagged eyes.

He tried not to look at the screen, turning instead to his email, and forwarding on the comment requests to the paper's in-house publicity team. They could decide which ones to answer while he got on with his job.

'What are you working on?' he asked as he opened a new browser window and logged in to the Sarnian archive.

'Ibbott,' Ella said. 'Going back through the clippings.'

'Are there many?'

'Too many. I don't think there was a single full week where we didn't write something about her.'

'When does Dixon first appear?'

'About...' – she thought for a moment, scrolling up the list of hits – 'seven, eight years ago? Not long after he arrived from the mainland.'

'I need to find him,' Ollie said. 'I didn't exactly cover myself in glory yesterday.'

Freya pulled a face.

'Who was it in the end? Who found him?' Ollie asked.

'Alfie. On his way back from the briefing. Bit of an exaggeration, the bit about being there three hours.'

So it was Alfie Erne, Ollie's boss and the paper's news editor. At least that was something. Alfie was an old hand, an experienced hack, and far less likely to make a big thing of the fact that it was he, and not Ollie, who had at least managed to quote an expletive if nothing else. If it had been another reporter – someone on Ollie's grade – it might have been a different matter.

The browser refreshed, calling up a dashboard stuffed with Ollie's past searches. The most frequently used terms were picked out in larger fonts, the rarest barely legible. Two words dominated the screen: 'Huffin' and 'Puffin', beside each of which a zero in braces relayed the unhappy news that they didn't appear in the Sarnian clippings – at least not in the context within which Ollie had searched.

Streaming out in columns and rows below them were other terms that Ollie had hoped might have brought him some news of his father's fate. Carey, Remus, RemusCarey, boat, accident, disaster, crash, collision, disappear, disappearance, body, wreck, explosion...

He clicked a new tab within the archive, saving his previous hits for later, and started a fresh search on the term 'George Dixon'. The server returned four hundred and thirteen results. Ollie checked a box in the sidebar to specify that both words had to feature in each article, not merely one or the other, and the list shrank to seventy-eight. Far more manageable. He ordered them by date, with the most recent entry first, and read through the headlines in reverse order, trying to work out where Dixon might have been on the days leading up to Richelle Ibbott's death.

Route de Jerbourg, 9am

Christine didn't believe in ringing ahead. She'd always preferred to arrive unannounced and see whoever she'd come to visit without giving them time to tidy and hide and prepare. Messy room, messy hair, still half dressed with breakfast in their beard or dripping down their pyjama top: it always struck her as far more honest and raw.

She parked at the top of the road and walked the rest of the way to the small granite terrace where Richelle had spent the last twenty years of her life. She clocked the neighbour pretending to reseat some heather at the back of a rockery, and she turned and smiled as she knocked on the door.

There was no reply, but she could see movement through the gerbera frosting, and knew it could only be Dixon. The only other possibility, Richelle, was lying on a slab in the mortuary, two floors below Police Headquarters.

She knocked again and the movement stopped. The shape at the end of the hallway paused, then turned and called towards the door.

'I told you yesterday,' he shouted. 'I have nothing to say. Not to you or the Press or anyone.'

'What about the police, Mr Dixon?' she

shouted back. 'Do you have anything to say to us?'

There was a moment's silence before he said, 'No.'

Christine paused, her eyes on the shape at the end of the hallway. He was still again, almost as though he thought that the silence could hide him.

'I'd like to speak to you about your partner.' She raised her voice to be sure that he knew she'd be overheard. 'Richelle Ibbott, Mr Dixon.'

'I told you –'

'Specifically, your movements over the weekend, Mr Dixon. And Friday night in particular.'

The shape got larger. She saw him lift his hand to the latch, and then the door swung open. His hair was crooked and the pink in his cheeks gave him the look of a slightly flustered piglet. He was a little fatter than she remembered, and she wondered whether he was wearing looser trousers.

...or maybe he hadn't had time to lace up his corset...

'This is harassment.'

'Well, I'm sorry you feel that way, Mr Dixon. We're only trying to do our job and –'

'Then do it. Find out who killed her.'

Christine smiled and scratched the back of

her neck, looking down as though it pained her to give him uncomfortable news. 'The first twenty-four hours of any investigation are by far the most important.'

'I have worked on police dramas, you know.'

'Then you'll know it's vital that we use the time not only to collect whatever evidence we can, Mr Dixon, but also to close off avenues that lead to dead ends. We can then direct our limited resources towards those that may prove more worthwhile. I'm sure you'd like to help us in that respect, wouldn't you? To find out what happened to Miss Ibbott?'

He stared at her, narrowing his eyes. His lips thinned as he pulled them tight.

'Very well,' she said, after several seconds of silence. 'I'll call you later and we can set a more convenient time. I'll investigate other options until then.'

She stepped back from the door and turned around as Dixon started to close it.

'I wonder if you could help,' she said, calling to the neighbour. He'd worked his way to the back of the bed, and had to turn to see her.

'Me?' he asked.

'Christine Le Page,' she said as she walked over to the low wall that divided the properties. The gardener stood up and wiped his soiled hands on the front of his t-shirt.

'I wonder if you could account for Mr Dixon's presence on Friday night and over the weekend?' she asked. 'Did you see him leave or return to the house at any time?'

'Fine,' Dixon said, pulling the door wide open. 'Fine. You win.' He stepped back and nodded her into the house.

The Sarnian, Editorial Conference

Freya stepped out of the hive and called across the floor. 'Conference room in five minutes,' she said. 'We need a fix on this story. It's been twenty-four hours, and where are we?'

She turned an ear towards the office, expecting an answer.

'Nowhere,' she said when none was forthcoming. 'Exactly one-eighty from where we should be right now.'

She clapped at them twice, then picked up her book and strode out.

Ollie printed the ten most recent stories to feature the name of George Dixon, Ella did the same for Richelle, and they carried them all through to the conference room, skim-reading on the way.

The seating was more relaxed this time. Freya and Harry took the head of the table, but Ollie could sit where he wanted, so he and Ella took seats side by side, and set to work with their highlighting pens, picking out facts and scoring through long strings of comment.

‘Okay,’ Freya said, once they’d all settled down. She looked along the gathered ranks of writers and section editors. ‘What do we know? Ella, tell us about Ibbott.’

‘About the woman herself, not much to say beyond what we already know.’ Ella spread out the papers on the long teak table. ‘Philanthropist, dead. No chance of an interview, naturally, but I’ve started pulling together quotes we’ve run in the past. See if we can string them into some kind of voice-from-the-grave.’

‘Good,’ Freya said. ‘Make it look like she’s settling a few old scores; see if you can find any criticism, anything she didn’t like about her friends and family. Tart it up a bit. You can’t libel the dead, but pass it by the lawyers anyway. They’ll keep you this side of legal. Just.’

Ella scribbled notes in the margins of one of her printouts. ‘Deadline?’

Freya looked at Harry Ozanne.

‘We’ll spread it across four and five,’ he said. ‘That section goes to bed at three. I’ll need your copy by eleven. Tony,’ he said, looking across to his brother. ‘I’m up to here...’ – he raised a horizontal hand to his neck – ‘so could you find the pictures for this one?’

Tony nodded, and looked back at Ella. 'Can you send me your links? I'll start there.'

'Good,' Freya said. They all turned towards her. 'Carey. You're on Dixon watch. Have you found him yet?'

Ollie could feel himself redden. 'I've been doing background. I'm going back to the Ibbott house as soon as we've finished here.'

'And how far ahead of us do you think the Press will be by then?'

Ollie stumbled. He started to say something but, thinking better of it, he swept his papers into a pile. 'I'm on my way. I'll find him.'

Freya pursed her lips. 'Tell us what you're working on now you're here,' she said, slouching in her seat. She raised her open palm, handing him the floor.

Ollie fanned his pages again and started to pick through the highlights.

'Alfie interviewed him a couple of months ago,' he said.

'Four,' Alfie Erne cut in. 'It was just after Christmas.'

Ollie nodded. 'He was taking a couple of weeks off.'

'Do you usually interview people about their holidays?' Freya asked, turning the room's attention towards the news editor. 'I should have thought that was more Ella's department.'

'Except that's not what this was,' Alfie said. 'It's the only time he's agreed to talk to us directly. I think it was under duress.'

'I've got it here,' Ollie said, lifting one of the papers. 'Do you mind?' he asked Alfie. Alfie shook his head, and Ollie started reading.

We met in the foyer of the shared media building close to St Sampson, and I found Dixon to be surprisingly muted for one whose character – Thomas Thoumine – has to date been far larger than any real life on the island. The hard drinking libertine we've come to know and loathe through the last six years of The Fleet would appear in person to be a man of few words and fewer opinions, whose every statement is carefully considered before it leaves his mouth.

Alfie stopped him. 'I don't think that's actually true,' he said. 'I wrote it, but truth be told, I think it was an act. If I could have proved any different...' He trailed off.

'On what account?' Freya asked.

Alfie shrugged. 'That editor woman,' he said, trying to remember her name.

'Rosalynd Holdbrook,' Tony Ozanne said.

'She'd left by then,' Ella said. 'It would have been Kira Spooner.'

Alfie pointed to her and nodded. 'That's the one. She was there, too. Didn't leave us alone.

Harry, can you find the story in the archive?'

Harry logged in through a browser and started his search while Alfie carried on talking. Eventually Harry found the pictures attached to the story, and there in the back of each one was a reedy woman with bobbed black hair and thick-rimmed glasses: Kira Spooner.

'I think she wanted to keep an ear on what he was saying. Make sure he stuck to an agreed line.'

'Which was?' Ollie asked.

'How pleased he was about the direction they were taking his character.'

'Of course,' Freya said. 'This was just after...'

Alfie nodded. 'The accident.'

Route de Jerbourg

Dixon showed Christine into the small lounge at the back of the house. It looked as if he'd been sleeping on the sofa for the last few days, and eating there, too. A small pile of dishes and plates sat on the end of a coffee table, and the handles of various cutlery items stuck out of the stack like fat spokes.

He gathered together some mainland broadsheets to make space for them to sit down and offered to brew them some tea.

Christine made a play of looking at her watch,

then politely declined. 'We ought to get on,' she said, slipping the band off her notebook and turning to a blank page. She cleared her throat. 'This isn't a formal interview, Mr Dixon. At this stage I just want to know a bit more about your movements over the last four or five days. Since you last saw Richelle.'

'Friday night,' he said, turning to look at the small, sparse back garden through the modest patio doors.

'I believe you were going to work. Your wif- partner was heading out to the shops?'

Dixon nodded.

'You said this was around half past five?'

'Since you already know,' he said, turning around, 'I don't see why we need to re-tread old ground. Unless you're trying to catch me out. I told you yesterday morning that –'

'Mr Dixon, I'm sorry. I just need to make absolutely certain –'

'What I said yesterday still stands. I left the house at half past five. She left shortly after. I went to work, she went to the shops.'

'Are you sure?'

'Absolutely. Unambiguously. Entire–'

'You see, Mr Dixon, I'm not sure how that can be the case.'

Dixon came back to the coffee table and eased himself into a chair. 'Go on. You clearly suspect something. Tell me what it is.'

'Ought I to suspect something, Mr Dixon?'

'Let's not play games.'

She closed her pocket book. 'You said you left the house first. If that's true then I don't see how you can be so certain that Miss Ibbott departed the house at half past five - shortly after yourself - and went straight to... where was it?'

'Are you partnered?'

'Married.'

'To a man?'

She nodded.

'Did you ever imagine as you left the house this morning that you might never see him again?'

'Well, no, I -'

'No,' said Dixon. 'And I bet if you had you'd have stopped for a moment, looked at him, tried to burn a picture of what he looks like, what he was wearing, what he's about to do in the next few minutes, into the deepest, safest part of your mind. Wouldn't you?'

'Of course, but then -'

'But you didn't, did you. You probably kissed him goodbye and he told you to be careful... and that was that. You didn't ever think he might not be there tonight. I didn't think Richelle wouldn't be here when I got home on Friday...'

He was good. She would give him that. Few

people – few innocent people, unless they were particularly distressed or had been needlessly harangued – would have argued back quite so convincingly.

She thought of the copy of The Sarnian that Bichard had shown her the night before, the Leggy Le Page heading and the suggestion that the paper had subjected Dixon to 'three hours of intense through-the-curtains interrogation'. Could that be to blame for his spiky demeanour? Perhaps it also explained why he'd been sleeping in the lounge at the back of the house, and taking his meals in there, too. The stairs were just inside the front door, which meant that to use them – to go up to bed – he'd have to bring himself close to the pack of reporters that had camped on his doorstep the previous day.

'Tell me about The Fleet,' she said.

'Have you listened to it?'

'Last night. First time, I'm afraid.'

Dixon shrugged. 'Doesn't surprise me.'

'I enjoyed it. But... I was surprised. That you were in it, I mean. I'd have thought with Miss Ibbott being found –'

'It's pre-recorded,' Dixon said. 'Last night's episode would have been in the can six or seven weeks ago.'

Christine had known that already. She was well aware that regular episodes of any radio drama were assembled in parts and played out from the station computer. Renouf had dispatched Falla to the station that morning to talk to Kira Spooner and find out exactly how it worked – and in particular, what had happened during Friday night's live broadcast.

Even so, she narrowed her eyes and put on a show of confusion, much like the one she'd adopted the morning before when he'd come to report Richelle's disappearance.

'You said when you came in yesterday morning that when you left Miss Ibbott you were on your way to work. It was my understanding that The Fleet was broadcast live.'

'No,' Dixon said, sitting forward in his chair and speaking more slowly. 'Friday night's episode was live. It was the tenth anniversary. My character... are you following?'

She nodded.

'My character, Thomas Thoumine, was injured. He fell into the sea on New Year's Eve. All a big cliffhanger, all leading up to Friday's episode when he went back on the boat for the first time after months of rehabilitation. It was live, and it was longer, because it was a special edition.'

Christine nodded slowly. 'Got it. So the rest of the cast and crew, they would be able to vouch for your whereabouts during the broadcast?'

'Four and a half million people would be able to vouch for my whereabouts during that broadcast. They heard me. Live.'

'Well then,' she said, tucking her notebook into her bag. 'It all sounds rather open and closed to me. If you wouldn't mind just jotting down what you remember of your movements over the rest of the weekend…'

'Of course.'

'Which only leaves the matter of identifying Miss Ibbott's body. If that's who this is. Do you have the time?'

'Now?'

'Unless you're busy,' she said. 'Considering there's no media parked on your doorstep, though, I'd say now was as good a time as any, wouldn't you?'

The Sarnian, Editorial Conference

'So tell us about this accident,' Freya Carlisle said. She asked the room as a whole rather than anyone in particular.

Ollie jumped in. 'It was their big story over New Year. Everyone knew it was going to happen, it was so well trailed. We ran a story about it.'

He started sorting through his papers again.

'It's here,' said Harry Ozanne, rearranging the

windows on his laptop so they could all see it in the mirrored image projected onto the wall.

'Dixon's character was knocked off the boat,' Harry said. 'Something to do with a jib and rough seas. He ended up face down in the water for ten minutes - most of an episode - and when they pulled him out he was unconscious.'

'But he lived?' Freya asked. She had never listened to The Fleet, and despite having told the rest of the team that they ought to consider tuning in an essential part of their jobs, she herself had no intention of doing so any time soon.

'Kind of,' Ollie said. 'They were twenty-four hours from shore, conveniently, so they got him back on dry land in the following episode.'

'That coincided with Dixon's holiday,' Alfie clarified. 'He was comatose for the next two weeks. Regained consciousness as Dixon returned from a fortnight in France.'

'Handy,' Freya said.

'Very,' Ollie said. 'Only, I'm not so sure he'll be glad he came back. Thoumine's almost... unintelligible. My guess is he's waiting for his contract to run its course, and then he'll be off.'

Freya nodded. 'Well, then. There's your first question, Mr Carey. I suggest you run along, find Dixon and ask it.'

Police Headquarters, 10.15am

Forensics Lab

In the next thirty minutes, three unrelated events occurred. First, Christine drove Dixon to Town so he could identify Richelle in the mortuary. She'd promised to arrange for a car to bring him home, but Dixon had refused. He didn't want to provide his neighbour with any further gossip.

A few minutes after they'd left, Ollie pulled on his brakes and glided his bike to a halt at the end of Dixon's front path. He propped his bike against the wall and knocked on the door, once again taking a look through the letterbox. He couldn't see inside this time; Dixon had covered it over with newspaper - from the look of it, one of the nationals. Ollie gave it a few exploratory jabs with his finger but it was more than just a page or two - probably most of a section folded over on itself - and he couldn't break through.

The neighbour appeared, standing up from behind a water butt, slopping water from a can as he waddled across the lawn. He told Ollie not to bother: Dixon had left in a car with a red-headed woman.

'Probably one of your lot,' the neighbour added. 'Asked a lot of questions.'

From the description it sounded more to Ollie like the police woman he'd met above Marble Bay the previous morning. He had to think for a moment before he remembered her name.

Four miles away, at about the same time, in a basement at police headquarters, Marc Renouf tapped his knuckles on the forensic officer's desk. Charlie Dubois hadn't seen him there, but now that he did he looked up from his keyboard, pulled out his earphones and smiled.

'Coffee?' he asked.

Renouf shook his head. 'I'll do it,' he said, walking across to the stubby glass flask that served as the lab's proxy kettle. 'I can never be sure you boys have washed your hands whenever you've got a dead body to play with.'

'When did you last see a body in here?' Dubois lifted some papers to find his phone, and tapped the screen to silence the music.

Propped on a tripod above a low-burning Bunsen, the flask had been on a permanent brew, day and night, for five years. Charlie would spoon in a fresh batch of beans every morning, ground by hand in a pestle and mortar, and top up the flask from a jar of distilled water. The grounds had formed a thick cake now and, having hardened through years of slow heating, they provided a measure of insulation that seasoned and mellowed the brew.

Renouf poured half a mug and brought it back to the desk. 'So what news?'

Dubois shuffled the papers and picked out two printed pages. He slipped off the clip that held them together and ran his eyes to the foot of each one. 'Well, it looks like a blow to the head. Just one, fairly accurate - most likely a fluke, I'd say - inferior to the skull between the second and third cervical vertebrae.' He looked up and saw Renouf frowning. 'Just here,' he said by way of explanation, touching the back of his own neck.

'That's what killed her?' Renouf asked.

'Probably. Almost certainly. All we can say for sure, though, is that whoever did it used some force and a heavy, blunt instrument of some kind.'

'A rounded rock from the beach?'

'Perhaps,' said Dubois, not in the least surprised that Renouf had said it before him. He'd already jotted those words in his margin and circled them round with red pen, not so much to tell Renouf, but to act as an aide memoire.

To say that Renouf and Dubois were friends would overstate their rapport. They didn't socialise or take their lunch together. Renouf was married, happily so; Dubois was five years divorced and somewhat relieved. Neither man could guess how the other might spend his time away from the office yet somehow, on a level entirely impersonal, the two dissimilar allies were drawn to each other like ormers to undisturbed rocks. Either one could largely predict which words the other was poised to speak, second-guess his subsequent thoughts and come to the same conclusion. It was purely professional.

Dubois turned over the paper and tapped the words 'smoothed rock' with the end of his pen. Renouf smiled.

'It's pure supposition,' Dubois admitted. 'Her skin wasn't broken, so I doubt we'd find any evidence without DNAing every rock. We found flecks of blood on her lips and between her lower incisors, so we know there was some discharge shortly after death. What we don't know is where it might have spilled as there's evidence that she was moved.'

'By the killer?'

Dubois shook his head. 'More likely the tide, I'd say. You remember she was resting on that line of seaweed?'

Renouf nodded.

'That's where the incoming tide left her. It pushed her up the beach.'

Renouf grunted into his mug. 'We're lucky she wasn't washed out to sea.'

'She might have been,' said Dubois. 'If it had happened in one of the other bays. Marble Bay's pretty narrow.'

'So it's straight in, straight out?'

Charlie dipped his chin. 'Not much lateral movement there. Tide comes in, tide goes out. If it had been Pembroke, or one of the west-coast bays – Cobo or Rocquaine, say – we'd have had a lot more lateral movement. She'd have been swept across the sand as much as up it. We could have lost her.'

'But she'd probably have been seen.'

'Probably,' Charlie agreed, 'which is most likely the reason she was killed somewhere secluded like Marble Bay, rather than somewhere more open.'

Renouf stood up and returned to the flask. The coffee was good that morning; he poured himself some more. 'Is it not more likely she fell from the cliff and broke her neck when she landed?' he asked, returning to his seat.

Dubois shook his head.

'On the way down, then?'

'I've seen no evidence that would support that idea. Beyond the broken neck, there was none of the scratching or other breaks you'd expect to see on a body that had fallen – what – a hundred feet? Unless she was already unconscious her natural instinct would have been to put out her arms, for all the good that would do. She had no chance of arresting her fall.'

'There's no possibility that she didn't? That for some reason she just fell and –'

'It's instinct,' Charlie interrupted. 'Like closing your eyes when you sneeze. She wouldn't have been able to help it, yet both arms remain intact.'

'Unless she was already unconscious...'

'No,' Charlie said. 'That doesn't work. There was none of the trauma to her internal organs that would have been consistent with falling from such a height, and no scrapes, scratches or bruises of the kind she'd have sustained knocking against the cliff and foliage on the way down.'

Dubois could see that Renouf wasn't convinced. He put down the report and picked up a map of the bay, which Renouf recognised as an excerpt from an official States plan. 'We had considered the possibility she might have fallen,' Dubois conceded, reassuring the inspector that his suggestion wasn't entirely outlandish. 'Taking into account the tides over the last three days and the eventual position of the body, she could only have fallen from this point here...' – he used his pen to mark out a spot at one end of the bay – 'or here. As you can see, at either point her fall would have been interrupted by outcrops that would have marked her body on its way down. She certainly – as far as we can tell at this stage, and by that I mean ninety-nine point something percent – she certainly died on that beach.'

Renouf sipped his coffee and thought. 'What if someone had carried her down? I'm right in thinking she lived just above the bay, aren't I? Could she not have been killed there, or somewhere in the trees perhaps, and carried down to the shore by whoever it was that wanted – needed – to dispose of the body.'

'That, I can't tell you,' Dubois admitted. After looking a moment longer at the map, he continued, 'I think it's unlikely. The last few steps from the path are steep and awkward, aren't they?'

Renouf nodded.

'Although these steps here...' Charlie traced his pen along the path to a concrete staircase that led to the back of the bay. 'These are far more regular. If he used these...'

'No,' Renouf said. 'Le Page and I made that mistake. Had to turn back in the end. They were roped off for repair, missing a couple of feet halfway down. I'd guess they were washed away in the winter storm.'

'Then it would have been difficult to carry her all the way,' Dubois concluded. 'Although, that said, there are few better places to hide a body. It might have been worth the effort if you needed to buy yourself some time. Perhaps to flee the island?'

The two men fell silent for a moment as each pictured the last few steps of the only open route to the bay. Dubois was right; they were tall and uneven. It seemed to them both that they'd been cut with more respect for the lie of the boulders that lined the foreshore than the needs of the bay's infrequent visitors.

Charlie had graduated from Cambridge with a First in molecular physics, but it was more often his steadfast common sense – like this – that proved his greatest asset. His Masters, at Leeds, was forensic science.

Renouf had little doubt that Dubois would find the proof he needed to finger whoever had left her there, and even without a body could likely have found them a killer; he'd simply have needed more time.

Dubois himself had never considered his terms at Cambridge and Leeds, and later the two slow years he'd spent with the Thames Valley force, anything more than an interlude. He knew that sooner or later the island would call him home, and when the forensics position had opened up he'd booked a seat on the next Aurigny to leave from Southampton. For close to an hour his plane had circled in fog above

Braye, the harbour that sheltered the Alderney fleet, and just as the pilot announced that their tanks held sufficient fuel for one more circuit before they diverted to France, a gap had opened below them and the small propeller plane turned its nose and dived towards Guernsey. Rarely before, and never since, had the island had so great a cause to be glad of a change in the weather. Without it, Dubois would have missed his interview and the States Police would have found itself short of his skills.

He'd arrived at headquarters with minutes to spare, but his record had preceded him and his shrewd, analytical mind had impressed the five-person panel. They asked him back for a second interview and hinted even as they set the time and the place that he ought to consider how much he would ask for his home on the outskirts of Reading. He didn't need asking twice; he instructed an agent that afternoon, calling through from the airport, and sold it the following week, well below market value for the sake of getting out fast. He didn't doubt for a moment that the second interview would be anything other than a formality, and so it turned out. He took lodgings on the island, had his belongings sent over by sea and now, seventeen years later, could think of few good reasons to ever return to the mainland.

'Are her friends and immediate family accounted for?' he asked at last, the two men having sat silent for a full minute, staring at the map.

Renouf sat back in his seat. 'As far as we can tell. She had no blood family left. She lived with George Dixon – or he lived with her, more accurately, as she owned the house – and he's not going anywhere. Her work colleagues are all accounted for...'

'What did she do?'

'Charity, on and off. Gave all her money to a fund for orphans and used to pop in every couple of days to help out.'

'Which leaves what? A random killing? Tourist? Marble Bay's pretty obscure, but it's not entirely impossible it could have been a visitor. Followed her down from the path, perhaps. They could have flown out or sailed long before we found her.'

'I don't know.' Renouf stood up and walked to the window, resting his mug on the sill. 'Somehow I find it unlikely. Even if she wasn't murdered, even if – and I don't believe this – even if it was an accident, or a robbery gone wrong, you'd have to be a pretty brazen tourist, visitor, whatever, to do it out in the open. That bay is exposed at this time of year. There aren't many leaves on the trees. Unless you knew for sure that the path wasn't heavily used...'

He turned around to see Charlie nodding. 'That's the conclusion we reached down here, too,' Charlie said. 'I'm pretty sure this was a local. Besides...' He turned to a two-drawer cabinet behind his desk, opened the top drawer and took out a small plastic bag. 'We found this.' He held it up for Renouf to see.

Renouf came back to the desk, leaving his coffee on the window sill. 'Hers?' he asked, taking the neatly sealed bag from Dubois' outstretched hand. Inside it was a radio, roughly the size of a pack of cards, with an analogue tuning dial at one end and a small dotted grille at the other.

'Most likely. There was some waxy residue on one of the earbuds which we've sent for analysis, along with a sample from Miss Ibbott's ear. We have a service level agreement with the mainland's National DNA Database. If the two samples match they'll be able to tell us.'

'Which would give us...' Renouf thought for a moment. 'What, exactly?'

'A fairly strong suggestion, if not outright proof that she was killed in situ.'

'How so?'

'Well, imagine you were the killer,' Charlie said. 'Would you bother to carry this radio down with the body?'

'Unlikely.'

'Indeed,' said Charlie. 'More likely you'd leave it in the house, or you'd be so preoccupied with the corpse you'd drop it somewhere on the path without noticing.'

'You think she was wearing it when she was attacked?'

'We don't know, but it's a possibility we're exploring. It might have been just enough to mask the sound of her assailant's approach if he came from behind. The battery was flat by the time we retrieved it, but the volume was set fairly loud, so it could have been running since she was killed.'

'Assuming she hadn't taken it off so they could speak.'

'I doubt she did that. There's no indication she struggled at all; no bruising on her wrists where a killer might have held her hands to disable her, and no other damage than the break in her neck.'

'And that came from behind.'

Charlie nodded. 'I don't think she saw him approach.'

'Unless she knew who it was,' said Renouf, 'and trusted him.' He looked again at the radio and pressed through the thin plastic bag on the now quite useless power switch. '93FM,' he said, reading from the dial. 'What station is this?'

'If it's accurate, its probably the BBC local.

Radio Guernsey's on 93.2.'

'That's where Dixon works, isn't it.'

Dubois nodded.

'Do we know what she was listening to when she was killed?' Renouf asked.

'You mean was she listening to Dixon's show?'

Renouf nodded. 'Yes, the... Fleet, is it?'

'That would depend when she died.'

'Which was?'

Dubois sucked his teeth, then turned back to his computer. He closed the document he'd been working on when Renouf entered the room and pulled up a spreadsheet of figures and unfamiliar formulae. He let the air rush out through his nostrils and Renouf saw in him the unconscious habits of a reformed smoker.

'Have you heard of Casper's Law?' he asked.

'Solicitors?'

Dubois smiled. 'It's a theory. A scale, really, that measures decomposition. Human decomposition in particular, in the air, in water, and when buried.'

'Faster at each stage?'

'No. Quite the opposite, in fact. It's half the speed when submerged; burial slows it by close to ninety percent, which would suggest, depending how long Miss Ibbott spent in the water, that she was killed somewhere between twenty-four and seventy-two hours before her body was found.'

'Or before we were notified.' Renouf sat down and toyed with the leaves on the small cannabis plant, neatly potted, that lived on Charlie's desk: a confiscated exhibit, yet to be destroyed, from a trial that had long since passed. It was clear that someone was watering it. The cleaners were never permitted into the lab or its antechamber without a chaperone, so Renouf could only suppose that Dubois was keeping it alive himself.

'That's still a rather wide window,' Renouf said, working out how many times the numbers divided down.

'Well yes, it would be,' Charlie smiled.

'But...'

'But we can apply further data to the equation.'

And here it was, his party piece. Renouf could tell he'd been leading up to something - something he was happy about - and now it looked as though it was an accurate time of death, the most useful lead they could hope for so early in the investigation. It would allow them to focus their attention on working out where each of the potential culprits might have been.

'What kind of data?'

'Second stage instar maggots.'

Renouf frowned.

‘Hatched blowfly eggs,’ Dubois explained. ‘Which we found in large numbers in her mouth and eyes. That would suggest she’d been dead for a day at least, but certainly no more than three.’

‘Which confirms what we already knew.’

‘Which is?’ Dubois knew the answer, but wanted to be sure they agreed.

‘Any time between…’ Renouf tried to visualise the days as he counted them back. ‘Monday morning when she was found and Friday evening when Dixon claims he last saw her.’

Charlie nodded. ‘Yes, although I think it’s actually closer to Friday evening, if not the evening itself. By the time we recovered the body the instar maggots were falling prey to larger insects. That doesn’t happen for the first two days, which pushes back the time of death to Saturday morning at the latest, either just after seven o’clock, or twelve hours before that.’

He turned back to the filing cabinet and took a second package from the bottom drawer. He passed it across the desk, and Renouf saw as he took it that it contained a small gold watch. The glass was broken, and the face had been stained by water. The stationary hands read five past seven.

‘You’re presuming this was broken when she fell?’ Renouf asked, holding it up.

'I don't see why she would have been wearing it otherwise.'

'So assuming it was correct at the time it stopped working, we can isolate two very narrow windows during which she was killed? Seven on Saturday morning, or seven on Friday night?'

This time Dubois shook his head. 'We can do better than that. Can you pass me that paper?' He pointed to the copy of The Sarnian he'd left by the Bunsen when pouring his coffee that morning.

Renouf tipped back in his chair to reach it and passed it across the desk, pulling a face that suggested he disapproved of Charlie's choice of paper. Charlie ignored him, and turned through the pages until he found the weather and tides.

'Marble Bay is almost entirely cut off at high tide. Agreed?'

'Agreed.'

'Two high and two low tides a day; each between twenty and fifty minutes later than they were the day before,' Dubois said, more to himself than to Renouf. 'Now we know it's either four or four and half days since she died, so we need to subtract between eighty minutes - an hour and twenty - and two hundred and twenty-five minutes - three and three quarter hours - from today's tides to see what they were doing the day or night she was killed. High tide tonight is nine fifteen; four days ago is was seven thirty-seven. An hour and thirty-eight minutes' difference. Right in the middle of our window.' He looked up, sat back and folded his arms.

'So she was killed on Friday night,' Renouf said.

'She was. Shortly before high tide. Her watch glass broke when it hit the pebbles, and our assailant just had time to escape before he got his feet wet. The rising tide caught her body at ten past seven, or thereabouts, pushing it further up the beach and wedging her behind the rock where Carey found her on Monday.'

The two men sat in silence for a moment while Renouf digested Charlie's hypothesis.

'That would certainly fit with Dixon's story,' Renouf said.

'And as he was on air at the time, in the live episode of... whatever it is...'

'The Fleet.'

'The Fleet, it would also substantiate his alibi.'

Renouf drummed a rhythm on the arm of his chair. 'Which brings us back to where we began. No suspects, and seemingly no motivation.'

Dubois raised his eyebrows. 'Time is running on, and nobody seems to be spooked. I think it's unlikely her friends or colleagues are involved.

Who might be left if you ruled them out?'

Renouf shook his head. 'To date, nobody.'

'No,' said Dubois. It was almost a murmur. He sat back in his chair and tented his fingers under his chin. 'Of course,' he said slowly and carefully. 'There is one person we know for sure had contact with the body.'

Renouf thought. 'Carey?'

Dubois pursed his lips and said nothing.

'Interesting,' said Renouf. 'Have you seen anything that might suggest he was involved in some way?'

Dubois shook his head. 'Nothing. I think he's an outsider at best.'

'Unless...' Renouf picked up the small bag containing the radio. 'When would you expect those results? The DNA on the wax?'

'Three days,' said Dubois, checking the date in the corner of his computer screen. 'Two at a push.'

'Can I borrow this?' Renouf held up the package.

'So long as you sign a chit. I'm in Sark for the next few days anyway.' Dubois reached down to lift a holdall from under his desk. 'Meeting the Jersey lot to swap notes. Give it to Minchin when you check it back in.'

Renouf slipped it into his inside pocket. 'Will do. Can I use your phone?' He picked up the receiver and pressed the button for an outside line. 'And can you find me a number? The Sarnian. Oliver Carey's desk. No, get me his mobile. If he's any good, he won't be sat at his desk at a time like this.'

BBC Radio Guernsey, 11.10am

Constable Falla drove from police HQ to the BBC: one kind of station to another. Christine had called ahead from the Ibbott house – their agreed signal that it was safe for him to visit Dixon's place of work without arousing suspicion. The chances of Dixon arriving while he was there were nil, and should he leave HQ before Falla called to say he was finished, Christine would phone again and bring the constable back to base. The only question was whether Kira Spooner would be there – or agree to see him – as the ad-hoc nature of his visit meant he hadn't been able to book himself in.

In the event, she did.

She met him in reception and walked him through an untidy office to her desk in a distant corner. She instructed an intern to make them some drinks, and brushed her skirt flat on the chair.

'This will be about George Dixon?' she asked, pre-empting him.

'Yes.' Falla took out his notebook. 'You heard what happened to Richelle Ibbott?'

She made an affirmative sound.

'And you know that she –'

'She was George Dixon's partner. Yes. Is he a suspect?'

'No, no. No more than anyone else. He may have been the last to see her alive, though, so I'm trying to ascertain his movements that night.'

'Then should you not be talking to him?'

'We are. One of my colleagues is with him as we speak.'

'Well then.'

Falla cleared his throat and turned through the book until he came to an empty page. He wrote Kira's name at the top of the sheet. 'We believe Miss Ibbott was killed some time between Friday night and Monday morning. Mr Dixon was here at the start of that period. Am I right?'

'Do you listen?'

'I'm sorry?'

'To The Fleet. Do you listen.'

'Oh, no. Not often. Sometimes. I listened last night.'

'You and half the island, I should think, Mr...?'

'Falla. Constable.'

'Constable Falla. It seems yesterday's story in The Sarnian has somewhat piqued the local interest in our drama. It's a shame we can't count them in our figures.'

Falla gently raised his hand off the page, tilting his palm towards her. 'Specifically Friday night, Ms Spooner. It was a live episode, is that right?'

'That's right.'

'And that's unusual?'

'Very. We've done it once before. To mark the thousandth episode.'

'And this one marked...?'

'Ten years.'

'And it featured...' — he turned back through the pages to the notes he'd written the previous evening — 'Thomas Thoumine.'

'Yes.'

'That's Mr Dixon's character?'

'Yes.'

The intern returned with a pair of drinks in BBC mugs; Falla's had a smudge of lipstick close to the handle. Kira thanked her for bringing them over and suggested to Falla that they step into one of the studios.

'We'll be able to talk in private.'

They picked up their drinks and she guided him through a sequence of doors, each of which fit its frame so tightly that he could feel the pressure change from room to room. The carpet on the floor and the walls, the slightly spongy surface of the tables and desks... together they seemed to absorb every sound, leaving a silence so pure he could feel it cushion his ears. It smelled of dead air and stale coffee, the latter from three dirty mugs that sat at the centre of the table, the skin of milk on their drying contents slowly turning sour.

It was a small room, half of it given over to four seats and four microphones set around a square table that seemed to have been set up for panel discussions. The other half accommodated a U-shaped desk covered in sliders and switches. Rectangular buttons below them flashed between amber and red.

'So that's what's going out now?' Falla asked. He pointed over Kira's shoulder, through a large window and into a neighbouring studio. It was the same as the one they were in, except that rather than two people sitting at the square table there was just one, seated at the U-shaped desk and speaking into a sponge-covered microphone.

'That's the morning show. The one you can see through there's the control room.' She pointed towards another window, set at an angle so that it chopped off the corner of each studio and allowed an operator to see into both simply by turning their chair.

The control room was larger than either of

the studios. It was more airy, too, with a window onto the outside world, and walls that were painted rather than covered in carpet.

Falla sipped at his drink, turning the lipstick mark away from his mouth. 'So tell me how it works,' he said. 'The Fleet, I mean. Do you record it in here?'

'In here or in there,' Kira said, thumbing towards the other studio. 'It depends which one is live. We alternate between the two. Morning's coming from that studio right now, so Light Lunch will come from here and the Cone Zone will be back over there. We fit the recordings around them.'

'And for the live broadcast on Friday?'

'We used them both. Nobody else was on air.'

Falla counted the seats. Four at each table, plus one at each of the curved desks. It wasn't enough for the full cast. 'Plus the control room?' he asked, trying to imagine where the surplus actors would stand.

'No. I was in there with two engineers.'

'But that's only ten seats. And ten microphones.'

'Aah. I see what you're getting at. We have booths for travel and news. We used them. That gave us fifteen mics, so we had one to spare, which we used for any effects that we couldn't play out from the computer.'

Falla leaned forward and back in his chair

to get a better view of the control room and any smaller windows that might lead off to the booths. He couldn't find them. All he could see were the two large studio windows and a third that looked out on the car park. Its fourth wall was almost entirely consumed by the door that led back to the office.

'You can't see them from here,' Kira said. 'They're just little box rooms off the main floor. Not much more than a mic and a tiny mixing desk.'

'So when they go to the travel...'

Kira nodded. 'The chit-chat? They can't see each other.' She smiled. 'It's a common assumption. Most people make that mistake.'

'So it's like they're on the phone?'

'If you like, but better quality. And no handsets, of course.'

'And during the live broadcast Dixon was... where?'

Kira thought for a moment. Her eyes settled on the digital clock mounted above the door. Falla followed her gaze, and he watched the small scarlet pimples set into its rim disappear, second by second, counting up to the next whole minute.

'Do you know,' she said at last, 'I couldn't rightly say. Probably here, being one of the major characters, but I couldn't be sure.'

Falla pinched his lips. 'Would you have a think? Over the next day or so.'

'If it would help.'

'It would. Perhaps for George Dixon as much as ourselves.'

'You are treating it as murder, then?'

They weren't - not officially - not yet, at least, although Falla suspected that that would all change at the afternoon briefing. Until then he had to be diplomatic, and at least a little ambiguous.

'I shouldn't believe everything you read in The Sarnian, Ms Spooner.'

Port Soif, noon

Renouf had taken a chair that put his back towards the kiosk; his small backpack was propped against one of the legs. He couldn't have sat any further away from the kiosk's counter and hatch, nor the hungry twist of visitors closing on ice cream and gâche unless he'd moved into the car park. Yet even at that small distance, the contrast between his suit and tie, and the shorts of the visitors around him, made him look like an out-of-place uncle, lost on his way to a wedding.

It was a quiet spot at the end of the garden, out of the view of the beach and out of the reach of the breeze from the sea. All about were the seasonal sparrows, newly returned from Africa, dancing through the pampas as though it were charged, and beyond them, the distant babble and splash of the visitors playing like kids in the shallows.

Ollie weaved his bike through the seats and laid it down on the bank by Renouf. He arranged the pedals to make it lie flat.

'Inspector,' he nodded.

'Marc, please.' Renouf set down a half-drunk mug of black coffee and cast an open hand towards an empty chair. 'Can I buy you a drink?'

Ollie took a bottle from the frame of his bike. 'Thank you,' he said, sitting down. 'I'll stick with this.'

Renouf's call aside, they hadn't spoken since meeting the previous morning on the path above Marble Bay. Ollie had been preoccupied with the goings-on about them, and he'd paid the inspector's appearance scant attention. Instead he'd been memorising all that he could about the scene on the sand, crafting his observations into a series of shaky headlines.

Yet he was sure that Renouf hadn't looked so tired then as he did right now, sitting in a deckchair in the sun. The bags beneath his eyes and the whisper of stubble lining his jaw belonged to a man who had missed a night's sleep.

Did he thrive on long days and short nights, Ollie wondered. Or was it merely a clever disguise – for when he spoke, his voice was clear, free from the slur of the over-tired.

Renouf pulled up his sleeve and looked at his watch. 'Thirty-seven minutes,' he said, calculating how long it was since he'd called Ollie's mobile from Charlie Dubois' desk phone.

'I would have been sooner if you'd given me some warning.'

'On the contrary, I'm rather impressed. It's how far? Five miles?'

'Thereabouts. I was down at the Ibbott house.'

'Anyone home?'

Ollie scrunched his nose. 'Nope.'

Renouf knew that Dixon was still at the station with Christine Le Page.

He looked up, beyond Ollie's head as he traced the route in his mind: up the hill from the house, as far as the main road. A little way north, then cutting inland through Vale and Castel... 'I believe you're a runner,' he said at last.

Ollie nodded. 'Most mornings. Although I ride most of the way. I just run the last bit down to the beach.'

'You could teach the rest of us a thing or two.' Renouf slapped his own belly, confirming Ollie's suspicions. Standing tall that first morning had hidden it well, but sitting in a low-slung deckchair caused his midriff to spill over his belt and spread like an over-cooked soufflé. 'What is it? Your motivation? A girl you need to impress?'

Ollie smiled. 'There might have been. Once. Back in Southampton, but she's... well, it's hard to tell these days.'

Renouf twitched his head, encouraging him to go on.

'We email,' Ollie said. 'Sometimes she sends me a postcard.'

'Which would be all the more reason to keep it up, wouldn't it?'

'Being more or less a free man?'

'Absolutely. And how much better would your chances be looking like that than...' He paused for a moment, then looked down at his belly. 'Well, like this.'

Ollie hid himself behind the spout of his bottle. He sucked hard, gulping down the lukewarm water.

'What's the secret?' Renouf leaned forward conspiratorially. 'Music? A special running playlist? A radio?'

Ollie shook his head. He took the bottle away from his mouth, and it bubbled and gurgled as the sides popped back out to their usual shape. 'What do you mean?'

'Your power track. That's what they call it, isn't it?'

'My motivation?' He shrugged. 'I don't know, really. Maybe the ocean. I like the sound of the waves.'

'You're a man of the sea?'

'My degree is marine biology.'

'Do you have a boat?'

'I do. The Huffin' Puffin.' He tipped up the end of the sentence as though asking Renouf whether he knew it. 'She's moored at Portelet.'

Renouf did.

He knew it well enough for the name to cause him to flinch, and to shift in his seat entirely instinctively.

He hadn't heard that name in... what was it now?

Two years?

He'd hoped he might never have heard it again. But here it was, and here – it was so obvious now – here was Remus Carey's progeny.

'So you're that Carey. I thought your face was familiar. Your father and I...' He stopped for a beat or two and thought better of saying whatever it was he'd started. 'He was a great man.'

Ollie smiled.

'So he left you the Huffin' Puffin?'

'He did.'

'She's a lovely boat, lovely boat. I only...' Again his words trailed off, and Ollie let them hang in the air. Renouf smiled, and reaching into the backpack he lifted out a plastic bag - a sealed evidence bag like the ones Ollie had often seen on TV - inside of which was a small radio and two tangled earbuds. 'Do you know where we found this?'

Ollie shook his head.

'It isn't yours?' Renouf passed it across the table. 'Pick it up. Take a closer look. The bag's been secured; you won't do it any harm.'

Ollie picked it up and turned it around. The dial showed 93FM, or thereabouts. BBC Radio Guernsey: he recognised the frequency from Simon's signoffs at the end of the news. There was condensation behind the dial. Other than that it was unremarkable. It was cheap, with few controls and probably even fewer functions. The earbuds were light and their cables thin; it seemed unlikely they'd be much good when tuned to anything other than speech.

'Never seen it before,' he said.

'We found it in Marble Bay. Where you discovered the body.'

'It's Miss Ibbott's?'

'Interesting question,' Renouf said with a shrug. 'Some might suggest that this would be yours, not hers. You were out on your run, listening to the radio, perhaps, and you were... surprised... by the body.'

'Go on...'

Renouf shrugged, trying to remain casual. 'You'd been swimming, I believe. You must have left your belongings somewhere. It would have been easy, under the circumstances, to have left it behind. Am I right?'

'In that some might suggest such a thing,' Ollie said.

Renouf smiled. He'd heard talk of Ollie – unfavourable talk, suggestions he might not be up to the job of staff reporter. Yet the way he could listen and wring his own meaning out of a quote greatly impressed the inspector. He might make a decent reporter yet. As underhand as the rest of them.

'Assuming that was when you left it there, of course,' Renouf said. 'Assuming you didn't lose it a few days before. Friday night, maybe. It looks like it might have been wet; perhaps it was caught by the rising tide, trapped by some rocks. There would have been five high tides between Friday night and when it was found. If you'd had it clipped to your belt on an evening run –'

'I told you,' Ollie interrupted, putting the evidence bag on the table and pushing it towards Renouf.

'That you run in the mornings?'

'That it's not mine.'

'Well, we shall see.'

'You don't believe me?'

'It doesn't matter what I believe.'

'Or don't believe, I presume.'

Renouf tipped his head to one side. 'We'll know soon enough. We've sent some samples for testing. The results should be back within the week. I'd wager you're right, and they'll prove that this did indeed belong to Miss Ibbott. If that's the case we'll have no cause to discuss it further.' He smiled. 'I thought it only fair to give you a chance, though. To have your say. Let me know if you'd seen it before - or if you knew how it might have come to be found on the beach...'

Ollie stared back, and Renouf tried to read him. He settled on cocky. There was something about the way that Carey met his gaze and held it; how he didn't blink or flinch or let his eyes drop. It felt like he was challenging him - daring him to take things further. He didn't seem to be showing any signs of guilt or fear, but then neither had his father, Renouf reminded himself - not even at the very end, so they'd said.

'I'm afraid you've wasted your time,' Ollie said, pressing closed the cap on his bottle.

Renouf sat forward and struggled out of his

chair. 'If you say so,' he said, reaching for his backpack and tidying the radio into its unzipped front pocket. He took out a small card and laid it down in its place. 'If you do recall having seen it before, though. Anything at all...' He smiled and turned and strode towards the kiosk.

'Oh, Inspector,' Ollie called.

Renouf turned around to see Carey pick up his bike and start to wheel it towards him.

'I won't be needing this,' he said, slipping the card into Renouf's breast pocket. 'We've got you on file.'

Vale Parish, 7.15pm

Rosalynd Holdbrook stood at her kitchen sink and looked at the Vale Parish Church. Site of her baptism, site of her marriage.

Her guests had departed, the bridge table was stowed beneath the stairs, and now she stood washing teapot and cups, her arms half submerged in the suds. Her mind was on nothing of any great matter, half an ear on the window-sill radio playing out the news.

Every room had a radio - some large, some small - hidden somewhere about it. The one in the bedroom sat on the nightstand. In the lounge, beside a television that she rarely turned on. The bathroom radio perched on the cabinet, itself above the sink. Here in the kitchen it sat on the sill so the incoming light could recharge its solar battery. Simon Langlois was reading the last few stories, the sport, and now the weather. The closing jingle segued into a tune that she herself had commissioned. Hornpipe, variation B, it was called. Twenty-seven seconds long, with a dampened tail of seven seconds over which came the opening lines of The Fleet.

How easy it is to forget, she thought.

Seven fifteen, every night, a deadline around which her life had revolved for eight years. Splicing virtual tape until the last moment, then sending it out across the island from an ageing computer under the studio desk. Once London learned of its local success it went to the south-west, too, then the south coast, and the Hebrides, Orkneys and other bits of Scotland cast adrift from the mainland. Fishing fleets and island life rang a familiar bell in those maritime communities.

Happy though those years had been, she'd sworn on downing her headphones that The Fleet would have no place in her retirement. She wouldn't allow herself to grow old by hanging on to the past. 'Onwards, forwards, ever new' had long been her motto, thwarted now by wet, sudsy hands that prevented her switching it off, forcing her to listen to her first episode in two years.

She tried to ignore it, but the theme ran on for too long, the first line of dialogue came too late, and as Rosalynd clucked her tongue the action cut from the throb of the wheelhouse and settled itself on the trawler's slick deck. To left and to right, angry spray spewed from her speakers and lashed the characters' faces and necks. Their boots slipped about on the fish-oiled boards as a fierce gust of wind tossed the boat towards port. Its two diesel engines hacked and coughed and beat at thin air as they struggled to crest a sharp wave.

A rattle, and then a clatter of chains on the boards, skidding across the deck, and the muted cry of a furious sailor to 'pick those bloody things up'. And then the Leviathan rush, as a towering surge broke on the side of the vessel. The boat, the sailors, all action among them rolled left and then right as the heavy, deep keel kept it from turning right over, and the skipper turned the wheel towards starboard to point their prow at the leading edge of the storm. The only way they could weather it, Rosalynd knew, would be to drive headlong into its boiling fury, presenting the narrowest, sharpest surface they could: the bow. Kira had got that bit right, at least.

Effects bank 1, track F17, Rosalynd thought.

She knew each one as well as she knew the spices that sat in her cupboards. The fierce waves, the fishermen's fear, the crashing storm above and about them... to all intents and every purpose these dropped-in sounds were her legacy. She had commissioned each one, stacked them up in the station's computer, and given each one a name. So this was F17: 'Sea, fierce, dawn'. It differed just slightly from F18 – 'Sea, fierce, noonday' – and once again from F19, which pitched the action still later.

She could tell them apart even now, standing beside her sink with only one ear on the drama she'd once controlled. She pictured the bank of screens on the edit room desk and the digital buttons upon them that comprised the whole world of The Fleet. Boats and pubs and hotel bars; the Gibson winches that brought in the fish; the gentle ting-ting of loose rigging that knocked against a mast in the harbour; right down to the closing of doors, the shuffle of feet and the sniff of a running nose... little that made up the world of The Fleet existed outside of a small backed-up server shared by the drama and newsroom staff.

Yet few who listened would appreciate – as she did – that each of the sounds was authentic. S17, she recalled quite clearly, was seven years old, maybe eight. She'd dispatched a novice with tape and a mic to the part of the harbour where boatmen picked up the tourists. From there they took them out beyond Herm for sea fishing trips behind Sark. Rosalynd had bided her time, picking the stormiest day of the season, with waves so fierce they'd been throwing up rocks from the beach to the road behind Cobo Bay. Most of the guides had refused to head out with the poor seasick youth, claiming that the conditions were too rough for effective line and pole fishing. It took some work to finally convince one of them that all they wanted to catch were some sounds.

'Hauling in the nets,' called a voice Rosalynd didn't recognise. 'All clear.' Apparently a new recruit to the cast.

Thomas Thoumine - George Dixon in real life - grunted his response. Then S84, the deep click of a well-greased mechanical lever; S12, the electric whine of the motor; and S44, the teeth of a ratcheted wheel as the winch began pulling the towing wraps onto the net drums.

The mythical MV John Gregg was what fishermen called a wet fish side trawler: sixty years old, thirty tons, and built in a shipyard in Poland. Its nets were tailored for rockfish and halibut, and brought in a ton of fish at a time. Without it, The Fleet would never have been a success.

The very first scene of the very first episode had marked the boat's arrival at St Sampson, from where its fishing grounds were a day and a half's full-throttle sailing away. Three days at sea, and six hours trawling had bonded the characters so that now the five men and one dog — effects S103 to S122 — were as tightly knit a family as the loved ones they left on dry land.

It had quickly built up a loyal following, which Rosalynd, and latterly Kira Spooner, had maintained for ten years. The actors claimed the success as their own, of course, but Rosalynd knew that without them it still would have worked. Radio wasn't just a medium. It was a friend and companion that most people met on their own. In the car, in bed at night, riding the bus while plugged into their headphones. In keeping her cast tight and small, rarely cycling her actors and barely ever changing the careful balance of the well-defined characters, she had led each listener to believe that they themselves were a sixth crew member. They cared for the characters - not the actors - and returned day after day to spend fifteen minutes cramped below deck or sprayed by the crest of each wave, or returning to shore after most of a week on the water to celebrate a catch that had never existed.

She'd been shocked when she read of Kira's decision to cripple Thomas Thoumine shortly before The Fleet's tenth year on air. It struck her as needlessly destructive, and a risk that she wouldn't have taken herself.

Perhaps that's what happens when you age, she thought. You stop taking risks.

Kira was young for the job – forty, forty-five, inexperienced, perhaps – but she had a vision, and though it might differ from that which Rosalynd had followed, it seemed to be working. Figures were steady, and the early counts indicated that the live tenth-anniversary episode, the one that had dealt with Thomas Thoumine's return to the boat, had been its most listened-to yet.

S27 – the nets breaking the surface.

Skipper Robert Newman stepped out of the wheelhouse to help bring them up on deck, taking control of one of the gallows as the fish were pulled high in the air.

'On my mark; three – two – one – swing,' he called to the man at the opposite gallow, and in kicked S14 – gallow motor – which in the listener's mind swung the catch above the deck rail and over the deck.

'Halt,' the skipper called.

'Halt,' his opposite number acknowledged, and the one-second wind-down effect of S15 truncated the progress of S14's unseen motor.

'Easy now,' the skipper instructed. 'Thomas, prepare the catch.'

Dixon made an incomprehensible sound, somewhere between a cough and a moan.

'All clear?' the skipper asked.

An assorted retort from the rest of the crew confirmed that indeed all were clear of the suspended net and its haul. Dixon's reply was a rounded, brassy wowl, isolated to just one channel such that it came from only the left-hand speaker. That represented the port side of the boat, Rosalynd recalled. Thomas Thoumine had climbed the rungs on the rear-most gallow and put his hand on the latch that released one end of the net and dropped the catch onto the boat.

'Disengage the aft cable,' the skipper called.

Thoumine acknowledged, and then S81, the net clip, S82, the trawl itself, and S83a, the fall of the catch, followed in concert.

The haul of a ton of invisible fish - fish that had never existed nor ever would - fell three feet from the net to the platform and skittered about as they slid and flapped towards the raised edges that stopped them falling off the platform and onto the deck.

The skipper jumped down from his gallow and called the crew across to the platform, and up came the music as S202, S203 and S204, the sounds of the deckhands sorting the fish, slowly began to fade.

Rosalynd Holdbrook stacked the last of the tea things to drain and dried her hands on a towel that hung from the door of her range.

Something - she couldn't quite put her finger on what it was - something had not sounded right.

It wasn't the story; that progressed well enough. It was logical and engaging, even if it hadn't done much to push the plot forward. It wasn't the dialogue. That was natural and technically accurate, too, and none of the characters had spoken in a way that wouldn't fit with their carefully layered personalities.

The sound effects were neither too loud nor too quiet. Neither were they used in the wrong places. Rosalynd had spent half of the time she'd been developing The Fleet on research and observation. She knew exactly what life on a trawler should sound like, and she'd heard nothing unfamiliar in that most recent broadcast.

Something, though... she shook her head, and resolved to tune in again the next day. Perhaps she'd work it out if she listened often enough.

DAY THREE

La Fontenelle, 2.42am

Christine Le Page closed the file on which she'd been working. She stretched and yawned and sat back in her chair, which gently creaked under her weight. It had been Dan's father's before he had died.

They were living in his house as the estate progressed through probate, and his brothers had offered to sell them their shares of the place - in advance of the will being settled - at a price so good it would have embarrassed them both to accept.

Besides, they had no plans to stay beyond the end of this posting. Dan was still a Guernsey boy - their return had proved as much - but Christine was Jersey right through, and even Dan would admit that their life was on her home island now, close to their friends and not so far from their children, the last of whom had just left home.

Aside from Bichard, Dan was the only person who knew the real reason they'd come back to Guernsey, and Christine had promised when they'd first discussed the posting that she'd work as fast as she could. A month at the most, she'd told him, and she'd meant it – back then. Now, though – now that she was embedded, now that she'd started to read through the case file – she wondered whether she hadn't been a little too optimistic.

It had taken her two evenings, and well beyond midnight both nights, to work her way through the first section of Remus Carey's logs. They were undated, but from what Bichard had told her of the time he and Carey had spent in Lyon together, she guessed that they must have been two and a half to three years old.

Some of the language was esoteric, not merely verbose as Bichard had suggested, but she'd read through her translation twice over, and she'd read it again in the morning, before handing it back to Bichard.

Between now and then she would sleep, until the alarm woke her up and the cycle started again.

TWO YEARS AGO

From the diary and logs of Remus Carey, as translated by Christine Le Page.

Interpol General Secretariat, Lyon, France

So there were fourteen of us in the end. Room sixteen again. The one that looks out on the park. Bit of a fag getting there, what with the tram and everything, but I arrived a few minutes early and ended up sitting around in reception, watching security going about its business. Terribly efficient. Most un-French.

So, fourteen people from seven different countries sitting around one table. Britain, France and Spain – three delegates each (me, Bichard and a lackey from the mainland for Britain, jurisdictional blurring aside) – two from Ukraine, and one each from Romania, Hungary and Poland. The fifteenth seat sat empty. Bulgaria hadn't made it if the nameplate was to be believed.

The space for the delegate name had been left empty, which perhaps is entirely appropriate. Names count for less than nations at these meetings, so you'll excuse me if I duck them entirely throughout the report. I think it will make things clearer.

We opened with semantics, or more accurately budgets and authority. It had been decided in advance that the investigation would be a joint operation between the branches for human trafficking and pharmaceutical crime. Human Trafficking argued that since the cargo's point of origin was human, it should fall under their jurisdiction. They enjoyed the support of most of the Eastern European delegates. Pharmaceutical crime acknowledged that no counterfeit or illicit medicines and medical devices were involved. Rather, they argued that as the cargo's ultimate use fell within the purely medical sphere it should be they who took the lead throughout.

After some forceful protestations from all sides, an agreement was made to establish a joint task force with equal authority, which would temporarily sit outside of either branch and be funded equally by both.

Sorry if this is getting needlessly technical so early on. Best to get the record straight from the start so we all know where we stand.

Anyhow, at this point, the Ukrainian delegation took the floor. Only one of them spoke – a short man with a woody moustache, turned yellow at the tips through indiscriminate smoking.

He went to the head of the table, used a remote to dim the lights, and called up a map of the buff-coloured landscape. It covered two thousand miles, give or take, from the Black Sea at Odessa to the French coast at Carteret.

'Gentlemen,' he said. His English may have been slightly imperfect, but in one word he'd used more of my second tongue that I could ever have used of his first. 'Since our meeting of three months, my agents and those of Misters _____, _____ and _____ [he indicated the delegates from Poland, Romania and Hungary] have conferenced our findings.'

He pressed again on the remote, and a sequence of dots scattered themselves across the map. They were seemingly random at first, but as more appeared it became obvious that they fell into distinct clusters.

'Each dot is body,' he said. 'Each group is near prison. Bodies are prisoners, each one.'

I asked him how many they'd found so far.

'One hundred four,' he said as the dots on the map continued to appear. 'Most have missing just one organ, maybe two if is pair: kidney, lung, eye.'

The dots slowed down, and carried on slowing until they came to a stop. Three clusters were more densely packed than each of the others: an area north-east of Kiev, Ukraine; another south of Sofia, Bulgaria; and the third on the edge of Bucharest, capital city of Romania.

He said something to his partner at the table, who opened a case and took out a dozen folders. We each took a copy and passed them on, then I opened my copy and took out a sheaf of carefully labelled photos. Ten-by-eight prints, in colour, each annotated with arrows picking out notable features, the captions written in

English and French.

Stomach-churning stuff.

Some of the victims weren't much older than kids. Seventeen, eighteen, nineteen at most. Most of the wounds I could deal with - the missing liver, the hastily stolen spleen, the empty chest, now just a cavity missing its heart - but those with the empty, unblinking eyes were quite something else. It was almost as though it wasn't a part of their body they'd lost, but their essence. Their soul.

I tucked those sightless martyrs back into the folder and spread out the others, which somehow seemed the less violated. I noticed Bichard turning his head away from them, fixing his eyes on the map. I can't hold that against him.

The Ukrainian paused for a moment and then, when we'd finished sorting the photos, he picked up the thread of his story - if you can call it that. I found myself distracted. The selective removal of just one or two organs from each victim supported the earlier supposition, with which we'd agreed at the previous meeting, that the organs were stolen to order. Harvested, Bichard had said, and I think that pretty succinctly describes it.

It seemed such a waste. Nothing can justify murder, but to be so selective about what to take somehow made it worse. A qualified surgeon working through legitimate channels could harvest sufficient parts to extend the life of a dozen or more, give sight to the blind and still have enough left over to bury or burn.

'Each of these sites,' the Ukrainian continued, circling the largest clusters with a laser pointer, 'is within five miles of major prison or centre of detention for large region.'

Click - the map zoomed in on the fifteen dots south of Sofia. Each now sprouted a fine white line, which linked to a string of text describing the victim: name, age, which body part had been taken. Below this, a pair of numbers: 244/681, 338/429, 51/384, and so on. Proportion of sentence served, over number of weeks originally imposed.

'This man. Apostol Isaev, has forty-two years. Sentence for robbery with arms, thirteen years. Two hundred forty-four week served - less than five year. One month later, is dead on road. No liver.'

He moved the pointer to another dot.

'Kuzman Dobrev. Twenty-six. For steal of car and drive away, six and one half year — four hundred twenty-nine week. Is release after three hundred eighty-eight week. After one month more, is dead behind tram house, no kidney. All this people,' he clicked his remote and the map receded as far as the overview, 'release early from jail. All die in one month or less after freedom. All fight in court with one company to represent: Malkulpa.'

The stress should have been on the last but one syllable, but other than that he got it right. It was through Malkulpa that all eyes had turned towards Guernsey, and in particular a small rented office in St Peter Port, just large enough for three highly paid solicitors, who in turn controlled a small but apparently skilful band of advocates posted across Eastern Europe.

Their unmasking was more to do with the fact that the advocates were sloppy than any great work on our part, if I'm honest. But who can blame them? They were working remotely, fifteen hundred miles from the island, in four distinct and separate countries. Were it not in the first instance for Europol, and latterly Interpol, they might still be working unnoticed. Now they were merely working under observation. Not that they knew it.

We knew who they were, and we knew how they worked, but not who they worked for. It certainly wasn't the poor bastards who ended up dead on a beach, in a housing estate or behind some dump of a depot. They were seemingly hand-picked, with all of Malkulpa's fees and expenses waived, which led us to one conclusion.

These men - for largely that's what it was, men - were murdered to order simply because their medical records suggested that whatever was taken (call it payment in kind) was a match for whoever the ultimate client might be. The client, in effect, was paying to free them.

None of us knew whether the clients also knew they were paying to kill them.

'What is this word, Malkulpa?' one of the French delegates asked.

'Is Esperanto,' the Ukrainian said. 'Malkulpa is innocent.'

'Actually,' I said, leaning forward on the table, 'it's not. Not quite. Kulpa is guilty, and mal does usually negate whatever follows, so it's closer to not guilty, rather than innocent. Innocent would be senkulpa - without guilt.'

'Fascinating though these linguistics might be,' Bichard interrupted, 'perhaps we could return to the map.' He pointed towards the projection. 'There's a fair distance between each of these clusters. There must be a hub somewhere. Do we know where the parts are being...' It was clear he was trying to think of the most appropriate word. 'Processed?'

I wish he'd chosen something else, but it fit.

'I think I can answer that.' This from one of the French - the only woman on their team. 'We picked up a trafficker passing through Carteret. A Polish man, early thirties. The Direction Générale [de la Sécurité Extérieure] has traced his route back as far as Krakow. We believe this to be the hub due to its position between three of the primary clusters.'

'And from Carteret?' Bichard asked.

'The cargo was discovered on a private boat,' she explained. 'The crew had not filed papers with the Capitaine du Port.'

The man to her left, a smartly dressed Lyonnaise for whom Interpol was his nine-to-five, not merely an inconvenient place to meet, tapped her on the shoulder. She leaned over and he whispered in her ear.

They reverted to French, perhaps assuming that nobody else in the room would understand. They were wrong, of course. From what I read of his lips there was some disagreement (on her part) over whether they should share with the rest of the room a particular piece of information.

She shook her head and her bob - white before its time - twirled about her ears. She pulled herself upright, straightened her jacket and folded her arms on the table. After a moment's silence during which we all expected some new information, she merely announced she had said all she needed.

Bichard frowned. I think that he had caught the gist of their argument, too, but he seemed unwilling to intervene.

So I did.

'Alors, allez-vous partager ces coordonnées avec nous?' I asked.

If nothing else, it confirmed what I had expected: they'd failed to recognise the fact that we'd settled on English as our lingua franca simply because for most of the group it was a useful second language, not because no one outside of the French delegation spoke French.

'Coordinates?' asked the Ukrainian. It seems he had a little bit of French, too.

'I'm sorry,' I said. 'I sometimes forget that we don't all speak French.' I smiled at the French at their end of the table. 'Please... don't let me steal your thunder.'

You have to give her credit: you'd never have known that things weren't going just as she'd wanted. 'Of course. I, too, forget that only some of us speak French.' She shot an accusatory glance at the man beside her. 'As Monsieur Remus would seem to be aware,' she turned to address the room, her eyes pausing on me as they swept the table, 'we retrieved a series of coordinates from a mobile phone in the pocket of the courier.'

'Do they confirm what we suspected?' Bichard

asked.

'They do.'

What we suspected, of course, for if we hadn't neither Bichard nor myself would have been there, was that the waters surrounding the Channel Islands were the ultimate theatre of operations. An unfortunate choice of words, perhaps, but one that the group understood, and which outside of English had few connotations.

The man to her left, who had caused such a public and rather embarrassing leak, sat forward in his chair, tapping the keys on his laptop. 'If you have a pen...?'

I nodded and he read out a series of numbers: two sets of pairs and triplets, three groups in each set. Without a map I couldn't place them precisely. From years of fishing the waters, though, first on my father's boat and then on the Huffin' Puffin, I knew roughly that anything that far south and as far to the east as the numbers suggested must have been somewhere between the smaller islands of Sark and Herm. Fertile marks for fishing bass.

'Do you have that, Carey?' Bichard asked.

I had.

'Then I would suggest you investigate upon our return,' he said. 'There must be some reason why they would choose a rendezvous at sea.'

'The time has surely passed for investigations,'

said a voice from the opposite end of the table – one we had not yet heard at that meeting. We turned to face the Hungarian delegate. 'The time is now for action.'

'Mr _____,' I said. 'I would counsel against anything hasty. Already our friends in the Direction Générale have put the operation at great risk by taking into custody the only courier we yet know –'

'I object,' the woman who headed the French delegation interrupted. 'It is merely a misfortune that the Surété picked him up on a random sweep. Any wilful intervention on our part to have freed him would have shown our hand, and most certainly the outcome would not have been to our advantage. We had no choice but to let them take him.'

Our friend from Ukraine stepped in, perhaps in the hope he might return us to the amicable lines along which the meeting had been running before the Hungarian interruption. 'Each side has merit,' he said. 'I also would like to see action. France, England [I refrained from correcting him] and Spain, you have not to worry. These victims, they are many miles from your home, but for us, it is by the door of where we live.'

'Absolutely,' said Bichard. 'I sympathise entirely, but if we move too soon and haul in the little fish, we risk allowing the sharks to escape.'

The Hungarian started to speak, but Bichard carried on, talking over him until, three words later, the Hungarian gave up.

'This operation is a most delicate matter, and the work that you have done, along with our friends from Ukraine, Romania and Bulgaria, is a credit,' Bichard said. 'Give us time to do our work, and together we shall bring this matter to a successful conclusion.'

The Hungarian seemed barely placated, but without jurisdiction beyond his own borders, what could he do? The route, so far as we could tell, passed through nine countries. Without cooperation along its full length and, when the time came, coordinated and simultaneous action, we risked allowing the whole thing to unravel. If that happened, the main players would regroup and reform somewhere else, along different lines, and we'd have to start over from scratch.

'The assistance that you have given us, the fruit of your investigations, has been of incalculable value,' Bichard continued, and I could see that he was winning around the eastern delegates. 'It is only through your tireless efforts that we know the names of the front organisations and the legal firms who have fought for - and won - early release for each victim. We cannot touch the lawyers, but you can instruct your judiciary.

Forbid them from granting early release to anyone represented by Malkulpa, however persuasive or valid their argument.'

This time it was Romania: 'This is not 1989,' he said, sounding rightly indignant. I saw the logic of Bichard's argument, and I understood that he was merely illustrating the impossible situation in which we all found ourselves, but the suggestion that they should take so Stalinesque an approach to judicial independence was too rich even for them.

'In that case,' Bichard concluded, raising his hands, empty palms to the ceiling. 'You have little choice but to let us conduct our work as we see fit; swiftly, as effectively, and as discreetly as we can.'

Translation ends.

DAY THREE

Vale Parish, 8.20am

By the following morning, Rosalynd Holdbrook had listened to five episodes of The Fleet, each downloaded and played on her laptop as she sat in bed eating breakfast.

Something wasn't quite right, and the closer she got to working out what it was, the more frustrating she found it. She had completely ruled out the dialogue; that was written by the same team as it had been through her own tenure. Neither was it the direction in which the show was progressing, or even the new character they'd introduced since she'd left. Jack Hunter, he was called, and the worst she could say on that score was that Jack had been poorly named. The Fleet already had a Joshua, and despite the apparent difference in their ages they sounded broadly similar – like father and son. She knew from past experience that that would certainly complicate matters – particularly for new listeners – but then maybe that was the point. Perhaps The Fleet was heading for a rather obvious and slightly disappointing reveal.

She finished her brioche and urged herself to resist the only logical course of action: to pull the programmes to pieces and see how they worked.

She'd spent her career splicing snippets of sound: first on carefully razored tape, and later on screen with keyboards and mice. Even now, in her semi-retirement, she maintained a modest editing suite with which to augment her pension. It was nothing more than a laptop and software tucked away in a drawer, but that was all that she needed to freelance edit occasional ads and return to the station one day each month to instruct the new recruits.

She left her bed, showered, and made more tea while the editing software loaded, then sat at her desk and dragged the downloaded files into the application.

Each one unravelled on screen as a graphical jumble of peaks and troughs. They pinched to fine lines as they briefly fell silent between each scene, and bloated to fill the full height of the soundstage whenever the boats put to sea.

She took out a pencil and pad and started to play the first track. It was the broadcast from Monday night, in which Skipper Newman had first shown remorse at Dixon's character's crippling injuries.

'If only we'd been able to hook him out of the water sooner,' he'd wailed, the sound wave compressed to avoid distortion. 'This might never have happened.'

The scene, just Newman and his wife alone in their home, was simple and unpretentious. Rosalynd knew exactly who had written it from the style of the dialogue. She jotted down the time at which it opened and closed - its 'in' and 'out' points - as well as the characters involved and the name of the writer.

Next came Dixon, grunting as he struggled to wash himself.

‘2m37s — 3m05s Thoumine washing. Sentimental contrast to previous scene? Writer: unknown,’ she wrote. The grunts gave away too little to betray the author, and she wondered whether the script had been left blank for those few seconds, with direction rather than dialogue, instructing Dixon to improvise.

She carried on through the rest of the programme, eventually reaching ‘14m52s End credits; back-announce’, then closing the file she switched to the second and third downloaded episodes and repeated the exercise. By the time she’d finished she had seven neatly annotated sheets of paper before her. These would look like the running order that Kira and the cast worked from when putting the programme together. What she really needed was the call sheets: the pages that told the actors what would be recorded on each day, and who was needed at any particular time.

Although she could guess, she had no way of knowing for sure when each segment had been recorded. What she could work out was who had been acting with whom by rearranging their story lines, so that rather than weaving the path of greatest suspense through each of the others the constituent parts of each thread would instead run in chronological order.

Reaching beneath the desk, she took a pair

of green-handled scissors out of her sewing box and carefully sliced between each scene in her notes. By the time she'd finished with the seventh page she had forty-one individual strips scattered about the desk. Each strip was a single scene. She tidied them into a pile and carried them through to the kitchen where she arranged them in groups on the worktop.

Now it became clear that there were three strong threads running through the series: Thomas Thoumine's disability, fronted by George Dixon; the sub-plot of Skipper Newman's guilt (Rosalynd suspected they'd write him out sooner or later, probably through stress-induced suicide); and a third story that had thus far only been hinted at surrounding the new recruit.

There was surprisingly little overlap, with few of the characters stepping outside of their own parts of the story. The trawler was berthed in St Sampson through two of the three days she'd analysed, the characters back with their families, pursuing their outside interests, but on the third they'd put out to sea. The forty-one scenes struck her as slightly too many for that much material - and certainly for squeezing into three fifteen-minute programmes. They allowed little more than a minute per scene, but she knew well enough that fast, jumpy cuts were quickly becoming the norm, so she discounted this as the source of her unease.

She picked up the first of the piles and went back to her computer to clip out the marked sections and rebuild that thread in a logical, chronological order.

It would never be broadcast, so she didn't take much care over placing her cuts and didn't bother to normalise the sound levels across the completed file. It took her ten minutes, then she dragged the playhead back to the start of the composition and tapped the space bar to run it through. Out came the rough-cut story of Skipper Newman's guilty conscience and the wedge it was driving between him and his wife.

Nothing strange there.

She went back to the kitchen and took the second pile: the new recruit, his introduction and gradual integration. Again, by the time she'd gathered together each constituent part and run through it twice she could find nothing unusual in the resulting file.

It wasn't until she started to pull together the segments identified in the third pile of notes that she realised she might have been right all along. These were George Dixon's scenes. Three days of solo acting in which he depicted a character once so happy to live alone adapting to life without aid or assistance following on from his accident.

There were no recognisable words in these scenes, and when laced together they comprised just four and a half minutes of drama. Taken out of context, they were meaningless and repetitive.

Very repetitive.

That's what was wrong.

She played it through another two times. Then once again she pulled it to pieces and rearranged his various grunts and groans, matching one to another until she'd repeated on screen what she'd done in the kitchen. She had organised his brain-damaged lines into groups of identical sounds, each used four or five times in quick succession now that she'd shuffled them about.

She compared the sound waves on screen, no longer listening to them, but looking at the rise and fall of each section, the duration of the peaks, how far the gaps were spread out.

Each of the matched sounds was visually identical to its neighbour and that, she knew full well, would have been impossible if they'd each been recorded live. Dixon's parts hadn't been performed at the same time as the others. In all likelihood he hadn't even been present at the recording. Somehow, someone had played them straight off the server. Each had been recorded, equalised, edited down, and saved to disk, just like the sounds of the crashing waves, the deck winches, the dog barking...

Thomas Thoumine was no longer played by George Dixon...

Thomas Thoumine was played by a computer.

'Well, well, George Dixon,' she said to herself, wondering how each of the sounds had been indexed and filed - and how many people knew of their existence. Was it a secret kept between Kira and George, or a larger conspiracy conducted with the full knowledge of the station management?

Maybe even of London?

She picked up the phone and dialled a six-digit number. It rang twice before Dixon picked up the receiver.

'She did it, then,' Rosalynd said.

There was silence at the opposite end. Dixon said nothing.

'To be honest,' said Rosalynd, 'I didn't think she'd dare.'

'Is that Rosalynd?'

'And you haven't told a soul, have you?'

'What are you talking about?' he asked, stressing the are, as though she was asking the most ridiculous questions.

'Kira Spooner. She finally did it. What I should have done years ago.'

George Dixon was silent again. All she could

hear was the static on the line. Eventually he spoke. 'I don't know what you're talking about.'

'I think you do, George.'

She reached forward to turn up her speakers and played him a part of the file: Thomas Thoumine's repetitive sounds.

...woaaah, woaaah, uhgugh uhgugh, woaghuh woaghuh...

'How long has it been going on, George?' She tapped the space bar to make it stop.

'I can't discuss this over the phone.'

'You can.'

'But I won't. If you want to talk, meet me for coffee.'

Rosalynd looked at the clock at the top of her screen. 'I have jobs to do.' She paused, thinking. She didn't want to be seen with him. 'I'm free tonight,' she said, then added, 'would that give you enough time to think of an explanation?'

'Eight o'clock,' he replied. 'I'll cook you dinner.' He dropped the receiver back on its cradle.

'Arrogant as ever,' Rosalynd said to herself, before switching across to her email app and opening up a new window.

She slipped Ollie's business card out of a drawer and started to type a new message.

Oliver. Take a listen and let me know what you think. George Dixon's contributions to the last three eps. No edits or repeats. I've just rearranged them. Notice anything strange? Rosalynd.

Police Headquarters, 10.35am

It had just gone half past ten, and the team was sitting together, drinking the day's first coffees and teas. Renouf had assumed a position halfway along one side of the table; Christine had taken the seat opposite. The wall behind her was prickled with pictures of Richelle Ibbott in various stages of life and death.

Falla and Clarke sat either side of her, and the team had been bolstered by three new additions: Frewin, Digard and Vaudin. Bichard had signed off Renouf's request for extra resources, giving him three staff to help with door to door and data sifting. He hadn't revealed his ulterior motive: to take some of the pressure off Christine and give her more time to observe Renouf.

'So, team,' Renouf said, looking around the table. 'Day three and we're starting to make some progress. Christine brought Dixon in yesterday; he identified the body. Since then she's been working on Miss Ibbott.'

He pointed towards her and nodded, indicating that she should take over.

Christine flipped open a spiral bound

notepad. She cleared her throat. 'I know some of you knew Richelle Ibbott, but I think for clarity's sake, and for our recent arrivals, I'll assume this is all new and take you through her profile.' She looked up, and Renouf nodded his assent.

'She was sixty-two. She lived at Les Moulins, a terraced Napoleonic cottage in St Martin, a short walk from where she was found.'

'Marble Bay,' Renouf reminded the table.

Christine frowned. 'She lived on the island her whole life. Parents both worked for the States of Deliberation, her father preserving ancient monuments, her mother on the coastal paths committee - something she's shown interest in herself. Both died in a gas leak when Richelle was in her teens. Ignore The Sarnian's lurid tales of slain parents: it was a faulty boiler. Carbon monoxide poisoning. Richelle was on a school trip to France at the time. I haven't followed them up as they're clearly out of the scope of this investigation. Do you want me to do some digging?'

Renouf shook her head. 'Not if they're so long dead. Any residual motive attached to them would almost certainly have played out before now.'

'Okay, so...' Christine ran a finger down her notes. 'Yes. She took early retirement years ago from a job she never really needed, but maintains – maintained – an active interest in various charities, most notably a fund for orphans of which she's – she was – a patron, along with her partner, George Dixon.

'From what I can tell, he isn't greatly admired by those who know him, but the same can't be said for those who don't. His character was variously described...' – she leafed through her notebook to find the reference – 'described as "a timely and appropriate introduction into what risked becoming a dying series" – that was The Sarnian, which seems to have cooled on him since they wrote that – and "turning the ebbing tide of listeners" – one of the national broadsheets. Listening figures doubled in his first nine months and the series was syndicated to three other regions. It celebrated its tenth anniversary with a live episode the weekend Ibbott was killed.'

'Did I read somewhere that Dixon was leaving?' Falla asked, picking up his own notebook and leafing through it.

Christine shook her head. 'I doubt it. Not imminently, anyway. We've all been listening, right?'

Renouf had instructed them, the day Richelle had turned up on the beach, to tune in to the series each night. 'The first twenty-four hours are crucial,' he reminded them all. 'That's when friends and family make mistakes. Listen out for Dixon, see what he sounds like. Get to know his voice so we know what's normal if we have to bring him in for questioning.'

Of course, the plan had quickly been cast aside when the team discovered what had happened to Thomas Thoumine, Dixon's part in the series: knocked unconscious on rough seas in Little Russell, cast into the water and fished out a whole cliffhanger later, brain damaged through oxygen starvation.

'I think the Thoumine thing is going to be a slow burner,' Christine said. 'My guess is he'll either make a dramatic recovery, or they'll keep him in there for years for the sake of being inclusive. It's a very white, male, able-bodied cast otherwise.'

'Thank you,' Renouf said, before she could explain her hypothesis any further. 'I'd rather we focus on the facts, though, rather than the fiction.'

'Fair enough.' Christine shrugged.

'So, Richelle Ibbott,' Renouf said. 'Generally liked. No obvious enemies. No scandal. I think we can fairly safely assume that this was a random attack. Probably a chance encounter, and if it was premeditated, the planning came down only as far as killing someone, not necessarily any particular person. Miss Ibbott was merely the unfortunate victim. Where does that leave us?'

'George Dixon,' said Clarke. 'As Christine says, he was –'

'Dixon was at the studio,' Renouf said. 'The time of death, we know, was seven o'clock or thereabouts on the Friday before she was found: the evening of the live broadcast. That puts Dixon four miles away if he went through Town – further if he went round the back – and gives him over four million witnesses who can vouch for his whereabouts.'

'I don't know,' Christine said. 'I've spoken to Dixon twice. There's something about him that doesn't ring true.'

'You heard the broadcast yourself, Christine.'

'Yes, and I've spoken to Dixon twice since Ibbott disappeared. The man is a narcissist.'

'He's an actor. Of course he's a narcissist, but that doesn't make him a murderer.'

'Then why did it take him four days to report her missing?' She looked around the table. 'Wouldn't we all have phoned it in after a few hours?'

Everyone nodded – everyone except for Renouf.

'And when I told him we'd turned up a body...' She shrugged. 'All he wanted to do was carry on signing books.'

'We're getting off the point,' Renouf said. 'Dixon was a devoted partner. They'd been together since he arrived on the island and by all accounts he was a passionate supporter of her charity. Few of his personal appearances were made without some associated Ormer Orphans branding.'

'Well, I'm sorry,' said Christine, 'but it just doesn't ring true. Not to me. He might give that impression, but close at hand he's a very different man. Ruling him out at this stage is premature. Particularly when we have no other leads.'

'But we do.'

Everyone turned to Renouf.

'Oliver Carey.'

'The guy who phoned in the body,' Falla said to the three new recruits.

'Thank you, Falla,' Renouf said. 'We all read The Sarnian, for our sins.'

'That's absurd,' Christine said.

Renouf raised his eyebrows.

'Why would he more or less turn himself in like that?' she asked.

'You tell me,' said Renouf.

'How many murderers would alert the police to their own crime?'

'I really have no idea, but I wouldn't be too surprised to find Carey among them.'

'For what conceivable motive?'

'He panicked. Went back for a swim on Monday morning, found her body still there. Couldn't risk someone seeing him with it without him reporting what he'd found, so he got on the phone.'

Christine shook her head.

Renouf leafed through a pile of papers until he came to the tide tables he'd photocopied from Charlie's paper. 'Richelle Ibbott was killed on the Friday night. We're all agreed?'

They were.

'We know from forensic and circumstantial evidence that this was roughly seven o'clock in the evening. At that time, Dixon was at the studio. The Fleet was celebrating its tenth anniversary with a live broadcast extended from its usual thirteen and a half minutes to nineteen. His character was in nine out of seventeen scenes – more than half of the story. Only three characters weren't in that episode, and although I think it unlikely they had any motive for finishing off Miss Ibbott themselves I asked Falla to follow them up with Kira Spooner.'

'Peter Stone and Joseph Claymore were both in the bar of the Imperial Hotel,' Falla said, reading from his notes. 'The barman there can verify that. Alice Bayley was off the island for the whole week. She only returned three days ago, which was before the body was found but still too late to have killed her.'

Renouf nodded his thanks. 'The crew - three of them - were all on rota dealing with the live broadcast, and...' he turned to Clarke, 'Ibbott's colleagues on the board of the charity?'

'All accounted for.'

'Which leaves Carey.'

'Have you asked him what he was doing on Friday evening?' Christine asked.

'I met with him yesterday. At Port Soif. I thought it better to meet on neutral ground. I didn't want to make a fuss at his office or call him in here.'

'And?'

'I put it to him that he was on the beach on Friday night.'

'On what grounds?'

'On the grounds that we found some evidence to link him to the case.'

'Did we?'

'Christine, do you have a problem with my line of enquiry?'

'That rather depends on your evidence, and why you think Oliver Carey would have drawn our attention to the body when he had no reason to do so.'

'A radio, discarded on the beach close to Miss Ibbott. We've sent it away for analysis.'

Christine took a deep breath to keep herself calm. 'I find that quite implausible. Not only does he call the police to report a murder that he apparently committed three days before, but he also left behind a vital piece of evidence that would link him to the crime?'

'Yes.'

'Why did he return to the beach?' Falla asked. Christine noted his tone, which wasn't entirely unbelieving, but certainly tinged by a note of caution.

'The radio. Carey's a runner. Every other day, by all accounts. He rides from Portelet to Jerbourg, then runs the cliff path. Runners need motivation; they pace themselves to music.' Renouf counted off the reasons on his fingers. 'When it became clear he'd lost his radio – perhaps on Sunday night as he readied his kit for the following morning – he retraced his steps in his mind and came to the only logical conclusion: he'd lost it on the beach when he killed Richelle Ibbott. On Monday morning, when out on his regular run, he retraced them again – in person, this time – only to discover the sea hadn't taken the body as he'd expected. What could he do?'

'Carry on running,' Christine said.

'Maybe that would happen on Jersey,' Renouf said. 'But Guernsey is a small island. We don't have that far to run. So, only other option: report the body as though he'd just found her.'

'I'm not saying Christine has disproved your theory,' Clarke said, 'but I'm not sure you've established beyond reasonable doubt that Oliver Carey is the perpetrator.'

'Perhaps not, but all other avenues are increasingly leading to cul-de-sacs,' Renouf insisted.

'Sir, respectfully, if Dixon –' Christine began.

'If Dixon killed Richelle Ibbott then he's not so much an actor: more a magician. Carey – Oliver Carey – is our only lead right now. Samples from the radio have been sent to the mainland for analysis, and as soon as he's back from Sark, Charlie Dubois will be extracting Carey's fingerprints from the bag in which I handed it to him when we met. Even if they don't match anything we find on the body – or the radio – there's little doubt in my mind that in due course they'll prove themselves invaluable, one way or the other.'

'Sir –'

Renouf cut her off. 'Le Page,' he said sharply. 'I want you to find out all that you can about Oliver Carey, his background and his family, and find me the link from him to Ibbott and Dixon.'

'Respectfully –' she started, but Renouf didn't let her finish. She saw Falla and Clarke exchanging looks and then dropping their eyes to the table as he interrupted for the third time.

'We have limited resources. Nowhere is that more true than where staff are concerned. If you can't follow my authorised line of enquiry I may find myself with no choice but to put in a request that you return to Jersey earlier than planned.'

Forest Parish, 1.20pm

Dixon ignored the plump red steaks, the chickens turning about on the spit, the strings of fat sausages practically bursting their skins. What a waste. He knew that Rosalynd didn't eat meat. Hadn't done for twenty years.

What about fish? Was she a proper vegetarian, or was it just the pretty creatures she couldn't abide being killed? The ones you didn't see day to day - did they count?

Dreadful woman with her picky ways.

No wonder they hadn't got on.

He looked at the mullet and snapper. There was some decent smoked haddock, crayon yellow, fat at one end. A piece of that and some cod, maybe a little salmon... that would make them a decent fish pie. A touch of parsley sauce, some cheese and mashed potato on top.

Perhaps he should stick to pasta. Everyone

ate pasta. Simple spirals with an arrabiata – no. She might not like spicy food.

Boring, boring tomato sauce, then.

Tomato and herb.

Tomato and garlic.

Tomato.

Just tomato.

He walked to the next aisle and fingered the sauces.

Sausage casserole.

Goulash.

Steak and ale mix, rich gravies, supreme... all decent meals that he'd far rather eat than a pasta twist in a bland red sauce.

He looked at his basket and sighed. Three apples, three bananas, a small bag of potatoes and some razors. It was hardly gourmet night at the Ritz.

But then... there was another option.

He didn't need to cook.

They didn't need to eat... and done right – done carefully – the right place, the right time, the right way, he could solve the Rosalynd problem once and for all.

Police Headquarters, 2pm

'Renouf knows about the boat,' Christine said.

Bichard nodded. 'And he's worked out who

Oliver Carey is...?'

Christine nodded back.

'And who his father was?'

'It looks that way.'

They were sitting in Bichard's office. It was lunchtime, and Renouf had taken the team to the pub. Christine had said she would stay back and try to trace Ollie's whereabouts on the night of the murder - pretending, at least, to respect Renouf's wishes. She needed him to believe that she took his threat at face value.

In reality, she knew that the length of her placement would not be Renouf's decision. Whatever he said on that account, Bichard would overrule him unless he, too, wanted her off the island. The chances of that were slim to non-existent.

The only exception, so far as she could tell, would be if Bichard's hand was forced. If Christine wasn't careful, if she gave Renouf any opportunity to bring a claim of professional misconduct or insubordination, Bichard would not be able to save her. Doing so would arouse suspicion, the one thing they couldn't afford, and he'd have no other choice but to send her back to Jersey.

For the time being, then, Christine was determined to stay on the right side of Renouf and treat him as though he deserved a degree of respect.

'Perhaps this is the point where things might start to get interesting,' Bichard said, pushing back in his chair, one foot on the edge of his desk.

'They already have.'

'Oh?'

Christine opened the notebook she'd brought to the office and started to read through her notes, paraphrasing as she went.

'Dixon is in the clear as far as Renouf is concerned. Perfect alibi, he reckons.'

'And what do you think?'

'It's hard to argue against it...'

'But?'

'It's all too neat.'

'Dixon's perfect alibi?'

She nodded. 'Richelle Ibbott's murder coincided exactly with only the second ever live broadcast, and the first time was long before Dixon joined the cast.'

'Coincidence?'

'Perhaps, but it's also the only reason Dixon has nothing to answer for.'

'Maybe he doesn't.'

'Do you know him?'

'Only by reputation.'

'Aye, and a poor one at that,' Christine said. 'The man's an actor. Not just for thirteen minutes a day, but all day long, every day of the week.'

Bichard tipped his head side to side. 'Perhaps he's shy.'

'That isn't it.'

'Actors can often be quite private people.'

'There's private, and there's uncaring. Three days, it took him, to report her as missing, and when we found her body...' She shook her head. 'You should have seen the effort it took to squeeze out a thimble of tears.'

'Delayed reaction? Shock?'

'It just didn't register. Perhaps he's too wrapped up in his own world to notice she'd not come home. Perhaps he's more interested in an inheritance.'

'Or perhaps he killed her.'

'Perhaps he did, but either way Dixon's off limits until Renouf believes the same.'

'Only officially,' Bichard said.

'Are you sanctioning further investigation?'

'Of course. Discreetly, though. I don't want Renouf getting wind.'

'I doubt he'd notice, so long as I turn up the goods on Carey.'

Bichard kicked his foot off the desk and let the chair swing back to its upright position.

'He actually believes that Carey had more to do with this than simply finding the body?'

'No. Not yet. I don't think so, anyway, but he

wants to. I think he might see this as too good an opportunity.'

'Because of what happened with Remus?'

'It could be.'

'And he's making it that obvious?'

'Again, not yet. I doubt the others have noticed anything out of line.'

'But then they're not watching Renouf, they're watching the case.'

'I don't think Falla was entirely convinced,' Christine admitted, 'but you can't deny that Dixon's alibi looks plausible, and there's no reason why it couldn't be Carey.'

'He's playing a dangerous game,' Bichard said, folding his hands together. 'For the time being you're going to have to play along. What can you throw him?'

'Precious little. Carey's clean, so far as I can tell. He doesn't pop up in the files, except for what we know from his father's background notes. There's nothing incriminating in there, and even if there was I couldn't use it unless it was also in the central files – the official ones – or Renouf would ask where it came from.'

'Well, we don't want him knowing about these,' Bichard said, shooting his eyes towards the locked filing cabinet beside him.

'Indeed.'

'Then you're going to have to follow this

through. Get in touch with Carey. Call him in for some questions, or take him out somewhere and do it on neutral ground. There's no point antagonising the kid if you've got no reason to suspect he's involved.'

'I'll see if he's free tomorrow,' she said, folding her book.

'Do that,' Bichard told her. 'But make it look convincing. Richelle Ibbott's murder might be the last thing you and I care about, but whatever we do we can't let Renouf know that.'

Route de Jerbourg, 9.40pm

It was obvious right from the start, from the moment she'd knocked on the door, that she hadn't come round to talk. She was more than an hour late. Dixon was glad he hadn't bought the fish or a jar of insipid red sauce.

She'd come to gloat, to play with him like a cat that plays with a rat, batting it back and forth with a paw so gentle, so tender, yet fringed by a fierce set of claws that at any moment might spear it and kill it.

But Dixon was no helpless rat.

'My dear Rosalynd,' he said, as he opened the door and stepped out. He blocked her way into the house.

'George.' Rosalynd smiled.

Dixon pulled the door behind him until it clicked on the latch. 'I thought perhaps we'd eat out. Richelle was always the cook in this house.'

He put his arm around her waist and steered her towards his car. She gathered her skirt into the footwell, and he gently pushed the door closed. The child lock would keep her there until he was ready.

He skipped around the bonnet and dropped himself into the driver's seat, then started the engine and threw them both up the hill, casting behind them a shower of gravel that brought his neighbour out to his porch.

'How have you been?' Dixon asked. He repositioned the rear view mirror so that he could see her eyes without turning his head. They crested the hill and turned left towards the airport. 'It's been how long, your retirement? Two years?'

'Two years and two months. George, would you slow down.'

'Two years and two months! It races, doesn't it.' He gunned the engine as though punctuating a clumsy pun. 'How have you filled your time? Walking? Baking?'

'Working.'

Dixon clicked his tongue and bumped his fist gently against her thigh. 'We're two of a kind, you and me. Restless. Too busy to ever sit idle.'

He clapped her knee and scrubbed her dress where it draped across her leg. She moved her legs away from him, towards the door handle, and caught him watching her in the mirror. She prayed that he'd keep his eyes on the road.

He took a sharp left, almost doubling them back on themselves and pointed the car towards Icart Point, the high spit of rock that looked out along the south coast.

'Where are we eating?' she asked. The only place open at that time of night would have been the hotel, but they'd already passed it and Dixon seemed to have no intention of slowing the car as he took them around the corner and on towards the headland. 'The kiosk will be closed by now,' she said, tracing the road in her head.

'Restaurants can be... I don't know, they lack a little something, don't you think? Privacy, mainly. I thought we'd park up for a while and have that chat. We can get some food when we're done.'

Rosalynd gripped the armrest as Dixon swung them into the empty car park. He drove to the furthest row and brought the car to a halt, straddling two spaces that looked out to sea.

'Let's walk.'

'In these shoes?' Rosalynd asked.

'Suit yourself.' Dixon pushed in the lighter, and pulled out a cigarette. He slipped it into his mouth, then folded his arms as he waited for the lighter to pop back out.

'Fine,' she said, eyeing the cigarette. He knew she hated smoking, almost as much as she hated meat. She knew he was playing a game, but even if it meant walking home on her own she'd rather do that than sit in a car while he smoked. She pulled on the handle.

'Allow me,' Dixon said, as the door refused to open. 'Bit sticky, that one.'

He tucked the cigarette into his breast pocket, then stepped out of the car and ran around to let her out. 'There's a bench over there,' he said, pointing. 'We can watch the sea and chat.'

He let her lead the way, keeping himself three paces back and taking his time as he locked the car to give her some space. No point in crowding her, after all.

'I love it up here, don't you?' he asked. 'Nothing like this in Southampton.'

'Shall we cut the small talk?' she said. 'We've never been friends. Not really. You know as well as I do that this isn't a social call.'

'Fair enough,' he said, striking a match and putting it to the end of the cigarette. 'Talk.' He flicked the match back and forth to extinguish the flame, then dropped it onto the dusty path.

She tilted her head and briefly raised her eyebrows, as though his curt reply surprised her. 'I know.'

Dixon thought for a moment. 'You'll have to give me more than that.'

'Okay. I know about you and The Fleet. I can't say I'm surprised. New broom and what have you.'

'I see,' said Dixon. 'This is about Kira.'

'No, George. This is about you.' She sat down. The bench was raised on a concrete plinth to give an unobstructed view over the heather and gorse. In daylight, when the path was busy with walkers, you could see halfway along the south coast from there, past the dizzying cliffs as they fell away, creasing themselves into bays. Now there was nothing – just the catch of the moon on the tops of the waves as they crashed on the rocks far below. 'Where were you on the night Richelle disappeared?'

'Richelle didn't disappear.'

'You know what I mean.'

'I was at work.'

'No, you weren't.'

'Check the tapes.'

'I've already have.'

'Kira...?'

'No. I downloaded it. Every episode for the last five days, and I've heard them all five times.

Five. Times. It's a wonder what you hear - what that degree of repetition brings to the fore.'

Dixon sucked on his cigarette, pulling the burning tip towards the filter. 'And what did you hear that the rest of us - those of us who were there, in the studio, working our way through our scripts, not sitting at home reliving past glories - what could you tell that we could not?'

She settled back into the seat as Dixon paced behind her. She enjoyed his discomfort. 'You've been fired.'

The pacing stopped and Dixon let out an explosive guffaw. She'd heard it before, that laugh. Four years ago: scripted, rehearsed and acted out twice to allow for cuts and re-takes. It was no more convincing here on the cliff than it had been back then. 'You do have the most extraordinary sense of humour, Rosalynd. Really, the most wonderful imagination. It's hardly surprising you earned your living from radio drama.'

'Far less surprising than your achievement in carving a living from acting in it.' She was smiling. He couldn't see her face, but he could hear it in her voice, and from where he stood behind her he could see her ears rise a little higher as her cheeks pulled tight.

He kicked at the dusty path until he dislodged a heavy stone, then picking it up he held it behind his back, weighing it in the palm of his hand. It was about the size of an orange, but where the skin of an orange was pitted, the stone was smooth, barely rough at all.

He pulled on the cigarette one last time, then flicked the butt into the air and over the edge of the cliff. The stiff easterly wind snatched it up and took it out and away from them, spinning it over and over and over towards the sea. They both leaned forward to watch it go. Neither spoke in the twenty seconds it took to touch down and die.

'Kira fired you, didn't she,' Rosalynd said at last.

'You gleaned all this from the show?'

'I'm right, aren't I?'

'What if you are?'

'If I am, you have no alibi for the night Richelle disappeared.'

'And do you?'

Rosalynd thought for a moment. 'I finished work early, had a swim at Beau Sejour, picked up some shopping on the way home. I'm sure I still have the receipt if you need me to prove it.'

Dixon grunted and turned the rock in his hand.

'Where were you?' she asked. 'Swimming? Shopping? Or knocking my friend on the head and leaving her to drown?'

He took a step towards her. 'Do you know how long we were together?'

'Yes.'

'Seven years.'

'I introduced you, God forgive me.'

'Seven happy years, until she came along.'

'Richelle?'

'Spooner.'

'Kira?'

'Kira Spooner. Queen of the spreadsheet. That's all that matters to her. She doesn't think that there might be real people behind our characters.'

'So she did fire you?'

Dixon swung back his hand, the weight of the rock giving it greater momentum, then he flung it forward and let go, sending the rock flying over Rosalynd's head, out past the heather and gorse and into the void. The wind had no effect this time, and the rock cut through the air and fell to the sea unimpeded. They neither saw nor heard the splash it made. 'She wrote me out,' Dixon said.

Rosalynd nodded. 'But she kept your character.'

Dixon blew heavily through his pursed lips. Rosalynd couldn't be sure, but she thought he might have been holding back tears.

'How long did it take?' she asked, turning

around to look at him. 'Recording those parts. The grunts and moans and –'

'Who cares?'

'I care.'

'Ha! You care! You would have done it yourself if you'd had the guts.'

'No, I –'

'Don't deny it,' he shouted, making her jump. 'I know you would. You all wanted me out, but no one would dare say a word. You're weak. You're weasels. You could at least have had the...' – he struggled to find the word he was after; not decency, not honesty – 'pluck. And the gumption to stand up for what you believed in.'

'George, the listeners wouldn't have –'

'Fuck the listeners. Who cares about the listeners? At least if I'd had a send-off, a decent storyline to write me out, I could claim it was my choice, my doing, that I'd not renewed my contract. But this? Reduced to a series of moans and grunts by some implausible disaster just to save her precious figures. To save her the inconvenience of a listeners' revolt when they discovered that she'd axed the one character that brought it all to life.'

'Get a grip, George,' Rosalynd said, her calm, measured tones in stark contrast to the stiff onshore breeze and his own ferocious outburst. 'You didn't have to play along.'

He sniffed again, and now she was sure he was crying.

'You didn't even tell Richelle, did you?'

He didn't reply.

'What sort of relationship was it that you couldn't even tell your own partner you'd been fired?'

'She wouldn't understand.'

'Yes. Yes, she would. You forget, George. Richelle and I have been – had been friends since school. I knew her better than you.' She turned around again and looked back out to sea. 'I rue the day I ever introduced you,' she said, more quietly.

'Don't tell me. That's your biggest regret?'

'No, George.' She fell silent for a moment. 'My biggest regret was hiring you in the first place. Bringing you over here. Perhaps if I hadn't we wouldn't be here. Your foul manners, your arrogance...' She looked at him again. 'You'd never have pushed away anything and everything that was good for you, to the point where people like Kira just don't want to work with you. Richelle would never have found you hiding on that beach, pretending you'd gone to work if you hadn't been such an obnoxious fool. And you wouldn't have killed her to keep your secret.'

Dixon pressed his knuckles to his eyes. 'Shut

up, shut up, shut up,' he screamed, and he kicked the concrete support at one end of the bench.

Rosalynd stood up and turned away. 'You can drive me back to the main road,' she said. 'I'll walk from there. I don't think either of us would be very good dinner companions.'

She started to move towards the car, but Dixon jumped over the bench and grabbed her by the neck. He threw her to the ground and her keys fell out of her pocket.

She landed heavily on the dusty patch in front of the bench. It knocked the air out of her lungs. They felt as if they were frozen. She gasped, trying to free them, desperately sucking at nothing, panicking now, worried that Dixon might leave here there.

'I loved her,' he shouted. 'And she loved me.' He kicked her twice in the thigh and once in the stomach, and instinctively she curled herself into a ball as her lungs spasmed and freed themselves. She protected her head with her hands as she gulped at the sweet sea air and Dixon kicked again. This time the tip of his leather-soled shoes sliced one of her fingers and cracked the knuckle. She screamed and pulled her hands away, leaving her head exposed, just as he threw back his foot and caught the keys with his heel. They skittered away, coming to settle under the bench as he swung forward again, twisting his body, his arms swinging out and around with the spiral of momentum. His shirt came untucked. He could feel the ribs of his corset rubbing against his skin.

'Evil - meddlesome - bitch,' he shouted, punctuating each word with a kick to the back of her neck where she'd curled it around to press her face to her chest. Then, as though the wind had caught it and pulled it over the cliff, his rage disappeared and a sickening comprehension rushed in to fill the void.

He hadn't intended to do it like this.

This wasn't measured.

This wasn't calm and careful.

He would kill her, yes, but not like this. Dixon knew that he wasn't a savage...

He was sweating, his chest heaving. Rosalynd Holdbrook lay at his feet. She was still, her eyelids starting to slacken. He was out of breath; he could feel his corset digging in. He wanted to unlace it - just a little - just enough to let him breathe more easily.

The tears tipped out now: the thick, dumb sobs ballooning until they collapsed in his throat like a pit of bubbling mud. He didn't need to feel her pulse to know that she was gone. Neither need he turn her over to see what he had done. Her neck was broken, the skin was broken. The trickling blood was already staining the dusty patch in front of the bench, its surface worn away by the scuff of a thousand boots, his own prints only one pair among them.

He wiped his eyes with the backs of his hands, and as he opened them again he saw to his right the wobbling spot of a torch. It flickered between the branches of gorse, at the head of a small group of ramblers walking the path to the Point. The light was still dim, but getting closer, and though they couldn't see him yet, he knew that in just a few seconds they would.

They were close enough to be heard, their excited chatter preceding them, and he prayed that the wind had carried away his own furious screams – the screams that he hadn't heard as he'd made them, but which rang in his ears now, telling tales of what he'd done as though they might give him away.

He crouched by her body and picked it up. The angle was awkward, it hurt the small of his back, and he grazed his knuckles as he slid them beneath her. The sleeve of his jacket rubbed on the back of her neck, and a drop of her blood fell onto its weave. He rolled her up his arms until she was resting against his chest, then walking out as far as he dared he pushed his way through the bushes towards the edge of the cliff. The ground there was thick with hottentot fig, utterly useless for anything other than making his footing unsteady. It had grown across the rocks, giving them a spongy coating that hid their peaks and toughs. He couldn't be sure of his footing, and he worried that at any moment he might step over the edge in the belief he was putting his feet on solid ground, only for nature to play her unkindest trick.

He stumbled, and threw a foot forward to catch his weight, Rosalynd's body shifting awkwardly and pulling him down. Her head rolled to one side, limp, and she bled again onto his jacket, the droplets rolling around his cuff and falling onto the fig.

Her body lay heavily across him, and twice more he came close to slipping under her weight. He couldn't go on. He didn't dare. He crouched down and leaned forward - and he dropped her. Her head hit a rock and her arms flopped about like streamers caught on a breeze, but she didn't make a sound as she rolled towards the edge. The forward momentum, the slope of the ground, the gentle push that Dixon had given her... they took her past the edge, cresting silently over the rim of the headland. He could only imagine how she would fall. Not over and over like the stub of his cigarette. Not on a graceful arc like the rock, but down - straight down, possibly knocking the wall on the way - until she struck the water and ducked for a moment below it, before she came back up and floated out of his life.

He thought he might have heard the splash as he hunkered among the grasses. He waited there for five minutes, then gave it five more, and when he was sure the walkers had gone, he dusted his knees and straightened his shirt and checked that he still had his wallet, his phone and his keys. He didn't want to leave anything lying around.

Like Rosalynd's keys.

Sitting in the dust.

DAY FOUR

Icart Point, just after midnight

George Dixon crept back to his car. He couldn't see the hikers or their torch. They might have strayed into the garden. The kiosk was closed, but the benches were still set out. They might have pushed on to Saints Bay, or for all he knew they might have doused it and perched on the bench, Rosalynd's blood on their boots, or maybe they were just there, on the rocky bollards that stopped the cars from driving too close to the edge.

They might be sitting there now. So close to him. So close to the scene of Rosalynd's death, kicking their feet and admiring the play of the moon on the sea as they rested their weary legs.

His forehead and arms were clammy and wet, and the thick, sticky sweat made him cold. He unlocked the car and threw himself in; he closed the door and gripped the wheel to steady his hands. They'd started to shake, and nothing he did would make them sit still.

Was it the effort of carrying Rosalynd?

Might he have strained his muscles?

No.

He knew that wasn't true, and he knew, too, that he had to be strong. He hadn't intended to kill her that way. And Richelle – he hadn't wanted to kill her at all, and now he wondered what else he might do when his mind was seemingly absent.

He started to shiver, and tensed all his muscles, pushing himself deeper down, further into the seat, trying to calm the spasms. He focused his eyes on the faint dark hulk of the cliffs as the first wave of sickness swept through.

The curious heat of a chilling sweat swept up from the pit of his stomach. It ran up his back, and it ran up his arms and it sat in his craw, expanding, expanding, ever expanding.

He'd have to control himself. From what he could tell from the news and the gossip – for all that either was worth – the police had nothing to go on. He was a victim as much as Richelle. More so, perhaps, for while she was no longer suffering, his life was becoming a torment: a tightening spiral of fear and dread that at any moment he might be discovered.

He slumped in his seat, his head loose on a slack neck, drifting about the headrest. He turned to his side and saw another car, empty, sitting beside him. A small Peugeot, just like the one that Rosalynd used to drive. A different colour, but –

- Rosalynd's car… a feverish wave washed over him, not heated but cold, and he felt his face go from hot to cool. He shrank into himself; his shoulder blades tightened, and his hands gripped the wheel as he thought of her car. He wondered how she had got to his house, and a moment later he realised…

She had driven.

She must have done.

But where had she parked her car?

And then the wave broke, and it crashed from his mouth like the sea in the autumn storms, which threw itself onto the wall behind Cobo, casting its pebbles and flotsam onto the road. But here it wasn't flotsam and pebbles, and here it wasn't the road. It was Dixon's last meal, and the wheel and the windscreen, the scruff and the spray spotting his trousers and shirt as it dripped from the curve of his chin.

La Fontenelle, 7am

Christine had been up for two hours, Remus's logs on the screen. They'd infected her. They were starting to eat her up, consuming more time than she'd like, not just as she sat there, decoding them, but after she'd closed the files. They'd strayed into her daily life as if they were an addiction.

She pictured Remus while eating with Dan.

She thought of his boat as she drove the coast road.

Sampson was there as she chased hopeless leads, trying - for the sake of Renouf - to pin the blame for the corpse of an heiress onto the good name of Oliver Carey.

And now the story had started to enter her dreams. The tales cast her out on the Huffin' Puffin, a boat she knew from pictures but had never seen in real life.

She'd skipped ahead to Carey's last log, and she'd read Bichard's private files, too, so she knew already what had happened at the end. Yet she still had no clear image of the heavily customised craft. She couldn't picture its powerful engines, nor how they'd been artfully hidden. It looked like a battered cruiser, just right for ferrying visitors out to the fertile marks around Sark. The words, though - the words in the logs - they told a different story, and gave away his cover.

She wanted to run her hands on its hull, and feel the new welding. She wanted to see the repairs, how the hole in its side had been patched after Remus's... Remus's what? Death? Disappearance? They were still no closer to knowing for sure, whatever the probate department had ruled.

She resolved to head to Portelet soon, on a pretence of questioning Ollie. If Renouf was convinced she was following orders, she thought it unlikely he'd stop her.

In the meantime, she'd carry on with the logs. She still had an hour before she needed to leave, so she took her coffee into the lounge and sat down. Scrolling back to the top of the screen, she read through the translation once more before sending it up to Bichard.

TWO YEARS AGO

From the diary and logs of Remus Carey, as translated by Christine Le Page.

There's a rough patch of sea on the other side of Herm. Follow a line from Belvoir Bay, tuck round the corner and head towards Sark; you'll find it easy enough. Nothing round there is especially deep, but the fish seem to like it.

I cast out a line and hauled in two bass in the first twenty minutes, each as long as my arm, not that I'd gone there to fish. Everything else, I threw back. My real quarry was half a mile east. The line and rod were just cover.

I'd anchored the Huffin' Puffin in quieter waters, in such a way that the tide kept it angled towards a couple of buoys. One orange, one pink, weathered and aged by years in the sea. They sat within a few hundred feet of the French delegation's coordinates.

Two reasons for choosing that spot. First, it was a lot more comfortable. I may have a good pair of sea legs, but the fifty-year sea knees between them prefer by a long shot a gently rocked gunwhale to slippery, knocked about decks. Second, it was more convincing. Who would fish off the back of a boat being tossed about by the tide when a calmer spot close at hand would be just as richly stocked?

So I fished off the starboard side - if that's what you'd call such a fruitless endeavour - and I kept half an eye on their rough position without it being too obvious.

Three things came to mind, as they're wont to do when you let your eyes softly defocus a scene of the sea and the sky:

1. The buoys could be a coincidence. Those waters are crawling with spider crab. Lobster, too, so it's no surprise that the coordinates would coincide with someone's existing mark. The island's surrounded by pots and buoys. It wears them like a necklace. In that respect these two would be rather inconvenient, since whoever baited and farmed them might chance upon the rendezvous.

2. That particular spot was chosen for the rendezvous precisely because of the pots. The longer I thought on this point, the more merit it seemed to warrant. I'll come back to that in a minute.
3. The pots are somehow a part of the whole operation. How, I couldn't say. Not without further investigation.

Point one doesn't justify serious consideration. You can't do anything about a coincidence other than discount it, which leaves us with points two and three.

Of course, I know the answer now, but back then it was point two that seemed the most likely. I secured my rod against the deck rail and went down to the cabin to boil up some coffee. Sampson was down there, sleeping on the bunk. He chirped as he saw me, the way that cats do, and I think he must have smelled the fish on my fingers, for he picked himself up and sat on the pillow. His legs pressed left and right to counteract the rock of the boat. Makes me think of a spinning top every time he does that. I tickled his chin as the kettle boiled, and he stretched out his neck towards me.

Anyhow, the buoys. If they'd been there all along then I reasoned they'd make the perfect backup. They'd be an analogue check, if you like, if the cloud was ever so dense that it blocked out the satellite signal. Whoever was destined to rendezvous there would have to do things the old way - maps and rulers and compasses - which would leave an inexperienced sailor prone to miscalculation.

If their nautical reckoning put them anywhere other than next to those buoys, then they knew they'd gone wrong and could start again.

Point three, to my shame, I also discounted. However depraved this whole operation, I couldn't see why anyone would take the risk of hauling human remains across Europe for the sake of baiting a trap. (Besides which, if human flesh was so effective a lure, there was a rich supply far closer at hand.)

So we had possibilities - but we also had a few complications.

I carried my coffee back up to deck and sat down to think. I'd been out a couple of hours, the sun was starting to go, and I wondered whether to head back to shore or spend the night on the boat. It wasn't a difficult decision. I'd caught two fish, so had dinner, and I knew that Odette would be taking her class until ten.

I called. Told her I'd picked up a last-minute night-fishing party from Albert Pier who'd offered to triple the usual rate. She told me to take care and asked how much drink they were bringing on board. I lied about that, and she asked me not to have any myself, and told me to throw their supplies overboard if they started to get too rowdy. I promised I would.

There are times I wish I could tell her the truth.

So, those complications. The first was a question, really. I clambered onto the top of the wheelhouse and took a good look around. Aside from the ferry to Sark there was no likely craft close at hand. I was pretty sure nobody would notice me taking a closer look, so I pulled out the binoculars and trained them on the buoys. They had matching numbers and seemed to be properly licensed: 44901 painted on each. I put in a call to Bichard and asked him to bypass the usual channels and find out from someone in Fisheries to whom they'd issued that licence. I read him the number.

The second complication was actually more of a problem. Assuming the hapless courier they'd picked up at Carteret wasn't a stooge fed into the chain with a dummy location, how did we know when the rendezvous was due? The Surété had concealed the location for goodness knows how long (and for goodness knows why) and claimed in a fairly convincing manner that the knave was refusing to talk. No doubt he feared he'd be next to lose a liver or spleen if he did.

If they'd let us know sooner that might not have been such an issue, but as things stood it seemed far more likely we'd missed it and I needn't have lied to Odette.

We could only hope it wasn't a single-use meeting place - something that changes every time there's a cargo to swap.

There was only one way to find out, of course: surveillance.

I keep the Huffin' Puffin unladen, so she's fast and sits high in the water. I'd guess she's clearing a good twelve feet. My six on top of that gives an eighteen foot lookout, give or take. I pulled out my charts, which from that height put the horizon at four and a half miles in any direction that wasn't obstructed by land.

I traced out a circle around the buoys, four and a half miles from centre to edge. To the east and north it crossed the shipping lanes taking the ferries to France. I didn't fancy spending an unlit night there. To the south-west, though, it was close to St Martin's Point, which gives out a clear view across the islands and on to France. If I shielded myself from St Peter Port's lights I should be able to anchor close to the headland and watch out for boats approaching the traps.

I hauled in my reel, packed up the rod and set the course roughly south-west.

It didn't take long for the buoys to disappear, even with the help of the glasses, so I gave up on heading as far as the Point and cut the engines three miles out. She settled down in the water, the fizz of the wake subsided and died, and with one final cough from the inboard engines all that was left was the gentle lap of the waves on the side of the boat.

I marked the sight line back to the buoys on my chart and settled down to preparing the fish, tossing the guts overboard for the gulls. I skinned them and cut them into generous steaks, then dropped a pan to the sea and scooped up the water with which I would steam them.

They made the best dinner since Friday. The smell of the flaky flesh brought Sampson up to the deck and I threw him the tail for his dinner.

Nothing much happened with the buoys. I sat on deck as the sun went down, Sampson curled up on my lap, and we watched the clipper come in from the mainland. As darkness came I threw down my bag on the deck and we both climbed in. I'd set the radar to watch for craft approaching the buoys, but nothing passed by – on the surface, at least – and right through to dawn the alarm remained silent.

I woke with the sun as it rose across Normandy, and checked the logs to be double-sure I hadn't missed an alert. The clock on the console read five fifteen and the waters were quiet. The ferry to Carteret wouldn't start loading its passengers for another two hours. That operation alone would take at least half an hour. The Trident to Herm and its partner that plied the route towards Sark weren't open for custom. That left... not much. Unless the pots' owner turned up while I was inspecting them, there seemed to be no time better than now to take a closer look.

I pulled up the anchor and put the engines to cruise at low power, scanning fore and aft as I slowly motored towards them. I was feeling hungry, and sorely tempted to push things along so I could head back home and eat with Odette before she left for work. This whole operation might be a waste of time, after all.

What I hadn't considered were the fishing boats. The tide was high and the fleet was leaving port at a steady rate. Two vessels passed close by the buoys; another cut around behind me and disappeared beyond Sark, but nobody seemed to be stopping and hauling the traps.

I cut the engines and tossed a cork over the side to check the current (one of the few benefits of keeping the stock of empty bottles onboard to convince Odette of my cover). It dipped below the surface, then bobbed back up and slowly drifted beyond the bow. The current was set in my favour.

I let it carry me on towards the buoys at less than two knots, all the while watching the sea for oncoming craft. Nothing. Nobody. All was clear. Eight minutes later, the first of the buoys was tapping the Puffin's hull and I was cursing for having left my gloves in the workshop.

I know how unforgiving it can be working with lobster pots. They're generally strung ten to a line, and as each one falls off the back of the boat and into the water it pulls its neighbour with it. By the time three or four have sunk below the surface they're dragging the rest of the line at a pretty impressive whack. Without a winch, someone to help haul them up, or my gloves, I didn't rate my chances. But then I didn't relish the thought of heading back to base with nothing to report, either. Not after a night on deck. So the pots won out.

I unclipped the boat hook from the corner of the wheelhouse and used it to hoist up the buoys. They came easily, taking the slack on the line until, having wound towels around my hands, I could reach out and grab at the line itself.

There wasn't much tension in the line, but the water's not so deep there, so it wasn't until it caught up with the first pot that I realised something was wrong.

Under normal conditions it should have stopped there – refused to go any further, torn through the towel and into my skin and stopped me tugging right away. But it didn't. There was still some give. It almost felt like the line was stretching, and so I pulled some more until the pot lifted up from the sand.

I kept pulling, hand over hand, and it gained some momentum. It felt like the cargo wasn't so much weighed down by the sea and the sand and the weight of its neighbours, as gently complying, gliding up to the surface. I stepped out of the tangle of line now forming on the deck and checked that no one was watching. The few boats in view were too far away to see what I was doing, and they seemed to be heading away from the port, out to the fertile fishing grounds. Then, as I looked back down, the first corner of the pot appeared above the surface, and I reached down and clawed it up with the deck hook.

I dragged it onto the twist of line, and saw at once why I'd been able to pull it by hand: there was no tail – no line leading off to the next pot. It was flying solo, a single pot attached to two buoys and, more to the point, unbaited.

I checked the neck and the netting but there was no sign of any damage. It didn't seem that a lobster or crab had been there and taken the bait. Neither were there any claws or tails. It's not uncommon for smaller specimens to push themselves out - part of themselves, at least - through the sides to make their escape and break off part of their shell in the process.

It could only mean one thing: the pot had never been baited. It had never been laid to catch anything, and the fact that the buoys correlated exactly with the coordinates was more than just a coincidence.

I pushed it over the side and watched it fall into the water, pulling the line behind it. It zipped across the deck, uncoiling once more as gravity dragged it into the sea, dancing around like an eel in a pan. And then the trap touched the bottom, the line slowed down and it stopped, and the buoys were left stranded on deck. I kicked them over the edge.

How the buoys and this one single pot were involved I didn't yet know. The questions they raised, though, made two things certain: the coordinates were accurate, and the courier wasn't a plant.

Things were starting to take an interesting turn.

Translation ends.

BBC Radio Guernsey, 8.45am

Dixon didn't go home that night. He drove his car north, as far as the roads would take him, as far as the island would let him get from the site of his act of defence.

He'd had to do it. He'd had no choice. So why did it make him feel bad?

He slept on and off in the passenger seat - it wouldn't recline all the way - and when the sun woke him up to cries from the gulls he found himself lost for a moment.

Unfamiliar rocky shores. Bunkers he'd never seen before. Lonely, disparate houses.

He sat for a while on the stony beach, then turned and walked back, past the car to Beaucette where he'd buy himself some breakfast.

But nothing was open. The place was deserted. The marina not yet awake.

Desperate now, he returned to the car and drove in a daze through St Sampson. He followed the coast to the studio and slipped into the building just as the night shift clocked off. He sat in reception and waited.

Kira arrived at a quarter to nine. Saw him as soon as she opened the door.

'Kira,' he said, half raising himself from the seat.

She stopped for a moment and looked at the

pitiful sight. She shook her head, warning him off, then looked straight ahead and walked past him as if he wasn't there.

But she smelt him.

What are you doing? Dixon thought. Why have you come here? Like this? A mess, stinking and dirty, with a crumpled coat and yesterday's shirt, and trousers spotted with sick. He looked down, scared that the hems might be splashed with Rosalynd's blood. But they weren't. They were dusty and crumpled, but that was all. He didn't notice the spots of her blood on his sleeve.

He stood fully upright, then nodding towards the receptionist he walked to his car with his head held high. He would put her - he would put them all - as far as he could behind him.

He would focus now on himself - not dwell on the things he couldn't change, but change the things he could.

The Sarnian, 9.00am

Ollie wheeled his bike through the newsroom. Freya was in the hive. Most of the news and lifestyle teams were unpacking their bags or lifting the lids off cups of takeaway coffee.

He nodded at Ella and dropped himself down in his seat, then shook his mouse to wake up his Mac.

The badge on his email app showed a hundred and two new messages. Fifty of them had 'murder' in their subject lines. He forwarded them straight to Ruby and dropped them, unopened, into an archive folder. She could decide which ones he should answer – and how.

Crime was so rare on the island – murder almost unheard of – that Ollie's story had made him the focus of rather unwanted attention, from Amy Sloane and others. The fact that he worked for the paper complicated matters, as anything he said outside of its pages could only be passed through appropriate channels.

And that was where Ruby Jones played her part.

As The Sarnian's in-house PR machine, her job had revolved around licensing photos for brochures and postcards less than a week before. Now it was a storm of schedules and quotes as she oversaw requests for comments and background facts and photos of Oliver Carey.

Half of what remained in his inbox were internal memos, which he marked as low priority and set aside for later. That left him fewer than thirty messages, the second of which was a note from 'rholdbrook'.

Oliver. Take a listen and let me know what you think.

George Dixon's contributions to the last three eps. No edits or repeats. I've just rearranged them. Notice anything strange? Rosalynd.

The rest of the screen was blank, apart for her name, address and home number. He dialled it, but she didn't answer. He tried again after forty-five minutes of typing up notes only to be met once again by the impersonal tone of her answer machine.

Route de Jerbourg, 10.20am

Dixon went home and washed, and sure enough, he found her small hatchback tucked nose-first into the verge. He knew it was hers from the BBC permit stuck to the top of the windscreen. It was close enough to the house for the two to be logically linked and suggested to anyone passing by that she'd been there over the last few days.

He tried the door on the off chance she'd left it unlocked, but the handle clicked at the end of its arc and the lock refused to budge. He cursed himself for not having searched her pocket or bag for her keys. No worries, though. That was behind him. There were other ways of fixing a problem like this. He picked a large stone from the garden and went back to the house for a towel.

He'd buy some thick tape on his way to the bus.

Vale Parish, 11.15am

'Sorry, fella.' The driver raised his eyebrows. He didn't look the least bit sorry to George Dixon. Neither did he look old enough to be calling him fella. 'Cash or nothing.' He pushed Dixon's credit card out of the tray, holding the edge so it stood up against the rim. The woman behind him sighed loudly. Dixon knew he was meant to hear it; she was standing too close for anything else, one step down, just up from the kerb.

He patted his pockets. 'How much was it?'

The driver tapped the small display on the top of the ticket machine and Dixon cursed beneath his breath. There were many reasons he didn't ride the bus. This outdated faith in real money came close to the top of the list.

He gathered together his coins and counted them out as slowly as he could. The driver stabbed at the buttons and caused the machine to spit out a rough slip of paper. Dixon thanked him and walked down the aisle in search of a seat.

'Your ticket,' the driver said, tearing it from the machine. He didn't turn around, but Dixon did, and all he could see was the driver's hand drooping into the aisle. The fingers flicked the paper; the paper twitched. Dixon snatched it away, and threw himself and his bag in the second seat back. The middle-aged woman beside him had dyed her scalp the same colour as her thinning hair. She stared at him.

Dixon glared back for a moment, then smiled and said 'Yes,' nodding. He didn't meet his public so often. Who could blame her for being a little bit star-struck?

'I'm sorry?' she asked.

'Yes,' he repeated. 'It is me.' He paused. 'George Dixon.'

She frowned. 'Do I know you?'

Dixon looked away from the ignorant fool. She was as culturally deficient as that dreadful policewoman. What was her name?

Le Page.

Le Page the television watcher.

The thought of her made his lip curl.

The woman tapped his elbow.

'You're sitting on my coat, Mr Dixon.' She tugged at a pocket and Dixon felt the thick, rough fabric being yanked from beneath his buttocks. It rucked his slacks as it went.

He vowed he'd never again take the bus, and that his next car would be less distinctive. One that would have allowed him to drive it to

Rosalynd's house and park it there without fear of being seen.

Then again, he couldn't have driven any car after last night's explosion. Not before a scrupulous scrub. Inside and out. The bodywork was covered in dust whipped up by the wind at Icart. The fabric and dash were still flecked with vomit and smelled of stale milk and thick bile.

He cursed Kira, too, while he thought about it, for casting him out of the cast. He cursed Rosalynd Holdbrook for meddling. She'd brought him down to the level of this woman, who dyed her head and was forced to use public transport to move around the island.

The doors flapped shut with a violent hiss, and the bus wobbled off on its eager suspension. It bobbed around the coast road, and now and then cut away from the sea, playing hide and seek through gaps in the walls, dodging behind the tall trees and small houses. Now and then it popped out again with a view of a beach or a fort or the bladderwracked rocks of low tide. Whenever it did, he turned back his cuff to see how much time he had wasted.

Its route seemed to be never-ending. Stopping and stopping and stopping again, ferrying visitors between their hotels, driving pensioners out to the store, picking up idle passengers who were fit enough to walk. They all looked comfortably off. They all could surely afford a car. Why were they holding him up when time was of the essence? He checked off the miles for the next fifty minutes, then checked one last time as he hauled his bag from the bus to the road where it followed the walls of Vale Church.

He felt like that old pope - the one with the white hair, the tunic and shoes, who used to kiss the runway whenever he came in to land. Dixon had thought it strange at the time, but a ride on public transport had changed his mind on that account. Now it seemed understandable: something he might do himself.

He knew where Rosalynd lived. Richelle used to go there for bridge, and Dixon would pick her up. He'd sit at the end of Rosalynd's path and blast his horn at the house. Eventually Richelle would arrive, slightly tipsy, swearing they'd only drunk tea.

Only once had he been inside, the best part of ten years ago. That was the night it had all begun: when Rosalynd had cooked him dinner and paired him up with Richelle.

'Richelle, this is George Dixon, our new leading man. George, Richelle. Let me leave you two to get to know each other while I finish the starter.'

She'd been so transparent.

The table had only been set for three, and

look what it had led to. Dixon unemployed, Thomas Thoumine humiliated, the insides of his car barely fit for habitation. And now he was trapped on the island. How could he leave when he ought to be pushing that fool Marc Renouf and his idiot sidekick Le Page to find an alternative culprit? Leaving would only arouse their suspicions, and so he had nothing to do. Nothing but act the part of a lover, bereaved and heartbroken, and innocent. Not for too long, mind. He didn't want to be typecast.

He crept around the side of the house and cupped his eyes at the kitchen window. It was neat and well ordered inside. A stack of clean cups and saucers sat on the draining board; a pile of airtight boxes on the table. Each one looked like it might contain cake. He pressed his face on the glass until he could see the back door, and there in the lock was what he'd been hoping to find: the key on its ring.

The door was a flimsy contraption: old wood and a single pane of glass. It wasn't even frosted, perhaps because it wasn't overlooked. Dixon had encountered one like this several years ago: in a studio in Bristol. He couldn't remember the name of the drama, but they'd had a consultant. A breaker done good, who'd served his time and hired himself out as a media expert. Now he instructed actors and crew on how to crack safes – prop ones, of course – how to enter a house unseen... how to break glass without being heard.

The pane was tight in the frame, which was good. The wood would hold the edges in place, allowing him to take out a small section without spilling too many shards on the floor. Dixon knew that it wasn't so much the break of the glass that you had to worry about – that could be managed. It wasn't the sound of it smashing that would alert the neighbours, but the shards falling out of the frame and onto the floor. They would have to be kept under control.

He unzipped his bag and took out the roll of tape. He'd bought the thickest reel he could find. It was almost black, and had a mesh of fibre running between the plastic upper surface and the tacky underside. It was so sticky that it stretched as he pulled it away from the roll, like the skin on a freshly killed fish. He pulled it more slowly here than he would have at home for fear of it streaking away from the next layer down with the sound of torn linen.

He cut it into two-foot strips and stuck them onto the window, from top to bottom and left to right, until he had covered its surface. He dropped it back into his bag then reached in and took out the stone and the towel, folded the towel and pressed it against the window, just above the handle. He struck it once with the rock.

It cracked, but it didn't smash. It sounded like someone had broken a thick bar of chocolate, snapping it off straight from the fridge. The heavy black tape creased from bottom to top, a valley now running up from the corner by the handle to the point where it touched the top of the frame. He slid the towel higher and struck again, and this time the valley coursed left to right, tracing a line from the edge of the glass to the central break but leaving the opposite side intact.

The window was now in three parts: a single tall sheet the full height of the frame and two smaller panes to the left. With another two strikes he had shattered the lower quarter, and when he pressed on the tape in that section, it felt like the seeds in a bean bag, grating together but all held in place, firmly affixed to the glue.

He dropped the towel and stone and picked at a corner of the tape, rolling it back with some ease this time, taking with it a glittering coating of crystalline glass.

It was almost too easy.

He reached through the gap and turned the key in the lock.

The house was just as he remembered: small and functional rather than small and cosy, but it did smell of baking and that, at least, was some concession to making the home feel homely.

He closed the door and worked through the kitchen, turning aside spoons and forks and whisks, fingering through a drawer full of towels, sliding flat hands between them, and then through another drawer filled with stout cardboard cake boards: thick, covered in silver foil, the slice marks upon them like rings in a tree, counting through the years. One contained a bag of batteries; another, some fuses, but none was home to a spare set of keys.

He slammed shut the last drawer and turned around, searching for hooks on the wall, looking in the fruit bowl, in pots on the windowsill, and turning over the bunch of keys that was hanging from the back door - the bunch that had let him in.

None of them looked like a car key.

Finally, he walked down the hall to look in the drawers of the dresser, and there he found it. A single key in a white envelope, with folded corners and a crease in the middle. There were a few pound notes underneath it. He slipped them into his pocket, then took out the key and put the envelope back where he'd found it.

It had taken him less than ten minutes. Now he would have to catch the bus home, and then he would move the car. What a waste of a day.

He hadn't yet bought the papers, had no proper breakfast, had barely slept last night...

The phone on the dresser chirped once, then started a more sustained ring. Dixon reached out, but stopped himself just in time. After two further rings it clicked and the answer machine picked it up. A voice Dixon recognised squeezed itself out of the tinny speaker.

'Rosalynd, ummm... it's Kira. Are you there...?' She paused. 'Okay, well, I was just ringing to see if everything was alright.'

Dixon felt his throat start to tighten. Did Kira know something? Had she heard a rumour?

Of course not, he told himself. Don't be so silly.

But he felt his face flush nonetheless.

It was too soon.

Nobody would suspect anything.

Not yet.

'Okay, well, it's oneish. We had been expecting you in this morning. Give me a call when you get this, yes? Just to let me know.'

She rang off, and a moment later the machine cut the line.

Dixon ran a hand across his brow, then reaching forward he tapped a red button with the end of the key.

'Message - - Deleted.' said the staccato computerised voice.

The Sarnian, noon

Alfie called a meeting. He gathered his writers around him and perched a buttock on Ollie's desk. It seemed unusually casual for a man who was so professional. Alfie was sixty, smart, with perfect hair and straight teeth and a reputation for doing things right. The old way. He didn't sit on desks. He didn't call meetings outside of the conference room.

Ollie rolled back in his seat to give himself some distance and looked at his boss. Something had changed.

'Team,' Alfie said, looking from one to the other. 'We have half a page to fill. Inner facing. I need some ideas.'

'Dixon or Ibbott?' Ollie asked him.

'They're one and the same,' Alfie said, shaking his head. 'Makes no difference.'

'Profile then,' Harry said. 'Nice big pictures, some bullets beneath each one.'

'Done it,' Alfie said. 'Done it to death. If you can find anything new to profile about either of them you can have the afternoon off.'

'Something about Ibbott's funeral, then. Some kind of campaign.'

'Go on...'

Harry shrugged. 'She's got no family. Who would go? If we started a campaign for a decent turn-out...'

'Not bad. I like that one. Make her out to be some kind of island hero?' Alfie thought for a moment. 'Only trouble is, of course, we won't know when it is until they release the body, and that won't be soon. Definitely back-burner it, though. Work up some ideas when you've got a moment, will you? We'll need to pass it by Freya.'

He looked up as he said her name and Ollie noticed that from where he'd perched on the edge of the desk, Alfie was right in her sightline. She was directly in his. He realised then, for the first time, what it was he'd been feeling for the last three days.

Drifting paranoia.

He had felt it that very first morning, presenting his story to the rest of the team with Freya beside him, when she'd made it clear that the only reason he was still there was that he'd had the forethought to take some pictures on his phone.

Ella was feeling it, too. She'd waited behind on the second day and caught him at his desk, just as he opened up The Sarnian archive to continue his search for his father. He'd thought she was going to suggest another drink, but instead she'd sat beside him and spoken in a quiet voice.

'I don't know,' she said. 'Something's changed. It ought to be good. It ought to be pulling us together...'

Ollie knew what she meant. It felt less like they were moving as one, as a team, against their media rivals – more like each was trying to win an undeclared competition. Harry Ozanne was arguing for larger pictures and smaller stories. Alfie was beefing up the headlines, adopting less comment, fewer question marks – yet twisting each one to the brink of libel as he tried to follow Freya's example, discarding his integrity, presenting supposition as fact.

And now he had moved.

He'd convened a meeting where he knew she could see him, at a time when he knew she was busy. At noon, every day, she was on the phone to the paper's owners. Sales, staffing, the state of the market... none of them knew what they talked about but they all knew the schedule – Alfie as much as the rest of them – and clearly he knew how to use it. He'd called an unconventional meeting, sited himself where she'd see him, and now he was being efficient for the sake of half a page.

They all fell silent, casting about for a worthy story, and one they could run right away.

'What would Dixon look like without a wig?' Ella asked.

'Bald, I should think,' Alfie said, turning so he could see her. She sat at the desk opposite Ollie, so from Alfie's perch she was behind him.

'Monkish,' Ollie said. 'The stuff around the edge is a different colour. It's thinner. It's probably real.'

'Where are we going with this?' Alfie asked.

'Well, just, Ollie's been chasing him for four days,' said Ella. 'Even you didn't get to speak to him. He just shouted at you through the letterbox.'

'We didn't discuss his wig.'

'No, but what if we could use it to our advantage? What kind of man wears a wig?'

'Someone going bald,' Alfie said.

'Someone insecure,' Harry said.

'Exactly. Let's use that to our advantage. Harry, do you know those wanted posters?' She pulled her keyboard towards her and typed a few words into a browser. Ollie could see the list of results reflected in her glasses: a page full of pictures that she scrolled through until she found a row of matching results.

'Of course,' Harry said. 'But Dixon hasn't been charged.'

'No, Ella might be on to something here,' Alfie said. 'It's us who wants him, not the police, but I don't see how –'

'The wig?' she interrupted. She scrolled

through the page until she found a poster with four different views of its suspect. She clicked to enlarge it, and they saw that each of the pictures was subtly different. The first was apparently untouched: a regular police mug shot with an ID number and date. The three below were markedly different, and the subject had clearly been aged by an unfriendly artist.

'This is what they do when they've been chasing someone a long time,' she said. 'They mock up what they might look like now. It makes them more obvious if they're out on the street. You know, if they've shaved their beard or lost their hair.'

'Or stopped wearing a wig,' Alfie said.

'Do we know that he has?' Ollie said. 'It's not like he's disappeared. He's just not talking.'

'No, hang on, though,' Harry said. 'This is good. Do you think he might have done that?'

'Why not?'

'And the corset?'

She shrugged. 'Maybe not that.'

'I like this,' Alfie said. 'I like this a lot, but it's more than half a page.' He turned to Harry. 'Get on it. Ditch the lead and run this page one with a nice fat strap: "George Dixon: Wanted for Questioning".'

'Don't you need to check with –' Harry began, but Alfie was already on his feet and walking towards the hive.

'Don't worry,' he said. 'She'll love it.'

Icart Point, 2pm

Tony Guille parked at Icart Point, close to the rocks that stopped the drivers tipping their vehicles over the edge. You could see the south coast from there, almost as far as Petit Bot Bay.

He loved it almost as well as he knew it.

All of it – the paths and the cliffs and the hedgerows that kept them apart. He knew them as well as he knew his own garden: where the gorse was the sweetest, where it smelled of coconut milk and of sun cream, of sweetness and childhood and days spent running free on the beach. Its unseen clouds fogged the paths with the scent of a long summer, and he walked among them when they were blooming, breathing deeply, lost in the past.

He knew where the hottentot fig was most dense. For twenty years he'd been rolling, rolling, rolling it back, hacking whenever he found a root, and burning great bundles in skips on the headlands. The following year it always came back, almost as though it had never been touched. A good frost would see to it better than him, but who could remember the last time they'd had a winter that cold?

So they'd made an uneasy peace, Tony Guille and the hottentot fig, and he found himself admiring it now, with its penchant for rocky terrain and the way it hid the concrete slabs, abandoned after the war. It impressed him, too – how it thrived in the loose sandy soil with only the salty spray of the sea to dampen its clumsy fingers. Perhaps he'd softened, for he'd even come to admire its flowers, transient though they might be.

He rarely touched it now. He'd let it lie while he busied himself with other jobs: patching the steps that carried the paths up and then down the steep cliffs, trimming the blackthorn or clearing the scrub from around the dolmen up on the common. Sometimes he'd spend a day reseating the stones of an abreuvoir or, like today, painting the benches that dotted the outcrops and gave the hikers a lookout from which to enjoy the views.

He took out his brushes and paint, then locked the van and tested the handle.

There were few better jobs on a day like this, when the weather was kind and birds were busy. They'd newly returned from a winter away, and were loud and excited, chattering, fluttering, staking their claims as he walked past their nests.

A couple of walkers had stopped there to

watch them. They nodded hello and he nodded back. He smiled and half waved the brush. They'd perched on the granite block, avoiding the bench as though they might know what had happened there just the night before. The ash of Dixon's cigarette was still scattered about its legs. The fibres of Rosalynd's dress were caught in the cracks of its paint. There were spots of blood in the dust below.

Guille saw none of this as he stood before it: just a raised wooden seat with a thick green skin that had bubbled and chipped in the sun. It would need smoothing off before he could make it good.

He set down the paint and took out his block, then started to sand the single long slat that made up its back. It had aged, and was crude and unattractive, no longer smooth but heavily textured. The wind had whipped at the tiniest pieces, chipping away the flecks of its skin to leave the surface broken and cracked like cheap patent leather left out in the rain.

The paint was still thick, though, and laid down in layers over the years, so it wasn't the wood that splintered away as he sanded it down with his block, but small green fragments, and with them, every hint of what Dixon had done.

First to go was a thread from Rosalynd's dress – a dress she'd made herself, using fabric brought back from a trip to Morocco. A dress that often drew comments. Tiny molecules of the flour she used, invisible to the naked eye, had entwined themselves within its weave. It had taken her years to find the flour she liked best, imported in batches of two score bags by an obscure island wholesaler. That thread, as sure as her dental imprint, would have been enough to confirm that she'd been there the day before.

The industrial fibres from Dixon's wig - a wig that needed replacing - were floating away like real hair, caught on the breeze and carried off to sea. So, too, the curious blend of tobacco he used, mixed by hand by a man in Sloane Square and sent on a monthly subscription. Few on the island had heard of that mix. None had ever smoked it.

None but Dixon. It would have been enough to convict him - if it had not been blown away.

The tiny strands of their DNA, from sweat and spittle, were transferring themselves from the bench to the paper, to Tony Guille's hands, to the dust on the floor, to the air all about. If Dixon had wanted to clean the crime scene, he couldn't have done any better than this.

It all came away so easily - the paint along with the evidence. He moved around to the front of the bench, from where he could sand down the seat, scuffing the dusty ground with his feet and throwing up clouds of sand and grit. His boots wiped away the spots of Rosalynd's blood, erasing the prints of Dixon's shoes and their smooth creamy soles of calf leather.

He had no reason to think of them; no reason to even suspect they'd been there. Instead, he tutted and shook his head, lamenting the state of the bench, and wondering who had painted it last, dashing on the vivid green dye without first sanding it down.

It had been a perch for the birds since then - he could see the scratches in its thick, vinyl surface. A sanctuary to weary walkers, the place of two conceptions on balmy nights late enough not to be seen.

A place of romance, the site of two proposals, one of which, on a single knee had led to a crushing rejection.

The wearing down of the skin on a bench was as much a part of the island's story as the forts and defences that hemmed it in. It felt like a crime to be rubbing it down like that, taking away the tales of the tourists and locals who'd sat there over the years.

So he didn't go down to bare wood, but carried on sanding only until he could close his eyes and run his fingers over the surface and not know when he was touching the uppermost skin or one of the layers below. By then it was evenly scuffed: just enough to accept the new coat, which would take it beyond his retirement.

It was also enough to obliterate once and for all any trace of Dixon's misdeed.

Guille put down the block, and the paper uncurled as he levered the top off the paint. He stirred in the thin oily film that had formed on its surface, then dipped in the brush as far as the cuff that secured the bristles and wiped the excess on the lip of the tin.

He looked at the bench for a moment, looked out to sea, and decided to start with the back. That way he would always be working away from the path, and the view of the coastline would stretch out before him. He put one hand on the thick wooden slat and lowered himself to the ground, straight onto Rosalynd's keys.

The car key tore his khaki knee. The house key pierced his skin. Guille cried out in pain and rolled his leg to one side, freeing the keys, which now caught the sun as they settled again in the dust. He could see them. They were obvious, but until that moment they'd been half obscured by the leg and flecked by the fragments of sanded-off paint. An irrational fury swept through him. They'd hurt him, and he wanted to do them some harm. He knew it would not ease his pain, but the thought of throwing them over the cliff...

He picked them up and swung his arm backwards, ready to hurl them away...

But the keys weren't his.

It wasn't their fault that he'd knelt on them, nor that he'd dropped his brush on the ground, its bristles now covered in dust.

He let his hand fall and he looked at them. There were three - fairly plain, nothing special - plus a small round fob and keyring the shape of the island. He turned the fob in his fingers and found the letters BBC stamped in white blocks on the opposite side. Perhaps they belonged to the hikers, he thought, but as he looked back at the carved granite block, he could see they were gone - long gone.

He shrugged. He didn't have time to chase them now. The lid was off and the paint was starting to skin.

He dropped them into his pocket and flicked the brush at the bush, spotting the new leaves with the darker, thick green of the paint, then he dipped it back into the tin and made himself a mental note to hand them in at the kiosk.

Before that, he'd seal off once and for all the remaining forensic clues that would have revealed how the keys had got there.

The Sarnian, 4.45pm

Alfie was right. Freya had signed off the new front page without even seeing it. She trusted him, and she knew a good headline when she heard one. Her only stipulation was that Harry Ozane use the layout to exaggerate every aspect of the story.

He'd taken her wish to extremes.

The headline was set in an Old Western font and the box that surrounded it had been tweaked. It now had a sepia background and torn-paper border. The corners appeared to be curling up from the page, lifting and turning back on themselves. Three shots of Dixon were evenly spaced across the middle: an untouched photo from the BBC website on top, and Harry's amendments below it. In the first he'd lost his toupee; in the second he'd burst the strings of his corset. His torso tumbled out and pressed itself tight on his shirt. He looked like blancmange in a thin muslin bag.

'It's supposed to be a poster,' Harry said, as he laid down duplicate copies on each of their desks.

'We got that,' Ella said. 'Only, isn't it a bit...'

Alfie flicked his eyes towards the hive, then quickly back to their desks. Ella nodded. She understood. It wasn't something to question.

'I need you to read this very carefully,' Harry said. 'To say we're skating on thin ice –'

'Would be a cliche,' Ollie said.

'Would be to massively understate things,' Harry said.

'Have you passed it by the lawyers?' Alfie asked.

Harry nodded.

'And?'

'They reckon we should be okay. On balance. Just. But you know how they are. They won't put it in writing because –'

'They want to cover their legal arses.'

'Yes. So this will fall on us in the end. Any trouble, any at all...'

He didn't need to finish.

They all ducked their heads and started to read through the copy, word by word, comma by stop by apostrophe, considering every syllable for potential legal demerits.

The story was pure speculation, pitted with questions it failed to answer.

What was Dixon hiding?

Why was he avoiding the press?

Didn't he realise they wanted to help?

He wasn't involved?

...was he?

Alfie had given the story to Ella and she'd more than rewarded his faith. She'd taken it just far enough, leading the reader, planting questions – and with them the seeds of doubt, that would germinate quickly and blossom by morning into a rambling vine of suspicion. It would smother the island and Dixon would have what he'd always craved: his very own water cooler moment, only not on his terms but theirs.

If this didn't bring him in, if he somehow resisted the urge to reply, then no course of action would ever be likely to get them the answers they needed.

They each signed their names at the foot of the page without a single amendment and handed the proofs back to Harry, ready for sending to print.

'Excellent work,' Alfie said, leaning across towards Ella. 'You can go if you want.' He turned to Ollie. 'Can I keep you for ten minutes? One more thing I need you to read.'

'Sure,' Ollie said, reaching out to take the page that Alfie was holding towards him.

It was less than two hundred words – a NIB, they called it, or News In Brief – that would run in a column beside the day's lead. Freya called them Bog Fodder.

'Crap for the porcelain seat of relief,' she said. 'Why not make a virtue of the fact that that's where they're read. Give them a proper headline.'

Alfie had talked her out of it, and in exchange he'd agreed to pep them up with more pictures, a greater use of bold and italics, and as many puns as the subs could muster. The best they'd managed this time around was 'Killer unVALEd?' The 'vale' part was not only set in bold type, but larger, too, and red, to drive the point home.

Island cops took the unusual step of adding a postscript to this afternoon's briefing on the Richelle Ibbott murder case. Speaking after questions, and flanked by Inspector Marc Renouf and lower-grade lackeys from the fledgling murder squad, deputy Christine Le Page put out an island-wide alert for Rosalynd Holdbrook, 60, who hasn't been seen since she missed a booking with the BBC at the media building north of Town.

Holdbrook previously worked in the building as editor of The Fleet, hired George Dixon to lead the cast in the role of Thomas Thoumine and is said to have introduced him to Ibbott. Holdbrook's successor, Kira Spooner, couldn't be reached for comment, although it's understood that she was responsible for bringing Holdbrook's disappearance to light.

Le Page tried to play down the significance of Holdbrook's apparent flight, but the tangential link to Ibbott, via George Dixon, can't be discounted. That naturally leads us to ask, was Ibbott's murder a case of lover's revenge?

Did Rosalynd Holdbrook have more to do with the death of her friend than Le Page, Renouf and the rest of the force would have us believe?

He felt himself flush as he came to the end of the page, his hands damp, his fingers clammy about the pen. He dropped it on the proof and shook his mouse to wake up his Mac, then clicked on the Mail app and scrolled through his messages, back to the start of the day.

Oliver. Take a listen and let me know what you think. George Dixon's contributions to the last three eps. No edits or repeats. I've just rearranged them. Notice anything strange? Rosalynd.

He looked at the time stamp. She'd sent it the previous lunchtime, but something had held it up and it hadn't arrived in his inbox until... he expanded the headers... seven o'clock that morning.

That meant that he – possibly he alone – could identify the time she disappeared. It was some time between that lunchtime, and one o'clock the previous day.

He signed off the proof, then picked up his phone and called an internal extension.

'Be there, be there, be there,' he chanted beneath his breath, willing someone – anyone –

to pick up at the other end. It rang four times, five, then a sixth, and he almost dropped it, thinking it might be quicker to go there in person. His finger hovered over the cradle - seven rings - and just as he was about to press it, the other end clicked. He heard some background chatter, cut through moments later by a clear female voice.

'IT.'

'Um, hi,' he said, getting his words in order. He lowered his voice so that no one would overhear. 'I'm - I received an email this morning. From someone called Rosalynd Holbrook.' He spelled out her address. 'I think it had an attachment.'

'Name?'

'Holdbrook, Rosalynd.'

'No, your name.'

'Sorry. Ollie. Oliver Carey.'

'Carey...'

He heard her typing. Her space bar was loose. It rattled each time she knocked it down with her thumb.

'Came in this morning?'

'Well, no. I got it this morning, but she -'

'Yeah, I see it. We stripped it.'

'Which means what?'

'The file. Stripped it out. Quarantined it.'

'Why?'

'Dunno. System's automatic. Works on

algorithms.'

'So where is it now.'

She cleared her throat without moving the phone, and the line cracked, overloaded by the eruption.

'They go,' she said. 'System keeps them six hours. After that...' She trailed off, but the implication was obvious.

'Can you get it back?'

'Sorry.'

'Great.' Ollie put down the phone. He turned to his boss. 'Alfie, if you'd received...'

Alfie looked up and frowned. He waited, but Ollie seemed frozen. 'Question?' he asked.

Ollie thought for a moment. 'Forget it,' he said. 'It's nothing.'

'Have you finished with that proof?' Alfie pointed to the page, still sitting on Ollie's desk.

'Sorry.' He passed it back. 'Do you still need me?'

Alfie shook his head. 'You can go.'

Ollie had to restrain himself. He wanted to jump up and run to the lift, and find the mental space he needed to think through the email and what had been stripped from its tail.

But more importantly than that, he needed to work out what it meant and how he could use his first proper lead to shore up his place in the newsroom.

DAY FIVE

Route Militaire, 1.54am

Renouf was in bed with his wife. She was asleep, but he was lying there wide awake: listening, thinking. Remus Carey was back in his life. He'd returned in a manner Renouf had never expected.

It wasn't the man himself. It was Oliver Carey, his son, whose face brought back to Renouf the endless loop of that terrible night - a night he hadn't witnessed himself, but heard about in retrospect. The very last night that he knew for sure Remus Carey had been alive.

For weeks afterwards, those events had played through in his mind. He'd lain awake just like this. He'd stared at the ceiling for countless hours, Marie and Remus and her two hired hands circling Remus, circling Renouf, around and around and around his bed. Eventually it had all got too much and they'd forced him out - out to the kitchen to sit alone and drink whisky.

The demons had settled, eventually, and they'd left him alone for a year and a half. But it was four days now since Renouf had met Ollie at

Marble Bay, and for the last four nights Remus Carey had been his constant companion. The fog was clearing. The man was stepping through, back into Renouf's world, yet the closer he got, the more he had changed. His face was merging with that of his son. The two were becoming one. Younger, brighter, still chasing the truth. Only this truth was different. This truth, though Ollie might not yet know it, centred more on Renouf, and less on the Consortium.

He gave up.

He got out of bed, picked up his phone and took himself into the lounge, then throwing himself in an easy chair he uncorked the whisky and stared at the dormant TV.

…

…

…

He woke with a start. Something had brushed his leg.

The cat.

It did it again, close to his hip. He reached down to swipe it away but instead of the cat he found his phone, vibrating against his thigh, its ringer turned off. The light of its screen fell on the arm of the chair and glared as he picked it up. His eyes were still blurry from waking, so he jabbed it without knowing who was calling and held it up to his ear.

'Renouf,' he said, lifting himself in the chair.

'Did I wake you?'

'Charlie.' It was the forensics officer, his voice urgent and rushed. 'What time is it?' Renouf could hear the wind licking the microphone, and pictured his colleague standing outside in the cold.

'Twoish. Listen, Marc. What do you know of Christine Le Page?'

'What?'

'Her background.'

Renouf stretched his back left and then right. It ached from falling asleep at an awkward angle. He tried to recall her application and why she'd so clearly stood out from the rest of the field. 'Fifteen years on the force. Impressive arrest record. I don't know, Charlie. Why?'

'Do you remember a Tim Collins. Late forties, receding hair. Bit of a lisp.'

'Should I?'

'He's here.'

'On Sark?'

'At the conference.'

'Can we do this in the morning?' he asked. 'I've just got off and I really –'

'You interviewed him. He and Christine were the two final candidates, only he was under-qualified. Massively.'

'I think I...'

'Didn't even want the job as he'd have to fly back every Friday. He's got a wife and kids.'

Renouf remembered him now. It hadn't been difficult ruling him out. Three years before he'd still been working in banking, retained now and then by the Jersey Police to help them investigate fraud. He'd thought it made him part of the force – but it hadn't, of course. There was none of the legwork. None of the drudgery, none of the tedious, cyclical tasks. If he'd known about them, Renouf was sure, he wouldn't have joined when a role opened up, and landed himself some constable shoes that he'd worn down to leather on the beat.

The star on the corner of Collins's CV had struck Renouf as ill-placed. Bichard had sent it down with one other, Christine's, and told him to take his pick. He could tell from the profiles alone that Collins would never have fitted the role. He talked to him for twenty minutes and sent him back to Jersey. He appointed Christine the following day and two months later she moved to Guernsey. Renouf's deputy went to Jersey in her place, largely against his own will, to fill an equal role for the length of her placement.

'He's here,' Charlie said. 'Collins. As surprised as you that he made the cut. Reckons there were three or four better options, far stronger candidates, and that's aside from Le Page.'

'So why did he put in?' Renouf asked, wondering where Charlie was leading him. Charlie wasn't one to get needlessly excited, but so far this sounded like the kind of thing they could have discussed when he got back to the lab.

'To make up the numbers, apparently. They promised he wouldn't get through. He was as surprised as you that you called him in for an interview.'

'I'm sorry,' said Renouf. 'Either I'm half asleep or you're half cut. Are you just out of the pub.'

Charlie sighed. 'Yes, but listen. Christine's appointment was out of your hands. It was a foregone conclusion. They weeded out any serious competition and fed you two candidates knowing full well which one you'd choose. She's a plant.'

'Meaning what? There's bad feeling among the four that didn't get it?'

'Yes. Plenty. Enough for this to be... Well, let's just say that when the beer gets flowing they're happy to bring it up.'

'It's politics, Charlie. Let it lie. Go to bed and sleep off whatever you've drunk.'

'I'm sober, I'm bloody cold and there's nothing I'd like more than to be in my bed, but Christine isn't what you think she is. She isn't a serving officer. She's civilian. She works in corruption. Police corruption. She investigates us.'

Renouf straightened up in the chair. 'She's internal affairs?' He sat forward.

'What did you think she was?'

'Inspector.'

'Technically she is.'

'Only she inspects the police.'

'You didn't know?'

Renouf said nothing.

'They've brought her in for a reason, Marc. There's a rat among us. Who it is and what they've done, I don't know, but we'll all have to watch our backs.'

He listened to the wind swiping at Charlie's phone and wondered how he could ever have been so naive. It was all so obvious now why Christine had come to Guernsey. It had nothing to do with improving inter-island relations. Christine Le Page was there to investigate him.

'You've got nothing to worry about, Charlie,' he said at last. 'If we all had records like yours there'd be no need for people like Christine Le Page.'

He took the phone away from his ear and silently switched it off.

La Fontenelle, 7am

Christine leaned back to look at the clock. She'd been working since five. Thirty minutes more, she told herself, and then she'd wake Dan. She'd shower while he ran, and then the cycle would start again.

She poured the dregs from her cafetiere and went to the kitchen to reboil the kettle. The coffee jar was running low, and she realised how much she'd been drinking. She'd been lurching from one caffeine hit to the next since she'd started work on Remus's logs, but at least she was making good progress - and enjoying it. It had been some time since she'd last felt so good about her work, and though she'd never admit it to Dan, she almost wished the case would last longer.

She opened a cupboard to find some more coffee and saw the postcard of Corbiere that he'd stuck to the back of the door.

'Our place,' he had said as he tacked it up. 'Every time we make a drink we'll think of home.'

The lighthouse there was indeed their place. Dan had proposed there. The sun had been low, the sky close to ochre, and right away she'd said yes. They'd sat on the rocks until the day was played out, then returned to the car and made plans. They'd been living in St Helier then, but moved across the island soon after, and sought out a house that gave views of the lighthouse, and the low-tide rocks against which it offered protection.

She missed it, and she knew Dan did, too, but what was a view really worth? More than true satisfaction? Of being happy day to day? Of looking forward to going to work and locking horns with Renouf? She had to wonder.

And she had to put it out of her mind. Bichard could never extend her placement. It would leave Renouf's deputy stranded in Jersey; she couldn't imagine that any reason would justify such a move.

The kettle clicked off and she told herself to be practical. Even Dan would admit that they couldn't stay there forever. Their home was in Jersey. They'd have to go back one day... One day fairly soon, in fact. She would have to make the most of it - enjoy it while it lasted - and think about Jersey as her placement drew to a close.

She poured the water on two fresh scoops of strong coffee, then carried it back to the lounge. Her laptop was open on the dining table, the radio low, Remus's log on the screen. She sat down again in her slippers and gown and set about tweaking obscure translations in the search for more meaningful, fitting expressions.

TWO YEARS AGO

From the diary and logs of Remus Carey, as translated by Christine Le Page.

'Funny thing,' Bichard said. He wasn't one for small talk. He'd called me up on the boat two days later and kicked off without a 'hello'. I was mending one of my rods.

'Go on.' I tucked the phone under my chin as I bit off the end of some twine.

'Those buoys,' he said. 'The orange and pink –'

'You've got a name?' I asked, spitting the end of the twine on the deck.

'They're unlicensed.'

'Illegal?'

'Pretty much, although if they were unbaited as you say it's highly unlikely they'd catch anything, so it's a grey area at best. Whoever's they are could probably claim they were storing them there.'

'Perhaps,' I said, knotting off the end of the line and taking the phone back in my hand. 'But it's pretty conclusive, don't you think?'

He was silent for a few seconds. 'Will you keep an eye on it?'

I told him I would. I could tell he was skirting some other issue, perhaps unsure how to broach a delicate subject. 'What is it, Miles?' I asked.

'Malkulpa.'

The name took me back to Lyon, and the legal firm we'd discussed in the stuffy room at Interpol. 'Are you moving on them?'

He grunted. 'No. We're keeping our powder dry. We're still of the opinion that moving too soon could blow it all open.'

'So...?'

'Their number showed up in the phone logs.' He took a quick breath and carried on before I could interrupt. 'From a phone in this building. It could have been a mis-dial. Whoever it was put it down before it was answered.'

'Someone inside calling a friend?'

'Perhaps.'

'A relative?'

'No. We checked that.'

'Who did?'

'Me and Renouf.'

'He knows about this?'

'Just the basics.'

'Is that wise?'

'He won't talk.'

'Are you sure? You know what we –'

'I trust him.' Bichard cut me off.

I hoped he was right. At our very first meeting in Lyon, three months before the most recent, we'd agreed that each delegate would disclose the details of what we were doing only to those who absolutely had to know. As far as I'd been aware, Bichard was the only one inside our force involved with the case, hence my semi-detached position.

'Whose phone?' I asked.

'It was a hot desk. Could have been anyone.'

'Could have been Renouf.'

'You don't like him.'

'I don't know him.'

'Well maybe you should,' Bichard said, with a little more force than was needed. 'He's good. One of the best.'

'Fine.'

'What?'

'Fine,' I repeated. 'I'll get to know him. I'll take him out on the boat.'

'Well, I don't know whether –'

'What?'

'Is that wise?'

'Do you really trust him?' I asked. 'Implicitly?'

'Yes.'

'Then it's wise,' I said.

It's not that I don't respect Bichard – or his judgement – but a second opinion, my opinion, never hurt anyone, least of all me. If there was some connection between Malkulpa and someone inside the States Police building then it made sense first to be careful, and second to try and discover where it might lie.

'You'd better tell me what he knows,' I said. 'We don't want any slip-ups.'

To my relief it seemed that he really did know no more than the absolute minimum. He knew we were investigating a smuggling operation, but not what the cargo was. He knew we were working with the police across Europe, and he knew about me. He didn't know about the captured courier, the coordinates or the apparently useless buoys.

'Perhaps you ought to arrange a meeting,' I said when Bichard had finished what sounded to me like a mild confession.

'Sure. How about...' I could hear him turning pages. Presumably his diary. 'Are you free tonight?'

It was Wednesday. Odette would be out on her course again. 'Tonight's good.'

'Dinner somewhere?'

'Bring him down to the boat,' I said. 'We'll head out with the rods and some beers.'

Now Bichard is tall – six-foot plus – but Renouf has an inch or two extra, and the broad-shouldered frame to carry it off. Bit of a belly, I noticed, although that was only obvious when he sat down. They arrived in separate cars, set their clocks by the kiosk and walked down the slipway together. I stood in the wheelhouse and watched them crossing the sand. I could tell from the fact he was wearing his patent shoes that Bichard wouldn't be joining us out at sea. He didn't try to hide it.

'This is Marc Renouf,' he said, standing back so his colleague could climb from the harbour wall to the deck. Sampson eyed them both from the steps that led to the galley.

'You're not joining us?' I asked, looking down at his shoes.

He shook his head. 'Prior engagement. I'm sure you boys will have more fun without me, anyhow.'

He'd never had any intention of spending the night with us, and in fairness that was perhaps for the best. If I was going to get to know this Renouf it was better we spoke man to man, rather than through a third party.

I turned to Renouf. 'I'm sure that's right, eh?'

Renouf put out his hand. 'You'll have to show me how this all works,' he said, as we shook. 'I suspect I'll be not much more than a hindrance.'

'Nothing to it,' I said, gripping him firmly and keeping our hands upright. I could feel him turning my wrist a little, to give himself a literal upper hand. He released me when he realised he was making no progress.

'You eat fish?' I asked.

'Of course.'

'Good. We shall catch our dinner. Bream? Bass? Pollack?'

'Mullet.'

'Mullet, eh? You like a good fight?'

'As much as the next man.'

'Feisty beast.'

'Is that me or the fish?' he asked, a smile on his face.

Bichard laughed. 'You boys enjoy yourselves,' he said, as he turned and walked back along the harbour wall. 'I'll see you in the morning.'

'Would you settle for sole?' I asked Renouf.

Renouf shrugged. 'If mullet's out of season...'

'Mullet's a daytime catch. Sole feeds at night.' I jumped down the steps to the galley where I'd stowed a selection of bait in the cool box. I pulled out some squid and threw it onto the deck to thaw.

'Do you mind if I smoke?' Renouf asked, as I came back up.

I could have thought of a less objectionable way he could kill himself, but I held my tongue and let him light up in return for helping cast off.

I busied myself in the wheelhouse as he settled in a seat on the deck, below the brass bell which swung about on the arm above his head. I turned the Puffin back on herself and guided us out to sea.

It was choppy, but Renouf seemed happy enough. He kicked one foot on the deck rail to steady the unsecured seat and kept his eye on the harbour as we motored south towards Pezeries and round past the Fairy Circle. He dragged the cigarette as far as the filter and threw the tip overboard, then came and leaned on the wheelhouse door. Sampson had retreated to the bunks by then, repeating his impression of a spinning top, no doubt.

'She's a fine boat,' Renouf said.

I smiled. It was a standard opening - one I'd heard many times before, often when someone was trying to find some common ground on which to start a conversation. In truth, though, she is. Better than the line of her bow might suggest. The engines develop a good twenty percent more power than her weight requires, the torque is eighty percent efficient. She has two propellers to reduce heeling, although her stern profile would have you believe she still had only the single motor installed by the boatyard. I wondered whether Renouf knew something more than his innocent act suggested - if he could tell from the sound of the engine that she... but then I mentally kicked myself. Suspicion and paranoia were not the basis on which to conduct an investigation, for was that not what this was?

'She's not so bad,' I said, putting my doubts to one side. 'Knows her way round these parts. Can't ask for much more than that.'

'Is that so? Where is she taking us this evening?'

'How much do you know about fishing?'

'I'm entirely in your hands.'

I nodded. I'd thought as much. 'Cowhorn,' I said, increasing the power a little now that we were clear of the headland. The cliffs of the south coast were starting to rise on our port side and I could see the top of the Pleinmont tower above us.

'Cowhorn?'

I hadn't expected him to know what it was. Cowhorn was a nautical name, well enough known among the fisherman but hardly in common use by the landlubbers. If he'd known what I meant – answered with anything other than a question – I might have had my suspicions.

'Havelet, more or less. The bathing pools. Sole is a shallow water fish,' I explained. 'We need to stick close to shore. It's too deep around here.'

I had another reason for wanting to stick close to shore, but I didn't tell him that. Renouf was an unknown quantity. I didn't worry that things might get out of hand – I can handle myself well enough, whatever his size – but the thought of being stuck beyond Alderney with a man who might turn out to be a champion bore wasn't something I relished. However powerful the Puffin's engines might be, they'd never get us back quickly enough if he started to talk about football or cars.

Renouf was silent for a moment, mulling this latest revelation. 'Could we not have fished from the beach?' he asked.

I nodded. 'For sole, I usually would.'

'Then why...?'

'I think Bichard was hoping we might get to know one another,' I said. 'He doesn't need to know we didn't head out to deep water.'

Renouf laughed, and I'm pretty sure it was genuine. 'He also said something about beer.'

I inclined my head towards the galley. 'There's some Breda down there. Mind the cat.'

He brought up two bottles and popped off the caps on the deck rail. 'So tell me,' he said. 'Tell me about yourself.'

'What is this? Speed dating?'

'I'm married,' he said, as though he'd taken me seriously.

'So am I.'

'Kids?'

I tugged at the picture of Oliver, slipping it out from behind the seal that ran around the side window. 'My boy. Oliver Carey. Ollie.'

'This recent?'

'Couple of years.'

Renouf took a closer look, trying to identify the background.

'Southampton,' I told him. 'He's studying oceanography.'

'Who's the girl?'

'Kirsty.' He was asking a few too many questions, but I resolved to humour him in the interest of good relations. 'Nice girl. Been seeing her, what, two years? Odette approves, which is something.'

'Odette?'

'My wife.'

He returned the picture and I tucked it back into the window seal.

'And you?'

'Wife, daughter. Struggling on with building a house out by Pembroke. We might move into it one day. Not much to tell.' He paused. 'Shall we talk business?'

'I suppose that's why we're here.'

'This cargo...'

'Aah, that business.'

'What is it?'

'The cargo? Can't rightly say,' I lied. 'I know as much about that side of things as you do.'

'Then what are you...'

'Doing? Keeping an eye out. Watching for strange movements. Unfamiliar craft, that kind of things.'

'That's its way in, is it? By boat?'

'That or plane. Assuming it's coming through Guernsey. Whole thing strikes me as rather redundant, given the sketchy details.' I'd been speaking with my back to him, keeping an eye on the cliffs and our bearing. 'What do you know of it?' I asked, turning around to look at him.

'No more than you,' he said. He took a swig from his beer, retreating behind the bottle like someone who sips from a glass when they've made an amusing comment and don't how to follow it up with something equally sparkling. Is that what he was doing here – pretending that he'd have more to say if only he wasn't so dry...

...or could it be that what I'd just observed was entirely lost on Renouf himself – a piece of spontaneous, subconscious body language. The liar so often hides his mouth behind his fingers or fist. Was Renouf now doing the same with his beer?

We carried on like this until we'd rounded the corner, passed Jerbourg Point, Marble Bay and Fermain, and I'd eased off the gas for the run past Fort George to the shallow waters in view of Castle Cornet.

'So what's your involvement in all this,' he asked at last.

I knew the question would have to be asked at some point - and answered, too - but until I'd seen them crossing the sand I'd been banking on Bichard being with us. At this point he might have jumped in with an answer, and I'd not considered it any further since casting off from Portelet. He'd caught me unprepared.

'I'm... a floating agent,' I said. I hadn't intended to use a pun quite so crass as that, but it largely explained what I did without being too specific.

'For the States Police?'

'For Europol. Although right now I'm seconded to Interpol. For the duration of this case, at least.'

'That's the done thing, is it?'

'Of course.' I walked to the back of the boat and leaned over. I filled my empty bottle with water, waiting until the last of the bubbles popped out of the neck before letting go. It quickly fell and faded from view, dropping in just a few seconds down to the sea bed, where over the years it would once again become sand. As I watched it go, I realised that now it was I who was giving myself away by hiding my face from Renouf. 'We often work together,' I said, turning to face him again, presenting as open and honest a face as I could. I made sure I didn't cross my arms, but put them behind me and held on to the deck rail.

He didn't seem convinced, despite the fact I was telling the truth - to a certain degree. I worked for Europol; I just happened to be working with Interpol. He didn't need to know the exact relationship.

'Am I not right in thinking that Europol has no jurisdiction here?'

'We have jurisdiction,' I told him. 'We just don't have powers of arrest.'

'So what are you? Liaison?'

'Liaison. Investigation. Cross border assistance.'

'I see. And who are you assisting this time?'

'You,' I said, digging out the rods. I squeezed the bag of bait. It was starting to soften around the edges, but still there was ice at the centre.

Renouf tapped his front teeth with the neck of his Breda. 'Are you sure it's not the other way around?'

'How so?'

He dragged across the chair he'd been sitting on as we motored out of Portelet, spun it around and sat on it backwards - like Christine Keeler in that photo. 'You can only assist me if I'm taking the lead.'

'Go on...'

'And I can only take the lead if I know what's

going on.' He cocked his head on one side. 'But I don't.'

I handed him the rod I'd made up. 'Can you bait your own hook?'

He nodded, and put it down on the deck. 'So, why don't you tell me what this whole case is really about, and then perhaps you can do your job and offer me whatever assistance you think I might need.'

I had to give him his due; he was good - as Bichard had insisted - and I wouldn't have liked to find myself facing him across an interview room table.

'I'll level with you,' I said, setting down my own rod. 'It sounds like you know as little about this as I do. This whole case is somewhere up there...' - I lifted my hand up to arm's-length - 'way above either of our heads.'

Renouf nodded. 'Your head, perhaps.'

'Perhaps,' I concurred, humouring him, although I was certain that he knew far less than I did. 'The thing is, whatever this smuggling case might be about - whatever they're bringing into or out of these islands - there's talk of a leak, or some inside involvement.'

'Inside where?'

'States Police.'

He didn't flinch. I watched him carefully, for widening eyes, fiddling fingers, an unconscious shuffling of the feet either side of the chair. There was nothing.

'Are you sure?' he asked.

'No. Like I say, it's just talk. Thing is, I need to know for certain - one way or the other.'

'And that's why we're here?'

I nodded. 'I need someone on the inside. Someone I can trust.' I paused to give what came next some emphasis. 'Bichard tells me you're the best.'

He stretched and smiled. 'You know, I don't think I'm in the mood to eat fish tonight.'

'Can I rely on your help?'

He looked across at St Peter Port. Allowing for the loop around Castle Breakwater, the harbour was less than a mile away. 'Why don't you drop me off in Town,' he said, 'and tomorrow I'll make some discreet inquiries.'

'Of course,' I said, and I thanked him, for what good it might do.

I dropped him off, and as I cruised back towards Portelet, I replayed the course of the evening - the closing act in particular. I had a hunch that Renouf had told me more than he'd planned as our conversation drew to a close.

The stretching, the smiling, the wistful glances across to the harbour. He might have been sent there on Bichard's command, but that was merely good fortune. I couldn't help feeling that as soon as he'd seen what was happening, once he had an inkling of what I was doing - and why - he'd been mining me for information, just as I was mining him.

The difference, I was fairly sure, was that I had given him nothing, while his body language, and the urgency with which he'd drawn our excursion to a close so far from his car, his transport home, had told me far more than he realised.

Perhaps he wasn't as good as Bichard seemed to think.

Translation ends.

TWO YEARS AGO

'I'll be fine,' Renouf insisted, as he stepped off the boat at Castle Pier. 'I'll walk to headquarters and pick up a pool car.' He started to climb the slip to the boating pool. 'Happy fishing,' he mumbled, too quietly for Remus to hear.

He didn't look back; he carried on walking, past the marina and fish sheds. He unwrapped a stick of gum and chewed it as he walked, and when he was sure he was out of sight, he crossed the road and walked along the front to the church.

The night was mild and had brought out

the drinkers. The pubs were turning out and a handful of tipsy sots were swaying across the market square. He thought it unlikely they'd notice him, far less approach him, but all the same it made sense to fit in.

He leaned against one of the pillars that ran along the old market hall as though he required support. A moment later he pushed himself off and lurched across the cobbles, vaguely towards the first bench.

Two young women in short skirts rounded the corner, the first of them colliding with him as she tottered about on high heels. She fell at his feet in a fit of giggles and Renouf let the toe of his shoe clip her shoulder. She swore and he acted out an overdone stumble, taking two fast steps and dropping himself onto a bench. He rocked to one side, then gripped the back of the seat and pulled himself upright.

The girls found their feet. They threw their arms round each other and stumbled towards the hill that wound its way out of Town. Renouf surveyed the rest of the square as they turned their backs, and finding it empty he let his arm hang, casually, to the crest on the side of the bench. It was neatly embossed: three lions, couchant. He counted them down, then took the gum from his mouth and pressed it onto the paw of the lowest beast in the stack. He could feel its claws through the newly applied rubber skin.

He never looked down, never drew attention to what he was doing.

He kept his eyes on the square.

No one had seen him leave his mark.

He stood up, straightened his jacket and walked through the back streets towards headquarters. There was no need to act any more.

Marie Budzinski didn't turn heads. Not often. Not day to day. She was stout and wiry; her compact body passed below the average gaze and she moved about Town unseen. Only her shoes might catch an eye - often trainers, often red - but a moment later she'd be gone again: just a seasonal worker servicing tourists.

Her cover was perfect, so far.

She changed the linen on beds too expensive to lie in, from five until noon, six days a week, in advance of the one o'clock rush. That was when the clipper arrived and the visitors made landfall, dropping their bags, eager to walk into Town and explore.

So she started each day with a brisk downhill walk, from her flat above Town to the Market Square. From there she would go down the steps by the church, then turn on the High Street and double back until she reached the hotel.

It took twelve minutes, fifteen in the rain, and could have been trimmed to five if she followed a less circuitous path. That would have given her longer for breakfast, to stand in the shower or choose her clothes with more care.

But it would have meant something else.

It would mean she would bypass the market. She wouldn't be able to look at the benches, inspecting the shield on each one. She'd never know if Renouf had left his mark.

He'd done it last night, pressing it into the claws of the beast just as they had shown him. She saw it at once as she strode through the square, and diverted her eyes, lifting them by a degree or two to scan the top of the old market hall. She looked like anyone else, enjoying the view on a sunny spring day.

She slipped her hand in her pocket and fished around for the small piece of chalk she kept among her coins and keys. Then, as she got to the top of the steps that led to the High Street, she stopped, bent down to tighten her lace, and drew a line on the end of the uppermost step.

She didn't believe she'd been seen, but she tugged on a lace nonetheless, then stood up and walked down the steps to the shops, dropping the chalk back into her pocket.

She didn't look back.

She'd acknowledged Renouf's mark. He knew what he had to do next.

Renouf was having a difficult morning. After leaving his gum the night before, he'd flagged down a taxi close to headquarters and asked the driver to run him to Portelet. He picked up his car and drove home, arriving not long after midnight. The house was in darkness and his wife was already in bed, so rather than wake her he took to the sofa and laid his head on a cushion. The family cat climbed onto his chest and they slept together surprisingly well.

He rose and left early, but didn't turn in at the office, instead driving on and leaving his car on Albert Pier, from where he could get out of Town far more quickly.

He talked to the press, then met with Bichard and Charlie Dubois to report his progress on two active cases. He glossed over the rather truncated night he'd spent on the boat with Remus Carey. They'd got to know each other quite well, he said, but they'd not, alas, managed to catch many fish. Bichard had expressed his surprise.

'You were out with Carey and you caught no fish?'

'Not many,' Renouf said. 'Not enough to eat.'

'Are we talking about the same Carey?'

'What can I say?' Renouf asked. 'I guess he had an off night.'

Bichard made a mental note to talk to Remus. He'd find out for himself what had happened.

As one o'clock rolled around, Renouf turned down the offer of a drink in favour of running some fictional errands. 'Wife's made a list,' he explained with a shrug. 'If I go home empty-handed...' He pulled a face and acted the part of a man in a noose, his neck stretched and his head cocked to the side. He put the tip of his tongue between his lips.

Charlie pressed down on his head with the pad of his thumb. The inference was clear and Renouf had no choice but to laugh it off.

He left the building two minutes later and walked down the hill into Town. He turned at the High Street and set his course for the church, glancing to the side as he passed the steps to the Market Square, where he spotted Marie's faint chalk line. So she'd seen his mark, and now she'd be waiting for him to make the next move.

He checked his watch to be sure he had time, then rounded the corner and picked up his car. It was ten past one. He had fifty minutes to cross the island, leave his message and get back to work.

The traffic was light for a weekday lunchtime.

He made good time by cutting uphill to the west and crossing the spine of the island. He came out on the coast at Cobo, where the sand was golden, busy with visitors, and carved into family blocks by row after row of striped windbreaks.

It was only once he'd crested the hill to the Guet – the watch house that sat on a sheer pink rock, from where it looked out on the bay – that he saw how busy the beach really was, and he noticed for the first time that year that summer was on the horizon.

He parked the car under the pines and scratched out his message on loose slips of paper.

Stranger danger feasible. Caution advisable max. Guidance required immediate.

He read it back, making sure it made sense. He didn't want to make it any longer than he absolutely should – not when he had to encode it. It was concise, but it contained all they needed: a warning and a request for advice.

He drew a slash after every other letter, breaking down the message into pairs.

St / ra / ng / er / / da / ng / er / / fe / as / ib / le...

Then he started transcribing them, writing below each pair of letters the positions in which they sat within the alphabet. Below S and T – the nineteenth and twentieth letters – he wrote 1920. RA – the eighteenth and first – were stacked above 1801. He looked at his watch as he came to the end of 'guidance required immediate' and saw the minute hand tick over half past one.

He was almost there. He dug out his phone and tapped on the screen to open the text file containing his one-time pad. To the unwary it would look like a random collection of numbers, each one four digits long like a series of codes for a cash card. The list was far shorter now than it had been when he'd received it. Half of the opening batch had been used and deleted, but that still left dozens to work through. The first of these – 2217 – he wrote on a new slip of paper, before starting work on the rest of the message. This was the marker. It would tell whoever decoded his message where to start in their own matching string of digits.

Scroll through to 2217, it said, and start with the numbers that follow.

He copied the clusters onto the first slip of paper, siting them under the numbers he'd already written below the original letters. When he'd got to the end, he added them up. The second cluster on the one-time pad had been 1418. This now sat below the 1920, which itself was beneath the S and T. When he added the two together it yielded 2338. He wrote this down on the second slip of paper, following on from 2217, and moved on to the next block. He worked his way through the rest of the message until he came to the end, swapping out period markers for encoded blocks of XX. By the time he was done he had a broken string of 158 numbers spread across ten lines, written as small as he could.

He rolled them around a matchstick and then, leaving his car unlocked, he climbed the steps to the watch house. He paused at the top of the steps. The view from up there was magnificent – one of the best on the island, from Cobo, down below him, right up the west coast, almost as far as the point where it turned at Rousse and was lost behind the bulk of the island. He'd been visiting the Guet all his life. His father used to bring him there as a child, with their dog, who would chase and catch stones without breaking her teeth, but showed little interest in sticks.

Now he rarely went there for pleasure. It was too tied up in this whole affair. In Marie and the Consortium, and now it seemed that someone was watching them.

He was tempted to find a way out.

What if he didn't warn them? What if he let

things run their course – let Carey carry on and discover what they were up to. Renouf was only a minor player, or at least he should have been. Just our eyes and ears, they'd said. Someone on the inside. And then the request had got more serious, and the rewards had increased – enough to... Well, enough to make some foolish decisions.

He cursed himself. Cursed for being so stupid.

He spat over the edge and watched the great gob of phlegm settle on the branches. He was in too deep to pull out now, and far too deep to let Carey know what was happening. Turning witness would not be enough to save him. Not now.

He turned back to the wall of the watch house and felt along the crusty mortar until he found the gap. He had thought for a moment that someone had been and repaired it.

But no.

There it was.

He levered it out with a key and pressed the slip of paper into the crevice behind it, then reseated the mortar and stepped back. It was perfect. The crack was so fine he could barely see it himself – and even then only because he knew it was there.

He looked at his watch. It was twenty to two. Too late. Far, far too late.

He ran to the car and retraced his journey to Town, cutting through the quieter lanes to avoid the lights where he could. He drove around Albert Pier three times looking for somewhere to park. By the time he'd left the car, the clock on the church read five past. He still had one errand to run.

He sprinted up the steps to the Market Place, taking them two at a time, praying throughout that the bench would be empty.

It wasn't.

He circled the edge of the market square, but the women who'd taken it seemed in no hurry to leave. One of them shuffled about, making herself more comfortable. The other reached into her bag and took out two apples.

Renouf checked his watch. It was a reflex action. He knew what time it was, and he knew he was late. He counted the coins in his pocket. He had a few coppers, and one that felt like a mainland pound, thicker than all the rest and not paper like the notes they used on the island. He took it out of his pocket and walked up behind them, dropping it close to the bench as he passed. It bounced twice and rolled beneath them, and as one of the women leaned down to see what it was, he stepped across and picked it up.

He held it up in front of her face, directing her

attention away from his opposite hand, with which he picked at the gum. It tore away from the lion's extended foot in two elastic gobs.

The woman smiled. 'Thank you,' she said, taking the coin and dropping it into her bag.

On the opposite side of the square, under the shade of a small green umbrella, a compact woman in red clamshell trainers observed the exchange across the rim of a latte.

She found herself mildly impressed by his act of misdirection.

She drained her mug as he hurried on out of the square, in search of a bus to the Guet.

TWO YEARS AGO AND TWELVE MONTHS LATER

As Bichard had driven away that night, wearing his patent shoes, he had thought of the men on the boat – and the time they'd have spent together, catching some fish, drinking some beer... he wished he was going out with them.

Instead he had an obligation, one that required not just patent shoes, but a jacket and tie and best behaviour. The annual services party, to mark the start of the season.

Search and rescue, Ambulance, Fire, and Police, of course, holed up in a castle and plied with drink until dawn –

- or until they bored each other to sleep, whichever came sooner.

The night was uneventful.

They drank on the ramparts as Remus and Renouf turned the corner at Pleinmont. They headed downstairs for their meal, just as the boat was passing the airport. They ate as Renouf left the boat and walked past the castle, not fifty yards from where Bichard had been seated.

The room had been tiered by rank, with the chief of each service corralled at one end and the more relaxed tables - the ones where Bichard would have preferred to sit - close to the door and the kitchen. He looked towards them with envy, only one ear on the conversations going on right beside him, and by one o'clock he'd made his escape and arrived at his bed almost sober. He kicked off his patent shoes, glad he could put them back in the cupboard at least for the next twelve months, and vowed that the following year he'd bring his wife for support.

Twelve months passed at some speed. The leaves turned gold and then brown; the hottentot fig lost its flower; the gorse died back and then the winds and rain came. It was a hard winter, bringing with it the first snow they'd seen in ten years. Spring brought the crocus and tulips, and when the bluebells arrived Bichard was digging about in his cupboard, searching once more for his shoes.

'And you're sure you don't mind?' he asked as he pulled out the first and dusted it off.

'Mind coming?' Marlise was standing behind him, watching. 'When else would I get to dress up?'

'Oh, I don't know.' He located the second shoe and pulled it out from under a sports bag. Good; they were both clean. He wouldn't need to polish them. 'There's the dancing, if you fancied.'

'Says the man with two left feet...'

He turned around and found her smiling. 'All set?'

'Of course.' She pecked his cheek as he pulled on the shoes. 'Annabel called. They'll meet us there.'

Bichard had ordered a taxi. If he was going to endure the night, he refused to do so without a drink.

'You remembered to pick up the tickets?' he asked as they settled into the back seat.

'I did,' she replied, tapping the side of her bag. 'But we won't need them.'

'I know, but –'

'I know. I know you like to pretend you're no better than the rest of them.' She reached across and squeezed his knee, and left her hand there until they arrived. They got out on Castle Breakwater and Bichard arranged for the driver to come back at midnight. Then, linking arms with his wife, he allowed her to lead him along the pier and into the castle itself.

The room had been tiered by rank, as it had been the year before, and this time around Bichard found himself partnered with Ferbrache, second in charge of putting out fires, and a man who enjoyed riding the engine even outside of his salaried hours. They'd stood for a while in silence, surveying the crowd, searching for people they knew and hoping someone might come across and introduce one to the other.

'Collins?' Ferbrache asked, running through a list of names of the people they might both know.

'Forensics?' Bichard asked.

Ferbrache shook his head. 'He's a call handler. Shift manager, I think. He came across from our side a couple of years back.'

Bichard shook his head. 'Don't think I know him.' He smiled at Marlise and squeezed her hand.

'Renouf, then,' Ferbrache said. 'One of your inspectors.'

'Oh, now Marc I know very well,' Bichard said, happy they'd found some common ground. 'How did your paths cross?'

'Aah, we go back years. Not so much crossing - more like running parallel. Went to school together.'

'St Sampson's?'

'Mm-hmm,' Ferbrache nodded. 'Twenty years back now, but it could have been... well, you know how the time races by. He'll have told you, no doubt, the things we got up to.' He gave Bichard a broad smile – the kind of smile that reminded the chief of a child coming home to tell his parents he'd won an award.

He almost said that yes, Renouf often talked of his time at school, if only to keep Ferbrache happy. But what was the point? The truth would out – sooner or later – and so instead he fudged the matter, admitting that it was obvious. They were, after all, clearly the same age. More or less.

'Not quite,' Ferbrache said. 'Couple of years between us. He was my mentor: showed me around, kept me safe.'

What a shame. Renouf was efficient. He was professional. He got the job done, but he wasn't a man who suffered fools, and if Ferbrache struck him as anything it was a f... no, that was unfair. Ferbrache wasn't a fool. Perhaps he was just naive. Something about him was altogether too keen.

Bichard looked to Marlise for some help, but she met his eyes and pecked his cheek and said she would get them some drinks. 'Can I bring you anything, Mr Ferbrache?'

'Oh anything - anything,' he said. 'Anything at all. Call me Ross.'

'I'll help,' Bichard said, stepping away, but his wife waved her hand and left him behind as she walked to the bar.

'Never forgotten his kindness,' Ferbrache said. 'Never entirely repaid him.'

'I'm sure he won't hold it against you.'

'All the same,' Ferbrache said, and he let the sentence drift.

Bichard turned around to watch his wife, and Ferbrache waited for him to look back. She was close to the bar but not yet there. She'd stopped to chat to a waiter Bichard found vaguely familiar.

'It looks like Marlise has been caught,' he said. 'I think perhaps I'll just –'

'She'll be fine,' Ferbrache said, touching Bichard's cuff.

Bichard looked back and smiled. 'I'm sure she will. So tell me, what did you do? You and our mutual friend?'

'Marc?' Ferbrache said. 'What didn't we do? That's the question.'

He reeled off a few of their exploits as Bichard fought the urge to look at his watch. A night on Lihou, a trip on a boat, and then, of course, the fire.

'Of course, I was happy to hurry it through, get him back on site.'

He paused, as though waiting for a response. The momentary silence brought Bichard back into the conversation.

'Sorry,' he said. 'I didn't quite...'

'The fire,' Ferbrache said. 'Of course, if it was anyone else, I'd have gone through the usual channels, done all the checks, but...' – he shrugged – 'well, as I say, never really repaid that favour, did I, so it was the least I could do.'

'A fire, you say?'

'You must remember.'

Bichard shook his head.

'His house,' Ferbrache said. 'The one he was building. One on the common.'

'Well, I know the house,' Bichard said, 'but... he never mentioned a fire.'

'Oh, yes,' Ferbrache said. 'Pretty nasty one, actually. Wiring, I should imagine, although as he wasn't making a claim...'

Bichard stared at him for a moment, willing him to go on. Ferbrache's habit of leaving his sentences up in the air was starting to grate. 'As he wasn't making a claim, what?'

'Well, I didn't... I didn't...'

This time, it seemed he felt he had said a little too much. He pursed his lips, then pulled the top one in and pressed it onto his bottom teeth, trapping it there and stopping himself from saying any more.

Bichard raised his eyebrows.

'As I say, I wouldn't have done it for anyone else,' Ferbrache said at last. 'I would have written it up, but as it was Marc. You know, police and all... Only, a fire like that, it can put you back weeks, and he didn't want to claim the insurance, so... you know... well, he asked me to...'

'Let it go?' Bichard asked.

'Yes,' Ferbrache said simply. 'More or less.'

'And you did?'

Ferbrache hummed for a moment. 'It wasn't much,' he said by way of justification. 'But if it helped him get back on his feet...'

Bichard smiled. 'I'm sure you've more than repaid him.' He reached out and gripped Ferbrache's wrist. 'Now I really should rescue my wife.'

DAY FIVE

Route de Jerbourg, above Marble Bay, 8.30am

Richelle Ibbott had always slept on the right of the bed. That had changed the first time she'd slept with George Dixon. She'd opened the bathroom door to discover him snoring, the duvet pulled up to his chin, her glasses and book now moved to the opposite side, his head on her pillow. He hadn't washed or cleaned his teeth.

He slept through to six, then woke her for sex and explained in a coital lull that he'd never be able to sleep on the left. He feared that the weight on his heart might cause it to stop, assured her she understood, then straddled her hips and the heaving resumed. It only occurred to her some days later to wonder why he thought her heart immune to similar pressures. Her breasts were substantial and awkward, her thighs gently pitted, her belly a slightly self-conscious surround that drooped to obscure her belt. She tipped the scales three stones deeper than he did, yet her heart, it seemed, would not have been smothered by turning her flesh the wrong way. Not to his mind, at least.

She admitted defeat. The phone and the coasters followed her glasses, and two days later she switched the drawers of the bedside tables. She slept out the rest of her nights under alien covers, facing a wall she'd never before paid any attention to.

Now she was gone, and Dixon was free to roam the bed in whichever direction his comatose thrashings might take him. Twisting himself in the unwashed bedding that still held the scent of her skin, stretching across to the cooler dry linen whenever the night sweats took hold, or throwing his unconscious fists at the demons that entered his dreams uninvited.

They swooped towards him like barbarous magpies, seduced by the stench of the damp musky sheets. Their eyes were useless grey marbles, long since blinded through roosting too close to the fire - a fire that had burned their scaly fists down to stumps, amber beneath the fraying pelt that was flayed with every unbearable move. On each stump, six fingers, laced with the teeth of the dead, carried the shrieks of their torment and roused him abruptly from sleep.

The sweat was beading the end of his nose, his back was in spasm from sitting up too quickly, but this time the ringing would not go away. The demons had followed him into this conscious world where the light should expel them and leave him free, at least until he next settled down to sleep. He closed his eyes and pressed the heel of each hand against them, and as he did it heightened his senses, cleared his mind and snuffed out the nightmare. He now heard not screaming, but ringing. Delivered, released, he threw himself across the mattress and lunged at the phone, and he picked it up a moment before the voicemail would have snatched it away.

'Hello?'

'Rosalynd Holdbrook.' The words were spoken with care, precisely pronounced in an even tone, with a curt, formal pause in between.

A prickling lay itself down on his shoulders. 'Rosalynd?'

'Where is she, George?'

'Who is this?'

'Meet me at the kiosk in half an hour.'

'Kira?'

'Don't be late, or I'll call the police.'

She put down the phone.

Rousse Kiosk, 9.02am

Dixon arrived two minutes late, driving a rented car. His own was holed up behind the house, where the sick on the dashboard was starting to crust.

He could have been five minutes early (the traffic was light) but then she would think she had won. He didn't want that, so he peeled himself slowly out of his bed and took a leisurely route round the coast. He drove slightly more slowly for the last half mile, cruising much of the way in neutral, playing a game, seeing how far momentum would take him before he had to pick a gear and briefly tap the gas.

She refused his offer of tea and suggested instead that they walk round the headland towards the next bay.

'Are you going to tell me what this is about?' he asked as they passed the Martello tower.

'Rosalynd Holdbrook. I told you.'

'What of her?'

Kira looked at him as they carried on walking, her hands plunged deep in her pockets. Anyone seeing them from the beach or the road would likely have thought they were lovers.

'Why, George?'

'Why?'

'You killed her. Why?'

Dixon stumbled. He caught his feet in the long reedy grass and lurched ahead on the path. He double-timed half a step until they were shoulder to shoulder again.

'She's... dead?' he asked.

He might have sounded genuine to anyone else, but Kira knew how he spoke, and she knew how he acted. She'd spent the last two years directing his words, editing out his slip-ups and teaching him how to enunciate. She'd known, even before he spoke, that he'd pause between those two words – just as she'd taught him – and how long that pause would be. She suspected the stumble had been put on, too.

'You haven't heard the news?' she asked.

'My... I... You woke me. No, I haven't. I... I can't believe it. How? When?'

'Only one person can answer that, can't they, George.'

'You think it was me?'

'Should I?'

'No.'

'I don't believe you.'

Dixon looked out to sea. 'Well, there's not very much I can do about that.'

'Convince me.'

Dixon laughed. 'Convince you?'

'Try.'

'This is crazy. You're crazy. You clearly have nothing, you know nothing. No reason to suspect that I –'

'Then why are you here, George?'

'I'm sorry?'

'Why are you here if it wasn't you? Why not call me straight back and tell me to call the police if you're so sure of your innocence?'

Dixon span around and grabbed her elbow. 'Now listen,' he said, a small fleck of spit detaching itself and touching the blush on her cheek. 'I'm here out of courtesy. You wanted to talk, so I've come to talk. I did not come to have baseless accusations thrown at me. If you –'

'Where were you the night Richelle Ibbott was killed?'

'You know where I was.'

'But you see, I don't, do I,' she said, shaking her arm free of his grip and walking on. 'I don't know where you were that night because you weren't where you claim.'

'That doesn't tie me to Rosalynd Holdbrook.'

'Not directly, but it isn't so hard to link the two.'

'Don't you dare accuse –'

'Rosalynd worked it out, didn't she. Rosalynd knew that you weren't at that live broadcast. Now what did she do? Threaten you? Try to blackmail you? Or was she just looking out for her friend? Your partner. The woman she cared for and always regretted introducing –'

Dixon slapped her, then whipped back his hand and thrust it under his opposite armpit as though it was acting without his approval. He seemed to fear it might lash out again unless he pinned it down. Kira blinked, then looked away, refusing to cry however much it might sting.

'Kira, I'm sorry.' It was almost a whisper. 'I don't know what came over me.'

'That's quite a temper you have.'

'Kira, believe me. I could never have killed Rosalynd. Much less Richelle.'

'That's the problem, George.' She shook her head, her cheek getting redder now, not just from the wind but the blood brought up by his slap. He could see the shape of his fingers there. Four of them pressed together. 'I don't believe you at all,' she said. 'You killed Richelle because she uncovered your secret. You probably killed Rosalynd for much the same reason, only then the secret was far, far bigger. She didn't just work out what's happened on The Fleet. She knew that it meant you had no alibi.'

Kira looked out, across the beach and across the sea. She could hear Dixon behind her, playing with the coins in his pocket.

'So what if she had worked it out. What could I do if she came to me with that –'

'Talk to her. Explain yourself. She's not an unreasonable woman.'

'No,' Dixon snapped. 'She's an entirely reasonable and utterly honest person. That's the problem. You can't reason your way out of something like this. Only into it. This isn't petty theft.'

'No, George. It isn't. It's murder. Double murder.'

'So...?' He said it the way he might have asked her to explain a confusing equation.

'So, I'm not going to make the same mistake as Rosalynd.'

'I –'

She held up her hand to silence him. 'You didn't come here out of courtesy, but I did ask you here for that very reason. I wanted to give you a chance to explain yourself, convince me that you had nothing to do with Rosalynd's death, and maybe Richelle's, too. But what have you given me?' She paused. 'Practically an admission.'

'Fine,' he said, the pleading now over.

'I'm sorry?'

'Fine,' he repeated. 'Draw that conclusion if you want, but think it through. What if you're right?' He took a step towards her, and now she could feel his breath on her neck. 'What if you're right? What if I did kill Richelle, and then went on to kill Rosalynd Holdbrook?'

She shook her head. 'That's no concern of mine. I'd prefer not to know one way or the other, truth be told.'

'So why go to the police?'

'For Rosalynd. And Richelle. And because it's the right thing to do.'

'Very noble of you,' he said, and then he whispered in her ear. 'But do you really want to go to prison?'

Kira stiffened. She could almost feel his lips upon her. 'What?'

'Oh, yes, my dear. Even if I didn't do it, and let's imagine for a moment that I didn't... even if I didn't do it, you protected me, didn't you. You've known right from the start that my alibi wouldn't stand up, yet you didn't say anything until... Well, until poor old Rosalynd turned up dead.'

Kira widened her eyes and right away she could feel them drying in the breeze. 'George, are you actually saying –'

'I'm saying nothing. But what if it was true? What if I did kill Rosalynd? You could have stopped me, but you didn't. You played along because you couldn't afford for anyone to know what you'd done with Thomas Thoumine. Or the fact that you're still paying out for a part that has no actor simply to cover yourself. Your silence endorsed my alibi, didn't it.'

'George, you have to understand the position I was –'

'If the police were ever to check...' He let it hang for a moment, as though he was running through the full implications in his mind. 'Well, you're the only person who would have been able to vouch for me. To tell them whether I actually was at the station that night. Because I wasn't, was I. You might have made out I was standing alone in my little booth, split off from the rest of those vapid no-hopers. But we both know the truth, don't we?'

'George, stop,' she said, but Dixon was just getting started.

'I was down on Marble Bay, out of the way so I

wouldn't be seen. So no one would know. Tuned in, earbuds in so I knew when it was over, when I could go back home. I was keeping our secret safe that night, and that's precisely what you've been doing ever since.'

'I crippled Thomas Thoumine because you know as well as I do how much trouble we'd have had if we terminated your contract. And you know why we'd want to do that? Because you're an obnoxious, unpleasant prig.' She spun around and looked him in the eye, her finger pressing into his chest. 'And if you think I had anything to do with this, if you think that I can carry the blame in any way –'

'Then tell them. See what they think. Run along to the nice inspector... what was his name? Renouf? Run along to Inspector Renouf and tell him what you think you know and then try to explain why you shielded a man you knew to be lying. Explain to the listeners that you fired me, then covered it up by crippling my character so I never again needed to come to the station. Explain to the BBC why they're still paying an actor, week-in, week-out, when he hasn't worked for three months. When I killed Richelle –'

Kira stumbled backwards, and Dixon stepped forward to once again tower over her.

'When I killed Richelle – yes, I'll admit it – when

I killed her it protected your lie as much as my own. You benefitted from her silence more than I did, so it wouldn't be hard to spin them a tale that neatly implicates you.' He smiled. 'I think they'd find it convincing.'

Kira stuttered the start of an ill-composed reply, but failing to find the words she needed she looked up and met his eyes, than spat as hard as she could in his face.

Dixon started to laugh. He lifted his arms and then let them fall by his side. He shook his head and formed an A-OK ring with his finger and thumb.

'I've always admired your scripts,' he said. 'So lean and understated. I think you've just excelled yourself.'

He leaned forward and kissed her forehead, wiping his chin on her fringe and leaving behind the bubbling pearls of her spit.

'No doubt I'll see you around,' he said, before turning and walking towards his car.

Saints' Harbour, 10am

It was Falla who'd taken the call. One of the overnight handlers had phoned him at home at seven that morning. He'd called Renouf, and Renouf in turn had called Christine and Charlie, instructing the forensics officer to get the first boat back from Sark in time for a lunchtime meeting.

'We've got another one,' he'd said. 'Saints' Harbour this time. Looks like it's Dixon's old boss.'

'Holdbrook?' Charlie asked. He was running along Sark's only real street. On an island without any cars, it was that or a bike or a horse, and he didn't have time to scout round for either. Neither was he sure when the next scheduled boat would be leaving. If it came to it, he'd assured Renouf, he'd bribe a trawler to offload some pots and find him some space on its deck.

'You know her?' Renouf asked.

'Only what I read,' Charlie said, the phone struggling to maintain a signal. 'Isn't she the one who...'

'Went missing. Yes.'

'And what do you think? Suicide?'

'That's why I need you back here, Charlie, but I don't think so. Looks like a broken neck.'

'Is she out of the water.'

'She is now.'

'Good. Call Gregg Minchin. Get him down there.' Charlie gave him the number.

Minchin was Charlie's number two. He oversaw the lab when Charlie was away. He'd answered Renouf's many questions while his boss was working on Sark, but his knowledge of the Ibbott case was largely second-hand. Much of it had been gleaned from overheard conversations carried on in the lab. The rest, he had read in the paper or seen on the news on TV. His own work concerned a small drugs case that would shortly be heading to court.

He reluctantly agreed to set aside the morning and meet Renouf and Christine at the harbour. By the time he arrived they'd been there an hour, and someone had put up a white forensics tent on the slipway. Rosalynd's body was inside.

Minchin was younger than Charlie, and looked it, with shorter hair and fewer lines on his sunburned face. He was no less able or eager, though, and he'd put in for Charlie's job when it first came up. He'd failed through lack of experience, but there had never been any bad feeling between them, and Charlie had taught him well. It was little surprise to Renouf that seventeen years of working together meant they thought along almost identical lines.

'She's a fresh one,' Minchin said, standing up and taking a long, deep breath, the way Charlie had done as they'd straddled Richelle in the bay.

'How fresh?' Renouf asked.

Minchin rubbed his chin. 'Been in the water less than twenty-four hours, I'd say.'

'That would fit,' Christine said. 'Kira Spooner

reported her missing yesterday. The last contact we know she had with anyone was –'

'Oliver Carey,' Renouf interrupted. 'Monday morning, if The Sarnian is to be believed.'

'Too early,' Minchin said.

Christine nodded. 'She must have seen someone between then and her disappearance.'

Renouf raised an eyebrow but didn't look at either of them. He focused on the body and thought about Charlie's call. Was Christine there because of him? He replayed the events of the previous week, but nothing among them was any real cause for alarm. She'd disagreed, yes, but no more than his full-time deputy had – the one who'd been sent to Jersey to wait out the length of her placement.

Even now, she was merely agreeing with Minchin, making a point with which Renouf couldn't argue. Monday was a long time ago. Four days had passed between then and the first report of Rosalynd Holdbrook's disappearance. It wasn't unreasonable to suggest they could narrow things down still further.

'It is,' he said, quietly. 'I'm not saying he did it. And if he did, I'm not saying he did it on Monday.' He thought for a moment. 'Did Holdbrook and Carey know each other before this Ibbott affair?'

Christine puffed out her cheeks. 'No way of knowing. Not without asking him. Why?'

'If they met for the first time on Monday,' Renouf said, thinking aloud, 'there's no reason why they didn't meet again later in the week.'

'Why would they do that?' Minchin asked.

'I don't know. A lead on Dixon, perhaps. The Sarnian still seems to think he had something to do with it.'

'And you don't?' Minchin asked.

'Inspector Renouf is directing our resources along alternative lines at the moment,' Christine said.

'Thank you,' Renouf interrupted. He didn't want to hear her carping on about Dixon again. 'After Alfie Erne, Carey seems to be taking the lead on this story. What if his digging made Miss Holdbrook suspicious?'

'Of...'

'Of him. What if she started to question his motives? He found Ibbott. Perhaps she got to wondering whether he wasn't just chasing the story, but...' - Renouf stopped to think of the right word - 'trying to direct our attention elsewhere?'

'Onto Dixon?' Christine asked, marvelling at Renouf's unwavering belief in Dixon's innocence. She saw how determined he was to keep the thread of their investigation laced through the narrow eye of the one unlikely presumption that Oliver Carey was somehow involved.

'Onto Dixon,' Renouf repeated, his voice soft and understanding. 'What if Miss Holdbrook here saw something that we did not? Worked something out?'

'About Carey?' Minchin asked.

Renouf tipped his head to the side as if to say 'you work it out...'

Christine had to restrain herself. She wanted to tell him what a fool he was being. How stupid he must seem to Minchin. That he shouldn't be so narrow-minded, should broaden his focus, follow more logical leads and not to direct all their resources, all their time, all their people, limited as they were, into pinning the blame on Carey.

She wanted to tell him that what he was doing only made his involvement in Remus's disappearance seem ever more likely and obvious.

But instead she looked down at Rosalynd Holdbrook, crumpled, awkward, uncomfortably splayed on the cobbles. The flattering light of the flimsy white tent did little to soften the stark, uncomfortable sight. Her hair was full of cotters. One of the shoulders of her simple white dress was blushed pink. Blood, Christine thought, partly washed out by the sea.

They all fell silent for several seconds, listening to the waves, thinking about what Renouf had just said, and noticing now the sound of a truck making its way up the lane. Each of them knew what it was: the chilled forensics van, come to take her away.

Two officers, uncomfortably wrapped in white paper suits, entered the tent and looked down at her, their eyes devoid of emotion. They looked like removal men, trying to work out the best way to squeeze a large piece of furniture out of somebody's lounge.

'All done?' asked the taller of the two. 'Photos, everything?'

'All done,' Minchin said. 'Before you take her, though, give me a hand.'

Renouf and Christine stepped back as the men stepped forwards. Minchin directed them to either side of the body, then keeping his hands flat on her cheeks, he counted them down and they turned her over. They laid her down on her front, her head to one side, a cheek pressed into the cobbles.

Minchin pulled back her hair to uncover her neck. It was blackened, bruised, the skin broken, fragments of bone laced through the bloodied cut.

'As I thought,' Minchin said.

'An accident?' Christine asked.

'I doubt it,' Minchin said. 'I doubt it very much.'

The Sarnian, 11.20am

That morning's conference seemed to go on forever. Once again the front page was scrapped, and for a second time the nothing story about the BBC investigating wrecks off Sark was pushed into reserve. Ollie wondered where they'd ever run it. Another two days and the thing would turn stale.

'Rosalynd Holdbrook is dead,' Freya had said. 'Yesterday's Bog Fodder was woefully timed or a piece of divine inspiration. We won't know which until we get the postbag. For now, though, I'm linking these two murders.' She tapped the email they'd all received that morning from the States Police press office. Two abrupt lines confirming that a body had been found and that initial indications it was Rosalynd Holdbrook were likely correct.

'Rosalynd and Richelle?' Ella asked.

'Yes.' Freya nodded. 'There are too many crossover points for us to take any other stance right now. They both worked with Dixon, and Dixon remains our primary focus. Alfie, what response have you had to that front "wanted" page?'

'Zip. And I can't see that changing now. Not with this on the cards. If anything, Dixon's going to think he'll be pushed further back in the book.'

'Well you can disabuse him of that right away. I want his picture on today's front page. Him, Richelle and Rosalynd Holdbrook. Harry –' She turned to the art editor. 'Arrange them in such a way to highlight the connections between them.'

He started to mark out frames on the page as she spoke. They all watched as they grew in tandem on the projected image. Harry dropped the pictures into them – Richelle on the left, Rosalynd on the right, and Dixon in the centre – and then slightly enlarged the shot of Dixon until it overlapped the other two.

'Good.' Freya looked at her watch. They'd been there close to an hour. 'Questions?'

Ollie was getting fidgety. He'd barely contributed to the meeting. Rosalynd's email was still on his mind. He'd called Simon from the lift as soon as he'd left the newsroom the night before, and they'd arranged to meet at the Huffin' Puffin.

It had been moored against the small harbour wall, its keels touching the sand with the tide on a slow retreat. The receding waters had left the view to Fort Grey spiked by the crowns of the uncovered rocks, which were slowly drying in the afternoon sun.

Simon arrived as Ollie had climbed up on

deck, carrying coffees from the galley. They'd sat on the wheel house roof as they talked.

'Rosalynd sent me an email,' he'd said.

'Holdbrook?'

Ollie had nodded. He pulled off his shirt and lay on the warm wooden roof.

'She's turned up?' Simon looked back at him over his shoulder. Neither knew she was dead. Not then. Her body was still in the water, close to the rocks where they turned to form the mouth of Saints Bay. It would take another high tide and a half to run up the slip. The following morning, the first of the fishermen casting off would find her close to his pots.

'No,' Ollie had said. 'She sent it last night. I didn't get it until... well, after she disappeared, by the look of things.'

'I thought you said she was cagey.'

'Reluctant. Shocked, maybe. Richelle was her friend.'

'I heard.' Simon had turned around fully then, propping himself on his elbows at an angle so he could see the misty shape of Ollie's face.

'You know she introduced Richelle to Dixon?'

Simon nodded. 'And now she's had a change of heart?'

'I think it's a bit late for that.'

'I meant about talking.'

'I don't know. Perhaps she likes picking at

scabs,' Ollie said. 'She said she doesn't hear The Fleet any more, but she obviously does. Or she has done.'

'Is that what she emailed about? A soap?'

'Not really. It was more about Dixon. Something about his bits from the last three shows. She said there was something... not suspicious...'

'Doubtful?'

Ollie had shaken his head.

'Irregular?'

'Strange. Something strange.'

'That was all? She didn't say what it was.'

'I think I was supposed to work it out for myself. You know, like a check. To make sure she'd heard it right.'

'To prove she wasn't going mad.'

'Something like that.'

'And was it?'

'Strange?' Ollie had asked, slowly shaking his head. 'I don't know. I never got the attachment.'

He'd thought of nothing but that attachment as he'd lain in his bunk that night, nor as he fed Sampson, rode to work and sat in the meeting. At last, Freya dismissed them, and Ollie rushed back to his desk to call Simon.

'BBC,' Simon said, snatching it up on the first ring. He was waiting for quotes, and time was running on. He wanted to get them recorded and trimmed in time for the midday news.

'It's Ollie.'

'Ollie,' Simon said, forgetting the quotes. 'Have you heard?'

'Of course I've heard. Everyone's heard.'

'And that email...'

'That's why I'm calling,' Ollie said, before Simon could say any more. Ollie knew that the BBC newsroom was open plan – just like that at The Sarnian – and he didn't want anyone overhearing. 'Not a word.'

'What?'

'You heard me.'

'But it's –'

'No,' Ollie said. 'I haven't told Freya and I haven't told Alfie.'

'Why the hell not?' Simon hissed.

'Because I need to make this my story. I've failed on every count so far. Rosalynd's email could be the in I need.'

'In?' Simon said. 'There is no "in" except for the fact that she forgot to attach the attachment.'

'No, she didn't. It was stripped out. She did attach it, it just didn't make it through.'

'That changes nothing.'

'It changes everything. It means that unless she's deleted it, the attachment is still in her outbox. All I need is to get into it and –'

'How are you going to do that?'

'That's why I'm calling.'

'Well call someone else. I'm not breaking into some dead woman's email.'

'Simon –'

'I wouldn't know how.'

'You do.'

'I don't. I wouldn't know where to start.'

'You knew Rosalynd better than me. You worked with her. I don't need you to get into her email yourself, but I do need you to give me some hints. Some stuff about her. Stuff she might have used for her password.'

'I didn't know her.'

'But you knew her better than me.' He stressed the last three words, making clear he'd said them already. 'She must have talked about kids or pets or nephews and nieces.'

Simon thought for a moment.

'Come on,' Ollie said. 'You know I'd do it for you.'

And Simon did. He knew very well that Ollie would have helped if their roles had been reversed. He also knew that he needed to work up the story himself. So far, all he had were some headlines dragged out of the issued police statement.

'I'll ask around,' he said. 'I need to flesh out my own report anyway. If anything turns up, though – if one of my suggestions works –'

'I'll send you a copy of whatever it is,' Ollie said.

'Good. In the meantime, go back through The Fleet,' Simon advised him. 'Back to the very beginning. Characters, places, the names of boats. I wouldn't be too surprised if one of them was her password.'

Police Headquarters, Noon

Renouf put the team into virtual lockdown. They could come and go as their needs required, but he cancelled the afternoon briefing and told them not to answer their phones.

'Falla will process all calls,' he said. 'All incoming calls. Ring out all you want, but no quotes, no statements leave this room until tomorrow's press briefing. Clarke –' He turned to look at the constable. 'Get on to the papers and get them here at ten tomorrow morning. Cancel the scheduled afternoon meet.'

'Got it,' Clarke said. He stepped back to his desk and opened a blank email, then copied and pasted the media contacts out of the team's shared address book.

'It looks like we have a multiple murderer on the island,' Renouf continued. 'This resets the clock. We have a brand new first twenty-four hours. Remember, this is the crucial time: from now until this time tomorrow is the period in which we might make or break the case.'

'Are we linking the murders, then?' Falla asked.

'We are,' Renouf said. 'Until we know any different.'

He thumbed across his shoulder, towards the pinboard behind him. The day before it had solely tracked the Ibbott case, covered in photos of all the key players, each surrounding a picture of Richelle. Now they'd been joined by a picture of Rosalynd Holdbrook: a candid snap from the Sarnian website. It was four years old, but she hadn't aged much in the interim.

'What I need from each of you is to work out how the various faces up there link to both Miss Holdbrook and Ms Ibbott. Where the two intersect, that's where we're likely to find our killer. So far we have only one person that we know for sure meets that criteria. Oliver Carey.'

'When did he –' Falla began, but Renouf cut him off.

'Read the notes, Falla,' he said, widening his eyes. 'Christine –' He turned to look at her. 'Carey remains your primary objective. I suggest you get out there and find out where he was last night and the night before. Be discreet.'

'On my way,' she said, picking up her bag.

Renouf had done her a favour. She had no intention of chasing Carey, but she needed a reason to leave the room before noon. Bichard had arranged an errand for Henri that took him out of the building; both were becoming aware that he'd seen a lot of her passing through on her way into the Chief's office.

Henri had mentioned it once - and Bichard had laughed it off. 'We've known each other for years,' he said, resenting his aide for bringing it up. He trusted Henri implicitly, but didn't like the implication that something was gong on.

Or, that Bichard's 'way back' friendship was borderline unprofessional.

He was right, of course - Bichard knew that - but he couldn't afford to put their meeting on any more formal a footing. Word would get back to Renouf, he was sure, and that would lead to more questions.

So now they had to be careful and organise rendezvous out of work hours, out of the office, or simply when Henri would not be around.

It meant that their meetings were briefer, more pointed, and Christine couldn't afford to be late.

She picked up her bag and pulled on her coat, and went through the doors to the foyer. She headed out to the car park, then doubled around to the back of the building and came back in through the loading bay, wafting away the clouds of cigarette smoke. She knocked on Bichard's door, and popped her head through without hanging back for an answer.

'Come in,' he said, looking up from his papers. 'Come in, come in.' Beckoning her forward, he capped his pen and slipped a document into a tray marked 'Pending'.

'How's it going down there?' he asked.

'All guns,' she said, moving the chair on her side of the desk and settling herself into it. 'I think this Holdbrook development was just what Renouf was hoping for.'

Bichard frowned. 'I wasn't aware they knew each other.'

'I don't think they did. He wasn't specifically waiting for her - just some other reason to bind Carey more securely into the case.'

She explained how Ollie was the only person they knew for a fact had come into contact with both of the victims - both on the same day.

'I'm surprised.' Bichard shook his head. 'Renouf is a first-class inspector. This isn't at all what I'd expect of him.'

'I wouldn't know, but from what you say, and from what I've heard elsewhere, such irrational behaviour does seem highly out of character.'

'Unless he has an ulterior motive.'

'Which... you believe he has?'

Bichard reached forward and picked up his pen. He rolled it around between both hands, as though he might find the answer inscribed upon its barrel. 'I don't know. Truth be told, Christine, I almost feel like I've got you here on false pretences. Renouf may well be settling an old score –'

'Revisiting the sins of the father on the son?'

'Just that. But I'm starting to wonder whether the more we look for proof, the more we're just going to end up reading too much into the situation. I've seen nothing in your translations to link Renouf to Remus's disappearance. Not definitively. Nor the broader Carteret operation, come to that.'

'No,' she said, reaching into her bag and pulling out a large brown envelope. 'Neither had I, until this morning.' She passed it across the desk.

It was the same as the ones she'd used to deliver the last three translations – the type they stocked in the stationery cupboards, and Bichard assumed she must have been taking them home.

'Renouf?'

She nodded.

TWO YEARS AGO

From the diary and logs of Remus Carey, as translated by Christine Le Page.

I dropped off Renouf in Town and spent the rest of the night on the boat. Just me, a beer or two, the salty water lapping the hull. The bait had thawed by the time I was passing Saints Bay, so I killed the engine and caught a black bream. I gutted it, and as it steamed I carefully guided the Huffin' Puffin up to the harbour wall, tying up by the rocks so I could hop ashore and pick samphire. I threw it into the pan with the fish.

I ate, and I called Odette, then I lay on deck and looked up at the stars as I smoked. It was the first chance I'd had to consider the implications of what Bichard had discovered. It couldn't have been mere chance that a pair of unlicensed buoys coincided with the coordinates recovered at Catretet. Even if they hadn't, no fisherman would go to the trouble of sinking a single pot. I know from experience, from the five years I'd spent at sea with my father, before he was lost on the rocks, that you'd put down a line of twenty pots – sometimes more – each connected to its neighbours fore and aft. Like the visible part of a vine, the buoys are just the head of a long and productive system of roots, harvesting not water from solids, but solids from the water.

There was only one logical assumption – that the buoys were there to mark a rendezvous point, and the pot had been sunk as an anchor.

Sleep didn't come too easily, but after peeing over the side I eventually lost consciousness at one or half past, and woke with the sun a few hours later. I had no food onboard, save the dry ginger biscuits I keep in the galley to settle the stomachs of queasy clients, and the kiosk at the bay wouldn't open for three or four hours. I considered heading for home, but Odette would be gone by the time I arrived, and there seemed little point spending the day in the house on my own.

So I stripped off and jumped from the back of the boat into the cold harbour water. I fought the urge to clamber straight out, and swam across to the opposite headland. I settled into a steady crawl and considered my options, deciding by the time I got back to pick a low gear and motor out slowly to Herm. The kiosk at Belvoir would be open by the time I got there. I'd buy some breakfast and spend the day watching the buoys with an unbaited hook. Even I can only eat so much fish.

There was no movement at the buoys all day. They bobbed up and down, and so did I, a mile away, keeping myself busy on deck, pretending to snooze under the brim of my hat, sanding and re-varnishing part of the deck rail, polishing the bell, cleaning the windows of the wheelhouse. I was kicking myself by nightfall. I'd eaten the three rounds of cling-wrapped sandwiches bought from the kiosk and so far achieved not a jot. I should have stuck with my first idea, headed for home, caught up on sleep, and eaten my meal with Odette. I wouldn't have missed a thing, and could still have been on the water by dark.

I nearly gave up there and then, but something made me stay. Like a gambler who can't quite bring himself to cut his losses, I couldn't convince myself that things wouldn't turn good in the end. Just ten more minutes, I told myself.

Then ten more...

And ten after that...

They say it's a mug's game, but sometimes the mug beats the house. Sometimes ten minutes really is all you need (although this time around it was twenty). I wound in my reel, clipped the rod into the rack on the back of the wheelhouse and took my tackle box down below deck, tickling Sampson as I passed the bunks.

Then, as I came back up, I saw a lumbering, wooden-hulled boat. It was something with which the casual yachtsman might compare the Huffin' Puffin – if he didn't know the truth of the engines that squatted below the deck. It had rounded the cliffs to the north of Sark and was crossing the channel that separated that larger island from Herm.

It was an illogical route.

If it were heading for Guernsey it would likely have carried straight on, skirting the rocky south coast to make straight for St Peter Port. The only reason it would have cut north between the islands was if it was destined for less likely harbours. Beaucette, perhaps, or Bordeaux or St Sampson.

Unless, of course, it wasn't heading for Guernsey at all.

I took out the binoculars. The sun was low in the sky by now, and I could feel its dying embers warming the back of my neck. I knew that from that position it wouldn't catch on the lenses, so there was less chance of a glint drawing anyone's attention. Nonetheless, I kept myself low, lying down on the deck and looking out beneath the lowest rung of the rails.

It was a nondescript craft. The paintwork needed some attention, but I could easily read the name on its prow. Single-engined, a rather chunky stern, the cabin well forward to leave fifteen or twenty feet of empty deck to the rear.

It was knocking on fifty years or so, probably needing some care and attention, but hardly likely to get it if it was somehow involved with smuggling. A raggy boat like that was less prone to draw attention.

It cut an unsteady, lumbering course, the rougher water knocking it about, the rasping sound of its unserviced engine rising and falling as it tipped up and down on the swell.

There seemed to be no one aboard beyond the master, so no one to act as a look-out or backup. That would explain its circuitous route to the buoys. My shadow had doubled in length in the time it had taken to reach them, and the first chill of night was starting to pick at my cheeks.

The captain came out of the cabin and reached a hooked pole over the side, scooping up the buoys and dragging them onto the deck. Just as I'd done a few days before. He had leather gauntlets, which helped him get a firm grip on the blackened rope, and he hauled it faster than I could have done.

The cage tipped over the lip of the deck and clattered down behind the wooden sides of the boat. I couldn't see how or where it had landed, but he reached down to it, fiddled with something - most likely the door on the side of the cage - and a moment later stood up, a zip-locked bag in his hands. He peeled it open and slipped out a fat brown envelope, from which he extracted a thick wad of notes. They were bound together by a paper ribbon, the way they're issued straight from the bank. He riffled through them, then pulled out two further bundles. Each bundle green, so Guernsey pounds or high-value euros. I discounted the pounds as too small, and tried to remember the euro colours: were green ones hundreds or fifties? (I've since checked - it's hundreds; fifties are orange. The three thick bundles were tens of thousands all in.)

He put them back in the envelope and walked across to the cabin, reappearing after a couple of seconds with a small grey flask in his hands. It was about the size of a tub of ice cream - the gourmet kind you find at the pricier end of the aisle - and tapered to fit through the neck of the lobster pot.

I could see him in perfect detail now, squatting on the deck as he fiddled with the door on the trap. His face and chest filled my field of view, his wispy white hair floating off towards the rim of my binoculars as though attracted by static. A large red nose, oversized ears like ormer shells, which seemingly clung to the side of his head rather than growing out naturally. The man was old before his time, which suggested to me he'd spent his life at sea. The boat, the gloves, the leathery lines on his face... it all pointed in one direction. Perhaps, like my father had been, he really was a fisherman and this - whatever it was - was merely a lucrative sideline. I wondered whether he knew what was in that flask.

He lifted the pot by its rope and lowered it into the water, then loosened his grip as it started to slide. The top of the cage disappeared, he let it go, and it fell more quickly, pulling the line behind it. The buoys were in spasm as it dragged them over the side, and they disappeared, just for a second, then bobbed back up to the surface. Satisfied that he'd done what he needed, he stepped back into the cabin and motored away, slowly retracing his route towards Sark. He took twenty minutes to turn the corner at the head of the island and disappear.

I waited a while longer to be sure he wasn't headed back, making a note of the pertinent facts - his appearance, the name of the boat, when and from where he'd appeared - and then took a route no less circular than his own over towards the buoys. By the time I reached them, the pot had been back in the water for over an hour, and I cursed myself once again for not having brought my gloves. This time the rope cut my hands. There's no need to log the language involved.

The rope was longer than I remembered, and the pot seemed to take an age to appear. I'd positioned the Huffin' Puffin such that it blocked any view of the buoys from Sark should the courier choose to return. It was a sound plan, except for the fact that it also meant I had my back to the island, and wouldn't have seen - let alone heard - an oncoming boat until it was close enough for the occupants to spot what I was up to.

I decided that speed was likely my best defence, so took no time to examine the flask once I'd hauled the pot over the deck rail. I opened the door and took it out, then threw the pot, rope and buoys back into the water and resumed my position a mile south and east.

By now the sun was well below the horizon. All that was left was a blush of peach across the high clouds floating on towards France. I switched on the light in the galley and sat on the deck at the top of the steps. I could see the flask in more detail there, and still keep an eye out for oncoming boats.

It was a heavy object with a smooth plastic coating that wrapped around the underside to form a seamless cup. The top was separate and the collar between them was secured using clear plastic tape.

I picked at the exposed end until I had lifted the first quarter inch, then gripped it between my finger and thumb and tore it off, leaving behind a thin tacky stripe. It was pure belt and braces, seemingly serving no purpose, as the lid of the flask didn't move, even without it in place. It took several minutes to budge it, in the end requiring a short, sharp knock against the top step - something that seemed to work just as well here as it does with a new pot of jam.

I dropped the flask as a film of icy water oozed out through the split between the body and lid. Turning it upright, I steadied it on the wooden deck and unscrewed the lid completely. It smelled faintly antiseptic in there, and was packed to the brim with crushed ice. I held the lid like a cup and poured the contents out of the body - carefully, slowly - allowing the ice to slide off the lid and onto the deck, along with the liquid in which it was floating. I wasn't worried about that, but I did want to catch whatever else might be in there.

A quarter, a third, and then half had poured away when the sinking level of the liquid revealed an off-white ball, like a hard-boiled egg past its best. I tilted it back to slow the flow, and as I did, the ball turned around to reveal a black dot, with an icy blue iris around it. Another one bobbed up beside it and stared. I jumped up in shock, and shook the eyes out of the flask and onto the wooden planking. One of them bounced off the top step and down towards the galley. The other rolled to port with the yaw of the boat, towards the edge, under the deck rail and into the sea before I could stop it. I heard no splash or plop.

I clambered after the one remaining eyeball, frightened that Sampson might chase it about in the galley, and found it under the stove. It was cold and firm, the pupil dilated - a challenging, lonely stare, full of hate. It looked like it was throwing me accusations for just having lost its partner.

So the buoys were indeed a marker. And the lobster pot - it only occurred to me later - had a far more important role. It kept the flask submerged, where the water would keep it cool and prolong the effect of the ice. How long it would last above the surface, I didn't know, but I suspected that the container wasn't designed for long-term storage. It was just a glorified coolbox, without any power or battery backup.

I dropped the remaining eye back into the flask and topped it up from the galley tap. It had been in some kind of sterilised liquid originally, but I needed to get it to Lyon, and reasoned that at least this would keep it protected. There, they would slice it, extract the DNA, and match it up to a victim.

I went back up to retrieve the lid, and as I screwed it on the neck of the flask I heard the distant but unmistakable snarl of a powerful engine. I could see no lights, but it sounded like it was coming from behind, rounding the south-east corner of Guernsey.

I had a set of night-vision glasses stowed beneath the dash in the wheelhouse. I grabbed them, leaving the flask in their place beside my battered Ebenezer (I'll get to the end one day), and pressed them to my eyes. It took a moment to acclimatise to the grainy green world they revealed, but once I'd found the horizon I panned them across, chasing the sound of the engines.

I caught the wake first - a sparkling emerald streak that I followed across the water until I found its source. It was clear that I'd sorely misjudged those engines, however generous my initial estimation. The spray they kicked up was a geyser, an enormous fountain that arced up and out from the back of the boat and fell again twelve or so fathoms behind it. They were native to the craft and at least as powerful as the aftermarket engines I'd had installed in the Huffin' Puffin.

It started to slow as it neared the buoys, and as it did it sat down in the water. I could see the name now: Dalliance. The bow wave grew as the spray to the rear subsided, with the prow of the boat now settling. It skipped less and steadied out, and as it did the pilot turned it around, circling the buoys as momentum carried him on, each yard a little slower than the last. He looked up, directly towards me, and if it were daylight our eyes would have met. I almost took down my glasses, the connection was so intense, but I steeled myself, and forced myself to keep looking, barely able to comprehend what I was seeing.

Marc Renouf, the man who feigned ignorance when it came to boats and fish, was staring out from the helm of a powerful speedboat, pulling back on the throttle and locking it off as the craft finally came to a wobbling halt.

He leaned over the side and hauled up the pot with more grace than I had managed. Only when he had dropped it onboard did he switch on a light as he bent to retrieve the treasure - the flask that now sat on a shelf in my own wheelhouse.

The light was like a flare in the night-vision goggles, and it took a moment for the glasses to dial down their sensitivity, recalibrating a couple of seconds later as he thumped his fist on the side of the boat and kicked the empty cage over the edge in disgust.

He killed the light, and extinguished the view in my goggles. They gave out a series of ticks as they widened the aperture behind each lens, and ramped up the gain once more. The dirty green picture came back into focus: Inspector Marc Renouf standing on deck, apparently wondering what to do next.

He put his hand in his pocket and pulled out a phone, but dialled the first few digits and thought better of it. He snapped shut the cover and thrust it in his pocket; then, gunning the engine, he spun the boat on a tight circle and headed back towards Guernsey, empty-handed.

Translation ends.

PRESENT DAY

East Coast Diner, 8.10pm

Marc Renouf unbuckled his belt, lifted the lid and sat himself down on the toilet. He pulled his phone from his trousers. Guernsey was playing Nuneaton that night, and it pained him to miss a home game.

He woke it up and tapped on the browser, then scowled as the bars at the top of the screen slowly blinked out one by one. Of all the nights for his phone to fail, why did it have to choose this one? Charlie was back from Sark; he'd arrived just in time for their lunchtime meeting and when they'd finished he'd challenged Renouf to a bet: £50 on the table. The score had been nil-nil the last time he'd checked, but that was half an hour ago as he'd left the car with his daughter and wife with the second half yet to play. If nothing had changed by now he was almost certain to lose.

When Charlie placed a bet it was never that one team or other would win. Instead he would take an opposing view: that whichever Renouf was supporting would fail to take the lead. If they drew or went down, Renouf would still lose, and that gave Charlie a two-to-one chance of a profit.

He started to tap out a text, asking a neutral third party to tell him what was happening. He didn't notice the sounds of the bar as they briefly got louder, then softened again as the door to the toilets drew to.

Knock, knock.

Knuckles rapped on the cubicle door.

'It's taken.' Renouf looked up, irritated. The trap next door was unoccupied. Why did they not go there?

The knock came again, louder this time, and Renouf clenched his jaw, his thumb hovering over the little keyboard.

'Hey, fella,' he said, raising his voice. 'It's taken.' He kicked the door and it rattled against the lock, shaking his jacket on the hook.

There was no knock this time. Just a shuffling of feet. Two steps forward, close enough now for the toes to poke under the cubicle door. Red shoes, with white rubber toe caps shaped like a scallop, the shoes of Santiago.

Renouf narrowed his eyes.

The shoes were familiar.

He'd seen them before, but he couldn't recall...

Three further knocks, gentle taps this time, a tick-tick-tick of a tapered nail tapping the door at its hinge. It wasn't a man at all. Like the tide as it rushed through the rocks at Jaunette, it all came flooding back. The shoes were no longer so clean. A little faded, perhaps, but the sharp edges were there. The perfect laces, so flat and even and straight; the tongue folded forward to cover the knot, the loops tucked behind the uppermost straps of the lace... He'd seen these shoes before, but not for... How long had it been? Two years?

'Marie?' He flinched as his voice echoed about the room. The name alone brought the hairs on his arms to attention.

'Open door.' Her voice was clipped, and paid scant attention to vowels, crushing them out between the spikier consonants. She held on to the closing ‘r’ and rolled it around like someone tasting new wine.

‘I’m – please, Marie. This is not the time. My wife and my daughter are just outside. We’ll meet tomorrow. Whenever is best –’

’Now is best.’ She hammered her fist on the door three, four, five times. ‘Open door or I will open.’ The tone was finely balanced to make it clear that she meant it without being heard outside of the room.

Marie was a messenger, the messenger. Postmistress of the dead letterbox on the Guet, where until two years ago Renouf would still pick up instructions and leave his coded responses.

He’d assumed it was she who had left the number there, which he’d filed in his phone under ‘Mother’.

Don’t wait for an answer, the covering note had said. You’ll hear no voice. Let it ring twice, then hang up. Your bonus will stand.

A follow-up note had explained its use: emergencies only, if his careful observations suggested they’d been found out, or someone within the force was showing a touch too much interest. Call, and they’d ship it out – the boat, the office, the whole operation – and leave no trace on the island. Renouf would no longer be needed, until and unless they came back.

He'd never called it - not yet - but he'd copied the entry for 'Mother' from handset to handset for close to five years. He'd thought once or twice of removing it, but now he was glad he had not. If Marie was back on the scene, he had to wonder - were they back, too?

Once, he'd been late leaving home, and arrived at the Guet an hour behind his appointed time. He ran to the drop-off and used the end of a ballpoint pen to ease out the mortar, slipping behind it his thin slip of paper and pressing the grey sandy wedge back in place. Hurrying back to his car, he passed a short, stout woman, grey hair, late fifties, who looked as if she needed a few hearty meals. Something about her was wrong. She wasn't expensively dressed, but her clothes were not the poorly matched garb that most walkers threw on for a trek through the woods to the lookout. She wore no coat, despite the cold, suggesting she planned to head back to her car fairly quickly, rather than linger and take in the view. He nodded and smiled, but she didn't smile back, and Renouf detected a slight lift of her shoulders. Not a shrug - just a slight tensing that stretched the weave of her thin knitted jumper, suggesting she'd tightened her muscles.

She looked straight ahead and walked past

him, and as she mounted the first of the steps to the lookout, Renouf ran back to his car, past a man with a dog and a cigarette, and drove as fast as he dared around the tight bend and down the steep hill to the Cobo Coast Road. He pulled up and parked by the sea wall. Then, lifting his camera off the passenger seat, he jumped out of the car and over the wall, and walked out across the sand.

He stopped when he reached the water's edge. Lifting the camera up to his face he made a great act of shooting the water, the rocks, a dog on the beach, all the while slowly turning until he was facing back up to the Guet. Two figures stood out on the roof of the concrete additions tacked onto the fort in the Second World War. One was the man with his dog; the other was the woman, now holding her arms to her chest, most likely to stave off the cold.

Nobody moved for two minutes. The man with the dog smoked his cigarette. The woman pretended to look at the view, all the while keeping an eye on the smoker beside her. Renouf zoomed his lens to its furthest position and fired a volley of shots, all of which turned out to be blurred and too grainy.

The man drew his cigarette down to the filter, rubbed the still glowing end on the railing and flicked it over the edge. He nodded towards the woman. Trailing the dog behind him, he walked down the steps and disappeared from view. The woman waited a moment - listening, perhaps, to his waning footsteps - and then stepped across to the lose chip of mortar and lifted out Renouf's slip. She read it, then put it in her pocket and slipped the crumbling stone back into place. Stepping backwards, she turned around and looked down at the beach - directly into his camera. Her face filled its screen as she narrowed her eyes; slowly nodding her head, she acknowledged his presence. She seemed not to care that he'd seen her. She widened her eyes and stared, oblivious to the wind that was drying them, until he lowered his camera. He felt the shame of a peeping Tom and slowly walked back to his car.

As he tossed the camera back on the seat, he took one last look at the fort in the trees, but by then she had gone.

They had met twice since then, but not in the last two years - not since Remus Carey. Not since the Consortium had moved its boat to calmer, less compromised waters.

And now she was here again.

Renouf pulled up his trousers. He flushed the toilet and buckled his belt, then gently, slowly, as smoothly as he could, he slid back the bolt on the door. He could feel his leg muscles tightening, instinctively wanting to run, but that was the one thing he couldn't do. His wife and his daughter were waiting. Their meal would be ready. His best hope lay in leaving the cubicle, stepping around Marie so she couldn't trap him. Maybe then they could talk without a repeat of their last encounter.

All of this was in vain.

She was watching the lock. The moment the bolt was free of the cuff, she kicked the door towards him, its leading edge striking the bridge of his nose. She bundled her compact body into the trap and pushed him backwards until his knees collapsed on the rim of the bowl and he sat with a thump on the lid. Momentum carried her forward, and as she kicked the door closed behind her she pressed down his head on the cistern and threw a fist into his face, breaking his nose with a crack. She pressed her palm to his mouth to stop him from crying out.

'Mister Renouf,' she said, pulling a stream of paper from the roll attached to the cubicle wall. She stuffed it untidily under the hand that was holding his mouth to catch the flow of blood. It had already dribbled down his cheek and stained the side of the cistern. Lifting him up, she turned his head towards her and leant closer, their noses an inch apart. Her breath smelled of cloves.

Renouf blinked, desperate to keep his eyes from watering lest she think he was crying.

'Now, Mister Renouf,' she said. 'I think we must be brave, yes?'

Renouf nodded as best he could with her hand still clamped to his face.

'Good,' Reaching down for one of his clammy hands, she placed it so that he could hold the toilet paper himself. She leaned against the cubicle door.

'It has been two years,' she said. 'They have been not kind, I would say?'

'Two years, yes.'

'You must be careful.' She reached forward, and Renouf flinched at her approach. She paused, then reached out again to tuck a loose end of the paper between his fingers. 'It is expensive shirt, I think, this. It would be shame to be...' She thought for a moment. 'Was sagst du...? Stain?'

'Stained. Yes,' said Renouf. 'Marie, what is this –'

'Chu chu chu,' she said, putting a finger against her lips. 'You listen. I have come to talk, then you go back to your family. Your daughter, so pretty she is. I see them as they leave your home. I see her –'

'What do you want from me?'

'Me? I want nothing. But I have message for

you. Oliver Carey.'

Renouf shuffled up on the seat. 'I'm sorry?'

'Four days ago you meet Oliver Carey at kiosk. He arrive on his bike. You talk for fifteen minutes and then you leave him there.'

'What of it?'

'Perhaps you discuss his father?'

'He may have come into it.'

In one swift movement she took a step forward and slapped his cheek, so quickly he didn't have time to flinch. Renouf dropped the tissue and it tumbled down the front of his shirt, leaving a tatty red streak in its wake.

'Now see,' she said, pulling more tissue from the roll. 'You tell your wife you have nosebleed, I think.' She pressed the paper hard against his nose, pushing up against his septum and forcing his head back onto the cistern. He tried to stand up to relieve the pressure, but she put her knee in his crotch to press him back down on the seat and be sure he was taking the full force of her hand on his broken, untidy nose. The blood started streaking the other cheek, too. 'Oliver Carey no longer is of interest to you. Verstehen?'

Renouf tried to nod, but only succeeded in pressing yet harder against her hand. 'Verstehen. Yes. I understand,' he said.

She took his hand again and brought it up with some force, smacking his nose and putting it back into place to hold the tissue, freeing her to step back. She resumed her position against the door.

'We try again,' she told him. 'You discuss his father when you meet?'

'No,' Renouf said. 'No, not specifically.' She pulled herself upright and Renouf blinked, unable to help himself. He started talking more quickly. 'He's a suspect. He found a body. Monday morning, lying on the beach.'

'A body of who?'

'A woman. Richelle Ibbott. She was... She was nobody. Nothing to do with...' – he looked up – 'the operation?'

She shook her head. 'This woman, I do not know.'

'Carey is a person of interest in this case.'

'No. Is no longer.'

'You don't understand. I can't just drop –'

She raised her eyebrows, then leaned forward and replaced her knee in his crotch. She pressed down with her full weight, and Renouf squirmed back towards the cistern again.

'I have a team,' Renouf explained, the words rushing out. 'I can't just drop our primary line of investigation without some explanation. They would ask questions. If anything it would make them examine Carey even more closely.'

'Then you must think of reason,' Marie told

him. ‘They will believe you, or...’ She gave one final shove on his septum, releasing her knee so that his legs instinctively straightened, shooting him up from the seat and cracking his head on the wall. ‘You understand?’

Renouf clattered down on the seat and grabbed his nose with both hands. He nodded.

Marie leaned forward and straightened his shirt. ‘This is mess. First you wash, then return to table, yes?’

Renouf sagged against the cistern and looked at Marie.

‘I can find a reason,’ he said. ‘I can sideline Carey, but there’s a problem.’

‘I hope not, Mister Renouf.’ She lifted her chin and looked down at him.

‘My deputy. He’s been sent to Jersey. I have a...’ He was unsure how to describe her. ‘Her name is Christine Le Page. She was sent to replace him for three months.’

Marie made an act of pulling her cuff and turning her watch on her wrist.

‘I have learned that she works in internal affairs,’ Renouf said.

‘You did not know of this?’

‘I... I can’t think of anyone else who she might be here to... to investigate.’

‘You believe she was sent to you, I think.’

Renouf nodded.

'You did not think to tell us?'

'How? There's moss on the stone at the Guet. It's obvious no one has been there in years. There's no other way –'

'You think we do not watch you, Mister Renouf? Your meeting with Oliver Carey did not go unnoticed. Your wife has new car; your daughter, her glasses. Am I right?'

Renouf nodded. 'How –'

'It is not always needful that you drop a coded paper into a crack in the wall, Mister Renouf. There are many ways you send us a message. You would find a way, would you not?'

Renouf didn't reply. He hadn't seen Marie in close to two years, but felt sure he would have done if she'd been anywhere close to his house. His mouth made some shapes but no sound came out, and a spot of his blood dripped through his finger and landed between his feet.

'No matter,' said Marie. 'This Christine. She can drive, yes?'

'Yes.'

'Good. Send her to drive. Tomorrow. She will borrow your car.' She paused. 'Verstehen?'

'Verstehen.'

She smiled. 'It seems, Mister Renouf, that again we do business together.'

Renouf peeled the paper away. He examined the blood, and then feeling an unfamiliar bump on the front of his nose he looked up to see Marie leave the cubicle, gently closing the door as she went.

DAY SIX

Route Militaire, 6.40am

The rest of the night was a washout. Renouf cleaned his face as best he could, but returned to the table with stains on his shirt and a fresh wad of paper pressed to his nose. They drove home in silence, his daughter in tears, and when they arrived they went straight to bed. Nobody boiled the kettle. He propped himself up in the hope it might lessen the swelling and spent the night concocting silent explanations, each more convincing than the one he'd given his wife – that careless feet and a loose-hinged door had conspired to crack open his nose.

'Come off it, Marc.' She'd been sitting at the dresser when he told her. 'You were driving. You hadn't even been drinking.'

He'd stood behind her and tried to look casual, dodging her eyes in the mirror.

'I should sue.' He tucked his hands in his pockets so she wouldn't notice the skin he'd picked loose on his thumb.

'On what grounds?'

'On the grounds it's unsafe.'

'There's nothing wrong with that door.' She

raised her eyebrows to wipe off her mascara. To Renouf it looked more like a sceptical glance. He wondered whether it was, or if he was reading too much into it.

'Have you been in the gents?'

'Well call them. Put in a complaint and get them to fix it before someone else gets hurt. There's no point making a fuss. You know we like eating there.' She put down the cotton ball and turned around, patting the edge of the bed. 'Tell me what really happened.' She nodded towards her hand.

'I told you.'

'Are you embarrassed?'

'About what?'

'Was there someone else in there? Someone you put away? There's no shame in it.'

He turned away and unbuttoned his shirt.

'I know the signs, Marc.'

He busied himself, uselessly folding the shirt before dropping it into the wash bin. 'I don't know what you expect me to say.'

'Do you know how many drunks we see in A&E.'

'Not a great deal by the last count.'

'I've patched up enough to tell the difference between a fist and the edge of a door.'

'Would you just leave it,' he hissed, turning around to face her. 'I tripped. I hit the door. End of.'

His nose had doubled in size by morning, and Sophie suggested he leave the house early, before their daughter woke up. Renouf agreed, although he suspected the real reason was as much about that as it was their fiery conversation, and how it had ended - or hadn't.

There were loose ends.

Sophie would find it hard not to pick them, and it wouldn't just be the bacon that got a good grilling.

'You'll only scare her,' she said, fixing a plaster across the bridge of his nose so it pulled his nostrils and kept them open. The blood had congealed, making it hard to breathe. 'Perhaps by tonight some of this swelling will have gone down. You haven't forgotten I'm working from five?'

'No, dear. And Sophie...'

She looked at him properly for the first time that morning.

'Thank you.' He went to kiss her, but she leaned across for his jacket, and neatly moved her face to the side.

'Drive carefully,' she said, handing it over.

He paused as he left the house - a nondescript bungalow on Route Militaire. In island terms, the Route was a major road. It sectioned off the northern quarter and linked the port of St Sampson, hub of The Fleet, with the Vale, where

Rosalynd Holdbrook had lived on the opposite coast.

Despite the traffic, he still knew his neighbours - each and every one of them for eight or nine houses in either direction. Catherine, Stuart, Jason, Jill. He couldn't imagine that any of them might be the watchman keeping an eye on his family.

He wanted so much to tell Sophie the truth: what had really happened, and what he had learned the night before, but to tell her even part of the story would blow the whole operation. His part in it, too. She'd refuse to keep silent. She'd talk to the Press, or that dreadful rag, The Sarnian, or worse, go straight to Bichard. She'd known him longer than he had.

He unlocked his car and got in, and paused for a moment before he turned the ignition. Why had Marie been so particular that Christine borrow it? The station had five unmarked cars in its pool. Why not take one of them?

Police Headquarters, 9.30am

'So,' Bichard said, closing a folder and slipping it into a drawer. 'Where are we?'

Christine leaned forward and picked up her mug. It was still too hot to drink but her fingers were cold and she wanted to warm them.

'Something's up,' she said.

'How so?'

'Renouf. Have you seen him today?'

'Not this morning.'

'Something happened last night. He claims he lost a fight with a door. His face is a mess.'

'You don't believe him?'

She shook her head. 'His nose is in pieces, there's blood in his cheeks. He ought to know better than blaming some stupid accident.'

'You think he got into a fight?'

She scowled. 'Not exactly Renouf, is it.'

'So what? Domestic abuse?'

'Unlikely. He was first in this morning. Claimed he'd been here most of the night, reading through the case notes. Reckons he might have overlooked something and wanted to start again from the beginning.'

'Easy enough to find out,' said Bichard, writing the words 'entry log' on a pad. 'I can pull up a record of everyone's passes.'

'Well, whether he was or not, something's made him change his mind. I'm guessing it's whatever happened to his face.'

'About what?'

'About everything. The whole Ibbott case. Suspects, motives, modus operandi. Everything except for the fact she's still dead.'

'And would the case notes support that?'

'I don't think so. Not the way he's been running it. He was still pushing every resource we've got towards nailing Oliver Carey last night. This morning, Carey's out of the picture.'

Bichard thought for a moment. 'So, does he have anyone in particular in mind? Now that Carey's off the hook.'

'Oh, yes.'

'Dixon?'

She nodded, and finally sipped her coffee. Bichard tented his fingers and rested them under his chin.

'You know,' he said, 'if you feel he doesn't have grounds for switching focus, protocol would dictate you refer the matter up the chain of command.' He raised his eyebrows. 'That would mean bringing the case file to me.'

'It would, but if I counteract him like that I might as well head back to Jersey.'

'Okay.' Bichard sat forward. 'How about this. Let's assume Dixon did it. Let's assume Carey's hands are clean. Is there sufficient evidence to haul Carey in?'

Christine frowned. 'No. There's nothing beyond the fact that Carey found the body. Richelle's body, not Rosalynd's. Renouf had some straw-grasping notion that Carey might have lost a radio so he sent off some samples of wax from the earbuds for tests, but even if they come back positive...' She shrugged. 'It's far too coincidental.'

'Likely chance of a charge, then? Out of ten. Top of your head.'

'One? Two? Unless he did do it and made some stupid mistake, but the chances of that...'

'Good.' He gave a curt nod. 'If Renouf got nowhere with six staff and the help of forensics, I think we can afford to push this Carey angle a little further without us risking a bullet through the foot.'

'To what end?'

'To smoke him out.'

'Carey?'

'Renouf. If this volte face is in any way related to the state of his actual face we can only assume it was some kind of warning. The only possible motivation, as far as I can see, is the Carey connection.'

'I'm not sure I –'

'You said Renouf had no grounds on which to be chasing Carey?'

'None whatsoever.'

'Which suggests to me that this is a purely personal mission. Renouf is a good policeman. One of the best. It's not like him to follow some spurious trail without good reason, and what he's uncovered simply doesn't support his thread of investigation.'

'Which could be precisely why he's decided to change tack.'

'It could. But so dramatically? I'm not sure. Does anything point to George Dixon?'

'Not yet, but if we looked into him…'

'Exactly. This isn't like Renouf. There's no more reason to latch onto Dixon than Carey or the Seigneur of Sark. My guess is that someone knows what he's up to – someone who also knows what happened to Carey's father, Remus – and they're worried that Renouf's fixation on Ollie will lead someone higher up to start asking questions.'

Christine took another sip. 'Are you sure?'

'No. It's conjecture,' Bichard said. 'A guess, as I say, but a qualified one. I'd also guess right now that Renouf is scared of whoever it was warned him off.'

'Do you want me to try and talk him round? Get this back onto Carey and see where it takes us?'

Bichard relaxed a little. 'That'll do no good. This would have to be a severe and credible threat for Renouf to have turned one-eighty. Besides, we don't actually need him to change his mind back to Carey. We just need to make it look like he has.'

Christine paused and thought for a moment. 'Are you suggesting a team within the team?

To push the Carey angle while Renouf chases Dixon?'

'If only we had the resources,' Bichard said, with a laugh. 'No. We can't bring in anyone else. Let the Carey leads lie, for all they're worth, and start work on Dixon like Renouf wants. In the meantime, get on to the Press and The Sarnian and leak some details about those waxy earbuds. Tell them Carey is now a person of significant interest in this case. Let them run with it tonight and we'll see what happens. The earliest Renouf could get them to publish a retraction would be Monday, which gives us two whole days to see what happens.'

'It won't work.' Christine drained her mug and put it back on his desk. 'No paper would take a story like that without quotes from at least one named source, preferably two. Even if they attributed it to "sources" they'd still need to know where it came from. Renouf would find out.'

'Since when did papers have ethics?'

'They don't, but they do have lawyers. They wouldn't risk it.'

'Then we'll have to find another route to market.'

'Can you think of one?'

'No,' Bichard said. 'Not right away.'

He thought about all the resources he had at

his disposal. An island-wide force, contacts in Jersey and the mainland, a press office. It didn't seem right that none of them could help in some way. Perhaps if he approached...

'Of course, there is one outlet that doesn't much care about named sources,' Christine said, interrupting his train of thought.

Bichard raised his eyebrows. 'On the island?'

He ran through the various outlets. Papers, magazines, radio... he shook his head.

'Amy Sloane.'

He smiled. 'Of course.'

'Someone in these parts is feeding her stories already,' Christine said. 'She knew about the Ibbott body before we'd gone public, and unless Carey let slip it can only have come from this building. My guess is that stories are more important than sources where she's concerned, so if anyone would run an unattributed feature –'

'It's her.'

'We just need to feed it.'

'Well...' Bichard paused as he thought it through. 'Call from the office after –' He looked at his watch. 'Call now. Use my phone. She'll check the number and end up back at the switchboard.' He stepped away from his desk and Christine slipped into his seat. 'If Renouf is involved in Carteret this could be our break.'

BBC Radio Guernsey, 9.40am

Simon had moved to Kira's desk. She didn't work on Saturdays – barely anyone did – and it meant he could see the whole of the office while nobody else could look at his screen.

He looked up. He couldn't see far beyond the end of the desk, but the newsroom was quiet – just the whir of a printer and voices at the furthest end. The sports team was in but that was it. Half of them were out at the ground, waiting for kick-off. He was flying solo on news, and travel came in on the line from the mainland, leaving him time for personal projects. He opened the file again and scrolled through the words, highlighting each as he went.

Gregg, JohnGregg, MVJohnGregg, Thoumine, St Sampson, Fleet, Vale, Trawler, Catch, Vessel, BBC, Alex, Alexander, Lucas, ThomasThoumine, 1984, 1979, 2003, Award, Awards, Net, Joist, Cod, Haddock, Mullet, Snapper, Sole, Plaice...

He was starting to think it was pointless. They had no way of knowing whether Rosalynd had used these words as her password, no way of knowing which letters should be in upper or lower case, no way of knowing whether she'd added some digits, or swapped out some letters for common numerical equivalents – S for 5, L for 1, T for 7.

The chances of hitting upon the correct combination were... Still, it was better than tweaking the headlines.

Police Headquarters, 10.20am

Bichard opened a browser and typed in Amy's name. It turned up over a thousand results, the first two of which were her profile and blog.

'There you go,' he said, stepping back and shuffling the phone across the desk. He highlighted Amy's number on the profile. 'Keep it brief. Whet her appetite and let her chase the rest.'

Christine dialled the six-digit number, half expecting to get through to voicemail. It was Saturday, mid-morning, and from the pictures she'd seen Amy looked the type who would rather spend her weekends shopping than waiting around for a lead.

The line clicked on the second ring, was silent for a moment, then started ringing again: a slightly different tone this time. Two further rings, and then –

'Amy Sloane.'

'Amy,' Christine said, pressing the hands-free

button so Bichard could hear both sides of the call.

'Who is this?'

Amy was on her mobile phone. They could hear sounds in the background: the beeps of hand-held scanners pricing up clothes or shoes from their barcodes. Chatter. The burble of a street as a door behind her, beside her, or somewhere close by quickly opened and softly drew to.

'Is this a bad time?' Christine asked.

'That depends.'

'On?'

'Who you are.'

Christine paused. She listened. They needed Amy. They needed her contacts and outlets, but Christine knew that she'd lose her if she made it too easy. She had to make it look as if she was still in control – make Amy crave what she had to offer. She counted to five before she spoke again. 'I want to talk about Oliver Carey.'

The words seemed to have the desired effect. The background chatter softened, and Christine imagined Amy cupping the mouthpiece. There was a rustling sound – the sound of fabric rubbing on fabric – perhaps she was stepping away from the queue, into a more discreet corner.

'What about him?'

'He's a person of interest.'

'To...?'

'Have you asked him about the radio?'

'What about the radio?'

'Have you asked him?'

'We may have discussed it,' Amy said. She kept her voice level and calm – almost dismissive – but Christine knew she was lying. The radio hadn't yet entered the public domain. If Amy had known about it, it would have been printed already.

'I don't believe you.'

'Believe what you like,' Amy said. 'Either way, I'm interested to hear your side of the story.'

'My side of the story?'

'That's why you're ringing, I presume.'

'And what do you suppose my side might be?'

'You have inside knowledge,' Amy said. 'Something that's not widely known. That would suggest you're calling from...'

'Never mind where I'm calling from.' Christine looked up and smiled at Bichard. He smiled back and nodded, urging her on. 'States Police found a radio.'

'Where?'

'Marble Bay. Monday morning.'

'Richelle Ibbott's?'

'That's what they thought.'

'But not any longer?'

Christine didn't answer.

'I'll take that as a yes,' Amy said.

Still Christine didn't respond.

'Why?'

'I'm led to believe there was wax,' Christine said.

'On the headphones?'

'On the earbuds. Forensics sent samples away to be tested.'

'Which came back positive?'

'Why else might I be calling?'

'You tell me, Miss...?'

Christine reached forward and tapped the hands-free button a second time, cutting the line and silencing Amy mid-stride.

'Excellent,' Bichard said.

'And now?'

'Now we wait.'

The Sarnian, 10.25am

The hive was empty. Freya didn't work on Saturdays and the mood in the newsroom seemed lighter without her. They still had a paper to fill - and Sunday's edition was larger than ever - but Freya's absence, just for one day, seemed to calm them. They took longer to make their drinks, paused by the kettle to chat and catch up, then returned to their desks and their work.

Alfie had already planned an extra sixteen pages for the Sunday paper covering what they knew of Richelle. When Rosalynd had turned up dead at Saints Harbour he'd had to re-think. Sixteen pages turned into twenty, with eight for each victim and four for the ads. He'd split the team in two, heading up the Rosalynd story himself with Ella compiling Richelle's. They'd each chosen writers, like playground captains picking players for football, and Ollie had ended up on Alfie's side, writing the story of Rosalynd Holdbrook.

He hadn't told Alfie about the email – or the missing attachment. He wanted to surprise them: retrieve the file and blow the story wide open. It might be enough to help them forget his failures of the week gone by – his failure to stay at the bay the morning he'd found the body, his failure to interview Dixon, his failure to get any meaningful quotes out of Rosalynd Holdbrook before she'd been killed.

He opened Simon's latest list of suggestions and started typing them into Rosalynd's online mailbox. With every attempt, the login prompt shook on the screen as though it was shaking its head. The dialogue froze for several seconds; it seemed there was some kind of hook in the code that slowed things down, probably to freeze out hackers.

The next one was wrong. The screen shook, he struck it off the list, and he waited. The longer it went on, the more he felt he was firing random shots into darkness.

Police Headquarters, 10.35am

Renouf was making tea when Christine came back from her meeting. He seemed to be in better spirits and called her across to the kitchen.

'I'd make you one,' he said, 'but I need you to grab a car and go down to Saints Bay. Call about some disturbance or other.'

'Isn't there anyone else?'

'Not today. Holidays and sick leave.'

'What about Falla or Clarke?'

He dipped his hand in his pocket and pulled out a bundle of keys. He separated the car key from the bunch and put it down on the worktop. 'Take mine,' he said, ignoring her. 'Some of those pool cars are filthy.'

He looked from the key to Christine. She noticed him twisting his wedding band. Round and round and round it went as he shuffled his feet on the carpet.

'It's coming up on eleven already.'

'Just go, would you, Christine,' he said. 'We've got plenty of time.'

'Well, not really. We've got the media meet in half an hour, and I –'

Renouf shook his head. 'I cancelled it. There's not much to tell. We've barely had a chance to look at Dixon yet and I'd rather not show our hand at this stage.'

'And Carey? Shouldn't we at least tell them he isn't our only lead?'

'I think it best that we stop talking about Carey altogether, don't you.' He picked up the key and held it between them. 'I parked it out front.'

She took it and returned to her desk to pick up her bag. She'd go – she had no choice – but not because Renouf wanted her there, or was it just that he wanted her out of the office. Either way, her duty was to Bichard, and unless she could find a logical reason to do otherwise, following Renouf's orders was the best she could do.

It came as no surprise that he'd cancelled the briefing. They'd been spinning the same hopeless story for most of a week, with too little evidence to point a finger directly at Carey, but waving it roughly in his direction nonetheless.

The waving had been more focused since Thursday, the spiral tightening, stiffening, squeezing the story until the ultimate revelation would seem entirely driven by logic and reason.

Renouf's reversal had brought out some

mixed emotions. Falla and Clarke were fresh on the force - two years apiece - and saw little reason to question his whims. Perhaps they assumed that this was how things were done. The other three - the three who'd served their time - sat stiff in their seats and said nothing. One drummed his fingers, another pinched his lips as though afraid he'd speak out of turn. The third had been tasked with removing the photos of Carey from the noticeboard to make space for the pictures of Dixon. He'd swapped them directly, shot for shot.

They'd dispersed soon after that: Clarke to the loading bay to smoke, Falla to the canteen, and Christine to her meeting with Bichard. She had no doubt that they'd have discussed it in huddled groups in her absence, out of range of Renouf.

She switched off her computer and zipped up her bag, then carried the keys across to the double swing doors that led from the investigation room to the station's main hallway. She met Falla coming in with an armful of folders.

'Falla,' she said. 'Just the man.' She held up the key. 'I've got a small errand I need you to run.'

Falla found the car soon enough. It was a two-year-old Ford. Sunroof, no air con. The inside was spotless, quite unlike Renouf's desk, apparently on account of a recent valet, the receipt for which he found in the door pocket. It started first time and he cruised out of Town in the light morning traffic.

Saints Bay was fifteen minutes away, close to the harbour where Rosalynd's body had washed ashore. He turned off the sat nav and wound down the window, then perched one arm on the door, glad to be out in the sun.

Life was good. A pair of sunglasses would have made it just about perfect. At last he was on a meaningful case, not simply walking the streets, chasing noisy neighbours and knocked-over dustbins. He'd been mentioned by name - twice - in The Sarnian, and was close to first-name terms with half the hacks on the island.

He indicated off the main road and headed into the trees. Saints Bay was a mixture of pebbles and sand, deep in a gully cut by the wash of the sea and the soft, steady trickle of streams. He'd known it all his life, and it used to be a weekend treat through the greater part of his childhood.

The facts of the case ran through his mind, Renouf's abrupt change of mind among them. It seemed that he'd picked up a scent, somewhere or other, that was turning about the investigation. Carey seemed a logical suspect,

Dixon no less so, and Falla found himself fizzing inside, excited to see how it all turned out, as if he was watching a case on TV, with a hand on the outcome to boot.

He tapped the brake as the incline steepened and saw a slight dip on the dash. He pressed it harder to slow down some more and felt its tautness grip and then slip, his foot falling forward and hitting the floor, all tension gone from the pedal.

The car started gathering speed.

He lifted his foot and pumped the pedal, but all it did was flap between his sole and the rubbery mat. He reached for the handbrake without even thinking and yanked it up between the seats. It seemed to have disengaged and came up without any clicks, the ratchet apparently gone, abandoning him to gravity as the road fell away on its sharp descent to the beach. He popped the gear from third into first, the engine shrieked and the revs leapt up from a comfy 2000 to three times that number.

The speedo picked up alongside it, creeping from fifteen to twenty, quickening on the approach to thirty and hitting forty in just a few lengths. The granite walls flashed by on either side, and he swerved as a runner pressed himself into a niche. The car shot across to the opposite side of the road, grazing the wall and tearing at the overhanging ferns. Two early tourists were straining at their pedals as they struggled to ride a tandem up from the beach, and as Falla approached them he swerved once again, this time back on himself.

He was moving too fast to control his descent, and his desperate twist of the wheel sent him through a half turn, the back of the car momentarily facing the sea, the bonnet back up towards the main road, and then as momentum took hold, the tandem streaked by and the car continued its turn, the offside quarter light smashed against the wall, the wheel beneath it struck a granite marker set at the foot of the wall and the tyre, finally pushed beyond the tolerances of its design, shredded itself against the unforgiving rock.

The granite stripped the car of its paint, and as the vehicle dragged its nose on the wall it slowed down enough for Falla to recover some form of control. He turned the wheel to line up the car with the wall until the whole of the passenger side was beating itself against the rough surface. It brought him, at last, to a juddering halt and his head flew forward, smashing his nose and brow on the wheel.

The airbag blew, covering him in a white, chalky powder and knocking him out as it quickly deflated. The inside of the car had been comprehensively dusted, and so had he. At last he'd come to a halt, the car itself wedged against the wall, its nose pressed into a corner where the granite came out and shaved a clear foot off the width of the road. It wasn't going anywhere, and neither was he.

Police Headquarters, 10.45am

Forensics Lab

Renouf spent the first fifteen minutes after he'd loaned his car to Christine trying to keep himself busy. He had plenty to do - that wasn't the problem. Keeping his mind settled was more of an issue.

He was trying to skew the case notes, directing the thread toward George Dixon, and how it might be that a man with a seemingly perfect alibi could somehow be framed as a suspect.

He pushed away his keyboard and looked up at the large amber clock. Its bright, glowing digits seemed to be growling, warning him, admonishing him for something he hadn't done.

He wondered what was happening, what she was doing in his car. Why had Marie been so insistent that she take it. Please, God, don't let it be... Things were already strained with Sophie.

If he lost the car, too...

His chest was tight, his stomach churning, a thickness in his throat. The drink he'd been making when Christine had left was still on the end of his desk, cold and untouched.

He needed to get away. He needed to leave his desk and the silent phone, keeping its counsel, making him wait, making him think. He took himself down to the lab.

Charlie was topping up the Bunsen flask as Renouf came into the room. He held up the bag of coffee grounds and nodded down at the pot. Renouf shook his head. The thought of it turned his stomach. 'I think I've probably had enough,' he said. 'Need to ease off.'

Charlie raised his eyebrows. 'That's a first.'

Renouf gave as natural a laugh as he could and pulled out the seat on the visitors' side of the desk. The table before him was strewn with papers, a series of maps and some inkjet prints of Rosalynd Holdbrook, harshly lit and laid out on the slab. The top of her head had been carefully peeled away to reveal the skull. Renouf leafed through the pile, which showed her head from four different angles: above, below, and on both sides. The underside rear was by far the most gruesome, revealing a deep and painful crack in her skull.

'What do you think?' Charlie asked, walking

around to the opposite side of the desk. He picked up a half bar of chocolate and broke off a chunk, offering what remained to Renouf. His casual air made Renouf feel quite sick. He waved away the chocolate.

'This is what killed her?'

'Mm-hmm. A smack on the back of the head. Thought it might have been a rock first, same as the Ibbott woman, but now we're not so sure. We're working on the theory it might actually have been someone's boot.'

'She was kicked to death?'

'Maybe. Another twenty-four hours or so and we could say for sure, but everything's pointing in that direction.'

'So it was murder.'

'That's the assumption.'

'Which would rather suggest…' Renouf hoped Charlie would finish the sentence himself. Somehow he felt it would seem more real if it came unprompted.

'A double murder? Is that what you're asking.'

Renouf lifted his eyebrows. 'Perhaps.'

Charlie selected the first of the pictures and held it up to the light. 'Not necessarily,' he said, sounding almost distracted as he turned it around. He peered at it as though looking at something he'd previously missed. 'Gut instinct says yes, but in terms of cold, hard proof there's nothing here that would stand up in court. Not yet.'

'But given time...?'

'Given time, with fibre analysis, a thorough examination of the material we recovered from beneath her nails, hair samples, we could probably say with a greater degree of confidence whether or –'

'Damnit, Charlie,' Renouf snapped, slapping the flat of his palm on the desk and causing the papers to gently lift up and then settle. 'Stop hedging your bloody bets. Are the killings connected or not?'

Charlie stiffened. 'I can give you the facts,' he said, his voice calm but cautious. 'Whether or not they're connected, Marc – that's for you to prove, based on the evidence.'

Renouf had rarely lost his temper in Charlie's presence, and when he had, Charlie himself had never before been his target. He sat down and looked at his friend.

'Are you sure it's just too much coffee?' Charlie asked.

Renouf sank back in his seat. He let his hands fall down by his side. 'One of those days, that's all.'

Charlie played with the chocolate wrapper, directing Renouf's attention by crinkling the foil and catching the light from the window. It allowed him to look at the bruises unnoticed. The fringe beneath each eye was still scarlet, but the centres were starting to blacken and Charlie could tell they were fresh. In a day or so they would turn towards yellow and stay like that for close to two weeks as they slowly faded away. He'd seen similar bruising back on the mainland adorning the faces of too many beaten wives, and he wanted to spare his friend the almost certain humiliation of claiming he'd walked into a post or a door.

He gathered together the pictures and shuffled them back into order.

'So, Rosalynd,' he said, standing up and walking across to the flask. The coffee was starting to bubble and he didn't want it to boil. 'Are you sure?' he asked, holding up a mug. Renouf shook his head. 'Foul play is a given,' Charlie continued. He filled his mug and carried it back to his desk. 'The wound is too big for a hammer, too rounded for a mallet - unless it was a croquet bat - so unless someone was hurling a rock about and managed to catch her -'

'You're sure they weren't?'

'It wasn't an accident.' He turned to his computer and opened a folder of images, scrolling through them until he found the one he was after. He turned his screen so Renouf could see it: a close-up view of Rosalynd's smashed head, with small red numbers marking out chips on the edge of the large depression. Charlie tapped each one with the tip of his pen. 'Rosalynd Holdbrook suffered multiple blows, each one of them likely sufficient to kill her. Each of these points marks the edge of an overlapping circle. We've counted five depressions in total, all in roughly the same position but slightly offset. They converge here.' He tapped twice at the centre of the wound.

'What sort of... object are we talking about?' Renouf asked. He was going to say rock, then he was going to say boot, but until they knew for sure in either direction he preferred to keep it ambiguous.

'Fairly smooth. Size of a decent potato. Pretty blunt, at least on one end.'

'Weight?'

Charlie shrugged. 'Can't say without knowing who did it. It needn't have been all that heavy if it was brought down with some force. If it was a boot or shoe, you've got the swing of a leg behind it. Put a rock in the hands of a little old lady, though, and you'd need a bit more weight to the stone itself.'

'Do you think that's likely?'

'A little old lady?' Charlie paused as he considered the picture for a couple of seconds.

'No.' He pulled out the printed picture that showed the rear upper quarter of Rosalynd's head. 'The wound is right up here. Square and centre, in line with her neck.' He touched his own head in the same position.

'I see...'

'And she was five foot eight - pretty much the mean - so logic would dictate that whoever struck her brought down this object from a fair height, otherwise he would have caught her here.' He lowered his finger until he was touching the back of his head. 'The crown,' he said. 'Or here, or round on the parietal ridge, here on the side.'

Renouf imagined Oliver Carey standing beside Rosalynd Holdbrook. In his mind's eye they were roughly eye to eye. He took a deep breath and smiled gently. 'So that would preclude anyone of the same height? That's what you're saying?'

'Yes.'

Renouf could feel himself lighten, the way he might if a physical burden - not merely a worry - had fallen away. The chair seemed to loosen its grip, his jacket to lift, no longer weighed down by the phone and wallet and pens in his pockets. 'Well, that rules out Carey,' he said. 'He's, what? Five foot eight, five nine?'

'At a guess,' Charlie said. 'Six foot, perhaps, but it doesn't rule him out. Not if she was sitting down.'

Renouf felt the weight begin to return. 'Was she?'

'Too early to say. She might have been. Or she could have been on the floor. Almost certainly was if this was a boot, someone kicking her.'

'When will you know?'

'As I say, twenty-four, forty-eight hours.'

Renouf slumped back in his chair. Oliver Carey was back in the frame.

'There's considerable bruising,' Charlie explained. 'Her left arm is fractured and there are contusions on her legs, chest and back, likely caused by the fall to the water. She was probably dead already, which would suggest she was killed at some height and the body disposed of in situ.'

'Marble Bay?'

'Don't know.'

Renouf sighed. 'Do you think you could find out for me? Have a guess at time of death and take a look at the tides again. You should be able to work out roughly how far she could have travelled and where she came from to end up on that slipway.'

'She died on Thursday. Thursday night.'

'Can you use that as your starting point?'

Charlie smiled. 'We already have.'

The Sarnian, 11am

Ollie had three more passwords to try when his phone began to vibrate. He reached out and grabbed it, expecting to hear Simon's voice.

'Oliver, Oliver, Oliver Carey.' It wasn't Simon.

'Amy.'

'How are you, my darling.'

'Busy.'

'Preparing your defence?'

'I don't have time for games, Amy.'

'Who does, darling?' she asked. 'Who among us has time for –'

'What do you want?'

'My goodness, you are pushed for time. Very well. One question. What brand were they? Those earbuds. The ones you left on the beach. What were they? Something good, or the own-brand freebies that came with the radio?'

'I don't know,' he said. 'I don't know, because they weren't mine. Now if you don't mind I've got more than enough to –'

'Not so fast, my darling. Word has it there was a fine gloss of wax from those oh-so-delectable ears of yours. How do you explain that?'

'Whose word?'

She tutted, casting a string of sharp kisses towards him. 'You know I never reveal my sources. Bad for business. You know…' She hesitated a moment. 'You know you'd be safe if you talked to me, hun. No one would ever find out that you'd –'

Ollie switched off the phone. Cracking Rosalynd's password was suddenly rather more pressing.

Police Headquarters, 11.10am

Renouf marched back in and set about sorting his desk, snatching up papers and dropping them into the bin, shredding some others and firing pens into pots like someone piercing balloons.

Pop-pop-pop.

The pot was full and all they did was part the ones already in place. The latest arrivals stood proud of their neighbours, a good three inches clear of the tops, and the next one he arrowed towards them bounced off and skittered across the desk.

Clarke had been writing Dixon's profile: events and dates, connections to either woman, his life on the island and how he'd come to be there. He'd taken it right through 5,000 words and wanted to check some points with Renouf before he went any further. Looking up at his boss, furiously gathering scraps of paper, telephone notes and old clips and staples, he decided to leave things as they stood and ask him later on.

The door to the hallway swung open, and Christine walked in carrying files – the same red folders she'd taken from Falla, swapping them for the key to the car. Renouf and Clarke looked up – the other three constables, too – and Renouf paused mid-stab, cupping his fingers around the pen and letting his hand drop to his side.

'Le Page,' he said. 'You're back.' He flopped back into his seat with a gentle smile. 'That was quick. No problems?'

She walked to her desk and put the files in her top tray.

'Don't know,' she said. 'I bumped into Bichard.'

Renouf said nothing. He nodded.

'He wanted me to chase a few things. Talk to the guys back in Jersey. Do a bit of liaison.'

'You didn't go?'

'I sent Falla.'

He settled his hands on the edge of the desk and his fingers scratched the grain of the wood. 'You what?' The colour seemed to drain from his face. He suddenly looked quite ill; his tan seemed to bleach and his lips to chill.

'I know what you said, but he was –'

'You sent Falla?' The last of those words, he was close to whispering, like something that the very idea of which disgusted him.

'He was happy to go. I had to make those calls for Bichard.'

Renouf's lips parted again, his chin falling just slightly but his thoughts never quite getting as far as his mouth.

His phone rang, and without looking down he slowly reached out and picked it up, his eyes never leaving Le Page.

'Renouf,' he said.

'Rosalynd Holdbrook,' Charlie replied. 'From the way the tides have been moving these last few days, I'd say it was either Icart Point or the Jerbourg Peninsular.'

Renouf paused for a moment, still staring at Christine.

'Are you there?' Charlie asked.

'Sorry,' Renouf said, putting the pen on the table. 'Icart or Jerbourg.' He turned his chair and looked at the island map pinned to the wall behind him. He traced the south-east coast with his finger, around the Peninsular and back towards the Point. 'That's an awful lot of land, Charlie. Can you narrow it down?'

'Well, it's been pretty calm of late. Beyond the crack in her head, there wasn't much damage done to the body, although the bloating might have softened things somewhat, so I don't think she's moved too far.' He paused, and Renouf could picture his friend looking at his own map, considering what to say next. 'On balance, I'd head for Icart,' he said. 'She would have come from the west on the prevailing current, so somewhere between there and Petit Bot. Jerbourg is unlikely.'

Renouf moved his finger away from the headland that drooped from the island's south-eastern corner and settled it back on the rocky outcrop that shot straight out from the steep southern shoreline. He looked at the clock: it was still before noon. Most likely the site would be filled with visitors walking or drinking tea.

'Thanks, Charlie,' he said, dropping the phone back on its hook and turning to face the rest of the office. 'Clarke. Get downstairs and dig out a roll of evidence bags. Gloves and barrier tape, too. Meet me at the garage.' He turned to Christine. 'You can call Falla. Get him back here as soon as you can.'

He stood up, then thought again. 'Oh, and tell him to drive carefully, will you. Sophie will kill me if anyone dings that car.'

Saints Bay, 11.15am

An anxious crowd had gathered about the smashed car by the time the fire crew arrived. They'd nudged a minibus out of the way further up the hill and crept down the rest of the slope with the brakes on hard, blocking the road from wall to wall. The weight of the engine carried them on regardless until they shut it down with the gears engaged to stop it from rolling any further.

Ross Ferbrache jumped down from the cab and spread his arms wide, herding back the spectators until he'd formed a clear margin around the car. He took a look through the shattered windscreen at Falla's motionless form, his head still slack on the wheel.

'Did anyone see what happened here?' he asked, looking from face to face.

A man in a light plastic jacket raised his hand from the bars of a tandem. His wife was holding one of the saddles. 'We were the ones who called,' he said. 'He was out of control.'

'When was this?' Ferbrache asked. He signalled through the cab window for the rest of his crew to climb down.

The man and his wife looked at each other and shook their heads in unison. They looked at their watches. 'Ten minutes?'

Ferbrache nodded and looked at his own. The ambulance ought to have been there by then. 'Frewin, Pawsey,' he said, pointing at two of his crew. 'Get cutting. Martel, if you could have a chat with… I'm sorry, I didn't get your names.'

He turned back to the tandem riders.

'Michael and Ruth,' the man said, his finger switching backwards and forth between himself and his wife.

'Michael and Ruth,' Ferbrache said.

Frewin and Pawsey opened a door at the back of the cab and started to haul out their equipment – cutters and pincers and poles with which to knock out the rest of the windscreen.

'The rest of you,' Ferbrache said, 'I need you to keep back, and if you could give this man some privacy...' – he turned pointedly at a woman taking pictures on her phone – 'I think that would be the decent thing, don't you?'

Icart Point, Noon

They checked out a car from the pool and Renouf drove them down to the Point. Christine called Falla every five minutes, but got his voicemail each time.

'He must have left it in the car,' she told Renouf.

Renouf tightened his grip on the wheel and said nothing. She noticed him clenching his jaw.

At last they approached the Point and he told them what Charlie had said. 'Anywhere between here and Petit Bot, most likely, but his hunch put it closer to this end. My bet is he killed her somewhere along the path and tipped her into the sea.'

'Or killed her somewhere else and brought the body here to dispose of it,' Christine replied.

'I don't know,' said Clarke. 'It's pretty steep and narrow. There are easier ways to dispose of a body.'

'Clarke's right,' Renouf said as they climbed out of the car. He locked the doors behind them. 'If this is where Holdbrook entered the water, it's my belief that it's also the place she was killed. I think she came here of her own free will and –'

'Why?' Christine jumped in.

'Why did she come here?' Renouf asked. 'Who knows. Existing engagement. Wanted some fresh air.'

'All of which would assume that this was opportunistic and not in the least related to the Ibbott inquiry.'

'Unless she came with the killer,' Clarke said.

'My thoughts entirely, Clarke, which pretty much rules out Carey,' Renouf said.

'How so?' Christine asked.

'Because Carey goes everywhere by bike. Rosalynd... not so much.'

They had reached the end of the car park, and were standing by the carved granite block, looking out to sea. The cliffs fell away before them, and the coast path led off left and right.

Renouf took the police-branded tape from Christine and unrolled a long stretch. He handed it to Clarke. 'You and Christine that way, at least as far as Jaonet,' he told him, pointing west towards the next headland. 'Tape off the path, then work your way back. Bag everything and anything that might conceivably have once belonged to Miss Holdbrook, or points to a possible killer. I don't care whether it's a hair grip, a shoelace or anything worn in between. Nothing is insignificant.'

He spooled out another length of tape, then walked across to a freshly painted bench and tied one end to its back rest and the other onto a branch of gorse on the opposite side of the path.

'I'll do the same from this direction,' he said to Christine. 'Whatever it is. No matter how small or unlikely. Sun-dried dog turd embossed by a boot? Bag it on up and bring it straight back.'

'We need help,' Christine said. 'There's far too much ground for the three of us.'

'No,' Renouf snapped. 'There's no time. If this is where she died it's almost certainly been contaminated already. The sooner we make a start, the less chance we have of the evidence being further degraded.'

Christine stared at him for a moment and marvelled at his overt change of direction. Not twenty-four hours before he'd been pushing them all to pin whatever they could on Carey, regardless of motive or evidence. Now he was grasping at whichever straw seemed most likely to pull in George Dixon.

She had no love of Dixon - considered him little more than an arrogant, bit-part actor in a marginal radio drama - but she couldn't help wondering whether he wasn't about to be given the same unfair treatment as Carey. If he was, she only hoped that this time Renouf was pushing in the right direction.

She turned, and pulling a roll of zip-lock bags out of her pocket, she started to walk along the path, away from the bench, the memorial and the car park. She kept her head down, scanning left and right in front of her feet, only looking up as the prop-driven planes clattered by on their final approach to the airport.

The path was so tidy she could well have believed that someone came by to sweep it each night. It was free of rubbish; the best she could find were cigarette butts, smoked right down to the filter. Two were unmarked, but a band of pink lipstick encircled the brown paper sleeve of the third.

Further on she found a discarded sandal, which she dropped in an evidence bag, and close-by to that, the end of a child's plastic spade, which she left.

Saints Bay Road, 1pm

Ferbrache's efforts to keep them all back were effective, but the sounds themselves - of the pincers, like huge curved pliers, as big as an arm, slicing through the pillars with the force of a hundred tons - of the spacers, spreading the chassis, cracking apart the roof from the body, the arches from the axels, the door from its frame - of the compressed gas driving them all - of the pneumatic rams pushing out the sides of the car to free the doors and give access - of the shriek of fabric tape being pulled from its roll with the sound of torn linen - of the quick inflation of the windscreen protector, orange like a lifeboat, that they wedged behind the dashboard to stop the glass from falling in - the sounds themselves were far more effective, echoing up and down the valley, winding up through the trees, assaulting the ears gathered around the smashed car and forcing them back towards the opposite verge.

It took fifteen minutes to cut away the upper parts of the dented body, by which time they'd stabilised what remained, jacking it up until it was level and wedging stepped blocks under the tyres. The ambulance arrived, and at last they snipped through the seatbelt as two paramedics jumped out - one from the front and one from the back – leaving the engine running. The first of them reached in, carefully stroking the back of Falla's neck to feel for obvious bumps or breaks; finding none she rolled him back and fit a stiff plastic collar. It lifted his chin away from his chest and kept it securely in place. A broad oval opening at the front exposed a path to his neck, and they could see for the first time how it was stained with blood from his nose and a vicious cut in his brow.

The driver returned to the ambulance as her partner dug out a torch and lifted Falla's eyelids, shining the light into each bloodied eye and seeing the pupil contract. He counted his pulse, listened to his heart, and secured a plastic tube in his mouth, one end of which gripped his tongue to stop it from falling back and choking him; the other he clipped to his cheek. It pinched the skin and would leave an uncomfortable mark, but it might save his life in the process.

The driver threw open the double back doors and pulled a gurney towards her. Its legs sprang out as they passed over the steps and locked themselves into place, their wheels on the ground but secured to stop them from rolling.

At last they carefully lifted him out of the car, their hands and arms protecting his head and neck, and laid him down on the stretcher, squeezing him back up the hill between the fire engine and the rocky wall just as the first patrol car arrived. The uniformed officer radioed over the registration. 'I need a PNC,' she said. 'RTA on the Saints Bay Road. Red Ford Fiesta.' She read out the five-digit number adorning the plates.

'Are you sure?' the crackling answer came back.

The officer read the number again.

'We have that registered to Inspector Marc Renouf,' the handler said, just as the ambulance crew walked past, wheeling an unconscious man on their gurney. She caught a snatch of his uniform and radioed back that apparently, yes, this was his car, and the crash had left him acutely impaired.

She said she would wait with the wreckage until they could send out a truck, and suggested that someone told Bichard what had happened before dispatching a car to the hospital.

The paramedics slid the gurney back into their van, the legs reversing their ratchet trick and folding away beneath it.

'White male, twenty-five to thirty, unconscious following serious RTA,' the driver radioed in as she reversed them up the road. She performed a narrow nine-point turn at the closest passing point.

The traffic was light. It was Saturday. The schools were off and the usual blackspots close to Town were easily avoided. Falla seemed stable but the state of his spine remained an unknown quantity, so rather than opt for sirens and speed they turned on the flashing blue lights and cruised along as smoothly as the roads would allow, keeping well back from the other traffic to minimise their braking, taking wide turns and only once doing more than twenty miles an hour.

On a good day, with traffic in their favour, it would have taken them less than ten minutes. This time around it took twenty, and the crash crew was there when they reached the sweeping driveway that led to the hospital door.

Nothing had changed since they'd strapped him onto the gurney. He was still breathing, he was still bleeding. His vital signs were stable, but so was his lack of consciousness. They walked him through the halls at high speed, through the doors to the trauma unit, just as an officer checked in with reception and asked for an update on Inspector Marc Renouf.

Route de Jerbourg, 2.15pm

The boy had almost finished - and he'd made a better fist of it than Dixon had expected. Perhaps that's what happened when you paid above the odds.

He'd been watching him, on and off, washing his car for the last two hours, and he'd made sure the boy changed the water - twice, if not three times - and was careful cleaning the soft top. Dixon had brought out the polish then, and three soft cloths, and showed the boy how he should rub it on one way and off in the other direction.

'Rub on, rub off,' he'd told him, gripping the back of the boy's wet hand and guiding it round and round on the bonnet.

And then it was time to clean the inside.

The car had been idle for days, locked up without ventilation, chilled at night and gently warmed by the sun, and the unhappy purging of Dixon's stomach was starting to crust on the dashboard.

'I'll bring you the key,' Dixon said, handing over upholstery shampoo and heading back into the house.

He looked in the pot on the dresser - the one where he kept his keys and spare change - but all that he found were some small value coins that may well have once been Richelle's.

He stood for a moment and thought, retracing his steps. He'd taken the bus to Rosalynd's house, so he hadn't used them then. That must mean the last time he'd used the car had been...

...think...

...the night at Icart Point. He'd been wearing his tweed.

He turned to the coat pegs and patted the jacket, and found a familiar lump in the pocket. He lifted the sleeve and lifted the flap and reached inside for the keys, and then as he let the sleeve drop back down an unfamiliar mark caught his eye.

It was brown, almost rusty, a bloom in the weave that had wicked and spread and eventually dried.

He held the sleeve closer, cupping the keys in the palm of his hand, and scratched the mark with his thumbnail. It didn't flake away, and it had no obvious smell.

It looked like... it looked like blood.

He sighed. Rosalynd's blood. It had to be. That was how he had carried her - the backs of her knees over his aching right forearm, her limp head thrown to the left, with her neck rolling backwards and forth on this arm, right where this patch was, spoiling the sleeve. She'd bled on his jacket and now it would need to be cleaned.

He threw it back down in disgust.

Even in death, the woman caused great inconvenience. A trip into Town was the last thing he wanted to do on the weekend.

The boy would have to hurry up - he needed the car after all.

Icart Point, 3.50pm

Christine met Clarke at the halfway point. She looked at his underwhelming collection. He'd done no better than she had, but as they turned and walked back, he bent down and picked up the spade, and slipped it into a pouch.

'You never can tell,' he said, when he looked up and saw her watching him.

They arrived to find Renouf on the floor, grubbing about by the bench in a flattened patch of hottentot fig. He was picking at a brown, gritty substance that seemed to have stuck to some of the larger leaves and he looked with some distain at the meagre collection of bags they'd brought back.

'This is supposed to be a murder investigation. Not a bloody litter pick.'

Clarke chewed his bottom lip. 'It's practically spotless out here.'

Renouf cursed.

'That or we need more feet on the ground,' Christine said. 'If we're going to find anything that ties this to Dixon so long after the event we can't do it with just three people.'

Nobody spoke for a moment. Renouf was occupied with his knife and the foliage. He sliced off a twig and its succulent leaves and dropped them into an evidence bag. He ran a finger and thumb across the lock to seal it, then held it up to the sun.

'Is that...?' Christine let her question trail off.

'Blood, I suspect,' Renouf said. 'Rather closer to home than we might have imagined.' He reached into his trousers and took out some coins. 'Make yourself useful, would you.' He held them out. 'Get us some teas.'

She raised her eyebrows, minded to object, then shook her head and took them. Renouf nodded towards the kiosk on the opposite side of the car park.

The garden around it was almost empty. There were a couple of stragglers sitting among the flowers and bushes, empty plates and teapots before them, but the shutter was halfway down on the kiosk and Christine had to duck beneath it to see the woman at the counter. She was drying a metal teapot.

'Can you do me some teas?' asked Christine, resting her arm on the counter.

'Sorry, love.' The woman leaned forward. 'Urn's off.'

'I'll take the dregs.'

'It's been off ten minutes.'

'Is it actually empty?'

The woman paused, the towel hanging limp. She thought for a moment, then putting down the teapot she reached for a stack of cardboard cups. 'Have to be take away,' she said, holding them up.

'Fine. Three, please.'

The woman twitched her eyebrows and turned to the urn. It was mounted on a worktop at the back of the kiosk. 'You can have 'em on the house. It's off the boil.'

Christine ignored her, scattering Renouf's coins on the counter. She hadn't counted them, but she didn't intend taking any change.

One of the coins rolled forward, running across the counter until it knocked the side of a chilled glass cabinet mounted onto the worktop, screwed down, with a thin rubber seam at the base to stop the cool air escaping. The cakes inside it were arranged on three shelves, doilies on the plates, sugar on the top, and there, beside a fruit cake on the lowest shelf, was a small bunch of keys, slightly incongruous, slightly out of place.

Christine eyed them idly while waiting for the teas. She wondered who might have lost them, and why they hadn't already been claimed.

There were just three: one for a car from the look of things, and two that might work in a Yale lock, attached to a keyring the shape of the island, which itself was hooked on to a fob.

Christine tilted her head to read the marks on the fob.

BBC...

She stepped around to the front of the cabinet. Yes, it definitely said BBC.

She took out her warrant and opened it. 'Those keys,' she said, holding it up with one hand and knocking her knuckles on the side of the cabinet. 'When were they handed in?'

The woman thought for a moment. 'Don't know, love. Yesterday, I think. Maybe the day before. I only work weekends.'

'I'll need to take them.'

'They're yours, are they?' She released the handle on the urn. The water dribbled for a moment, and once it had properly stopped she turned around and put the teas on the counter. 'Have you got any –' she started, but then she saw the ID, and she reached into the case to retrieve them.

Christine took an evidence bag out of her pocket and held it open for the woman to drop them in. She sealed it using the zip-lock top.

'Thanks,' she said, shaking them down to the bottom. Leaving the teas on the counter, she turned away and headed back out through the garden.

Bloody litter pick. Let's see what he thinks of this...

Police Headquarters, 3.55pm

Sue Martel called again. She dialled the internal number and listened to the distant phone pealing its single ring. Brrr-brrr-brrr. She counted them. Two to go: it would ring five times before he answered. It always did. He was like that.

Brrr.

Brrr.

'Bichard's office,' said the voice at the opposite end of the line. It was male, but high and slightly breathy. It sounded like he could have done with clearing his throat.

'Is he free?'

'No. I told you three times already –'

'Four times.'

'Four times that he can't be distur–'

'And I told you this was important.'

'Yes,' Henri said. 'But you haven't told me what it's about. I can't very well go in and disturb him if I don't know that it's –'

'Fine,' she said. She'd be knocking off in five minutes, and someone else could deal with the incoming calls. She'd hang up her headphones and ride the bus home, and spend the next three days neither thinking nor caring about the petty office bureaucracy. 'Tell him its Renouf.'

'Marc Renouf?'

'He's been in a serious accident on the Saints

Bay Road. They've taken him in to the hospital.'

'Well, why didn't you say?' Henri asked. 'If I'd known that it was –'

She disconnected the call and logged off.

The Sarnian, 4.00pm

Ollie had reached the end of the list. He'd tried all of Simon's suggestions, and then gone on to exhaust his own.

He picked up the phone and called Simon.

'No luck,' he said.

'It was always a long shot,' Simon said. 'You didn't think we'd crack it, did you?'

'No. It was more palatable than the alternative, that's all.'

'Admitting defeat?'

'I'm not admitting defeat,' Ollie said. 'I need to take a more direct route, that's all. I need to get into her computer.'

'But that's...' Simon stopped for a moment. 'Her computer's in her house,' he said, his voice a loud whisper. Ollie imagined him bending down to the desk, hiding himself behind his screen.

'Have you got any better ideas?'

'Plenty.'

'Such as?'

'Letting it drop.'

'Letting it drop?' Now it was Ollie's turn to

whisper. Most of the office had gone to buy a late lunch but Alfie was still by the printer, waiting for proofs. Harry was at his Mac. 'You're the journalist here, not me. And you're telling me to drop it?'

'Do you know what you're suggesting?'

'Yes.'

'Breaking into someone's house. A dead woman's house.'

'They think I did it.'

'Did? What do you mean did?'

'They think I killed Richelle. And probably Rosalynd too, for all I know. I need that email. I need to know what it says so I can –'

'And they've told you this? They've taken you in and questioned you? Under caution.'

'Not yet, but it's only a matter of time before –'

'Where did you hear this from?'

'Amy.' And as he said it he noticed the unconscious change in his voice. He said it more slowly, more quietly, somehow less certain.

'Amy Sloane? You heard it from Amy Sloane and you're taking her word as gospel.'

'I know. I know it sounds... however it sounds, you know her record. She's got contacts. You've said it yourself. She gets the story first and she gets it right.'

'Not this time.'

'You don't know that. I need to get into that outbox, and it looks like the only way I can do it is through her computer. In person. Now I'm not going to ask you to come along because I know you'd -'

'You know f-all,' Simon said, cutting him off. 'I might not agree with you, but I'll support you. And if that means watching your back -'

'With your eyes?'

'- that's what I'll do.'

Princess Elizabeth Hospital, 4.00pm

Bichard arrived at the hospital, Henri in tow, the PA rightly humbled. The ten-minute drive had been just long enough for Bichard to make clear his displeasure - in excruciating, ear-singeing detail. He told him to find them some coffee while Bichard himself approached the desk and flashed his ID.

'You have a Marc Renouf,' he said. 'Brought in some time this afternoon. Road Traffic Accident.'

The man behind the counter smiled at him and picked up a clipboard. 'Damned system's down this afternoon,' he said, running the tip of his pen down a list of names, times and wards. He shook his head as he got to the bottom of the page and turned to the following sheet. 'Renouf, Renouf, Renouf... ah. A and E. It's...' He leaned forward to point the way but Bichard was already off, following the signs.

Christine stepped out of the tearoom garden and found Renouf in the car park. Clarke was helping him pack the evidence bags into a box in the boot of the car.

She held up the keys and shook them, and Renouf instinctively patted his pockets.

'Rosalynd's,' Christine said.

Clarke looked up.

'How can you tell?' he asked.

She was standing beside them now, so she pressed on the bunch to separate the keys within the bag and showed them the fob.

'Pretty big coincidence if they aren't,' she said.

'Good work.' Renouf's voice was flat and matter-of-fact.

'So Charlie was right,' Clarke said.

'Only one way to find out.' She looked at Renouf. 'Shall we take a ride to the Vale?'

Bichard pushed open the door and found himself at a second reception desk.

'Inspector Marc Renouf,' he said, placing his open ID on the counter. 'You checked him in this afternoon.'

'He's in recovery.'

'Can I see him?'

The receptionist told him to wait while she left her desk to check. Bichard reached over and picked up her phone. He dialled Christine's desk number, and when he got no answer tried her mobile.

Renouf pulled up on the hill above Town. 'You can walk from here,' he told Clarke. 'I don't want to get stuck in traffic. Not tonight.'

He unlocked the door and let him out.

'Get the stuff from the boot and log it before you head home.'

Clarke's shoulders briefly sagged. 'You coming back in tonight?' he asked.

'Unlikely,' Renouf said. 'But I want us all in tomorrow. Media briefing first thing.'

Christine's mobile started to ring and she bent down to find it.

'On a Sunday?'

'Yes, on a Sunday. Get onto the usual names. Call them at home if you have to. I don't want this Holdbrook lead turning stale.'

Christine found her phone and answered it, frowning at the unfamiliar number. Renouf pressed the button to pop up the boot and watched her as she put the phone to her ear. Whoever it was at the other end started talking right away.

'It can't be,' she said.

More talking.

'No. He's here with me.'

Another pause, then...

'That's not Renouf, sir.' She turned to Renouf. 'It's Falla.'

'Get here,' Bichard said as the receptionist returned. 'As soon as you can.' He handed her the receiver, along with a humourless smile of thanks.

'This way,' she said, dropping it back on the hook and leading him through two sets of doors to a four-bed room. One bed was empty; the other three were occupied by patients. One alert and two out cold, Falla included.

Bichard made his way to the side of his bed. He hadn't seen Renouf that morning, but from what Christine had said of the look of his face, he couldn't imagine that Falla was looking much better. His nose was starting to soften and spread with a mosaic of fine red lines following its contours. The split on his forehead was held together by thin adhesive strips, while a blistering scorch mark beside it showed where the airbag had blown. Someone had placed a drip in the back of his hand.

A nurse came in and stood by him. She picked up the board from the end of the bed and pretended to study the chart. Bichard glanced across after thirty seconds and saw that the sheet was almost empty. Just his name - wrong name, it turned out - and a few sparse vitals scattered about the page. A graph with two lonely data points was still too short to describe any kind of a trend.

Bichard knew why she was there. She didn't need that long to check the data. She was there for him - so that he might ask his questions without looking out a member of staff.

'Is it serious?' he asked.

She clipped the board back onto the end of the bed. 'You're his father?'

Bichard held out his ID.

'He's a very sick man,' she said, 'but we won't know for sure for the next few hours.' She leaned forward and checked the cannula in his arm. 'Nothing's fractured, but he's bruised - inside and out. Struck his head, by all accounts, so we want to keep an eye on that. He may have torn some blood vessels close to the brain.'

'Then it is.'

She looked at him for a moment, blinking like a seagull eyeing up a sandwich. 'Very,' she said plainly. 'He won't be leaving here for several days, assuming he wakes up in the next few hours.'

Christine and Renouf left Clarke on the hill and

arrived at the hospital ten minutes later. Renouf left the car at an untidy angle close to the entrance. Christine called Bichard to see where he was. He met them outside the recovery room.

'It's not good,' he said, putting his arm around her shoulder and guiding them both towards the canteen. Henri would have found the coffee by now, and Bichard felt a desperate need for some caffeine.

'It should have been me,' she said. 'Marc sent me out. I gave the keys to Falla when he...'

Bichard shushed her. 'It's not your fault. It could have been Marc if he'd gone himself.'

Renouf looked sick.

'You had a lucky escape,' Bichard told him. 'You both did.'

'I'm sorry, I...' Renouf said. He shook his head and walked back out through the doors to reception.

Christine shrugged off Bichard's arm. 'Marc,' she called out as the doors swung to.

'Leave him,' Bichard said, touching her arm. 'He's had a nasty shock. It was his car, don't forget. He probably feels it was somehow his fault.'

Renouf pulled out his phone and scrolled through the numbers. Liam... Matt... Michael... Mother.

He paused for a moment, his thumb gently shaking as it hovered above the entry.

He left the building and walked across the car park, rubbing the back of his neck with his free hand, and when he was sure he was out of earshot, he tapped the name and let it ring as he crossed the road and stood by one of the trees.

He counted the rings. Foreign ones: long, single tones - not the chirpy twin chimes of the local lines. Two rings became three, became four, became five. Two years on and the line was still active, that much was clear, or the network would never have patched him through.

Someone picked up.

'Hello?' Renouf stopped. He pressed the phone to his ear. 'Is there...? Is there anybody...?'

He heard movement at the end of the line. A hand shuffled its grip on the handset. Whoever it was, they were walking - indoors, he was sure; there was no sound of a passing breeze - and when they sat down he could hear the sigh of a well-stuffed cushion. That suggested leather or something synthetic, not fabric, which didn't breathe that way through its stitch holes - its spiracles - but instead exhaled in silent, limp gusts.

'I didn't ask for this.' Renouf ran a clammy hand through his hair. 'She could have been killed. I didn't ask... You bitch,' he said. 'You bitch.'

'Calm,' said the voice at the end of the line. A man. Eastern European, maybe German. Renouf had expected Marie, with her clipped vowels and smoker's rasp. This was something new.

'Who are you?' he asked.

'Woman is unhurt?'

'Who are you?' Renouf repeated.

'You ask many questions,' the man said. 'Woman is unhurt?'

'Yes, woman is unhurt,' he spat back, unconsciously adopting the broken grammar coming from the opposite end of the line. 'She wasn't driving. She gave the keys to someone... someone... he could have been killed. Do you understand that? Killed.'

'Is alive?'

'Yes, he's alive. Just.'

The man tutted. 'Is pity,' he said.

'But what am I supposed –' Renouf began, but the unbroken tone of the severed line cut him off.

Henri handed Bichard his coffee and asked Christine if she'd like one herself. She refused, and Bichard sent him home.

'Thank God you're alright. Sit down, sit down,' he said, pulling out a chair at a table in the corner, comfortably spaced from the next nearest customer. 'Tell me from the top.'

She explained how she'd met Renouf in the kitchen after their meeting that morning, how he'd sent her down to Saints Bay, handing her his keys to save her from taking a pool car.

Bichard considered this for a moment, the same question forming in his mind as Christine had already asked herself. 'Do you suspect foul play?'

'The garage can tell us for sure,' she said. 'Assuming they can piece it together again.'

Bichard coughed. Christine could see he was biting the side of his cheek as he thought.

'What do you really think happened to Marc Renouf's face?' he asked.

'I don't know,' Christine said, 'but it wasn't a door.'

'And now this.'

'You think the two are related?'

'Assuming it was foul play.' He nodded. 'This was clearly intended for him.'

They both sat in silence taking it in. Bichard stirred his coffee with a thin wooden stick. It was a fruitless exercise: the cup was just coffee and water. No milk, no sugar.

The thought that someone - almost certainly someone outside - could have wanted Marc dead was hard for either to comprehend. The island had not seen a murder for years. Now Ibbott and Holdbrook had washed up on the beaches, and whoever had seen to them was showing an interest in the investigating officers.

Unless...

'That might not be a worst-case scenario,' Christine said, finally breaking the silence.

Bichard raised his eyebrows.

'Can you access the call logs?' she asked him.

'Incoming?'

'Anything logged by the call takers up to, say, ten this morning.'

'What are we looking for?'

'The call from Saints Bay.'

Bichard clucked his tongue. 'Well, yes, but... you think the same person who placed the call played with the brakes?'

'Possibly. Or maybe there was no call.'

'Then why would Renouf send you down to...' Bichard trailed off.

'Are you with me?'

'If you mean...'

Christine nodded. 'It would mean he knew that the brakes were likely to fail.'

'And he wasn't the target at all.'

Vale Parish, 5.00pm

Rosalynd's lawn was starting to look a bit tufty.

Other than that, the house was exactly as Ollie remembered. He and Simon walked past on the opposite side of the road, Ollie watching for neighbours. When he was sure there was no one around they turned and walked back, and Ollie hid his bike behind one of the bushes.

'Round the back,' he said, taking Simon's elbow and turning him towards a path that ran up the side of the garden.

It was obvious - even before they reached the back door - that someone had been there before them.

Simon reached out and touched the window. 'Is this...' He paused as he ran his fingers across it. 'Tape?'

Ollie touched the corner closest to the handle. It gave way easily, moving forward with the slightest touch, to reveal a view of the kitchen floor and, beside the handle, a small bunch of keys hanging from the lock. 'I don't like the look of this,' he said. 'Someone's been in here already.'

He took out his gloves and slipped them on, then passing his hand through the gap in the window, he turned the keys and opened the door.

They walked through the kitchen. It was very neat and very tidy, except... he walked over to the row of drawers that ran beneath the longest worktop. Some of them were pushed right in, but others were slightly askew.

'So what do you think they were looking for?' he asked Simon. 'Whoever they were.'

Simon shrugged, pulling one of the drawers forward and bending down so he could see the cutlery inside it. 'Corkscrew? Sieve?'

Ollie did the same with the drawer beside him and found it full of used cake boards. He pushed it closed and walked across to the pedal bin. He stepped on the lever to flip up the lid. It was empty.

'Come on,' said Simon. 'Let's find what we're after and go.'

Christine looked across at Renouf, and then back down at the dash. He was speeding: 30mph west out of Town, further up the hill and into the country parishes. He'd come back into the canteen, his collar undone and with sweat on his forehead. Christine suspected he'd been crying. His already puffy eyes were red on the rims and he was blinking more than was normal. He'd dragged her away from Bichard with a 'come on, we haven't got time to waste talking,' and Bichard had nodded them off, telling them he'd station an officer there for the night and call as soon as he had any news.

'Marc,' she said, reaching across and touching the cuff of his shirt.

He looked at her quickly, then turned his eyes back to the road.

'One of us has been hurt already,' she said. 'I think that's enough, don't you?'

He eased off the gas.

'Sorry,' he said, puffing out his cheeks and sighing. 'Been a funny few days.'

'Want to talk about it?'

'It's Falla and...' He pursed his lips and shook his head. 'Just don't want to let this one get away. We lost a lot of time chasing Carey. Looks like we may have been wrong there. If Dixon's our man...' He indicated and turned them off the main road. 'We can start making some connections, that's all. Look at what they've got in common. See where the stories intersect.'

'We've still got no definitive proof that Carey wasn't involved,' she said. 'Nothing's changed on –'

'No,' he snapped. He looked at her again, the way he might look at a mischievous dog, reminding it who was in charge. 'No.'

He stared, for longer than was comfortable – long enough for them to have passed a school and a care home without him even noticing. 'Are you running this investigation, or am I?' he asked.

Christine folded her arms.

Ollie pushed open the door to the lounge. His visit at the start of the week had taken him through the hall to the kitchen and back; he'd merely glimpsed this room through a crack between the door and its frame.

It was small - about the same size as the kitchen - with a chair and two-seater settee. There was a small table pushed up against the wall, with one of its four chairs stacked on another to make space at the back. A cheap, modern bureau sat against the opposite wall, and on this was Rosalynd's laptop. The lid was closed, with three piles of paper strips neatly arranged on top.

Ollie picked up one of the piles and started to read through the notes.

2m37s - 3m05s Thoumine washing. Sentimental contrast to previous scene? Writer: unknown.

They'd each been written using a fine-tipped blue ballpoint that had pressed a deep line in the page. The writing itself was carefully rounded: somewhat feminine. Ollie felt sure he would have picked it out as the work of a woman, even if he hadn't known they'd been written by Rosalynd.

He riffled through the rest of them and guessed there were fifteen or so - forty-odd in the three stacks combined - most of which he skipped until he came to '14m52s End credits; back-announce'.

'What do you make of this?' he asked Simon, passing a few of them over.

Simon took them and held them close to his face. He moved his head along each line as he read them.

'These are characters from The Fleet,' he said, turning from one slip to the next. 'They look like production notes. Some kind of schedule or running order.'

'I got that from Thoumine,' Ollie said. 'What I mean is, what was she doing with them?'

'At a guess,' Simon said, after reading another two slips, 'this is what she was emailing about. Somewhere in here is the something strange about the last three episodes.'

Christine and Renouf came out on the west coast road. They paused at the junction, the sun setting straight ahead, the tip of each wave flaming red.

'Bichard has called for a psychological profiler,' Renouf said. 'Someone from the mainland, but they're pretty booked up. Reckons it could be another two days.'

'This could be over in another two days,' Christine said. 'If your hunch is right –'

'You're not convinced, are you?'

'I'm not decided either way. I didn't take to Dixon when he came in. I didn't take to him in the bookshop, either. I haven't met Carey other than on the beach. You've only met Dixon in passing, and then only through your wife. We've got to go on the facts alone,' she said. 'Keep it professional.'

'This is what you do, is it?'

'What?'

'This... this...' He couldn't think of an adequate description – something that wouldn't reflect poorly on himself.

'If you mean do I stick my nose in and advise my superiors on how to do their job, no.'

'You admit that's what you're doing, though.'

'No,' she said, worried that what had started as an amicable discussion was turning into something closely resembling a lovers' tiff. 'No, I'm not, but I do think you believe that's what I'm doing. I'm here to support you, Marc. Not undermine you. What I object to –'

Bip bip.

A car had pulled up behind them. Neither had noticed how long they'd been there, or how long the car had been waiting.

'Which way?' Renouf asked.

'Right.'

He put his hand out of the window and waved at the driver behind them, then put the car into first and turned.

Ollie lifted the lid of the laptop. It was an old Windows machine with a thick bezel around the screen, and faded keys with a deep travel that ended with a definite click. The battery was flat but the power cable was still plugged in. He switched it on at the mains and waited for it to resume.

It hadn't been switched off - merely put to sleep - but in the three days since it had last been used, it had spotted the drain on its battery and suspended itself more fully, writing the contents of every window to the drive and adopting a deeper sleep.

It took several minutes to restart, and Ollie used the time to read through the rest of the slips. Towards the end of the second stack he realised that each pile had been filtered to cover a specific set of characters. The second pile cycled fairly evenly between three of them, the third between just two.

'That stack you're holding there,' he asked Simon. 'Does it look like just one storyline?'

'Could be,' Simon said. 'It's just Thoumine, isn't it. Difficult to know what the story is, though. Just grunts and noise for the most part.'

The computer chimed and flashed up the Desktop.

'Thank goodness for lax security,' Ollie said, as it restored each of the suspended windows: a sound editing application, a notepad, and her email.

He clicked on the email app as a car drew up outside. It was already downloading new messages from the server, but Ollie ignored these and instead clicked back to the sent items folder.

Simon looked up as he heard the car doors open, feet step out, then the same doors slam closed.

Rosalynd's email to Ollie was still at the top of the stack. It was the last one she'd sent before she'd disappeared.

Simon stumbled across to the window, jarring his shin on the arm of the chair. He stood behind the curtains and pulled back the edge closest to the window frame. He squinted, but couldn't make out the make of car, or where its passengers might be now.

'Ollie...' he said.

Ollie shushed him.

Simon could see them now: two blurry figures walking towards the house.

'Ollie, really...'

'One second.'

Ollie opened the email and clicked the Forward button, then typed their addresses into the new message. It auto-completed both of them, indicating that Rosalynd had emailed Simon before, too – probably during her time at the BBC.

'What is it?'

'We have to go.'

'What?'

'There's someone –'

The sound of a key sliding into the lock excused him from carrying on.

The laptop was still grinding away, apparently unable to decide whether to finish downloading new content or forward an old message on.

'Come on,' Ollie said. He'd have to leave it to work it out for itself. He grabbed Simon's hand, dragging him through the living room and into the kitchen. The back door was still open. He pushed Simon ahead of him, then stepped through it himself as Renouf and Christine came into the small hallway. He quietly closed the door behind them.

Christine was the first to enter. She heard something click at the back of the house.

'Hello,' she called out. 'Police. Is anybody there?'

There was no response. Renouf stepped in and pushed past her, then strode up the hall and into the kitchen. He looked around the empty room, and his eyes fell on the door, with its taped-up window and the crystals of glass stuck to one corner. The keys were still swinging in the lock.

He opened it and looked left and right down the side passage, catching a glimpse of Ollie and Simon as they ran around the corner and out of sight. He recognised them both and breathed a sigh of relief. Lucky escape.

Christine came up behind him.

'Did you see them?' she asked.

'Long gone.'

He pulled the door closed before she could look out.

'Best get forensics down here,' she said, pulling out her phone. 'See if they can find any prints.' She nodded at the window. 'Looks like a professional job.'

Renouf had to agree. If this was Carey, he'd planned well ahead.

'Let's get Clarke down here for tonight,' he said. 'He can sit outside in a car. Forensics won't thank us for getting them out at this time of night. Not for a break-in.'

Christine opened her mouth, then closed it again.

'Fair enough,' she said, pocketing her phone.

She put her hands behind her back to avoid the temptation to touch anything, and ran her eyes along the surfaces. Nothing seemed to have been disturbed. A couple of the drawers were out of alignment, but other than that it was all pretty square.

Renouf went back to the hall and she followed, then she led him into the lounge. She wasn't surprised how small it was: she could tell from the outside that there wouldn't be too much space beyond the front door. It was cluttered, though. She would have lost the bureau and moved the laptop onto the table. How many people who live alone eat at a dining table anyway?

The laptop was still turned on, the email app open as it processed some background tasks. She thought little of it until it made a whooshing sound –

– a whooshing sound she knew well –

– the same one her own computer made every time it dispatched a new message.

'Marc,' she said, calling him over. He'd positioned himself to one side of the window and pulled back the curtain to look out discreetly.

She went to the laptop and looked more closely. The email app had been set to take up the whole of the screen. It was downloading messages, slowly – she could see that from the way that the numbers beside the word 'Inbox' were ticking up one or two at a time.

But the inbox wasn't open. It was showing a list of sent items, the most recent of which was time-stamped within the last minute.

'Marc,' she said again, turning now. She pointed back towards the screen. 'I think we may just know who we may just have missed.'

TWO YEARS AGO

Renouf steered the boat to Beaucette Marina, all the while thinking things through. The only thing he was sure about was the fact that the pot had been empty. There had been no flask, and there'd been no money either, which could have meant one of two things: the cargo had never been left but the money had gone all the same, or he'd gone to the wrong pot himself.

He berthed the boat and dug around below the wheel to find the most recent Sarnian. He turned on the cabin light and folded back the pages until he got to the personals page. He double-checked the ad. 50 to 60, 44901. That's what he thought. Right pots, right day, right time. So where was the cargo?

It should have been an easy job. Retrieve the flask, leave it beneath the steep iron steps that ran down the cliff to Joannet, then press the gum onto the bench and go home. Somebody else would take it from there, and Renouf neither knew nor cared who that was. He had never signed up for this - not for getting his hands dirty. He was supposed to be a lookout, no more - someone to watch the files at police headquarters and warn them if ever their names should appear.

He killed the light and the engine and tied up the boat against one of the piers. It was close to two o'clock by then. Far too late to head home, so he drove to the office and slept at his desk - uncomfortably, fitfully - until six o'clock when the night shift knocked off and the cleaners arrived with their vacuums. He rose and went out in search of some food.

The streets were still empty, almost. The States workers were out picking litter, the hotel staff were just clocking on. Overnight porters were leaving their various desks; the chambermaids and serving staff were readying for breakfast.

He passed a short woman with muscular build and small red trainers with clamshell toes. He smiled, but she frowned, and she walked straight past him, apparently caught by something in Creasey's window.

'Bitch,' he said, under his breath, not loud enough to be heard. He thought that she looked familiar, and wondered where their paths might have crossed. He wasn't often out on the street at that time - not since he'd taken a job at a desk in preference to wearing out shoes on the beat. He supposed she was just a seasonal worker, so maybe he'd seen her shopping, or out exploring the rest of the island before her tenure came to an end.

He turned at the end of the High Street and skipped up the steps to the Market Square. They were wet, recently hosed, with puddles sitting in each of the dips. The cleaners were still in view, scrubbing the street close to the church, yet here on the step they seemed to have missed a white line. A narrow, straight, undulant stroke that crested the rough granite tread.

He skipped up the first two steps, then stopped, the line now directly beside him, its purpose suddenly clear. This was the signal – the mark they used to acknowledge his gum on the bench. But he'd left no gum. He had nothing to tell them. There had been no cargo, so nothing for them to collect.

Unless, of course, someone else had carelessly left their own gum, unknowingly, innocently, ignorantly, on the paw of the lowest lion carved on the shield on the side of the bench.

He took the rest of the steps in pairs, ran to the Square and counted off each bench as he passed them, expecting to see the clear defacement stuck to the end of the last in the line.

There was nothing. No gum, and no sign that any had been there, either. The cleaners had not yet reached the square, so unless it had fallen off... he looked beneath it, checked the soles of his shoes, swept his eyes across the paving.

There was no gum. The ground was clean, the crest was clean, and all three lions stared back at him. None was obscured by a sticky grey gob.

He thought for a moment, then turned and walked slowly back to the steps. The puddles were starting to drain between them, the stonework either side of the line now dry. The mark must have been made after they'd been cleaned. It was fresh. Just a few minutes old. It was almost certainly there for him.

He looked to either end of the street, as far as the church to his right and up to the curve in the short run of shops to the left. Just a handful of people, aside from the cleaners, nobody hanging around, nobody looking suspicious. The woman with the shoes had –

The shoes!

He had seen her before, or her shoes at least. He remembered them now, from the last time he'd been to the Guet – when he'd left a message and hurried back to the bench only to find the two women there, sitting, chatting, sharing their apples. That's when he'd seen them, tucked beneath a table on the opposite side of the square.

It must have been her who had left the mark, plugging the obvious gap in their arrangements. The system only worked in one direction: when he needed to tell them that he wanted to leave a note. They'd never agreed on a signal with which they could tell him to pick up a message themselves or, indeed, where they might leave one.

Instead they communicated via The Sarnian personals column.

'Mature gentleman seeks cultured lady, 50 to 60 for outdoor pursuits, cliff walks, fishing expeditions. Sausmarez area. ALA. Box 44901.'

The wording changed every time; the key was the box number. 44901 identified the marker buoys attached to the empty lobster pot. 82184 was a matching pot behind Jethou. 2306 was sited close to Fort Grey. 9312 was in deep water a mile and a half off Alderney, easily found by projecting a line from the end of the Braye Harbour breakwater.

The ages - 40, 50, 60 and 70 - signified midnight, 1am, 2am and 3am, such that a cultured lady aged 50 to 60 - by far the most common - indicated a pickup some time between one and two in the morning. Renouf dreaded finding an advert for anyone aged much older.

But it was worth it. It paid well: eight thousand euros per pick-up, straight into the bank. Four days later he'd transfer it out to fund the continued costs of the house – the one he was building on the edge of the common. Their retirement home, the one to which they'd move, with space and views and none of the traffic of Route Militaire.

The system worked, in its own way. It was fairly efficient, but messages had to be planned in advance, submitted in line with the newspaper deadlines – and that meant a last-minute entry simply wasn't an option.

So is that what this was?

His own system used in reverse?

A simple chalk mark, which seemed to answer no mark of his own, sending him up to the Guet?

He ran to headquarters and picked up his car, glad that he'd ventured out early, as one shift went off and the other came on. It meant he'd avoided the peak morning traffic, and he made it across to the opposite coast in less than ten minutes, two Dairy lorries and one yellow tanker the only vehicles sharing the road.

The Guet was cold when he reached it. The sun was still rising and hadn't yet warmed the rocks on which it was built. The first few rays were touching the sands of Cobo Bay as he stood on the edge and looked down, and off to either side from there they were catching the glass of the lighthouse, and lighting the flag that hung loose on the pole at Grosse Rocque.

He eased the loose mortar out of the crack, and sure enough, tucked in behind it, he found a thin slip of paper. He took it out and pressed the mortar back into place, then carefully unravelled it as he carried it back to the car. It was covered in numbers, as he'd suspected, arranged into four-digit blocks. The first four digits, 6176, told him where to start in the sequence stored in the note on his phone. He worked his way through them in turn, subtracting the numbers pair by pair from those written down on the paper.

It felt unfamiliar, working in reverse like that – he'd never decoded a message before, only encrypted those he needed to send. Slowly, one by one, block by block, minute by minute, the numbers revealed themselves as logical letters: pointed, clipped and threatening.

Consider this a warning, Mr Renouf.

That was it. Six common words, but what they meant was no clearer now than when they'd been hidden behind the meaningless numbers.

He pressed the lighter into its socket and read through the note three more times. It proved he'd correctly made sense of the narrow chalk mark, at least. Holding him responsible for the missing flask, though, was –

Pop.

The lighter jumped up, its cycle complete and the end glowing hot in the dash. Renouf pulled it out and he held the end against the paper until the fibres caught light. They quickly started to smoke, the paper curling up on itself like a dying insect, reaching up for his fingers, trying to fight them off.

He opened his door and dropped it, and as it fell it touched the needles and some of them took up the flame. Underneath they were dusty and dry, but those on the top were still slightly damp, too fresh to have dehydrated. They smouldered, but didn't go up before all that was left were the charred remains and the first three letters of 'warning'. He crushed the ashes beneath his foot and held it there for a moment, starving them of oxygen to be sure the fire was out.

It was seven o'clock. Still early – time enough for a shower, a fresh set of clothes from his locker, and then he'd return to his desk and try to forget what had happened that morning –

– and, more to the point, his cold wasted night on the water.

He closed the door and clipped his seatbelt,

then turned on the radio just in time to catch the end of the news. Traffic was slowing the routes into Town, the Southampton flight had left behind schedule and the fire brigade had blocked the road through the common. A new-build house was ablaze and the fire had already brought down the roof.

DAY SEVEN

The Huffin' Puffin, 9.10am

Ollie weathered a night of rough dreams in which Christine Le Page had arrived at Rosalynd's door with her keys.

He watched her shuffle and shake them until she turned up a bright copper Yale key. She slipped it into the lock and he turned and fled. He reached out for Simon, but floated straight past, his feet lifting up as he found himself caught on an incoming tide. The faster he ran the more his feet simply cycled beneath him. He tried to part the thick, buoyant air with his hands, but that only brought forth enough to replace what he'd pushed behind, and as Christine unlocked the door and pushed it open she found him suspended before her.

'Carey?' she said. 'Oliver Carey?'

He tried to reply, but before he could say the first word she was joined by someone else, and a shuffling of feet and a shifting of chairs. He couldn't see who was making the noise from where he was hanging - all he could do was hear them.

And then he heard Renouf.

...

...

He shot up, wide awake now, and turned to the radio set by his bed. The alarm had come on; it was BBC Guernsey, broadcasting a live press briefing. Renouf and Le Page were talking. He heard the word 'Holdbrook', and turned it up. Renouf concluded his statement and asked the crowd if they had any questions.

'Lady at the back,' he said.

The microphones couldn't pick her up, but Renouf repeated the question before he went on to answer it. 'No,' he said. 'We're not in a position to say how she died. As soon as we have that information we'll naturally release what we can. Gentleman here?'

'Is there anything to suggest a motive?' This from someone closer to the front. Ollie heard it clearly enough, and recognised Alfie Erne.

Renouf cleared his throat. 'Again, we're unable to make any comment on that at this point. We are, however, examining Miss Holdbrook's property and will report back in due course.'

'Are you linking this death to the break-in?' Alfie again.

'No.' Renouf paused. 'However, it is early days just now, and we're not closing off any line of enquiry at this stage. Yes, sir. You...'

'Was Miss Holdbrook killed on the slipway?'

'At this stage, we can't say, although from the position in which the body was found we suspect not.'

'She was carried in on the tide?'

'That would appear to be so.'

'Can you say when she died?'

'No. We are conducting tests on the body that should reveal the time of death in due course. However, at this early stage we have reason to believe that she had been dead for several days. Lady over there...'

Ollie heard a rustle of fabric that suggested Renouf was pointing to someone else in the crowd. The voice this time was the clearest yet, and Ollie recognised Amy Sloane.

'Are you looking for anyone in particular?'

Renouf may have shaken his head, as it took him a moment to start his reply. 'Having only recently discovered the body of Miss Holdbrook –'

'If I might answer this question...' A third voice interrupted him. A female voice. 'As Inspector Renouf was about to explain, until we've had time to properly examine the body - and Miss Holdbrook's house - we shan't be in a position to narrow down, or indeed formulate a list of potential suspects. However, two -'

'I'm sorry.' Alfie cut her off. 'Could we have your name? For the record.'

'Christine Le Page.' There was a sound of tapping wood, which Ollie guessed was Christine drumming her pen on the wooden nameplate propped on the desk before her. 'I'm working alongside Inspector Renouf on this case.' She paused, waiting for Alfie's next question, then carried on a moment later much as she would if she'd never been interrupted. 'However, two names are of particular interest to us at this point.'

There was a generous murmur and the sound of an anxious congregation shifting in the pews.

'I think that's –' Renouf began, but Christine cut in.

'As of yet we're not linking the break-in at Miss Holdbrook's house to the discovery of her body on the slipway yesterday morning,' she continued. 'Inspector Renouf and myself arrived on the scene of the break-in shortly after the intruders left the property through the rear garden. Upon entering the house we observed that Miss Holdbrook's computer was switched on, and her email client was active. Examination of her outbox indicates that the intruder or intruders may have sent a file from that computer. We have no reason to suspect that the recipients were in any way involved in Miss Holdbrook's disappearance or death, nor the break-in, but naturally we would like to speak to them regarding this matter.'

As she'd been speaking, the background chatter had slowly been growing. Now it reached its climax. She trailed off as questions came in from all sides, with nobody waiting their turn.

'How did they make their escape?'

'Did they leave any fingerprints?'

'Have you got any clues?'

Ollie flopped back on the bunk and reached out his hand to stroke Sampson. He knew what was coming. The only obvious question. The one he would have asked himself. The one towards which Christine had steered them. In the end it was Alfie who made himself heard above the rest of the crowd.

'Who received the email?'

Marc Renouf banged his nameplate down on the desk. 'Thank you, ladies and gentlemen. I'm afraid that's all we have time for.'

The uproar grew louder still as the press protested Renouf's evasive manoeuvre. Then came the crack of the nameplate again - louder this time, to puncture the rowdy commotion - and the voice of Christine Le Page.

'The recipients of the email, with whom we would very much like to speak, are likely known to most of you. Simon Langlois of BBC Radio Guernsey and Oliver Carey of The Sarnian,' she said, before adding for clarity, 'the man who discovered the body in Marble Bay.'

St Peter Port, 9.25am

Simon felt the teapot. It was cold. It had sat there two hours, and been his largely neglected company as he pulled the sound file to pieces.

He still couldn't understand what he was hearing. Or, more to the point, why Rosalynd would have chosen to repeat the same set of moans and groans time and time again. Was it some comment on George Dixon's acting, or had she heard something else?

He flipped up the glass on his watch and felt the hands. Almost half nine; he needed to leave. He gathered the pot and his mug and plate on the tray, and took them back to the kitchen. He'd drop Ollie an email and see if he'd got anywhere with it himself.

The Sarnian, 10.40am

Ollie had downloaded the file as soon as he'd got back to the Huffin' Puffin. He'd listened to it once, then put it on his phone and listened to it twice through the following morning, while riding into Town.

...woaaah, woaaah, uhgugh uhgugh, woaghuh woaghuh...

He couldn't understand why Rosalynd would have chosen to snip out those parts of the broadcast and lace them together. Ollie had heard the episodes. They didn't run that way. Thomas Thoumine – George Dixon – may have become more repetitive since his accident... but what else could the scriptwriters do? He'd been damaged, he'd lost his ability to speak. If he couldn't make these expressive noises, then what?

Ollie arrived at the newsroom to find the front page pinned to the wall. The lead was a snap of the Saints Bay Road, which was grainy and smeared, suggesting whoever had taken it had used their mobile phone in a hurry. A mangled car at the edge of the frame was wedged against one of the steep granite walls.

The photo was uncredited, but the block of dummy text below it was headed by Ollie's byline, and he knew even before he entered her office that Freya would ask him to fill in the blanks.

'Sit,' she said, pointing to the round meeting table. She picked up a bundle of papers and joined him. 'So, tell me about the email.'

'Email?'

'Rosalynd Holdbrook's email.'

Ollie could feel his back start to stiffen. He forced himself to slouch and he slowly shook his head.

Freya turned over the first sheet of paper. 'I quote: "...two names are of particular interest to us at this point..."' She ran her finger down the narrow columns of shorthand until she came to the next significant sentence. '"The recipients of the email, with whom we would very much like to speak, are Simon Langlois and Oliver Carey, the man who discovered the body in Marble Bay." That email.' She put down the page and sat back in her chair. 'The email from Rosalynd Holdbrook's computer.'

'I can't speak for Simon, but apart from the usual spam...' He shrugged. 'That's all I've had at home for days. Jokes and stuff, but... I can check my account here –'

'Don't bother.'

'It might have –'

She put up a hand. 'I know what's in your inbox and your outbox and all of your folders, and it concerns me how much time you appear to spend researching whatever became of your father.'

'I think you'll find you're not allowed to do that.'

'I think you'll find I don't care. My concern

is this paper, above and before all else, and I don't want to hear about stories like this from third parties. Now was there any email from Rosalynd Holdbrook?'

'In my inbox, no.'

'And Simon Langlois?'

'You'll have to ask him.'

Freya raised her eyebrows.

'I'll ask him,' Ollie corrected himself.

'This is a dream story, Carey. Why don't you see that?'

'I do.'

'Then act like it. Amy Sloane practically beat you to the big reveal despite you finding the body. I haven't seen an interview with George Dixon yet. No useable quotes from Rosalynd Holdbrook before she turned up dead, and then your own name comes up in a briefing. Initial pictures of Ibbott aside, it's all been dog-eared leads from third-hand sources. I want us to make the news, not report it.'

'It's also been less than a week.'

Freya dropped her pen on the desk. 'Six bloody issues and a Sunday special. Just three with this as the lead. That's four - four - missed opportunities.' She stood up and walked out of the office, pulled the dummy front page from its pin on the wall and brought it back. She dropped it down on the table.

'Facts are few and far between,' she said, pointing at the crashed car. 'Ella Brouard's been hitting the phones since six but nobody's talking. Redeem yourself.'

'Whose is it?'

'Your friend Renouf.'

'Marc Renouf?'

Freya grunted. 'Your inspector.'

'He's no friend of mine,' Ollie said.

'Then make friends with him.'

'Do you really think, considering what's been –'

Freya leaned forward. 'I really do think, yes. You have an in. Use it.'

'But the email...'

'What about it?'

'You were at that briefing. They think there was an email. They want to talk to me about Rosalynd Holdbrook.'

'No they don't.'

'You heard what they said.'

'What they said was mainland talk. How big is this island?'

Ollie thought. 'Eight by –'

'Never mind. The point is nothing's more than half an hour from anywhere else. They know where you live, they know where you work, and they've known about that email since yesterday. Have you seen any police in that time? Anyone at all.'

Ollie shook his head. 'Nobody.'

'They're not interested in you. Why they said it, I don't know, but this...' – she tapped the page with a finger – 'could be your way to find out.'

Ollie picked it up. 'How many words?'

'As many as you need. I'll move stuff around. The front section goes at four thirty. Get it over by four.'

'I'll look again for that email,' he said, walking across to the door.

'You do that,' Freya told him. 'And if you find it, you forward it straight to me. Last chance, Carey. Don't let me read this story anywhere else.'

He stepped out into the newsroom.

'Or any other story, come to that,' she called as he pulled the door to.

BBC Radio Guernsey, 11am

Simon was late. He'd spent too long playing the clips back and forth, and by the time he'd left the flat, he'd missed the bus into Town. He ended up walking, and arrived to find his editor waiting.

'So?' she asked.

'So?'

'This email. What was in it?'

'Pfft.' He puffed out his cheeks. 'You tell me.

Nothing in my inbox. Not at home, and I checked this one before I came in.' He twitched his head towards his computer. 'Want me to chase it up?'

'You've checked your spam?'

He nodded and she rubbed her eyes with the heel of each hand. She was halfway through her shift, and Simon could tell from the way she was talking - slightly slower, slightly flatter - that the hours were starting to take their toll.

'Put in a couple of calls, then,' she said. 'But get in there and do some quotes.' She pointed towards the studio. 'I can't have you reading today. Not when you're in the news. You can do some forward planning. See what you can get from States Police, then run through your inbox and see what's ripe for some longer reports next week. Oh, and get that cliff story finished, too, will you.'

The Pleinmont cliff walk. So much had happened since he'd made the recording that Simon had almost forgotten about it. He'd clipped together a rough cut already, just for timing and content, but the levels needed rounding off. He ought to reduce the background noise, maybe tighten up a few of the edits. Right now, the whole exercise felt entirely irrelevant, but he knew that those who had been on the walk would still be waiting, eager to hear it.

He recorded his quotes, then settled down at

his desk and played back the sloppily stitched-up walk. He let his mind wander, straining at the leash of concentration, his eyes turning away from the screen and staring as far as they could towards the middle distance.

He made a few half-hearted cuts and removed a second here and there, snipping out irrelevant comments, replacing them with ambient noise – the sound of the wind on the cliffs, the sea below the old wooden bench where the visitors sat and looked out at the lighthouse, the cry of the circling birds.

The words were washing over him, his head's internal soundtrack replaying Rosalynd's re-cut Fleet, his own report answering back the unnaturally clustered groupings of fictional characters, now lined up together and making no sense.

He tapped the space bar to stop the playback and dropped the file onto the server. It would have to do. From there, they'd pick it up in the studio, and sooner or later play it out. It wasn't his best production, but it was gone – done – and his mind turned back to The Fleet.

He looked at the uploaded file, sitting on the server, just an icon now in a window, no longer a graphical sound wave. In a column beside it, running up and down the edge of the window was a list of familiar folder names. Dragspot,

Datavol, News, Backup, Drama, CMS, Documents, Archive, Shared...

One in particular held his attention.

The Fleet lived in the Drama folder. Weeks and weeks of episodes, running back through several months, with older editions archived off to a data vault somewhere in Bristol.

He moved his mouse towards it, minded to click on the folder and open the store, to scroll back through the last week or two and load the original files - the ones from which Rosalynd had clipped out the random sounds. He wanted to hear the raw recordings - to see how they'd been interleaved, slotted in between the other characters to build a complete storyline, to see whether they made any more sense when they weren't neatly ordered in such a logical manner.

His finger hovered, he rolled the mouse across the desk, then click, cli-

He stopped himself. This wasn't the time or the place. He closed the window and turned to his email. The sound files would have to wait.

His inbox was showing a dozen new notes. Two from shops in St Peter Port promoting their seasonal sales. Timetable updates for the boats linking Guernsey to Herm. A note from the States about parking restriction in place for the next few weeks in St Sampson. He marked them as read, then opened an internal memo.

'Chaps,' it began. The language was clipped, with accurate grammar largely ignored. 'London on the phone. TV's been trawling off Sark for...'

He ran his eyes through the rest of the email - as far as the signature - and then looked at the forwarded message below it. It was the original note from London, referring back to a factual team in Cardiff. He felt a shock of adrenaline, a heat in his belly that quickly spread, chilling his legs, causing his fingers to tingle. He picked up the phone and could feel his palms getting clammy against the receiver.

'Carey,' Ollie said, as he picked it up at the opposite end.

'Ollie. It's Simon.'

'Simon, fella.' Ollie sounded distracted. 'Can I call you back? I'm on deadline. Freya needs my copy by four.'

'No, listen.' Simon scrolled back to the top of the memo. 'Email from the boss.'

'Simon, really -'

'Listen. "London on the phone. TV's been trawling off Sark for weekday series, daytime - marine archaeology. Talking heads required, unscripted.'

'I can't do TV -'

Simon shushed him. 'They've found some stuff.' He skipped down to a list within the main body. '"Flotsam inc lifebelt (liner), spent flare casings (possibly trawler / lifeboat), rigging, ship's bell - brass, scuffed, possibly engraved 'Puffin'?? No fee. Come through me if available / interested. Qs?"'

'Huffin' Puffin?'

'Well, it doesn't say that, but how many boatyards would call a boat something Puffin?'

Ollie pictured his boat, and the hook on the rear of the landing deck where an empty eye had once been home to a bell. He remembered it clearly from growing up, how his father would let him stand on the chair and ring it as they left the harbour - and how his mother would call from the beach for him to get down and stay below the line of the rail.

He hadn't seen it since he'd returned to the island, and he'd found himself wondering, now and then, whether he wasn't remembering something far older than the reality. Had his subconscious mind built up the bell to something it wasn't? Was it something his father had got rid of years ago? Maybe his mind was recreating a different boat altogether?

But if this were the one...

'Are you there?' Simon asked.

'Do you really think...'

'Why do you think I'd be calling?'

'But it said Puffin,' Ollie said. 'No mention of Huffin. It could be... I don't know, but couldn't it be...'

'Ollie, listen. This is it. This is what you've been searching for.'

'But the name...'

'Is Huffin' Puffin. You know it is. It was scuffed. It says so here. The Huffin' bit's been scraped on the rocks. How long is it now since...' He clawed for a better way of phrasing it. 'How long since he disappeared?'

'Two years.'

'There you go.'

They listened to each other for a moment: Simon waiting for some kind of affirmative response, Ollie not wanting to believe that this could be the confirmation he'd been chasing since his return.

'What are you working on?' Simon asked, his voice calm and reassuring.

'Oh, nothing.' Ollie looked back at his screen. He tapped the mouse around his desk. 'Renouf crashed his car. I assume it was him, but nobody's talking. Freya's running it front page lead.'

'How many words?'

'Four hundred? Maybe five. There's not much to go on. We'll re-run some profile copy and drop in a box of stats.'

'That's forty minutes if you push yourself,' Simon said, equating the words to a three-minute feature. 'Get it done and dig through the files for whatever they've got on a wreckage off Sark.'

The Sarnian, 4.00pm

Simon was right. Ollie finished his story well ahead of his deadline, and with more words – relevant ones – than he needed to fill the existing frames. He sent an email around the team, told art to make space for six hundred words, and saved the file to a local folder. His deadline was nearly an hour away, and although he knew that the subs would start work on his copy as soon as they could, he held off sending it up to the server.

He wanted them to think he was still at work, trimming, refining and sharpening up the story, when all the while he was following up Simon's lead. He clicked on the browser and opened two windows: one, the paper's internal archive; the other, a newswire to which it subscribed.

He started to search.

Searching for 'Sark' alone was too blunt an option. It turned up close to six thousand results on the archive server, and two hundred more on the newswire. 'Wreckage' was no more selective. 'Sark shipwreck' drew a blank on the newswire, but called up a list of seven entries in the local database. One concerned a local fishing boat - nothing to do with the Huffin' Puffin - three were dive stories, and the rest involved the Cutty Sark, the London tourist attraction damaged by fire.

He sat back for a moment and pulled at his bottom lip. He tried searching for Huffin' Puffin, something he'd done several times before, but still the local results were blank, while the newswire talked of Mario Brothers, a Canadian marathon and various lyrical references to drugs.

He looked at the clock. He'd already used half an hour. Fifteen minutes more and he'd upload his words to the server. He started pairing up less likely combinations. Sark and trawler, Sark and yacht - despite the fact it was far from a yacht - Sark and motor vessel. In desperation he returned to simply 'Sark', and narrowed the field of relevance to just the day his father disappeared, and the three days either side.

The newswire list was blank. In the neighbouring window, The Sarnian database turned up a single result: 'Sarkees' Scrutinised Sea Smash Statement Still Stands'.

Guernsey authorities have downplayed reports of a weekend collision off the coast of Sark, stating that no debris has been found, and no boats are reported missing.

Three residents living close to the Seigneurie in the northern part of Greater Sark, the smallest of the four main islands within the Bailiwick, telephoned Guernsey Police and Harbour Master's office shortly after midnight on Sunday with claims that two or more boats had been spotted in rough seas off shore.

The vessels disappeared below the cliffs for some minutes, according to witnesses who reported sounds of a collision shortly thereafter. None of those to whom The Sarnian has spoken was able to say with certainty whether the sound was that of the two boats colliding, or a single vessel making contact with the cliff. There was further dispute as to whether the second vessel left the area shortly after.

At a hastily convened briefing this morning, Inspector Marc Renouf of Guernsey police told reporters that officers from the force had been dispatched to the island the following morning, and he had personally –

'Carey!'

Ollie jumped, and looked up to see Freya leaning against the door of the hive, one hand on her hip, the other pointing towards him.

'You,' she said. 'In here. Switch off your Mac and bring your bag.'

Ollie did as she said. He sent the story up to the server, then picked up his bag and followed her into the office.

'Don't sit down,' she said, seeing him move towards the visitor's chair. 'You won't be staying.' She walked around her desk and swivelled her screen so that Ollie could see the page she'd been reading. 'What is this?' she asked, pointing to the open browser window.

Ollie immediately recognised an image of himself at the top of the page. It had been taken with a long lens, most likely that morning, as he was wearing the same jumper he had on now. He was riding his bike past the piers, after descending the hill into Town for his final approach to the newspaper's waterfront office.

'I... I don't know,' he said.

She turned back the screen and started to read it aloud.

Oliver Carey, The Sarnian's sporty newshound...

– she looked at him and raised her eyebrows –

...found himself at the centre of the investigation on which he is supposed to be reporting as States of Guernsey Police yesterday named him a prime suspect in the deaths of two island women.

Carey, 32, with a strong, defined jaw and a seemingly

permanent chin-and-jaw shadow, claimed to have discovered the body of Richelle Ibbott when cooling down during his thrice weekly sprint along the rocky east coast. Carey is known to swim naked at secluded spots around the island.

'I don't see how –' Ollie began, but Freya raised her hand and continued.

Police now suspect that athletic Carey, single following the break-up of his long-term relationship some two years ago, may have had more to do with Miss Ibbott's death than previously assumed.

Historically reliable sources inform me that Carey and Inspector Marc Renouf, who is leading the inquiry into the deaths of both Miss Ibbott and former BBC Guernsey producer Rosalynd Holdbrook, undertook a clandestine tete-a-tete in the sheltered kiosk garden at Port Soif. There, Renouf presented Carey with damning evidence found close to where Miss Ibbott's body had been left on the beach.

A small portable radio and a set of inexpensive stereo earphones, likely bought on the kind of budget one cannot avoid when earning the wage of a novice scribe on a minor provincial paper, have been sent to the mainland for analysis. Police believe that examination of the wax deposited on the earbuds may help them to finger the killer.

Sports people, and runners in particular, frequently

use earbuds of this sort when working out in the belief that listening to music helps maintain momentum and motivation.

Carey declined to comment on the matter, although...

'...blah blah blah.' Freya sat back in her chair. She pushed away her keyboard and looked at him in silence.

'Amy Sloane?' Ollie asked.

Freya nodded slowly.

'Well, then she has a source on the inside.'

'Undoubtedly. And I thought I did too.' She pointed across the table. 'Did you meet with Renouf?'

Ollie let his eyes drift away, freeing themselves of her gaze and wandering on, past her face and the high back of her chair, past the small cluster of trophies the paper had won and on to the picture windows that drew in the view of the sea. Spotless, cleaned every week, they comprised the whole of the fourth glass wall, completing the pure, clear cube that Freya worked in.

'We met last week,' he said at last, after watching a boat score a line through the waves. 'He called me.'

'At Port Soif?'

'It wasn't long. He just... he was there when I got there, and he was gone five minutes later.

That's all. There was nothing useful. Nothing I could report on.'

'And this radio?'

'He did have a radio.'

'And?'

'I'd never seen it before.'

'It wasn't yours?'

'No. Nor the earbuds, but Renouf –'

'Suggested they might be yours?'

'Yes.'

'And you didn't think this was important?'

'Of course I did,' he shot back. He'd followed the boat across the horizon, but now it had gone, swallowed up by the bow of the ferry. He let his eyes carry on, tracing its unseen path through the larger vessel until they alighted once more on her profile. 'I see that now. Maybe not then but it was... if you'd been...' He searched for an appropriate word. Accused was too strong. Blamed? Charged? '...linked to a crime – a murder – would you put that in the paper?'

'That's for me to decide,' she said, her voice still level and calm. In all the time he'd been working for her, he'd heard her raise it just twice. Neither time had it carried the crisp, cool menace implicit within the more measured tones she used to berate her staff. She turned the chair to face him and spread her arms wide, standing up and gripping the opposite ends of her desk.

An image flashed through his mind, of the female mantis stretching her limbs, dominating the male of her species shortly before the post-coital kill. 'I edit this paper, Carey. Not you. You are employed to bring me the stories; I make the call as to whether and when they appear in print. This...' – she nodded towards the screen – 'this is the biggest story of your career: a career that could well be over before it's even started.'

She stared at him for a moment. 'Do you understand?'

'Freya, I –'

'No,' she said, her voice ice cold, heavy with disappointment. 'You swore to me there was nothing else, that we had the full story. I didn't need to worry, you said. But I did, didn't I. Amy Sloane is a hack. A gossip. She's a columnist who doesn't know how to spell integrity, let alone define it, yet here she is, with the biggest scoop of the last seven days, and where are we?'

'There's nothing else,' Ollie said, feeling himself shrinking before her. 'That's it. Really. Unless she knows something I don't.'

Freya scowled and Ollie mentally kicked himself for introducing more doubt.

'It won't happen again,' he promised.

'Too right,' she said. She released the desk and picked up the phone, dialling a four-digit number. Ollie heard it ring in the newsroom.

'Can you come in?' she asked, then replaced the receiver without leaving time for an answer.

For the next ten seconds – ten that felt like a minute – they studied each other in silence. Ollie knew that whatever he said would make things worse, not better. At last he heard the door click open, and as he turned he saw Ella Brouard behind him.

'Escort Mr Carey out of the building,' Freya told her. 'We'll send on his personal things.' She looked back at Ollie. 'Until this case is resolved, or until you bring me something worth printing, you're suspended on full pay. Hand in your pass at reception. Once this story's over, we'll meet with HR and discuss where we take it from there.'

Route de Jerbourg, 5pm

Dixon slid his chicken under the grill. A pot of sauce was heating on the stove.

Not so bad, he thought, as he sat on a stool and licked the end of a pencil. He turned over an unopened envelope and started to sketch out a meal plan. His abortive trip to the store the night he'd killed Rosalynd had left him rather low on supplies. This was the last chicken fillet, and though he'd have to check the pantry before he could say for certain, he was fairly sure the same was true of the sauce.

He was getting accustomed to cooking, and found himself wondering why Richelle had made such a fuss, complaining that he didn't do his share when all she needed to do was stand there a while, slice things up and throw them in a pan.

He thought of her now, how she used to stand by the gas ring, a cigarette in one hand, a glass of white wine in the other, the condensation wetting her fingers, and they'd talk about his day. His lines, what was going on at the station, what was going to happen to Thomas Thoumine after his fall.

He wondered why he'd not been able to trust her. Why had he never been able to tell her the truth? Perhaps, if he had, if she'd been the sort who would listen without looking at him the way she did, like she was judging, like she was itching to tell her friends... well, she paid a high price, didn't she. Perhaps if she'd been able to listen the way he'd have wanted, he wouldn't have needed to hide.

He wouldn't have been on the beach.

She wouldn't have found him.

She'd be here, cooking his dinner.

And Dixon wouldn't be writing out menial meal plans.

The sauce was starting to spit. He returned

to the stove and stirred it, turning up the radio as he passed it. The presenter was signing off with talk of events on the mainland, then handing back to the local stations for dropped-in regional news.

The pips, the jingle, and then a new voice. Unfamiliar, female, one he'd not heard before, with rounded vowels and deeper notes. Richelle had taken the lead again, Rosalynd beside her as the States Police...

...revealed a new lead in the hunt for the killer following a break-in at the house of Rosalynd Holdbrook, former BBC producer, whose body was found at Saints Harbour on Friday morning...

So they'd discovered the break-in. He was surprised they'd taken so long. His stirring slowed and he let the spoon settle on the base of the pan.

...when they attended the property yesterday afternoon. In a highly unusual Sunday briefing at Police Headquarters, Inspector Marc Renouf of Guernsey Police and Christine Le Page, currently on secondment from Jersey, named The Sarnian's Oliver Carey and BBC Radio Guernsey's Simon Langlois, as persons with whom they'd like to speak in relation to the break-in yesterday evening. Although police have not yet revealed the reason for their interest in the pair, it is understood that they had already left the house by the time...

Dixon jumped as the sauce spat at his hand. He lifted it off the heat and stirred it quickly to cool the bottom of the pan.

So Carey and his incompetent sidekick were suspects one and two... Dixon smiled. The police here truly were as hopeless as he'd suspected. He opened the drawer for a corkscrew. This called for a celebration.

The dominoes were starting to fall, and he had no reason to stay. He tore up his meal plan and started instead to plan his escape. If Langlois and Carey were in the frame, he could leave without arousing suspicion. He'd book a flight after dinner and leave the island – whatever the cost – before they changed their mind.

The Sarnian, 5pm

'Can I take something?' Ella asked, nodding towards the lift. Ollie had hoisted his bag on his back and was wheeling his bike through the newsroom.

He shook his head. 'I'll be fine.' He pressed the button to call the lift, and felt all eyes turn towards him.

They knew. Freya had not been discreet. She

hadn't waited for Ella to come in completely. Hadn't asked her to close the door. Her words had bumbled out of the hive, to Alfie, to Harry, to Tony, to everyone else. Ollie could just imagine the scene as soon as the lift doors closed. Heads would bow, voices would drop. The younger staff would scuttle away to the kitchen, to gossip beyond Freya's orbit. Alfie would keep his counsel. Harry and Tony, too, most likely.

For now, though, among them, they were the focus, and Ollie felt exposed.

He jabbed the button twice more, and at last the lift arrived. He put out his hand, inviting Ella to step in first, then followed her in and kept his eyes down until the doors closed.

Ella looked at his reflection in the mirrored doors. 'This is...' she trailed off.

'Embarrassing?'

She smiled. 'I hope you don't think...'

'No, no,' he jumped in. 'Not at all. I know you wouldn't... well, you know, it's just... work.'

She turned to him and touched his cheek, and as she did he looked up, into her eyes – her real eyes, not her reflection. He put up his hand and gently held onto her wrist.

'I can't,' he said. 'Not right now. Not when all this...'

He lifted her hand away from his face and kissed her palm, then putting it back by her side he gave her a smile and a gentle shake of his head.

They rode the last two floors in silence, and when they reached the end of the run and the doors slid apart to reveal the foyer he reached out and squeezed her hand. Then, without saying a word, he stepped out of the lift and wheeled his bike through the doors to the street.

The Tug, 6.30pm

'You're a hard man to track down, Oliver Carey.'

He turned around and found Christine Le Page standing behind him. She was resting one elbow close to a puddle on the bar as she shook the other out of a light cotton jacket.

'Not so hard.' He shrugged. 'You know where I work.'

'I do. Spoke to a very nice... girl? Woman? Ella Brouard. She told me I might find you on your boat.'

'Ah.'

She smiled. 'Suggested here when I told her you weren't at home.'

'She knows me too well.'

'Mind if I sit?' she asked.

Ollie pulled out the stool beside him and gathered together the two empty glasses he'd already pushed to the side.

'Are you drinking?' he asked.

'I'm buying,' she said. 'What are you having?'

'That depends.'

'On?'

'Is this official business?'

Christine pursed her lips.

'Only, I think I ought to stay sober if it is, that's all,' he said.

She caught the barman's eye. 'Another one of them,' she said, pointing to the empty glasses. 'Same for me.'

'Just a chat, then?' Ollie asked.

'Just a chat.'

She looked at him and smiled. They were sitting in front of the taps, the barman standing right by them, and Christine was reluctant to broach any subject until he'd moved away.

'I hear someone had a little accident,' Ollie said, to chase away the uncomfortable silence.

'Sorry?'

'A nasty little scrape at Saints Bay?'

'Oh, that,' she said. 'It, um...' She took her gaze away from his own and let the sentence die on her lips.

'Anything to it? Any story?'

'Mechanical fault.' She handed over a note to the barman, told him to keep the change and gave Ollie a rather forced smile. 'Cheers,' she said, lifting her glass from the bar and clipping the rim of his drink with its base.

They each took a swig as the barman moved down to serve the next customers.

'So,' Ollie said. 'This isn't a chance encounter. What is it? Ibbott or Holdbrook?'

'Either.'

'I didn't kill them, you know.'

'I know.'

'You do?'

'No, but I doubt you did it. Either of them.'

'But this morning...'

'This morning, as now, I was interested in a break-in. Know anything about it?'

'I may have heard something.'

'Anything I might find useful.'

'Nothing you don't already know, I suspect.'

She smiled. 'Okay, listen, Ollie. Let's not dance around each other, shall we?' She picked up her drink and took another sip. 'I'm not going to ask you to incriminate yourself, so I'll do the talking, and we'll see where we go from there. Deal?'

Nodding, he picked up his drink and nursed it.

'I suspect you were in Rosalynd Holdbrook's house last night. And I suspect you were there in a professional capacity. Whether you were sanctioned by The Sarnian or not, I don't know and I don't care, although it would make things rather inconvenient if we were to find any fingerprints.'

'You will,' he said. 'I was there at the start of the week. Monday. I told her about Richelle and wanted to see if she knew where Dixon might be.'

'Good. Then you'll have a plausible story if and when forensics turn something up.'

Ollie squinted at her. 'You're being surprisingly...' He thought for a moment. 'Helpful.'

'Well, let's just say I have a vested interest in catching the right guy. And if that's not you...'

'If it's not me, who?'

She sucked through her teeth. 'I suspect that to answer that question would count as gross misconduct.'

'Okay. Then let me.'

She held out her hand, inviting him to go on.

'George Dixon.'

'On what grounds?'

'That's the trouble,' Ollie said.

'You don't know?'

'No.'

'No. I didn't think you would. The Sarnian has been chasing its tail on this one, hasn't it.'

Ollie nodded. 'Largely my fault, I think. Or so my editor seems to believe.'

'She's not impressed?'

'Why do you think I'm here?'

'Drowning your sorrows?'

'You could say that. Beaten to one story too many.'

'How so?'

'Amy Sloane. Do you know her?'

'Aah,' Christine said. She looked now at the unintended consequence of her actions. She had come to the pub hoping she could use Carey to her advantage. Now, it seemed she might have pinched off that opportunity already, without even realising.

'You knew about the radio, I presume.'

'Radio?' she asked.

Ollie raised his eyebrows.

'Yes, I knew about the radio,' she admitted. 'Renouf said he'd talked to you about it at Port Soif.'

'He did. Only not only me, it seems. Someone told Amy Sloane. She got it up online.'

'And your editor wasn't impressed?'

'She had a point,' Ollie said, staring down at his drink. 'I should have told her. We should have run that story days ago.'

'Then why didn't you?'

'Would you? If you'd been accused of... It's human nature, isn't it. You try to ignore it, hope it'll go away.'

'Except it doesn't.'

'As I'm now finding out.'

There was a moment of awkward silence. Ollie seemed lost in the depths of his glass, watching the bubbles float up in his drink, while Christine was consumed by an unfamiliar feeling. What was it? Guilt? Regret? Had she managed to do worse herself than Renouf had done when he'd made this man the focus of their investigation? At least he'd called things off before any real damage had occurred.

'So you live on a boat,' she said.

'I do,' he said, looking up. 'The Huffin' Puffin. Do you know it?'

'Of course,' she said. 'But you weren't home, remember? Your cat was in.'

Ollie laughed. 'He was probably hoping you might be there to feed him.'

'You'll have to forgive my innocence, but what is it, exactly? Fishing boat? Cruiser?'

'Fishing boat.'

'Unusual choice. Is that a sideline?'

'No, nothing like that. I don't use it. Not for fishing.'

'So why not live in a flat?'

'It's cheap,' he said. 'You get a sea view for the price of your mooring. You're on the beach.'

'You can motor off for the day and –'

'No.' He shook his head. 'I mean I don't use it at all. Not on the water.'

She frowned at him.

'You won't tell anyone?' he asked.

'Of course.'

'Scared of the water.' He smiled coyly.

'Yet you live on a boat?'

'It's tethered,' he said, brighter now that they'd moved away from the case. 'It was my father's.'

'And you, what? Inherited it?'

Ollie nodded. 'Couple of years ago. That's why I came back from the mainland.'

'He died? I'm sorry.'

Ollie took a long draw from his glass, excusing himself from replying. What could you say to such commiserations that hadn't already been said?

'So he was the fisherman, then?' she asked.

'Now and then. More of a guide, really. He took out the tourists. Knew where to find the best fish. He had a guarantee: if they didn't catch, they didn't pay.'

'Did they often pay?'

'Always.'

She laughed. 'And you miss him?'

'Of course.'

'Do you mind me asking what happened?'

'You can ask,' he said. 'But I can't answer.'

'You don't know?'

'He disappeared. Out one night on his boat, guiding some visitors, and he never came back. They found the boat the next day.'

'Who did?'

'Coastguard. There was a hole in the side, no sign of him or the party.'

'And they, what? Crashed? Some kind of explosion?'

Ollie shrugged. 'I was this close to finding out.' He held up his free hand, his thumb and forefinger less than an inch apart.

'You were?'

'I was.'

'And you're not any more?'

'Not since Amy Sloane and her story about the wax.'

'You've lost me,' Christine said. She held up her now empty glass and wobbled it at the barman. He nodded and she held up two fingers, ordering each of them a refill. 'What does the wax have to do with your father?'

'Not so much the wax. Just the timing. I only took that job to get access to the archives. Thought I might find out what had happened to him.'

He told her about Simon's call and the memo from the BBC. 'It was the first concrete lead in two years. Something to go on – a starting point. Then Amy Sloane happened and now I'm suspended. Full pay, pending some kind of discussion when this whole Ibbott thing has been tidied away.' He looked at her as the barman put down their drinks. 'Any idea when that might be?'

She pursed her lips and slowly shook her head.

'I know,' he said. 'You can't say. Even if you knew.' He reached out and picked up the drinks, handing one over. 'You know,' he said, as they knocked their glasses together, 'I really ought to eat something, or this is going to hurt.'

BBC Radio Guernsey, 10.10pm

Simon snipped apart each of Thomas Thoumine's grunts and moans and sorted them into separate folders. Each contained between seven and ten repeats of the same sound. He played them back through his headphones.

The office was empty. It was Sunday night and the station was in automation, taking in feeds from a regional show. The speakers were on in the background, as they always were to monitor the output, and the silent dips between the clips of Dixon's lines allowed familiar West Country names to slip through.

...got Barbara from Looe on the line who wants to talk to us about the...

...from the community hospital in Liskeard where...

He loaded the clips one by one and studied

their shapes on the screen, leaning in close enough to focus on the graphic rather than the sound itself. He slowly moved his head from side to side to see how it grew and fell.

...on the A38 between Saltash and Bideford, so police are advising that motorists avoid...

'What were you trying to tell us?' he murmured, as though Rosalynd was standing beside him.

He loaded the next clip and stacked the windows one above the other on his screen. They were both the same sound, only one started slightly later than the other. He trimmed its lead in - the silence at the start of the file - until they lined up, then ran his head left to right again to examine it. It looked nigh-on identical.

He selected both files and played them through together, then trimmed off a fraction of the second file again to get them fully in sync. He played them through a second time, but now they sounded like just one file.

They were identical.

...next weekend until the end of the month when a group of intrepid ladies from Launceston will be taking charge of...

He opened the folder and looked at the rest of the files. He knew what it was now - he just needed to make absolutely sure. Dragging in each of the clips, he could at last see what

Rosalynd had discovered.

These weren't merely repetitive - they were repeated. A single recording played over and over and over, which could only mean they'd been played directly out of the server.

He jumped up and hurried across the office, through the door to the sound proofed studios and into the control booth from which he could see each of the vacant broadcast desks.

He joggled the mouse on the desk to wake up the screen, then logged in to the playback system. The screen cleared for a second, then repopulated itself with each of his saved recordings. This was his workspace: the files he'd saved to his account to be played into the bulletins.

The same list of folders ran down the left hand side of the screen as they had in the newsroom editing software.

Dragspot, Datavol, News, Backup, Drama...

He double-clicked the Drama link and once again the screen redrew. Another display beside it reconfigured in sync, throwing out a pattern of on-screen buttons and flowing in a new selection, each marked up with unfamiliar codes.

F17, F22, S19... he tapped them, stabbing random graphics, the speakers behind him throwing out sounds of the sea, of people in pubs, of dogs scattering across a wet beach. This was the world of The Fleet and all of the people who lived in it.

The buttons seemed to be split into sections, each one colour-coded, each suffixed by two digits, but some with only one letter before them, while others had two.

He skipped the rest of the F and S buttons and swiped at the screen to pull up the lower rows – those with the double prefix. Doorbells ringing, doors slamming to, cars starting up, kitchen timers, mobile phones. Each prefix seemed to relate to a character, and the sounds behind them formed part of that character's life.

Joshua's ringtone, the captain's habit of sniffing, the barman's nervous cough.

He scrolled down yet further until he came to the buttons prefixed TT. Thomas Thoumine: George Dixon.

There were more of these than there were for any other character. Over a hundred, the thirty-two most recent of which had been recorded within the last month.

Simon jabbed at the first of them, and Thoumine's now so familiar moan edged uncertainly out of the speakers.

...ooahhhrh...

It sounded like the man was in pain.

He worked his way through them until he

found the sounds in Rosalynd's files. All of them. Every single one, recorded, stored and ready for playback -

- ready to be dropped into the programme.

George Dixon, Simon now knew, need never return to the station.

George Dixon, Simon suspected, had never been there at all the night that Richelle had been killed.

West Coast Road, 11.52pm

Ollie had drunk too much to notice his phone - and far too much to answer it. It rang and vibrated inside his pocket, unheard, unfelt and unnoticed as he rode on, on the Route de Rocquaine, to his bed on the Huffin' Puffin.

'Ollie, it's Simon.' The words tumbled out as soon as he heard the beep. 'I know what it was. I know what Rosalynd wanted to tell you. Hang on...'

Simon cut the line and called back. He wanted to talk to Carey, not leave him a message. He'd already hit the voicemail three times since he'd worked out what had happened. He'd ignored it so far, but now he needed to tell someone - even if that someone was an inanimate machine.

It was almost midnight, the waves were pounding the foot of Fort Grey as the sodium lights that painted it amber finally blinked themselves out. Ollie looked up at the cloudless sky, now speckled with lights so fine and so far that they made his head start to spin. He wobbled his bike up onto the pavement, then giggled and corrected his course, onto the road, as Simon once more encountered the beep.

'Pick it up, damn it,' Simon said, knowing full well that Ollie wouldn't be able to hear him. 'Dixon wasn't there the night of the broadcast. His alibi, it's a recording, the whole thing. All of his lines. All the same noises, just... dropped in. At the right time. You'd never know if they weren't stacked up in a sequence...'

He dumped the call and tried again, just as Ollie rounded the corner, passed the hotel and the kiosk at Portelet, and jumped off his bike at the start of the cobbled ramp that led the way to the beach. He caught his feet on the pedals and took a tumble. His phone fell out on the windblown sand that had gathered against the curb. The battery came loose and the line went dead, condemning Simon to voicemail once more.

'Where the hell are you?' he said. 'Do you get what I'm saying? Dixon doesn't have an alibi. Rosalynd knew that, and then Rosalynd turns up dead.' He sighed. 'Give me a call as soon as you get this, will you?'

TWO YEARS AGO

Renouf thought nothing of the travel report, and the fire engine blocking the road through the common. Neither did he consider the fire that had brought it there, except to wonder how it had started and how much damage had been caused.

Not for the next half hour -

- and then he understood.

Consider this a warning, Mr Renouf.

Nobody found the point of ignition. They might have done, had they looked, but the time it took them to put out the fire and make the structure safe had been just enough for Renouf to quietly put the matter to bed.

He'd arrived at police headquarters fifteen minutes after leaving the Guet - a little early, but not so much it aroused suspicion. He'd showered and changed his shirt, and taken a coffee from the canteen, placing it on the desk he'd left barely ninety minutes before.

A matching mug was steaming on Falla's own neat desk between two tall stacks of files. Falla's commute was an easy walk from his parents' house, and he made good use of the extra time to review cooling cases, few of which Renouf believed would ever be fully closed off. The Alton Hollett file was on the top of the stack.

Renouf had done the same himself when he'd been in Falla's position. That had been almost fifteen years ago - when he, too, was still on probation, fresh on the force and eager - and now he was more than happy to hand on those files and let someone else take care of them. It never hurt the service to review its unfinished work, and however unlikely it might have been that Falla would make any progress, Renouf knew from his own experience that there was no better way to help him develop.

Falla's coffee was steaming, so it hadn't been there very long, but his chair was empty and facing the wrong direction. Renouf thought nothing of it as he shrugged off his jacket and hung it up - not until Falla came in through the scuffed double doors and jogged across to his desk.

'Sir,' he said. He was short of breath. Renouf assumed he'd run up the stairs. 'I saw your car. I thought you might have come up the back way.'

'Problem?' asked Renouf, his mind still up at the Guet, reading, reading, re-reading the note in his head. He didn't think for a moment that Falla might be about to decode it.

'Your wife called.'

'Sophie?'

'Your house –'

'What is it, Falla?' He couldn't bear tiptoeing

round a subject.

'Well, not yours. The one on the common. The one you're building...' Falla trailed off. Something had changed. Something about Renouf's face. It looked like someone had turned down the contrast, softening the tanned cheeks and dark, shiny hair, rubbing off the definition around his eyes, giving them an a ghostly appearance. Grey.

Renouf couldn't see it, but he felt the change. A damp coolness started in his palms and crept up his arms to his shoulders. From there it seemed to cascade down his back until he shook it off with an involuntary twitch.

'Call her,' he said, as he wedged his arms into his jacket once more and pulled it tight across his clammy back - still damp from the shower, and damp from the chill that had run right through him. 'Tell her...' He paused at the door and shook his head, wondering what to say. 'Tell her it's fine. Tell her I'm on it.'

He'd left his car on the road, in its usual spot outside the station. It was facing north, so a dash to St Sampson and clipping the top of the island, more or less passing his home, brought him out on the common and neatly avoided the worst of the traffic.

The road had been cleared by the time he arrived, the fire out and the engine tucked up on the kerb. Traffic edged past as the drivers slowed down to look at the damage, giving Renouf enough time to dash over between them, barely noticed by those whose paths he crossed.

The joists had burned away, leaving only the eves to bookend what was once the roof. Through the windowless holes at the front of the house, he could see where the flames had eaten the floors, and the bare breeze block walls were streaked black, not by the fire but the high pressure hose that had doused them with water. The weight of sodden insulation had brought down the living-room ceiling.

Consider this a warning, Mr Renouf.

He stepped onto the site and over the fencing that someone had pushed to the ground. He wondered whether that had been done by the fire crew, or if it had been like that before they arrived. Whoever had set the fire would need to get into the house, after all.

How much would it cost to put right, he wondered, ticking off a mental list of repairs. New joists and having them fitted would likely require another uncomfortable trip to the buoys (not the Alderney site, he prayed). Repairing the ceiling, re-plastering, drying out the floors – that would be a second job. Thank the Lord he wasn't employing contractors. Making up lost time would have cost him how much? He didn't like to think about that, so instead he thought of a positive, if one should exist in this pile of wet ash, and reminded himself that he hired his builders ad-hoc, whenever he needed to lose some money.

He walked to the gap that would one day become his front door, and leaning on the frame, he called into the echoing shell of the house.

'Anyone there?'

He could hear voices, the sound of feet scuffing grit on the floor.

'Sorry, sir. You'll have to –' Ross Ferbrache rounded the corner and stopped when he saw Renouf. 'Marc,' he said, coming forward and clapping him on the shoulder, his club-like paw knocking the policeman against the wet frame. 'Awful mess. Awful.' He shuffled him in through the doorway. 'Yours?'

'Well, it was.'

'Thought so.' Ferbrache clucked his tongue on the roof of his mouth and looked about the largest room. An empty rectangle in the furthest wall hinted at the fireplace yet to come. 'Lounge?'

Renouf nodded.

'My wife signed off on your plans. Smart-looking house.' He shook his head. 'Damn shame. Put you back a few weeks, I should think.'

'We'll see.' Renouf was distracted by the hole in the ceiling, through which he could see the clear sky. A joist had fallen down from the roof space and pierced the floor above.

Ferbrache smiled. 'Still, only money. No one was killed. You're insured?'

'Of course.'

'Good man.' Another clap on the shoulder. Ferbrache's false humour was starting to grate. 'I'll speed it through. Get you back on site as soon as we can.'

'I'm sorry?' Renouf asked, his attention drawn back to their conversation.

'The report. I'll bump you up. Get it done this week, see if we can't get you paid out a bit quicker. Just give me a couple of days to investigate, find out how it started. You got contractors?'

'No.'

'You're doing it yourself?'

'No. I mean... no report. Don't... I won't be claiming.'

Ferbrache squinted. 'You're not worried about your excess, are you?'

'No. It's not that.' Renouf tried to think of a plausible reason not to make a claim, or at least some reason good enough to stop Ferbrache writing it up – for that, he knew, would require an investigation and things might start to get sticky.

'Because if it's faulty wiring it won't be a claim on your policy anyway,' Ferbrache said. 'They'll chase it down the line until they get to the contractors who –'

'I won't be claiming. It... it takes too long,' he said at last. His hands were clammy again, and though he told himself it could have been caused by the damp in the room, he knew it was more likely caused by his nerves.

'As I said, I'll speed it through. Get it done today if I can.'

'Leave it,' Renouf snapped. Ferbrache flinched, and Renouf saw the disappointment in the big man's eyes. They'd known each other since school and their friendship (or acquaintance, as Renouf preferred to think of it) had never really moved on. Ferbrache was two years younger and Renouf had been charged with showing him round on the first day of term. The best part of three decades had passed since that initial encounter but neither man had quite stepped out of those roles: Renouf the guardian, Ferbrache the spaniel, always looking to please.

'I'm sorry,' Renouf said, softening his tone. 'I'd rather just get on with it. I can cover the cost myself. It's a... well, it's a hobby, I suppose. Let's not make it more than it is.'

He toured the rest of the ruin alone.

So this was a warning. Well, maybe things

weren't as dark as they could have been. What was a warning if not an incentive to do things better the next time around? The work would continue, the money might not be guaranteed, but it certainly didn't sound like the end. He could pay to have this put right by doing a few extra pick-ups.

The question was, did he want to?

He'd never signed up to do the collections. 'Just keep an eye out,' was all they'd said. 'An open ear, that's all we want.'

Why had he ever agreed?

And then, when he'd stepped in 'just this once' when the usual courier disappeared and Renouf had made a collection himself... well, that was the day it had changed. All of it. His role in the operation. How deep he was in all of this. How clear it had suddenly become that he had little say any more. And if this kind of warning followed a single missed pick-up - just one - what would happen if he pulled out altogether?

What had become of the previous courier? One too many missed collections? Two too many warnings?

He slowly drove back to headquarters, replaying the conversation he'd had with Ferbrache as he picked his way across the island. All he'd been doing was trying to help, and Renouf had ended up barking at him. He felt he'd been an insufferable shit, and tried to reason away his guilt – to find a way to excuse his behaviour, telling himself it was better (wasn't it?) that Ferbrache should be steered well clear. It would be better for them both – for Ferbrache no less than Renouf himself – if the fireman kept well away from the whole operation.

In the end he'd asked him to knock out a brief report, putting it down to faulty wiring, and to file it quickly before anyone thought to investigate further. Ferbrache agreed, they shook on it, and Renouf felt his shoulders and neck relax. He'd buy the man a bottle of whisky.

DAY EIGHT

Police Headquarters, 8am

Clarke had taken a seat by the window, but didn't feel the warmth of the sun. It fell on his shoulder and back, but the thought of Falla still lying unconscious seemed to have brought on a chill.

Each of them could feel it, as though Falla was there, playing on their minds, occupying them, clouding their senses, distracting them. Clarke looked around at his colleagues and wondered how they could carry on, knowing that Falla was merely unfortunate and they were the lucky ones. They could have been there in his place, hooked up to a drip, immobile from drugs and injuries.

He forced himself to listen again as Marc Renouf came to the end of his introduction, telling the team what he knew of the sample of hottentot fig. And more to the point, what they knew of the stain, which Charlie Dubois was as good as certain could only be drops of blood.

Human or animal, he didn't yet know, but tests on the mainland would tell them soon enough.

Renouf gave the floor to Christine, his knee

jogging the table as he sat back in his chair. Clarke shifted his focus as Christine leafed through her notebook.

'Oliver Carey and Simon Langlois,' she started, ticking off the first of her bullets. She looked at Renouf. 'No longer our primary concern,' she said, acknowledging his discomfort, 'but there are a few loose ends that we need to consider, chief among them this email.' She slipped a copy out of a folder and placed it at the centre of the table. 'You've each been forwarded a copy...'

Clarke nodded. Renouf raised his eyebrows and sighed.

'Any thoughts?'

'It's The Fleet,' said Clarke.

'Probably working on this when she died,' Renouf said.

'It is The Fleet,' Christine said, 'but no, I don't think she was working on it. At least not in any official capacity – it wasn't new. I checked. The date stamps on the original files – the ones she cut up – were the day before she was killed. They'd have to have been recorded weeks before that.'

Renouf grumbled, and hauled himself up in his chair. 'So where did she get the raw footage?'

'She didn't,' Christine said. 'This isn't the uncut material. This was taken to pieces and rearranged after the broadcast. Listen.' She took out her phone and tapped on the screen a few times to call up the audio player. She dragged its progress bar across the screen until she got to the start of the first scene, which in Rosalynd's rearranged file was seven minutes into the stream. 'There,' she said. 'There. Did you hear that?' She tapped it again and dragged the playhead back a few seconds.

'I'm sure we'd get further, far faster, without playing games,' Renouf said. 'Perhaps you could tell us what we're listening out for.'

Christine lifted her finger, releasing the playhead. 'Listen.' she said. '-even...' She pronounced it ev-ven. '...-ev-ven, in a female voice.'

She looked around the table at three blank faces.

'There were no female characters in this episode. The whole thing was set on the boat. It has an all-male crew.'

'So who's that?' Clarke asked.

'Jennifer Doyle.'

'The newsreader?' Clarke rarely listened to the local station, but he'd met her in a bar in Town, and humiliated himself in front of his friends when he'd asked her out and she'd declined. 'How's she involved?'

'She isn't. "Quarter past seven," she's saying. She's signing off at the end of the news, right before the start of The Fleet. Rosalynd didn't cut the first line as precisely as she should. Same at the end. Listen.'

She dragged the slider back through the file to slightly after the four-minute mark, where the closing scene now sat in Rosalynd's remix. 'This is the last line of that episode,' she said, tapping play.

They listened, and this time all four of them caught a snatch of a female voice cut off halfway through her first word.

'Doyle again?' Renouf asked.

Christine tapped stop. 'She's trailing the next episode. Same time the following day.'

'I thought Rosalynd Holdbrook had retired,' Clarke said.

'She had,' said Renouf.

'So what was she doing re-cutting this episode?'

'More to the point, why did someone send it to Oliver Carey?' Christine said.

'Not only Carey.' Renouf said, trying to widen it up and take the focus off Ollie.

'I'm not so sure,' said Christine. 'Simon Langlois may have received this copy, but I'm pretty sure Rosalynd Holdbrook only intended to send it to Carey.'

'I thought we'd established Holdbrook was dead by the time they received it,' Clarke said.

'She was,' said Christine. 'Charlie's been looking through her emails, though, and he's pulled out another message sent to just Carey the previous day.'

She returned to her folder and flicked through the pages until she came to another print-out. She put it on the table beside the one to which the re-cut episode had been attached, and turned it around so that Clarke and the constables could read it.

'Miss Holdbrook sent this email to Carey intimating that she'd found something strange in a recording.'

Renouf picked up the page and ran his eyes down its contents.

'This relates to the recording later sent to Langlois and Carey?' he asked.

'The very same. The attachments are identical.'

'And this was the last thing she sent before she was killed?'

'As far as we know.'

'Do we know where she was heading?' one of the constables asked.

'Quite possibly,' said Clarke, taking out his own notebook and leafing through the pages. 'Eleven forty-two hours, just before she sent that first email, phone records have her putting in a call to an unlisted number in St Martin.'

'Let me guess,' said Christine. 'The Ibbott house?'

Clarke nodded. 'I confirmed it this morning.'

Renouf pulled himself up in his seat. 'George Dixon,' he said, a smile forming.

'Hang on, though,' said Christine. 'Do we know if they actually spoke?'

Clarke nodded. 'Not for long, though. The call lasted twenty-eight seconds.'

'Was it definitely Dixon? Could someone else have picked it up? Maybe the answerphone?' Christine said.

'Answerphone or not,' Renouf cut in, 'Rosalynd Holdbrook was messing around with something that, by all accounts she found a bit fishy...' – he tapped the print-outs – 'after which she put in a call to the home of one of the actors who featured in that very episode, and whose partner, Miss Holdbrook's friend, just happened to have turned up dead some days earlier.'

'There's nothing concrete here,' Christine said. 'It's all circumstantial. Without knowing what they discussed – or even who she spoke to – we can't tie Dixon to Rosalynd Holdbrook on the night in question. What we can do, though, is tie Rosalynd Holdbrook to Oliver Carey on two separate occasions, once immediately before she died, and then again a couple of days after the event.'

Renouf scowled. 'Receiving an email is barely grounds for suspicion.'

'On the face of it, no,' Christine agreed. 'But until we know for sure who sent that second email, there's a very logical explanation we can't entirely rule out.'

'Which is?'

'Carey sent it himself.'

Renouf gave a weak, unconvincing laugh. He knew that Christine was right - he'd seen Carey and Simon Langlois fleeing the house with his very own eyes - but Christine, he was sure, had not.

'Think about it,' Christine said, determined to press her point. 'She sent him the first email, I think we can all agree on that.'

'Go on,' Renouf said.

'So, rewind the clock a bit. Carey's chasing the story. We know he called at Dixon's house the morning he found the body, and spoke to one of the neighbours. It wouldn't surprise me that finding him out he followed up every other connection, which sooner or later would bring him to Rosalynd Holdbrook.'

Renouf made a peak from his fingers and rested his chin on his thumbs. 'Fair enough...'

'Now we know both that Miss Holdbrook and Richelle Ibbott were friends, while at the same time there was no love lost between Holdbrook and Dixon.'

Christine got up and wrote their names on a dry wipe board at the head of the table. She traced a double-ended arrow between Rosalynd Holdbrook and Richelle Ibbott, and a broken line between Holdbrook and Dixon, slashing it twice in the middle.

'Carey's been bylined on almost every story that The Sarnian has run on this case, but he's been two steps behind on pretty much every development, which going on what we know about Freya Carlisle likely means he's been getting some heat.'

'If you're going to tell us he killed Rosalynd Holdbrook for the sake of an exclusive you must –'

'No,' Christine interrupted. 'Far from it. Rosalynd Holdbrook would have been one of his sources. So, when she sends him an email hinting at some juicy development, it's going to be exactly what Carey's been waiting for. Only, something must have gone wrong somewhere along the line. The message bounced or it got scrambled, or some overeager virus scanner stripped out the crucial attachment – this file...' – she tapped her phone – 'whatever it is. What's he more likely to do? Sit around and wait for her to get back in touch, or find some other way to get hold of it?'

'He broke in?' Clarke said.

'That's my guess,' Christine told him. 'We'll know soon enough, thanks to the inspector.' She pointed towards Renouf.

'Explain...'

'The bag containing that radio,' Christine said. 'The one you handed to Carey at Port Soif.'

'What of it?'

'I asked Charlie to see whether he could retrieve any fingerprints. Having eliminated your own – and Charlie's – we've been left with two clear and one partial print from Carey's left hand. I've asked him to compare them to some samples we retrieved from Rosalynd Holdbrook's computer. If they match, we should have sufficient grounds to bring him in for questioning.'

Renouf slapped the palm of his hand on the table. 'By whose authority?'

Christine didn't blink. 'Time is against us and you were out of the office. I had to make a decision. Of course, if you want to over-rule me...'

Renouf felt his heart start to race, not through fear but through fury – fury at himself. Somehow he'd fallen straight into her trap and couldn't countermand her logical move without arousing suspicion. 'That is not the issue here.' He neatly sidestepped the point of their argument. 'Lab time is a finite resource. We can't be wasting it investigating dead ends.'

'Forgive me, Inspector Renouf, but only last week Oliver Carey was the sole focus of this investigation.'

'And with good reason,' Renouf said. 'A reason that's borne fruit: it has enabled us to eliminate him from our enquiries.'

'On what grounds?'

Renouf's jaw cycled in the empty air, no answer forthcoming.

'Christine,' he said at last, taking a deep breath and slowly letting it out, forcing himself to stay calm. 'I think we all know why you're here.'

'We do?'

'Would you care to explain to these gentlemen your role on the Jersey force?'

Christine shrugged. 'It's no secret.'

'Well?'

'Internal affairs.'

'You didn't think to mention that in your interview?'

'You didn't ask.'

'I shouldn't have needed to.'

'I thought it was fair to assume you might have made some enquiries.'

'What good would enquiries have done when you were the only suitable candidate in a pair of no-hopers?' He turned and looked at the constables. 'Internal affairs, gentlemen. Le Page here investigates the law makers, not the law breakers.' He paused, allowing it to sink in. 'I should be careful what you say.'

'Inspector Renouf,' Christine said. 'I would never think to undermine my commanding officer, and I hesitate to use the word "unprofessional", but I find your reaction to my discussions with Charlie a little... shall we say strong? If I have stepped out of line I can only apologise.'

'Not at all,' he said, turning back to face her. 'But I find myself asking whether your own particular skills might not be better employed in a more appropriate manner.'

Christine raised her eyebrows.

'Internal affairs,' Renouf said, speaking the words with great precision, pausing between each one. 'An investigation of the investigators.' He paused. 'It seems there's a mole among us.'

'A mole?' Christine asked.

'Someone is passing information to the press,' Renouf said.

'I see,' said Christine, capping the pen and putting it back on a ledge that ran across the bottom of the board. 'You're talking about Amy Sloane? The fact she knew about Richelle Ibbott before we'd even released that information?'

Renouf stumbled, verbally, but quickly

recovered, in the process confirming to Christine what she already suspected – that Renouf himself was Amy's usual source.

'That she could have got from anywhere,' Renouf said.

'Hardly,' said Christine. 'It was less than an hour after Carey had called. Ibbott was still on the beach and we hadn't even –'

'What interests me,' Renouf cut her off, 'is how she got the story about the wax on those earbuds.' He paused, holding Christine in his gaze. 'That story appeared after we had already ruled out Carey as a suspect in this case.'

'With no good reason,' Christine said. She could see Clarke in the corner of her eye. He was staring at some invisible spots on the table.

'We had followed every lead on that front, and they'd taken us nowhere,' Renouf said. 'Dead end. We should now be focusing all of our efforts on finding out what Dixon's involvement is in all this, not following some thoroughly implausible angle involving fingerprints on a bag and a keyboard.'

Renouf became aware that he'd raised his voice above a level that seemed reasonable for a man who had nothing to hide. He stopped for a moment, pinched the corners of his mouth to dry them, then continued. 'Before we go much further, I think it's important that we plug this leak in our team. We can't afford to have any further misinformation put out about Carey and his friend at the BBC.'

'With respect, sir,' Christine began, but he jumped in before she could finish.

'No,' he said. 'That's the end of it. Barring any new, credible leads, the case on Carey is closed, and you, Le Page – I want you to find this leak and plug it. If you're here on false pretences, the least you can do is put your skills to good use.'

Police Headquarters, 8.45am

Ferbrache remembered far more than Renouf about their earlier years.

He remembered the day they'd crossed to Lihou without first checking the tides. They were fourteen and twelve, and the rising water had flooded the causeway and stranded them both on the island. Then the rain had rolled in and they'd run to the ruins and taken shelter, just as the monks would have done, and they'd waited for the tide to turn. By the time they'd got back the coastguard was out on alert.

Renouf had forgotten it was Ferbrache's father – not his own – who had first taken him off the island. Ferbrache recalled it in trivial detail: an overnight ferry to France, and neither had felt a sea so rough; they'd emptied their stomachs into the Channel, partly through the sway of the boat and partly because of their nervous excitement. France had not lived up to the promise and after a rainy day in Cherbourg they'd repeated the tumbling journey back to the island.

Neither did Renouf remember that Ferbrache had betrayed the secret of his own first love, and blabbed that Renouf had scrawled three misspelled words on a bunker at Pleinmont (Renouf had been forced to spend a weekend scrubbing them off), or that Ferbrache had told the rest of their friends - in strictest confidence, naturally - that Renouf's parents were to divorce.

Ferbrache had never been able to keep a secret.

Had he remembered these things - any of them - Renouf might not have felt so confident as he drove away from the charred remains of his house two years before. He might also have thought to inform Marie, by way of their code and the crack in the Guet, that their warning had drawn more attention than they'd intended.

Two years later, had he known why Christine was away from her desk just minutes after their heated discussion, he might have had cause to regret asking Ferbrache to hush up the facts of the fire.

In truth, she was two floors above him, sitting across the desk from Bichard, watching as he leafed through the pages she'd taken out of her bag.

'I'm impressed,' he said.

'It wasn't so difficult once I got into it,' she said. 'Remus Carey uses pretty plain language. It's a lot more descriptive than I'd expected. I can see where his son got his literary leanings.'

Bichard turned over a couple of pages and started to read at random. 'I could tell from the fact he was wearing his patent shoes that Bichard wouldn't be joining us out at sea. He didn't try to hide it.' He laughed. 'The man has the eye of a magpie.'

'It's quite a confessional. Did you know that he and Renouf didn't go fishing that night?'

'No, I didn't. Although I had my doubts. I met with Renouf the following morning and he had surprisingly little to say on the subject.'

Bichard looked up when Christine didn't respond. She was staring right at him, her front teeth pressed into her bottom lip.

'What is it?' he asked.

She leaned forward and picked up all but the very last page, turning over the papers between her finger and thumb and laying them face down on the table. She pointed to the one remaining sheet. 'This bit.'

'Marc Renouf, the man who feigned ignorance when it came to boats and fish, was staring out from the helm of a powerful speedboat, pulling back on the throttle and locking it off as the craft finally came to a wobbling halt...' Bichard trailed off and read what remained of the page in silence. Then, taking off his glasses, he slid back in his chair and pinched the bridge of his nose.

'I'm not sure even this is enough,' Christine said.

Bichard put down his glasses. 'No. No, it's not. Not without Remus.'

'And the log?'

'It means nothing out of context. Is this the end of it?' He flicked the edge of the paper.

'Ten pages left, maybe twelve. He writes pretty small, so maybe a third as much again.'

'Have you read it?'

'Bits of it.'

'No clues as to what happened?'

She shook her head. 'He seemed to write it in chunks, a few days at a time, so whatever happened in the last few days before he disappeared or...' She didn't know the man, except through his logs, yet she still didn't like to think that he might be dead. 'Well, we'll probably never know, unless he turns up.'

Bichard fell silent for a moment, picturing

Renouf hauling in the empty pot. What possible motivation could the man have had to get himself involved? Money – it had to be money – but why? What was he spending it on?

Of course!

He reached for his keyboard and pulled it forward, then switched to his email and searched for Renouf. The server truncated the list of results, showing only the thousand most recent messages with links to load the next batch or filter the results by date. He chose the latter and tapped in a spread that encompassed the three days before and seven days after the last part of the log Christine had translated.

'Let's see,' he said, picking up his glasses. He scrolled through the forty-four remaining messages, most of which were office circulars. He opened three, closed them all, and then found a fourth – a note that Renouf had sent from home two days after Remus had written his log.

He turned his screen and let Christine read it.

'A fire?' she asked. 'At his home?'

'No. A house he was building up by the common. Still is, I think, although where he was getting the money from, I don't know.' He paused. 'Or I didn't.'

'What does his wife do?'

'Not enough to pay those kind of bills,' Bichard

said. ‘Not on her own.’

‘Can we prove it?’

‘That she couldn’t afford it, or that Renouf was bankrolling something beyond the reach of his salary?’

She shrugged.

‘Probably not,’ he said. ‘We don’t know the state of his finances, and even if they’re shredded there’s any number of ways he could get the money. Parents. Relatives. Loan from the bank.’

‘Illegal organ trading.’

Bichard raised his eyebrows. ‘It would fit, wouldn’t it.’

He looked back down at the transcript and leafed back and forth through the pages, reading sections at random.

...I’d anchored the Huffin’ Puffin in quieter waters, in such a way that the tide kept it angled towards a couple of buoys. One orange, one pink, weathered and aged by years in the sea. They sat within a few hundred feet of the French delegation’s coordinates...

Forward a couple of sheets.

...I put in a call to Bichard and asked him to bypass the usual channels and find out from someone in Fisheries to whom they’d issued that license. I read him the number...

A few pages more.

...The light was like a flare in the night-vision goggles, and it took a moment for the glasses to dial down their sensitivity, recalibrating a couple of seconds later as he thumped his fist on the side of the boat and kicked the empty cage over the edge in disgust...

Bichard straightened. It was almost imperceptible, and Christine would have missed it if it wasn't for the tick of the swivel mechanism, knocking as he shifted his weight in the seat.

'What is it?' she asked.

'This fire,' he said, picking up his phone. 'What if it wasn't an accident? What if it's somehow related to this?' He stabbed the page with the tip of his finger.

Christine heard Henri pick up his end of the line and wondered how much of their conversations the PA could hear through the door.

'Get me Ross Ferbrache at Fire and Rescue would you, Henri. And another coffee, please. I've let this one go cold.'

He put down the receiver.

'Renouf should have been in there by now,' he said. 'Only this fire set him back six months. Quite a lot of damage by all accounts - not long after all this.' He nodded at the papers.

'You think they're connected?'

Bichard leaned forward and crossed his arms, setting them down on the desk. 'Have you come across Ross Ferbrache on your travels?'

Christine didn't recall the name.

'Oily as a kipper,' Bichard told her. 'And a tongue that runs away with itself.'

'Charming.'

'Quite.'

Bichard's phone rang and he broke off to pick it up. 'Thanks, Henri,' he said, then waited for the transfer.

'Ross,' he said, speaking to the man like a long-lost friend of the family. 'How are you? Good, good. Listen, Ross, can you spare half an hour today? Like to send over one of my officers for a quick chat.' [Pause.] 'Half past?' [Pause.] 'No, no. She'll meet you there. Christine Le Page. She's here on a secondment from Jersey.' [Bichard licked the tip of his middle finger and used it to dab up some crumbs from his desk. He dusted them off and they fell on the floor.] 'Oh, nothing. Just following up a few old cases. We've got a loose end on that fire. You remember the one? Renouf's house on the common?' [Another pause – a longer one this time.] 'No – that's okay. No need to call Marc. In fact, probably best not bother him. Painful memories and all that... Top stuff. I'll send her over. Listen, we must have that drink. Yep... Yep... Of course.' He gave an exaggerated laugh, which died on his lips the moment he put down the phone.

'Half eleven at Fermain,' he said. 'Take an early lunch and meet him there.'

She nodded. 'How will I recognise him?' she asked, standing up.

'Oh, I think you'll spot him,' Bichard said. 'Great bear of the man. Can't be missed.'

He held out his hand, and Christine raised her eyebrows. 'What?'

'Those papers,' he said, indicating the second sheaf, which she'd clasped to her chest. 'I presume they're the next instalment?'

TWO YEARS AGO

From the diary and logs of Remus Carey, as translated by Christine Le Page.

I've been watching Renouf for a week. Eight o'clock, he arrives at the office. Rarely takes lunch, although if he does it's a ploughman's at the Admiral. Sits down at two, back at his desk by half past. Six fifteen, he leaves. Sometimes stops off at the Doghouse for a pint if there's live music but he's always gone by seven and home by twenty past.

Daily.

Predictable.

Regular as an ormering tide.

I followed him home on Thursday and Friday, and at the weekend I convinced Odette we should head for the beach at Pembroke as I'd seen him there the week before with his wife and that kid of theirs. We parked our towels on the slab and I watched the sands from behind the Guernsey Press. Odette had brought Friday's trash from The Sarnian. I've given up trying to wean her off it.

He arrived around one, one fifteen. Unseen. I was queueing for lunch in the kiosk when his wife came in with their daughter. I turned around and busied myself with a stack of buckets and spades until they left, then headed out without giving my order. Odette was texting Oliver and didn't see me leave, so I scouted the back of the beach and eventually found them sitting by those rocks in the middle of the sand, sheltered from the wind.

Renouf was laying face down, his arms crooked at right angles and his hands up by his ears. His wife and daughter were eating their ice creams. None of them looked like they were going anywhere in a hurry.

I went back to the kiosk and bought our lunch, then carried it back to Odette, making some excuse about the queue. She hadn't noticed – just held up her phone to show me a picture of Ollie and his girl.

'Kirsty. They look so good together,' she said.

I grunted and Odette said something about them being on the same oceanography course.

I couldn't have chosen a worse position. It's a long way from the slab to the rocks – too far to make out details without the binos. I swept them about the beach, pretending to watch the birds, but kept returning to their little party as the ice creams disappeared and their industrious daughter steadily reinforced their bridgehead with a six-inch trench and a ring of small castles pressed out of a plastic cup.

Odette fell asleep under a blanket of Factor 15, leaving me free to observe them unobserved. Renouf rolled over and shaded his eyes as his wife said something, pointing towards the sea, then she and her daughter ran to the water and paddled about in the shallows.

Had they ventured any deeper, I might have approached Renouf right away, but they headed back a few minutes later and quickly towelled off their wet feet and ankles.

Renouf shook his head, and drawing their attention to the bags he was leaving behind, he heaved himself up and ran to the water, carrying on as the waves consumed his knees, thighs and hips, until they swept him off his feet. He settled into a leisurely crawl.

I stripped off my shirt and followed, and could understand why his wife had returned so quickly. It wasn't cold, but certainly cool, and I threw myself in more quickly than I should have so I could get under the waves and acclimatise myself.

I swam a lazy arc around his position and came up from behind. He hadn't seen me.

'Marc,' I called out.

He span around and trod water. 'I'm having a pee,' he said with a twitch of his eyebrow. 'Tide's coming your way.'

I swam a couple of feet to one side and straightened up. We were a fair way from shore, and I could just touch the soft sandy bottom.

'How are you?'

'Loving it,' he said. 'Relieved. You here alone?'

'Odette's on the slab. Dead to the world.'

He looked back but we were too far away to see her. Neither could we see his own wife and kid.

He turned and started to swim. Clearly he'd finished relieving himself. I swam after him.

'Busy?' I asked.

'So-so.'

'You look tired.'

'A few late nights. You know how it is.'

I laughed. 'You know, if you need a break, I'm sure we could convince Bichard I need some help with this smuggling case. We could take that trip. Catch some fish. Perhaps we could head out in your boat this time.'

He'd been slightly ahead of me, but as I said that he stopped and trod water.

'I told you,' he said. 'I'm not into boats. I don't have your sea legs.'

'But you have a boat.'

He frowned.

'The Dalliance,' I said.

His lips parted momentarily, but he quickly closed his mouth again and pulled a strong stroke, moving past me in the opposite direction.

'Not me.'

'Are you sure about that?' I started to swim in his wake and hoped he'd been telling the truth when he said he'd finished peeing. 'Long boat, powerful engine. I saw you on the prow, pulling up an empty lobster pot... I have the flask myself if you need it back. I'm afraid the contents have gone off for analysis.'

He slowed his stroke and let me draw up beside him. He said nothing for a moment, then asked, 'does anyone else know about this?'

'Yes. But not about you. Not yet.'

'Why not?'

I would have shrugged had we not been swimming, but I couldn't quite pull it off in the water. 'I wanted to hear your side of it first.'

'Very understanding of you.'

'Not at all,' I said. 'I want to know the whys and wherefores. I want to stop it. I thought you might be more willing to talk to me - off the record - than work through official channels.'

We swam on a little, side by side like the women at Beau Sejour with their blue frilly caps and scowling faces. Nobody on the beach would have imagined we were discussing anything more important than football or fishing.

'It's a relief,' he said, 'truth be told.'

'Having a pee?'

He smiled. 'No. You knowing. Anyone knowing.'

'I don't follow.'

'Are you up to swimming as far as the range?' He nodded towards the rifle range at the opposite end of the bay. The red flags were up and I could hear the crack of the guns.

'Sure.'

We started to swim.

'I don't know much,' he said, a few strokes later. 'They tell me where to go and when to be there and I do it. It's all arranged so that I don't know who else is involved.'

'No one?'

He shook his head. 'But now that you know about me...'

'They'll have to find someone else?'

'It's a way out, isn't it.' He looked at me and smiled.

I raised my eyebrows. 'I'm not sure that would cut it.'

'Not much of a plea bargain, is it?'

'How did you let yourself get involved?'

'I didn't. Not to begin with.'

'You must have known what they were up to.'

'You know what they're smuggling?' he asked.

I told him I did, and he asked if I really thought he would let himself get involved with the organ trade if he'd known what they were doing. I had to admit that I didn't.

'It was all quite harmless to start with. Request from a lawyer on something unrelated. Handed me a list of names on the way out of an interview. Asked me to cast an eye over them.'

'And tell him if anyone rang any bells?'

'Something like that.'

'And did you?'

'Of course not.' He swam a couple of strokes in silence. 'Not at first.'

'And then?'

'He came back. Some other poor sod he was representing, up for theft or affray, I don't remember, and he slipped me some cash. Asked me to look at the list again, give him a call.'

'Did anyone see him?'

He shook his head. 'We were having a smoke. No cameras, no recorder.'

'Did you know the names?'

'No.'

'You told him that?'

'I thought that would be the end of it. I called him, but the money kept coming. Every few weeks.'

'Why didn't you tell Bichard?'

He ducked under the water and came back up, shaking the drops out of his hair. 'What could he do but fire me? I'd already compromised myself.'

I didn't like to say, but Bichard would have had little choice but to do more than fire him, or he'd have been up against the board for gross misconduct himself.

'How long has it been going on?'

'Five years, give or take.'

'Five years?' I couldn't believe he hadn't found a way out in all that time, unless he really was a willing participant. I was starting to doubt that it would be possible for him to cut any kind of deal after so long.

'You don't think it goes from checking over a few names to picking up the cargo and money in a couple of months, do you?'

I was finding it hard to swim and keep talking, so I put my hand on his shoulder and stopped him. We both put our feet on the sand and stood, with the water at our chests.

'So why don't you tell me what happened?'

Turns out it was the same old story. Money. The more they gave him, the more he came to rely on it, and when they asked him to pick up some cargo for them - he didn't know what it was back then - and offered enough to pay his mortgage for a year... what could he do but say yes?

'Someone else leaves the money. I transport the cargo.'

'Where do you take it?'

'It's never the same place twice.'

'Can you take me?'

He was quick to refuse. 'It's too risky. If they see you in the boat...'

'Then at least let me follow. They don't need to know we've spoken.'

He considered it for a moment, but it was clear he was in no hurry to continue.

'When's the next pick-up?' I asked.

'I have a drop-off tomorrow.'

'Where?'

He threw back his head and looked up at the sky, exhaling deeply.

'Do you know the Venus Pool?'

I did, of course. It's a sink in the rock on the southern coast of Little Sark, filled by water from the sea. It's deep but calm, and perfect for swimming. My father used to take me there as a child.

'Just to this side are the caves of La Louge,' he said. 'It's low tide tomorrow. Low enough to go right inside with a boat. Even a bucket and tub like yours.'

I let his slight slide. 'What time?'

'I'll be dropping the cargo at two. AM. I don't know what time they'll be picking it up.'

'How long do you need to get away?' I did some quick calculations. I could anchor a few miles to the south and still see any boats approaching the caves on the radar - Renouf's included. When I saw him leave I'd motor over the way I would on the hunt for some fish.

'Half an hour. They won't retrieve it before then in case I'm late.'

He shifted his gaze over my shoulder, and I turned to look back at the beach. We could see his wife from where we were standing. She had come to the water's edge and was waving both hands, calling him back.

'Don't blow my cover,' he said. 'Not yet.'

I promised I wouldn't. As he started to swim away I called after him. 'One thing. Why don't they just collect the cargo themselves? From the lobster pot?'

He turned onto his back so he could see

me. 'The longer the chain, the longer the odds against anyone reaching either end.' He trod water for a second, and saluted. 'Bon chance,' he said, before turning and swimming away.

End of translation.

Renouf swam back to shore. He waded the last few feet and took the towel that his wife had brought with her.

'I know, I know,' he said, pre-empting her.

'You know she needs to be there at four.' She twitched her eyebrow to indicate their daughter, who was sitting beside their packed beach bag surrounded by tiny castles.

'I know,' Renouf snapped, and then immediately apologised.

'What were you doing out there?'

'Swimming.'

'You know what I mean.'

'Let's just drop it, shall we?' He rolled the towel and hung it around his neck, then jogged across the hot sand to their spot on the beach.

'Ready?' he asked, pulling his shorts over the top of his damp trunks. He ran his fingers through his daughter's hair.

'Mummy says you've made us late,' she said.

Renouf smiled. 'Don't you worry. We'll get you there in time.'

His wife joined them and picked up the bag, and Renouf followed her back to the car, holding his daughter's hand.

He drove them back down the west coast road, and just as the damp of his trunks was starting to soak through the weave of the seat, he looked up and saw the Guet. He'd have to return there later that afternoon, and he'd have to leave some gum on the bench, too. He prayed it would be deserted, and prayed again that Marie would see his signal in time to retrieve the note he would leave.

There was no pick-up the following day, but Remus Carey knew too much.

Plans would have to be put in place to see to his dispatch.

DAY EIGHT

The Huffin' Puffin, 9.30am

Ollie woke up to the sound of a knuckle knocking against the wheelhouse door. He opened his eyes to find himself dressed, laid out on the floor with his legs beneath the lower bunk and his head pressed hard on the stove. He turned to the side and felt his skin peeling away from its cold enamel shell.

He hauled himself up on the rim of the sink

and pulled at the tail of the curtain. The sun was up, higher than he'd expected.

The knocking came again.

'I'm coming,' he called, and he stumbled over to unlatch the door. He frowned for a moment and shaded his eyes as a silhouette loomed above him. 'Clive?'

'Look at the state of you,' the silhouette laughed, holding out a paper plate on which sat a bacon sandwich. That confirmed it: Clive Bailey. A mainland refugee, now the tenant of the Portelet kiosk. What a sight for a man with a head like this, fogged by drink and a night on the floor.

'Heavy night?' Clive asked.

'What time is it?'

'Half nine. That's on the house. Looks like you need it.'

Ollie took the plate and thanked him.

'You know your bike's on the beach?' Clive asked.

Ollie stepped up to the deck and looked across the sand. He could feel a graze on one of his knees, and looking down he saw a hole in his jeans. He groaned. 'It was a late one.'

'I thought as much.'

Ollie was far from hungry. He felt quite queasy from the night before, but Clive was a friend, and Ollie was touched that the sight of his bike astray on the beach had inspired him to bring him some breakfast. He bit into the hot, greasy sandwich and felt a dollop of sauce escape. He heard it land on the deck.

'There was one other thing,' Clive said, reaching into both back pockets of his well-worn jeans, pulling out a phone from one and its battery from the other. 'Yours?'

Ollie patted his own pockets and found them empty. 'Thanks, Clive,' he said, setting the plate on the wheelhouse roof and taking the parts from his friend. He snapped the battery into the back of the phone and turned it on. It took a few seconds to come back to life.

'Well, best get cracking,' said Clive. 'Crab man's due in ten minutes.'

He stepped backwards onto the top of the ladder, then realising what he had said, he threw back his head and laughed. 'Cracking,' he said again, shaking his head.

As Clive stepped onto the harbour wall and turned his back on the boat, Ollie's phone latched onto the network, and right away it started to ring. Ollie focused his eyes on the screen. Voicemail.

'Ollie, it's Simon.' The words came tumbling out. He sounded excited. 'I know what it was. I know what Rosalynd wanted to tell you. Hang on...'

The message came to an end, and right away the next one played. It was Simon again.

Ollie listened to all three messages. Then, leaving the wheelhouse unlocked and his sandwich perched on the roof, he jumped from the deck to the harbour wall and ran across the well-packed sand to his bike.

Simon had taken to drinking coffee after he'd left the messages. He wanted to stay awake, just in case Ollie should call. He tried him again, three times, but every time it went straight to voicemail and at last he'd given up. The coffee was wearing off, his eyes were getting heavy, so he put the time to good use – anything to keep himself upright – cutting down Rosalynd's audio file to the point where all that remained were the burbling grunts of George Dixon, perfectly trimmed and without any gaps.

Fifteen lines was all it came to, dotted throughout the programmes, between them comprising just nine different noises, skilfully laced together in seemingly random concoctions.

He fell asleep at his desk, his head on the keyboard, and some hours later he woke to the sound of his phone.

'Ollie,' he said, snatching it up without even thinking to check who it was.

'Simon, it's Ollie.' Simon could tell he was

pedalling hard. The wind was catching the mic and his voice was breathy and tight. 'Are you sure?' he asked.

'Absolutely. He wasn't there. He's got no alibi for the night Richelle was killed.'

'And Rosalynd?'

Simon stood up and felt his way to the window. He pulled it up to let in some air. 'I don't know. But Richelle was her friend. My guess is she worked out what had happened and took it to Dixon. Where are you?'

'Just leaving Dixon's.'

'Is he there?'

'No. Place is deserted. Where does... who's his boss?'

'Kira?'

'Where does she live?'

'Chouet. Do you think she knew that he –'

'Of course she knew. Who do you think put his lines in the programme? Can you text her address?'

'I'll find it.'

'Cheers, mate,' Ollie said, and he tapped his phone and rode on.

Chouet, 10.35

A knock on the door. Kira Spooner put down her coffee and looked at her watch: too early for the post, too late for the milk. She pushed herself up from the table and went to see who it was.

'George,' she said, surprised to see him standing there. She wasn't yet dressed, and she pulled the neck of her dressing gown tighter around her neck.

'Kira.' He nodded, stepping through to her hallway. He had a sports bag slung over his shoulder, and as he turned, it brushed the wallpaper. Kira instinctively reached out to smooth it.

'What do you want?' she asked, her voice more accusation than inquisition.

'Shall we start with coffee?' he asked, walking through to the kitchen and taking a mug from the draining board. He dropped his bag by his feet and emptied the jug from the coffee machine. 'We'll see where we go from there.'

'You've got a cheek,' she said, striding through and reaching out for the mug. He snatched it up off the worktop before she could take it and walked back to close the front door.

'No point heating the street.'

'You shouldn't be here,' she said as he stepped back through to the kitchen.

'Why's that?'

'Because...' She tried to think of a plausible answer. 'It's not right.'

He pulled out a seat and sat at the kitchen

table. 'You're single, I'm widowed,' he said, picking up the previous evening's Guernsey Press and leafing through the first few pages, not really reading the stories. 'I don't see a problem.'

'You need to have been married, George, before you can claim to be widowed.'

'Indeed, but I've rather given up trying to convince people we never did splice that particular edit.'

Kira reached over and picked up the paper. She closed it with a flick of the wrist and put it down on the draining board, well beyond his reach. 'What do you want?'

'Money.'

She shook her head. 'You've tried that one already.'

'Yes, but... I'm leaving in...' He looked at his watch. 'In a couple of hours, so, I can't dawdle.'

'Leaving?'

'The island. The island, The Fleet. The full unabridged shebang. I think it's for the best, don't you?'

'Where will you go?'

'Never you mind.' He sipped at the coffee. 'I must say,' he said, studying her face, 'I thought you might have been rather more pleased than you seem.'

'I'm... surprised.'

'Surprised? Or relieved.'

Kira didn't answer. It didn't feel right to admit he had guessed how she felt.

'You've won, Kira. You've got what you wanted. I'll be out of your way, you can kill off that hideous character, and I'll even back you up when you tell the world I've resigned so you won't face the wrath of the listeners. Poor, misguided fools that they are.'

'For which you want what?'

'Adequate compensation. Is that too much to ask?'

'Actually, it is,' she said. 'You're on a contract. You don't get redundancy. There's no chance I could get this past London, and if you leave I can't go on paying –'

'Oh, no. No, no. You miss my point.'

'Which is?'

'I know the Beeb won't agree to a severance. I read every word of that contract.'

'Then who...?'

'You.'

Kira let out an undignified snort, which segued into a full-bodied cackle and then a rattling cough. 'I'm your editor,' she said, gripping the sink. 'Not your employer.'

He pursed his lips and tipped his head side to side, as though judging the weight of her argument. 'You defrauded the BBC.'

The words themselves were simple enough, but they sobered her up like espresso. She pulled herself straight and coughed once more to clear her throat. 'Show me the proof. Which of us here took a salary to which we weren't entitled.'

Dixon pointed towards his own chest, and Kira nodded agreement. Then, as he slowly turned his finger towards her, the nodding turned into an unsteady frown.

'I do believe we both did,' Dixon said. 'How much do they pay you each month?'

'You're forgetting, George. I still earn my pay. I don't sit at the beach and just take it. I work, unlike some.'

'And what if they knew what you signed off each week? What might they call it? Hush money? A bribe to keep me quiet and spare you a furious postbag and difficult questions from London?'

'Do you really think London would care if I wrote you out of The Fleet?'

'Then why didn't you?'

Kira didn't answer.

Dixon stood up. 'I do hope you don't think I'm rude. Check-in closes in ninety minutes or so. Do you have any cash in the house?'

She narrowed her eyes. 'Get out of my house, George Dixon.'

'Hmmm,' he said, lifting his eyebrows. 'Well, if that's the way you want to play it, but I must warn you, it's a dangerous game.'

He looked at his watch, and picking up his bag he made his way to the door.

'I shall be in touch,' he said. 'We can sort out a transfer.' He turned around and pecked her on the cheek. 'You can trust me to keep your secret.'

TWO YEARS AGO

Remus squatted behind the wall and pretended to tighten his shoelace. It was quarter past seven; the traffic was light - just the first few commuters, and parents taking their children to school for breakfast club and morning sports.

He'd already walked past this spot three times, each time carrying milk in a bag. Just a regular guy - nothing to see here - just a guy who's run out of milk trying to make his breakfast.

More of the curtains were open now. The street was waking up, and Remus couldn't afford to parade back and forth any more. For a while he sat at the bus stop, nodding the first two buses away as they slowed to pick him up. Then he'd studied the postbox, picking at the cracked blue paint as he read and re-read the list of collections.

And now he was tying – re-tying – his shoelace, pulling it tight although it already was, unravelling the bow and tying it again like someone with an obsession.

He heard a door. Looking to the side, around the corner of the low brick wall, he saw Renouf step out of his house.

'Anything else?' Renouf called, leaning back into the hallway.

He waited for an answer that Remus didn't hear, then closed the door and stepped onto the pavement. He was already dressed for work.

Remus sank back on his heels, pulling himself behind the wall and listening as the footsteps drew nearer. He kept his head bowed until Renouf walked past, then reached out and tucked a slip of paper inside his black slip-on shoe.

Renouf felt Carey's finger slide in by his foot. He looked down, surprised more than shocked. When he saw Carey's face, he pretended to stumble, corrected himself and went on.

He walked as far as the newsagent, never stopping or looking back, then crouched in front of the magazines and pulled out the small folded slip. It was the same, more or less, as the papers he used at the Guet, only this time the message was written in English, not code. Remus wanted to meet.

Twenty minutes, close to where he'd just seen him, the note explained. And if not... Carey would have no choice but to wait at his house. No doubt Sophie would welcome him in.

Renouf chose a paper and tucked the note inside, then he dropped some coins on the counter and left without taking his change. He retraced his steps and found Carey inside a disused greenhouse, crouching among the weeds and grass.

'I can't be seen with you,' Renouf said, pretending to survey the rest of the greenhouse, his eyes fixed on the furthest end, never dropping to Remus himself.

Carey pulled at one of his ankles, dragging his shoe through the gravel until Renouf lost his balance. Renouf grabbed at the thin aluminium frame but quickly let go as the rough, corroded surface started to bite at his fingers.

'What are you doing?' he asked.

Carey hissed at him to crouch down.

'You can't just come here.'

'I don't think you're in a position to make demands,' Carey said as Renouf squatted down, pulled back his foot and freed his ankle. 'Now tell me. How many, how will they get there, and will they be armed?'

'Why would they be armed?'

Carey gave him a sideways look.

'I don't know,' Renouf said. 'I don't know who they are. I drop off the stash and –'

'That's not very helpful.'

'What can I tell you? I drop the cargo and I'm gone. It's the way they want it.'

'How do they get there?'

'By boat.'

Remus sat forward, his face close to Renouf. 'I could have told you that.'

'The Dalliance.'

'The one you were driving?'

'Probably. It's their boat. It isn't mine. They leave the keys and I pick it up whenever I have a job.'

Remus sank back on his heels and pictured the boat. It was sleek, long, with a pointed prow that tipped up, well away from the water. The back was chiselled and it had a low screen rather than a wheelhouse. It had been built with one thing in mind: speed.

'Let's assume you're right,' he said. 'Tell me about it. How fast does she go?'

'It's a rum runner.'

'A rum runner?'

'Built for... for smuggling. It's a smuggler's boat. Used for running rum outside of the law. Long and lean.'

'How fast?' Remus repeated.

'Does...' Renouf paused for a moment,

thinking. 'Forty, fifty knots. You won't catch it. The Huffin' Puffin isn't –'

'I have no intention of trying to catch it.'

'Then what are you –'

'Never you mind,' Remus snapped. 'What else? Anything special? Any modifications?'

Renouf shook his head. 'I told you. I don't know boats. If they'd made any changes I wouldn't even –'

'Armour? Guns? Special radar? Anything?'

'Nothing,' Renouf said, before adding with less certainty, 'as far as I know.'

Remus dismissed him. Either he really did know as little as he claimed, or he was a better actor than Remus suspected. Either way, he'd be giving away no secrets that morning.

Remus waited five minutes before he left the greenhouse. The road outside was empty. It seemed that no one had seen them.

DAY EIGHT

Fermain Bay, 11.25am

Christine was glad she'd taken a marked police car. She'd never been down to Fermain before, and hadn't expected the tortuous drop she found on the lane through the trees. It was as steep as the road to Saints Bay, but narrower and with a hairpin bend halfway.

She gripped the wheel like a fairground ride; she couldn't deny that Falla's crash had left her shaken and nervous, and now she found herself using the car's conspicuous paintwork to force the oncoming cars to reverse, first as far as the hotel gates, then down to the car park below.

The road opened out as she reached the last turn, where it ran along a broad grass verge that kept the cars from the granite sea wall. The cafe had set out its tables there, between the wall and the No Parking signs, and each was capped by a broad parasol that was already casting hard shadows.

She parked at the end of the tables, close to the slipway that led to the beach, and locked the car by one of the signs. She took a table as far as she could from the counter, and settled her eyes on the view - the broad, shallow beach and its distant sea line, now far beyond the high seam of pebbles. Cliffs rose up on either side, and here and there she could see the path between the ferns and the first feeble petals of African lily.

Her mind turned to Falla, lying unconscious in the hospital bed; she knew that it should have been her. She wondered what Renouf had thought when he saw her return to the office. She replayed the sequence, watching him repeat his actions deep in her mind. Relief; a momentary lightening as she walked back into the room. It was fleeting; chased away by the news she'd sent Falla. Irritation, annoyance, quickly controlled. Did he seem distracted driving them out to the Point? No, not overly so, but it might just have been that he...

'What would you like?'

She looked up, surprised to find a waitress beside her, pen clicked out, pad in hand, and she wondered how long she'd been there.

'Sorry,' Christine said, reaching for the menu. 'I haven't even looked.'

She smiled, then looked beyond the waitress and saw a man that matched Bichard's description.

'Mr Ferbrache?' she asked, standing as well as she could with her knees crooked between the seat and the top of the bench.

He took her hand - it was lost in his own - and told her to call him Ross. His skin was unnaturally smooth, and Christine wondered whether the heat of the fires he'd spent his life putting out had melted away his fingerprints.

'Can I get you a coffee?'

'Thank you, black.'

'A latte,' Christine said, dismissing the waitress and sitting back down. Ferbrache sat opposite, his back to the view, and Christine felt the table lean towards him. He smiled and settled his heavy arms on the broad wooden planks that made up its surface. They creaked beneath him.

'So you're here from Jersey?' he asked.

'I am,' she said. 'Someone had to pick the short straw.' She watched his face, and flashed him a smile when she saw that he hadn't spotted the joke. 'I understand you investigated a fire at Marc Renouf's house?' she asked. 'The one he was building on L'Ancresse Common, is that right?'

She'd got onto business sooner than she'd have liked, but Ferbrache already seemed uncomfortable, and she wondered how long they'd have managed to string out their small talk.

He ran a finger round his collar. 'Sometimes I drink a little too much.'

'We all do that, Ross.'

'True,' he said. 'I get a bit talkative, though. Really shouldn't have mentioned it. It wasn't my story to tell.'

'But there was a fire?'

'There... was,' he said with some hesitation.

The waitress arrived with their drinks. They paused while she settled them down and tucked the receipt beneath Ferbrache's saucer.

'I assumed he knew,' Ferbrache said as she left them.

'Bichard?'

'Yes. Being his boss and all.'

Christine picked up her coffee and blew on it, hiding herself behind the rim and looking at him through the steam. 'I suspect he did,' she lied. 'Probably forgot about it. There's an awful lot of people working below him.'

Ferbrache wasn't convinced. 'Then why the sudden interest?'

'Oh, nothing. He's just following up on some... well, they're not leads, exactly. He's tying up some loose ends, and he seemed to remember you mentioning it, that's all. At some party or other.'

'Did I? Did I?' Ferbrache toyed with his spoon. 'Well, I just... didn't want to see him held up, I suppose. It's frustrating enough building a house, isn't it. With the extra delay...'

'But you inspected the property?'

'Yes.'

'And...'

'Faulty wiring, as I put in my report.'

'You took some pictures?'

'Of course.'

Christine ducked down to reach into her bag. Her head briefly dipped below the table and she saw him rubbing a thigh with the palm of his free hand. He was nervous. She dug out her notebook and pen.

'Could I get a copy?' she asked, coming back

up and clicking the end of her ballpoint.

'A copy?'

'Of the report. It might help if we could see the pictures.'

'Aah, well, you see, we can't just give out personal data.'

'I see. It's about Renouf himself, is it?'

'Well, no. It's the fire, but –'

'Well, that's fine, then. It isn't personal data.'

'All the same.'

'Do we need to apply to the court?'

He closed his mouth and looked down at his coffee.

'Are you sure you took some pictures?' Christine asked.

'Yes,' he said, a little too quickly, and then looking up and meeting her eyes he had a change of heart. 'No.'

Christine clicked back the nib of her pen and closed her book. She reached across and put her hand close to his on the table.

'Was it the wiring?'

He shook his head. 'I was only trying to do the right thing.'

'Could it have been the wiring?'

'No.'

'Are you sure?'

'There wasn't any. It wasn't weatherproof.'

Christine shook her head. His own head was

dipped now, and she could see what looked like the start of a bald patch.

'Did you examine the property?'

'What little of it there was. It wasn't much more than a shell. The floors were in, and the ceilings, but no windows. No staircase.'

'Was there any power at all? Anywhere on the site?'

Ferbrache thought for a moment. 'A small generator. Petrol, I think, but it was well away from the house.'

'Okay.' Christine paused to drink some of her coffee. She wanted him to pay attention, so she waited until he looked up before she went on.

'Now I want you to think very carefully before you answer this question.' She raised her eyebrows and he nodded. 'Good. This is between you, me and Bichard. It will never get back to Marc Renouf. You have my word.' She made sure he noticed her moving the notebook away, then asked: 'Could the fire have been started deliberately?'

He hesitated. 'Yes.'

'Do you believe that it was?'

'Is this still between us?'

She nodded. 'You, me and Bichard.'

Ferbrache tore open a packet of sugar and stirred its contents into his cup. 'I dismissed the rest of my crew. Said I would do it myself. I had to write it up anyway. So, they went. I had a look around the site. There was a pile of kit at the back. A couple of bags of cement. Half bags. Tilers' batons, that sort of thing.' He sipped at his coffee and looked at the road as though it might let him escape. 'There were some bottles.'

'What kind of bottles?'

'I can't say for sure they were anything to do with it.'

'What was in them?'

'They were empty.' He stopped for a moment, but picked up the story when Christine took a breath, ready to prompt him. 'They were spirit bottles. The stuff you use for cleaning brushes. All of them empty.'

'Is that so unusual? It was a building site, after all.'

'They wouldn't have been cleaning brushes until they started painting, and they couldn't have done that until the house was plastered. You don't do that before it's weatherproof.'

Christine understood. 'How many bottles?'

'Twenty. Thirty, perhaps. All of them scattered around the end of a ladder.'

'What kind of –'

'Someone had been up to the roof,' he said, cutting her off. The kind of ladder was irrelevant. 'Probably doused the joists and set them off. Either way, they didn't hang around. They didn't even stop to fold it up. It was still extended.'

Christine puffed out her cheeks and exhaled slowly. 'What did you do?'

He dropped his cup back in the saucer and looked at her properly for the first time since they'd sat down. 'Picked them up. Threw them in the quarry that night. Collapsed the ladder.'

'You covered it up.'

He nodded.

'Why?'

'I had to repay him a kindness.'

Christine stared and wondered how any man could be so naive. Perhaps Renouf's position – his role on the force – had played a part. She liked to think that Ferbrache wouldn't have been so stupid if Renouf had driven buses, or worked the tills at the airport. But still...

'Perhaps I should tell him myself,' Ferbrache said.

'Who?'

'Marc.'

Christine reached out and at last touched his hand. 'You really have been most helpful. But I think we ought to keep this between ourselves. Best not implicate Marc any further, eh?'

Ferbrache shrugged.

'We don't want you owing him any more favours, eh?' she said.

TWO YEARS AGO

Marie stood in front of the pines. Portelet Harbour was just below and from that far up she could see right along the west coast. She'd been watching Carey for close to two hours, hurrying back and forth in the bay, from boat to building and building to boat, apparently unloading as much as he could and storing it in the small granite block at the back of the bay. He was emptying the Huffin' Puffin, unloading equipment and anything else he might not need on his trip to Sark.

Marie was surprised that he found so much to remove. She'd been well briefed - and so had the Consortium - on the state of the boat and its contents. Renouf had left a long and rambling note at the Guet, running to more than a hundred digits. It must have taken him almost as long to encode as it had for her to untangle each block.

Bit of a tub, rough sounding engines. Sparse below. Two-ring burner: gas. Small sink, toilet, bunks. Good storage, mostly empty - Renouf had done more than pick up some beers when Remus had sent him down - top speed 20/30 knots. Sturdy hull, no protection, no weapons.

So what was in the boxes?

He'd taken out three of them: cardboard,

buff in colour, rigid but burred at the corners. Apparently they'd been on the boat for some time. Perhaps it was the galley, and the tins and bottles he must have kept there. Renouf hadn't mentioned them, but she knew that Carey spent nights on the boat and he surely didn't catch all of his food. Maybe he knew – maybe he was anticipating some kind of a fight, disconnecting the gas and putting it somewhere safe, removing his utensils, rolling up the bunks and taking them onshore, all the while making the boat lighter, more nimble and agile. Better for a quick getaway.

Should she be concerned?

She thought for a moment, lowering the glasses and looking towards Fort Grey and Lihou beyond it, and then at the curve of the coast bending back on itself as it strode uncertainly north.

If her judgement was right the Huffin' Puffin was not much more than a motorised bucket built for fishing trips and days spent at anchor. However light, it wouldn't – it couldn't – ever threaten the Dalliance. If this was Europol's best resource she had little to worry about. It would be a quick operation. An easy night. She might even see her bed again before her shift in the morning.

And of course, she thought, it means

something else, doesn't it. It means they know very little.

Renouf had suggested that Remus was clueless so far, working off his own bat with a flexible remit and little to go on. Perhaps it was all just speculative. Maybe they had very little. The flask, yes, but what else? No prints (they'd been careful), no contacts, no chain of command. If they had – and they'd known that tonight might have brought some success – would they not have kitted him out with something more fitting?

Carey had told Renouf that he wanted to give him a chance before he took things higher. This would suggest he meant what he'd said. All they needed to do was neutralise Carey and they'd be safe. They might even be able to bring back the boat and resume the operation.

She lifted the glasses again and watched him complete his unloading. The last few items came out in dribs and drabs. He emptied the wheelhouse, removed the seat on which Renouf had sat during their abortive trip to Cowhorn and unscrewed the red bulb at the rear of the craft.

He dropped off the last of the boxes and carried a sturdy pole out of the building and back to the boat. It was six feet tall with a rubber-wrapped baton at one end and a vicious hook on the other. He pushed it into a pair of lateral clips by the wheelhouse door and finally he spent twenty minutes securing things on the deck and taping the wheelhouse windows, perhaps in preparation for some kind of explosion. He lifted a cat onto the harbour wall and placed beside it an open tin of what looked like tuna, no doubt to stop it from climbing back onto the boat.

It was quarter past midnight. He set a countdown on the dashboard timer, edging it on by just enough minutes to grant Renouf a clean escape, then he turned the key and pressed the button to start the engines. They fired up right away, without a cough or hesitation, and whipped the water, which foamed and fizzed as they kicked up a cloud of sediment dragged up from the sandy floor.

He threw off the rope and reversed away from the wall, tucking between the rocks and the hooked granite arm, and by using the rusting spear that stuck straight up from its outer edge as a marker, he kept the hull clear of the rocks that were hidden by two feet of water.

Marie watched him pulling away, cruising at leisure out of the harbour like someone with nothing better to do. Anyone who saw him – anyone other than her – would have paid scant attention, assuming that Remus was just a fisherman heading out on an overnight trip.

She lifted her cuff and looked at her watch. Its iridescent face glowed green and the hands stood out against it. She did a quick calculation. He'd have to pick up some speed as soon as he rounded the corner. The window Renouf had given him wouldn't stay open for long. Perhaps he assumed - wrongly, she reminded herself - that once he was out of view of the harbour, no one would see him at least until he reached Petit Bot.

She let the cuff slip back, pulled out her phone and called the next look-out, high on the headland at Pleinmont. A man there swiped the face of his phone.

'He's coming your way,' she said.

The man on the cliffs said nothing. He cut the line and picked up his night-vision glasses.

The first stage was underway.

Marie walked back to her car and drove north.

Remus looked back at the harbour, at Sampson sitting at the end of the wall, staring back at him over his unexpected midnight feast. He'd been the only one there - and the only one on the beach, too, as he emptied out the Huffin' Puffin, removing the few belongings he kept onboard. He didn't know what to expect, but travelling light - even lighter than he usually did - seemed to him a sensible move.

He was sure he'd be back before morning, so didn't take food or gas for the burner. Its canister was bulky and heavy, and though he was certain he'd have no trouble he knew it was better to face whatever was coming without an explosive bottle onboard.

He'd offloaded his notes and his maps, packing them into one of his cardboard boxes and stashing it in the old granite boat house behind the bay. He couldn't afford to lose his record of the operation so far: the notes that backed up the log he'd present at the next meeting in Lyon - after translation, of course. Even the French delegation, forgetting that not everyone could speak French, probably wouldn't welcome a lengthy tract of Guernesiais.

But then again, after that little stunt at the previous meeting, perhaps that's all they deserved.

He'd been remiss in updating it. It was complete until... he thought back... as far as their swim at Pembroke. He'd rectify that as soon as he returned. Maybe he'd anchor off Herm - somewhere quiet and undisturbed - and bring it up to date on the deck. He could write up whatever happened over the next few hours so then Bichard and the Poles and the French delegation, those chaps from Ukraine and... well, whatever the other nationalities, they'd all know what he'd been doing and where they stood.

He steered around the arm of the harbour, resisting the urge to push on the throttle, well aware that the wind was blowing towards the shore and would take with it the sound of the engines. No one would know what he was up to but years of tradecraft had taught him to be discreet.

Besides, he had plenty of time.

The countdown turned over its second full minute and beeped. He silenced it and shuffled it into the corner where it could sit out of his line of sight. He had other things to concentrate on for the next ninety minutes. The clock was just his insurance - and Renouf's. He didn't want them to meet. Plausible deniability had to be maintained, at least in Renouf's mind if not his own. He already had enough to pick him up when the time came to make that move, so why not maintain the illusion a little while longer?

At last he rounded the headland and lined up the prow with the bulb of the lighthouse. The course he had chosen would keep him clear of the rocks at Pezeries until he turned at the back of the fort.

He maintained twelve knots as he rounded

the south-western tip of the island, then doubled his speed as the south coast cliffs rose up to his left. The sheer granite walls threw back the roar of the engine, almost enough to drown out the sound of the motors directly behind him. He felt the snout of the boat rise up and its rear sink into the waves as his grip instinctively tightened on the wheel. The Huffin' Puffin started to skip on the gentle crests, between each of which a fearsome vavv-vavv-vavv spilled out as the props broke free of the water, only to be submerged once they hit the next crest.

He wasn't concerned that he might be seen or heard any more. The wall was close to two hundred feet, it was late, it wasn't the warmest of nights. The coastal path would be deserted on a dark night like this, but things would be different as he closed on Sark. The houses there were closer to where he needed to be. The island was smaller and lower. The noise of his engine would carry over the lip and be heard inland and he'd have to slow down as he made his final approach.

Between now and then - and between here and there - he would make some good progress and give himself enough time to scout out the caves before he moved in.

The man on the cliff heard him approach, and

he heard the change of the engine note as Remus rounded Pezeries Fort.

He scrambled across the shingle, climbing down from the bench that had been his lookout for the last two hours, and hunkered in the heather as close as he could to the edge of the cliff. It shelved away there, each layer sloping toward the precipice to reveal a further, slightly smaller ledge below it.

He darted from one to the other, clinging onto the rough grass as he lowered himself towards the precipice, praying that each would hold his weight and help him keep his balance. The last of them was loose: not rock and soil, but just the grass itself, hanging out over the edge. He stepped back, up to the level he'd almost left without due care - a move that would have sent him to his death - and as he did he frightened a rabbit. It shot away, scampering back up the tiers with a deftness of which he could only dream, and he took its place and wedged his buttocks into the hollow that had given it shelter. It was tight, but he felt secure, and at last he released his hold on the grass and lifted the binoculars up to his eyes.

Remus Carey was right below him, bouncing onto and out of each wave, accelerating now that he was out of the view of Portelet Harbour. The man judged his speed to be close to thirty knots already and realised at once that the Huffin' Puffin was no ordinary boat.

Renouf, it was clear, really did know as little about boats as he'd always claimed.

Marie crossed the island in fourteen minutes. She pulled into Beaucette Marina and left the car by the club house. The Dalliance was berthed there, fuelled and ready to leave. Crossing the island had given her a significant head start. Now all she needed to do was traverse the channel to Herm, skirt its northern coast and cut a route south between Shell Beach and Sark. She would intercept Carey as he approached the caves from the south.

She had to admit that Renouf had done well, given the circumstances, but she worried that they hadn't been able to call on all the support they needed. The plan was merely to make Carey disappear, not to kill him, but they had chosen to keep Renouf in the dark on that score. The less he knew about the operation, the easier it would be for him to deny any knowledge.

Plausible deniability: it would be better for all of them. She'd been playing the game long enough to understand the value of discretion.

She turned the key and the twin four-litre engines started without hesitation. They gave a hollow, deep cackle and spat from their inlets.

The water behind the propellers was sucked down under the boat where the blades smashed and mashed it, mixing it round and around and throwing back up a bubbling foam as she slipped the wet rope off the dock. Freed of its tether, the boat pushed away from the rocking pontoon.

By the time she left the harbour mouth she was already closing on fifteen knots, soon to match Carey's impressive speed.

She dug out her phone and called ahead to make sure the boats at Sark were in place.

Andrej snapped shut his clamshell mobile. Petter, who sat in the second boat, frequently called it a dumb phone, but Andrej would always ignore him. It didn't send photos or pick up his email, but at least the battery lasted two weeks and the signal was always rock solid, even down there in the mouth of the cave when all they had was the overspill from Guernsey.

'He comes,' Andrej said. 'The woman, too.'

Petter nodded and used a pole to push his boat away from the wall of the cave.

'You know what we do?' Petter asked.

The light of the moon caught his partner's eye, and Andrej started to laugh. It echoed around the ceiling and walls as he reached down and picked up his lantern.

*

Remus looked down at the radar, its arm of green light sweeping round the edge of the screen, dragging behind it a stream of small dots that were rocks and islets and boats he was passing. They were moored, abandoned in the channel, ready for someone to come and collect the following day or the day after that or the weekend.

He squinted, and sometimes he caught a flash from one of their windows - the moon reflecting off cloudy glass, or trapped within a bulb's protective casing. Other than that he was blind to the world beyond the glass of the wheelhouse. Its windows were drenched, dripping with spray that the sea threw up at forty knots. Only the small spinning plates left and right were clear enough to see through. The boat powered on, still tipped back, and the view through the plates was of clear skies and stars and there, to one side, the hulking mass of the cliffs, bleached silver grey by the moon.

From place to place, where it cut into alcoves and bays, the cliff would be lost in a yawning black cave which would catch the boom of his engine and fold it over and in on itself, the echoes colliding with one another until they escaped as a powerful roar.

He clipped a run of buoys, which shattered

and snapped and flew up in the air. They crested the boat, lost in the darkness, clearing the wheelhouse by several feet and catching the wind high above him. Freed of their tether, they sailed beyond the Huffin' Puffin as Remus powered it on, finally finding the water again once he was half a mile distant.

He looked across at the timer; he still had plenty of time, but that was no reason to let up the pace. He rarely had call to drive so fast this close to land, and the streaking past of the cliff and the buoys - and the random boats he found here and there - was a heady, quite breathtaking rush.

The radar completed another swift sweep and it seemed that he had the sea to himself. The Dalliance was out of sight, cutting across Little Russell and hidden beyond the island itself. The other two craft, lying in wait at the caves under Sark, were beyond the reach of the digital eye and protected within the dense rocky walls. He wouldn't see them for half an hour and by then it would be too late.

Marie reported her position, and told Andrej to make sure he was ready. If the man on the cliff was right, they'd underestimated Carey's boat. It was faster and more powerful than Renouf had been led to believe - and he'd led them to believe in turn. At his current rate Carey would reach the island sooner than they'd expected and Marie would have to pilot the Dalliance at top speed if they weren't to lose him.

She checked the fuel gauge, then pushed the throttle up to the top of its run. The boat lurched forward, the wind tearing at her hair, and she hunkered down behind the chrome rim of the curved, open screen.

It was obvious now that their strongest card was surprise. The wind was from the south, and so that, at least, would count in their favour, cutting the throw of the sound from her engines until she was almost upon him. She knew his own motors would further mask her approach but speed, as ever, was key. She'd never outrun the sound wave but the faster she drove the boat towards him, the less of a warning he'd get.

Remus powered on, past St Martin's Point, straight out from Jerbourg, and beyond the southern-most tip of Herm. Sark was directly ahead, and at last he could make out its hulking mass rising up from the waves. It blocked a patch at the top of each sweep of the radar. He'd passed the point from which he had first seen Renouf retrieving the pot from the sea – the place where this part of the operation had all begun – and now he was only a mile from the Venus Pool.

He eased the throttle and unhooked his night-vision goggles from the back of the wheelhouse door. The boat's subsiding momentum let it sit down in the water as he carried them out to the deck and swept them across the horizon.

The view through the lenses fizzed a dull green on the two tiny screens within them. He was too far away to make out any details in the cliffs of the island, but he could scan the water and see that the surface was clear between him and the cave.

The moon should still have been bright that night, but unforecast clouds had obscured it now and it gave off less reflected light. The goggles were relying almost entirely on heat and ultra violet, leaving the water pitch black and rendering everything else in faint detail. It was a mixed blessing. Better light would have helped him to find his quarry, but it would also have made him more obvious.

He completed a sweep, fore and aft, then lowered the goggles and felt his eyes stretching, accommodating the new darkness. He stepped back into the cabin and hung up the goggles, then perched on the edge of the captain's stool. By now the Huffin' Puffin had come to a standstill, and the tilt of the hull on the tip of the waves was the only motion about him.

Remus Carey wasn't the only one with night-vision goggles. A mile away north and east, Andrej looked back at the dumpy boat that now bobbed around, entirely unlit and seemingly waiting for something – or someone.

He turned and signalled to Petter.

'He is come.'

Petter held up the lantern and flipped the switch, casting a dull amber glow on the walls of the cave.

Remus caught sight of the light flashing on. A moment later it faded and died before reigniting, steadier now.

He settled the goggles down on the dash and picked up his heavy binoculars, turning the wheel between the barrels until the view sharpened up. The mouth of the cave was steeped in the soft, dim light. It looked to Remus like someone was using the least light they could: just enough to see their surroundings without the gentle tobacco glow being carried too far out to sea.

He slung the binocular strap round his neck and pressed the button to restart the engines. The Huffin' Puffin leapt forward, and Remus gripped the wheel again, his knuckles bone white as he hung on to keep himself upright.

The light blinked out as he closed on the cave and all that remained was the retinal glow where the light had imprinted itself on his eyes. He kept his head steady, never shifting his gaze, and allowed the now dying ember to guide him.

It faded quickly, but by then he was close enough. He could see the island and make out the shape of the rocks at its feet, among which the black yawning bulk of the cave opened up. What he didn't see - and didn't hear - was the long, fast boat approaching from the north.

The Huffin' Puffin was dead ahead. Marie could see the streak of its wake that led like an arrow right up to its stern. At the end of the streak throbbed the motors, still churning the water and leading her on.

As Remus slowed and angled towards the mouth of the cave, she pushed the Dalliance harder still. Squeezing out every last drop of its power, she braced herself and rammed its upturned prow into the port side of Remus' boat.

The Dalliance recoiled as its prow broke through the Huffin' Puffin's thick hull, the impact throwing Marie from her stool and out of its cockpit. She fell to the deck, crushing her arm beneath the small weight of her body, but her wiry, elastic frame bounced back and she hauled herself up again, the better to see what was happening.

Petter jumped over to Andrej's boat as Andrej started his engine, and he clung to the top of the low-slung windshield as the single-engined craft shot forward. The Huffin' Puffin was almost upon them, too close for Andrej's boat to get up much speed, but just far enough for the lighter, nimbler, harder craft to send the Huffin' Puffin's undamaged side crashing into the opposite wall.

It struck the rocks at an angle, the granite first grazing, then scoring, and finally breaking through the hull. The deafening, sickening sound of splintering wood, of racing engines thrown out of the water, the coming together of powerful boats - three of them in a confined space - filled and echoed around and around the small chamber. Andrej killed his engine and jumped across to the Huffin' Puffin's forward deck, swiftly followed by Petter, who used his pole to smash the wheelhouse window.

Remus put up his arm as the glass rained down - a move that momentarily blinded him and hid his assailants from view. All that was left of the broad, thick pane were the crystals that still hung on the tape he'd applied in the harbour.

He lowered his arms and saw his attackers, with pug-like faces and sinewy bodies and muscles picked out by the moonlight, now back as the clouds drew apart.

The man with the lance thrust again, and Remus dodged to the left. The lance missed his flesh, but it found his jacket and tore a hole in the sleeve, catching within the armpit just long enough for Remus to grab it with both of his hands and pull it towards him, through the windshield and into the cabin. The man fell with it, landing hard on the flat of his back and winding himself.

He gasped for breath at Remus's feet, his palms slapping against the deck as he struggled for air while Remus freed the lance from his jacket and span it around in his hands. He raised it high above his head and saw the man's eyes widen, sharp now, aware of what was to come. Remus stretched as high as he could, determined to do it the kindest way, to finish it once and for all, to bring down the point as hard and as fast as he could, into the man's straining neck.

It had happened so quickly – the collision, the broken glass, Petter disappearing into the cabin – and now Andrej saw their quarry with Petter's lance in his hands, held high above his head.

'Petter,' he called, freeing himself from the cabin and leaping across to the Huffin' Puffin.

He could see him now, prone on the floor of the wheelhouse, seemingly trapped and unable to move.

Andrej was moving instinctively, not thinking what might come next as he leaped head first through the broken window and crashed into Remus's ribs. The two of them hit the floor, and rolled out of the wheelhouse and onto the deck. Andrej scrambled back to his feet and turned to find Petter. His eyes were wide, the whites now clear around each iris. Andrej reached down and grabbed Petter's legs, rolling him into a sitting position, forcing his ankles under his buttocks until he was crouching.

Remus found his own feet. He scrambled up and turned around, scanning the deck for the lance. It had rolled to the aft, beyond his reach, and was now effectively lost to them both. He turned back towards the front of the craft as Petter recovered and Andrej thrust up his fist, crashing it into Remus's teeth. Bone met bone and Remus felt his neck snap back as the fist powered on, knocking his head to one side.

Andrej lifted both of his arms, keeping his elbows bent in a fighter's pose, supple and ready to hit out again, but in doing so he'd left his groin open. Remus kicked forward, landing the steel-tipped toe of his heavy boot into the soft flesh between Andrej's legs. The force of the upswing lifted Andrej's feet off the deck and he cried out like a stuck pig.

He slipped backwards off the boot and fell to the floor, and as he hit it he vomited, splashing the contents of his stomach onto the varnished wood and the boot that had caused him such pain.

Remus looked up as Andrej fell and saw Petter standing behind him. He was fully recovered, breathing heavily, and holding Remus's own deck hook. Remus's eyes darted to the clips on the side of the wheelhouse - but he already knew he would find them empty.

Petter lurched forward once more, and this time he found his target, sinking the pole deep into Remus's midriff. Remus bent over, unable to keep himself upright as Petter pulled back and spun the pole through a quarter turn, smashing the heavy rubber-clad end into Remus's jaw and knocking him onto the deck.

He fell and didn't get up.

Marie called across from the Dalliance.

'Melden!' she ordered - report.

'Der Mann ist am Boden,' Andrej called back - the man is down. He wedged the toe of his boot under Remus's kidneys and levered him up. Remus flopped back on the deck, seemingly lifeless.

'Bringe zu mir.'

Petter leaned down and picked Remus up, throwing him over one shoulder and bouncing him up and down until he was balanced on the fleshy part between his own ribs and hips. The fleshy part that had caught the brunt of the strike from the pole was now taking all of his weight as Petter's shoulder sank into Remus's stomach.

Marie watched as Petter heaved the prone body, clearing the void between the two boats with a single leap and throwing Remus down on the salt-stained deck of her craft.

'Gut,' she said, putting two fingers to the side of Remus's neck and feeling a steady pulse.

She gathered his limbs and bound them tight with a length of thick rope. None of them knew how long they could count on him being like that, or how he might struggle when he came to.

DAY EIGHT

Chouet, noon

Ollie's phone chirped and vibrated as Simon's text popped up on its screen. He'd cut across the island's humped back, through the valleys and hills of St Andrews, and now he was nearing the north-west coast. His legs were starting to feel the burn. He lifted the phone to read it without slowing down, then swung his bike around a sharp corner and narrowly missed an oncoming car.

Kira Spooner lived two streets away, just missing out on a view of the sea. Ollie rounded a second corner, and there he could see her modest bungalow hunkered down between two identical neighbours. He swung a leg over the saddle and glided the bike towards the kerb, both feet perched on one pedal.

Kira must have been standing by the door, for he heard her pressing the handle as soon as he'd pushed the bell, and she started to talk before he could see her face.

'George, if you think I'm going to change my –' She stopped when she saw who it was.

'Expecting somebody?' Ollie asked.

She started to push the door closed, but Ollie put his foot on the threshold and moved it towards the hinge. The door jammed on the side of his trainer.

'George Dixon, perhaps?'

'Please leave,' Kira said, pushing on the door. It wasn't budging, and neither was Ollie's foot.

'Not until we've spoken.'

'We've got nothing to discuss,' she said. 'I don't even know who you are.'

'I'm not sure that's true,' Ollie said. 'Not when

you're clearly so keen to keep me out of your house.'

She pushed a little harder, but Ollie's foot was wedged so close to the hinge - and their bulk so very mismatched - that her efforts were getting her nowhere.

Ollie pulled out his card and held it up. 'I'm perfectly happy to talk on the doorstep,' he said, pushing the door slightly towards her, freeing his foot and placing it back on the path.

Kira saw her chance, and slammed the door shut.

'Perhaps we could talk about Dixon,' he said, raising his voice so she'd hear him through the door. He could see her standing in the hallway, close to the frosted window.

'Go away,' she called back.

'And your involvement...' - he continued, raising his voice so that now he'd be heard by the neighbours - 'in the murder of Rosalynd Holdbrook.'

Silence.

'...and Richelle Ibbott.'

More silence.

'When did you first get involved in -'

She pulled the door open and stared at him, her legs planted wide to one side of the door, one fist gripped tight by her hip. Ollie could see a pulse in the side of her nose where she gently

– no doubt unconsciously – flared her nostrils like gills.

'That had nothing...' – she hissed it – 'nothing to do with me.' She poked out her head beyond the door and looked left and right at the neighbouring houses.

'George Dixon never was at that live broadcast, was he?' Ollie asked, phrasing it so that it came across as a statement.

'I don't recall.'

'I think you do.'

She stepped back and opened the door fully. 'Get in.'

Ollie leaned his bike on the wall and stepped into her hallway. She closed the door and stood in his way, barring him from going any further into her house.

'Do you know how radio works?' she asked.

'A little.'

'Radio drama?'

He shook his head.

'Six episodes a week,' Kira said. 'All recorded in bits and pieces and stuck together a couple of hours before the broadcast. It isn't recorded the way it goes out. You do know that?'

'I don't doubt it.'

'And you do know that means each actor, Dixon among them, is only in for a couple of hours a week – three at the most. It's almost impossible to say who was in when and for what.'

'Yet you have a signing-in book on reception.'

Kira waved away the suggestion.

'And of course, the night Richelle was murdered was the night of your live broadcast.'

Ollie paused, giving her time to make the connection herself. She didn't quite get there, or maybe refused to play on, for she asked him what of it.

'Dixon had fifteen lines.'

'If you say so. I haven't counted them.'

'He did,' Ollie said. 'So how did it work? Did you split them all up? The cast, I mean. Or did you cram them all into the same room?'

Kira let out an exasperated sigh. 'I've said all I want. I don't have time to discuss the mechanics of specific broadcasts. If you don't mind...' She reached for the door again, a hand now resting on his chest, ready to push him back through it.

'My guess is you split them all up.' Ollie stood his ground and could feel her fingers pressing harder. 'Scattered them around, a few here, a few there, until you'd filled the studios.'

'It's getting on,' she said. 'If I don't get going...'

'That way, no one would have noticed that Dixon was absent, would they.'

He felt the pressure lighten. She took half a step away from him and met his gaze for the first time since he'd arrived.

'Dixon didn't utter a single word in that episode, did he, Kira?'

'Don't be so ridiculous.' She laughed - an unconvincing laugh, almost as weak as George Dixon's. 'You counted his lines. What was it? Fifteen?'

'There or thereabouts.'

'Well then.'

'Well then, what?'

'That proves it.'

'That proves nothing. He wasn't there. You dropped in his lines yourself, didn't you.'

She shrugged. 'Does it matter?'

'Not where Richelle is concerned,' Ollie said. 'Although there's little doubt in my mind that that's the point when he killed her - when he should have been live on the radio. Rosalynd, though... If you knew Dixon had no alibi for the time Richelle was killed, I'd say it makes you an accessory to Rosalynd's murder.'

She dropped her arms and they dangled, limp and lifeless at her side. 'Dixon was there. He'll back me up. Ask him.'

'Of course he will. And you'll back him up, too, because you need him just as much as he needs you right now. He wasn't there, though, and I don't think we'll have too many problems proving it.'

'Nobody there that night - no one except for me - saw everyone else,' she said, steadying her voice. The effort she was making to maintain her composure was starting to show. 'No one can say for sure whether Dixon was there or not.'

'I can. Simon Langlois can. With a little bit of cutting and trimming of that night's broadcast, pretty much anyone can. There were witnesses, Kira. Thousands of them, but none of them know it yet.'

She looked at him, and her lips fussed and twitched without her making a sound.

'I'm sure you had no idea what Dixon was doing the night you unwittingly covered for him.' Ollie put out a hand and rested it on Kira's shoulder. 'And I'm sure he hadn't planned to do it at all. He had too much to lose for that, but by not coming forward you covered for him, and you let him go on to kill for a second time.'

She pulled her arm free and stepped back. She seemed to be frozen, and then, as though in a daze, like someone thrashing their covers in bed, she swung her arm forward and slapped him. She gripped her mouth, seemingly shocked at what she'd just done, and the tears she'd been fighting for most of the week finally came to her eyes. They tipped out with great heaving sobs, streaking her face with weak, cheap mascara, which her shaking fingers were starting to smear.

'Where is he, Kira?' Ollie asked.

She shook her head. 'I didn't know. I didn't know he would do it. You have to believe me. I couldn't say because...'

'Because of what? Why couldn't you tell?'

She turned away and ran to the kitchen. Ollie ran behind her and caught her at the door. 'Tell me where he is.'

'You've missed him,' she said, gasping between each word, barely able to finish her sentence. 'He's gone.'

Ollie smoothed her hair back, taking it out of her eyes. 'Tell me where he's gone, Kira. Try and undo at least some of the damage.'

'He's... gone,' she sobbed. 'He's leaving the island.'

'Now? How?'

'I don't know.'

'Boat or plane, Kira? Boat or plane? This is important.'

'I don't know,' she shouted, the outburst coming from nowhere - perhaps the same place as the spontaneous slap - and then she calmed herself down. She slumped on a seat at the kitchen table and felt the warmth ooze out of its cushion. Dixon's warmth. He'd been there less than five minutes before. 'I don't know,' she whispered, pressing her face into her palms. 'He had to check in.'

Ollie swore. He pulled out his phone and ran to the door, then jumped on his bike and kicked away as he started to dial a number.

'Ella Brouard,' he said, as soon as the switchboard picked up his call. 'Tell her it's urgent.'

He turned his bike east and started to pedal and prayed that he'd get there in time.

Police Headquarters, 12.10pm

Renouf ran down to the lab as soon as Charlie had called him. He swiped the door with his pass and pushed it open with enough force to crash the handle into a line of cabinets.

'What have you got?' he asked, rounding the corner to Charlie's desk.

Charlie was writing a note on a label. The label was stuck to a vial whose sloping sides were causing the ballpoint to slip. 'Wax,' he said, putting the vial in a rack. 'On the headphones.'

'And?'

'We turned up a match.'

'Richelle Ibbott?

'Yes.'

Renouf let out a luxuriant sigh, and Charlie found himself frowning, surprised at his friend's reaction.

'Then they must have been hers,' Renouf said, taking the chair by the cannabis plant and allowing himself to flop down.

'Maybe, maybe not,' Charlie said.

'We found a second sample mixed in with her DNA.'

'Dixon?'

'Maybe.'

'If they were hers - or his - they probably ended up sharing them.'

'Most likely, but without a sample of his DNA we can't say for sure. What we do know, though...' He turned around and opened a new window on his computer. He scrolled through a list of files and double-clicked when he found the one he wanted.

'Well?' Renouf tried his best to sound casual, forced himself to slouch a little, and when he caught himself pulling the lobe of one ear, he folded his arms and sat still.

Charlie angled his screen in Renouf's direction. It was filled with numbers and graphs. 'The sample you took from the hottentot fig at the second murder scene.'

'The blood?'

'London had some lab time, so we rushed it over.'

'It matches?'

'No, but some fibres caught in it did carry a sample of errant DNA that matches the second sample within the wax.'

'If you're going to tell me that was Richelle's, too...' Renouf started, but Charlie waved his hand and shook his head.

'No. That's the one thing we can rule out. It wasn't hers, and it wasn't whoever bled on the hottentot fig.'

'Then how did it get there?'

'My guess is that someone carried her.'

'Holdbrook?'

'Holdbrook,' Charlie said, nodding. 'Whoever killed her picked her up and carried her to the edge. She bled on his clothing, and when those drops fell to the ground, they took a fibre with them. There was DNA on the fibre. The same DNA as we found in the wax.'

Renouf puffed his cheeks. 'Circumstantial or not, that says Dixon to me.'

'That would be the most logical assumption. With what we know about the tides and currents and the probable route of Rosalynd Holdbrook's body, it would seem particularly coincidental if he wasn't involved in both matters.'

'And Oliver Carey?' Renouf asked, barely wanting to hear the answer for fear it would turn things against him again.

'In the clear, as far as we can tell,' Charlie said.

'We sampled his DNA from the bag you handed him at Port Soif but there's no match.'

'You're sure?'

'I'm sure you don't need me to answer that.'

'Dixon then,' Renouf said. He leaned forward and started to play with the leaves on Charlie's plant. 'There's a head-scratcher for you. Going on this evidence, he could have been involved in the Ibbott murder and still have a rock-solid alibi.'

'Except he can't, can he,' Charlie said. 'And my guess is Rosalynd Holdbrook knew that. She knew the systems in place at The Fleet, so if anyone was going to spot a hole in his story, it would have been her. Perhaps she was foolish enough to tell him what she knew before she told us.'

Charlie's phone rang. He picked it up and listened, then handed it over to Renouf.

'Someone called Ella Brouard,' he said. 'Says it's urgent.'

States of Guernsey Airport, 12.20pm

George Dixon pulled into the airport car park, swung past the bus stop and jumped on the brakes at the front of the terminal building. He cut the engine and sprang out, leaving the keys in the ignition.

A man in a fluorescent jacket put up his hand, but Dixon barged straight past him.

'Clamp it,' he said. 'Or have it. It's yours.'

He swept through the doors and into the foyer, and looked for his flight on the screen. There were two Aurigny flights to the mainland – Southampton and Gatwick, more or less leaving together – as well as a pair of Trislanders fuelled and prepped for island hops, and JOEY, the red-nosed tourist flight currently open for boarding. He hurried across to the desk where his check-in was marked as 'last call', handed over his passport and took off his hat so the woman who served him could pair his face with his photo.

'No luggage,' he said. 'Just this.' He held up the holdall. Stowed inside it was all he could show for the best part of sixty years on the planet.

He confirmed that he'd packed it himself, had left behind any sharp objects and hadn't been asked to carry onboard any belongings for anyone else.

'You'll need to hurry,' she said as she stamped his ticket and handed it over. 'They're boarding.'

Ollie let go of the handlebars and sat himself up in the saddle. He'd covered the first mile already, heading inland across the common from Chouet, and now he was close to the point where he'd have to make a decision: south-west for the airport, or carry straight on to St Peter Port and the ferry to France or the mainland.

He pulled out his phone and called Ella.

'Any news?' he asked.

'I'm checking,' she said. He could hear her clicking her mouse. 'There's a ferry to Carteret in two hours. Portsmouth in... Nothing. Not until this evening.'

'And the flights?'

'Hang on.'

He clamped the phone between his ear and his shoulder and reached down to pull on the handlebars. He leaned to the right and took a corner more quickly than he'd expected. The back tyre span and kicked out, skidding away on a patch of loose gravel. He hauled the bars left and dragged the frame back in line.

'Come on, Ella.'

'Four departures in the next twenty minutes, then nothing for...' She scrolled down the list. 'An hour. Just arrivals.'

'That's where he's headed. Did you find Renouf?'

'I told him what you said. He's sent a car to the port. He's heading for the airport himself.'

'Call them back. Tell them they have to ground those planes – at least until they know which one he's on.'

'Will do.'

He hopped his bike onto the pavement to cut past the traffic on Route Militaire. Taking the road down the spine of the island would lead him straight to the airport.

'Listen, Ella,' he said, as he swerved around a pedestrian. 'When this is all over, would you like to –'

All she heard was the sound of the phone as it skittered across the road, the riderless bike not so far behind it.

'Dixon has family in Southampton,' Renouf said, as Clarke switched on the blue lights and siren and threw the car into fourth. They were within the 25mph belt surrounding Town, and when they escaped its orbit the island-wide limit was still thirty-five on even the most major roads. It wasn't often they got the chance to push it to fifty or sixty. Clarke was determined to enjoy it.

'Call dispatch,' Renouf said, turning around to look at Christine. She'd returned from her meeting with Ross Ferbrache and had jumped in behind them, just in time for the chase to the airport. 'Tell them to call the airport and hold the Southampton flight.'

'Got it.'

'Then get on to Hampshire. Tell them I want a car at the airport their end in case someone cocks up. Tell them they've got half an hour.'

'But the flight takes –'

'I know that. But they might not, and I'd rather have them sitting around for thirty minutes than miss it.' He turned to Clarke. 'How long?'

'Ten minutes,' he said, his eye on the speedo. The needle was touching forty-five as they narrowly scraped past a bus.

Renouf looked up for the first time since leaving the garage to see the harbour fly by on his left, and the backs of the shops do the same to his right. 'Why the hell have you brought us out this way?'

'Roadworks at the back of Town,' Clarke said, picking up speed as he shot them along the short straight stretch towards the hill heading south through the trees.

'Frewin's on the pier,' Christine interrupted, taking some of the heat off Clarke. 'There's no sign of Dixon's car. The St Malo boat left half an hour ago. There's nothing now for a couple of hours.'

'Tell him to hold tight, and look out for Dixon on foot. He might have dumped his car. And call the airport.'

'Dispatch is on it, sir.'

Ollie picked up his bike and dragged it across to the pavement. He'd torn his jeans and gashed his knee, but nothing seemed to be broken. He had no time to look for his phone, so he hoisted himself rather stiffly back onto his bike and kicked away from the kerb. He cut through the traffic and followed the road south-west, past the visitor village at Oatlands, down through Friquet and on towards the airport.

Dixon stepped through the scanner and picked up his holdall the moment it appeared on the airside end of the x-ray machine.

'Have a nice flight, sir,' said the man in the blue rubber gloves who lifted it off the belt and passed it over.

Dixon smiled, but didn't respond, as a moment later he heard someone calling his name.

'Mr Dixon.' It was a woman's voice, coming from the door that led through from the booking hall. 'George Dixon.'

He couldn't yet see who was calling his name, so hauled his bag over the side of the conveyor and turned towards the departure lounge.

'Mr George Dixon.'

Dixon felt a hand on his shoulder, and turned to see the man from the x-ray machine.

'Mr Dixon?'

He hesitated, looking back towards the booking hall as the woman who'd checked him in jogged through the door, waving his hat above her head. The metal detector gave an angry bleep as she leaned through and passed it to him.

Ollie sped on through the southern parishes, turning through Forest until he arrived at the airport turn-off just twelve minutes after hoisting himself back into the saddle. He let the slight incline that led to the terminal building dampen his speed, then he dabbed at the brakes as he bumped the front wheel up onto the pavement and cruised through the open glass doors.

He came to a halt in the check-in hall, beneath a ceiling-strung model of JOEY.

A man in a fluorescent jacket came running over, waving his arms.

'Have it,' Ollie said. 'It's yours.'

He dismounted from his bike and held it out, pressing it into the startled man's hand; then he ran towards passport control.

Renouf leaned across and pushed on the horn. He let it sound for ten seconds. All around them, drivers wound down their windows and a handful leaned out and looked back to see who was making the fuss.

They were stuck at the last set of lights before the turn for the airport, and as Christine looked up through the sunroof, she saw a flight lift up from the runway and bank sharply right just above them. It angled itself towards Jersey.

At last the lights changed to green and the traffic started to move. The cars at the front raced off, while others turned left and right to clear the road.

Clarke thanked them by lifting his hand, then quickly snapped it back down to the wheel when he saw Renouf turn and stare.

'Just drive,' Renouf said. Pulling down the visor and eyeing Christine in the mirror, he asked why the planes were still flying.

'Dispatch is on it.'

'Call them back,' he said, as a second flight left the ground just before them. 'Make sure they know how important this is.'

Dixon passed over his boarding card and stepped out onto the apron. How many times had he done this now, shuttling forwards and back between The Fleet and more glamorous postings in London?

He thought for a moment. Too many and yet, at the same time, not enough. He'd never dreamed it would end like this, fleeing the island a single man, with barely a penny to call his own.

He looked at the plane as he walked towards

it. The fuel truck was backing away; the ground crew was stacking the last of the cases close to the front of the hold. He was the last of the passengers - the last to book and the last to board - and he thought that highly appropriate.

So long, godforsaken hellhole, he thought to himself. You won't be missed - not by me; not now, not ever.

He quickened his step and took the stairs in pairs, towards the steward who stood by the door, waiting for him to arrive.

'15B,' the steward said. 'Halfway along, on the right.' He handed back the boarding card and held out a hand, directing Dixon away from the door.

A stewardess walked towards him with papers draped over her forearm.

'The Sarnian, sir?' she asked, holding one towards him.

Dixon waved her away. 'I prefer the Press, thank you.'

'I'm sorry, sir.' The man at the desk leaned forward again and handed back the press pass. 'Passengers only beyond this point.'

Ollie took the card and slipped it into his pocket. 'This is an emergency,' he said, somewhat hopelessly, like a child in the playground asking for favours.

'In that case, sir, perhaps I should call security.'

The man reached towards a phone but made no attempt to pick it up. It wasn't the first time he'd had to deal with a difficult customer, crying wolf in the name of waving a friend goodbye, or passing over forgotten belongings.

'Perhaps you should,' Ollie said. He folded his arms and rested them on the high back of the desk, below which were hidden the phone and a screen.

'I have to warn you, sir, that it is a serious offence to –'

'Call them.'

The man raised his eyebrows. 'Right you are, sir.' He pointed to a row of plastic chairs. 'If you'd like to sit over there I'll see who I can find.'

He picked up the phone.

Clarke didn't slow down as he took the turning onto the airport estate, scraping the wheel along the kerb that divided the entrance and exit lanes. He took the car around the back of the bus stop and round again to the terminal doors, drawing up behind a scuffed convertible.

'That's Dixon's car,' Christine said.

'Call dispatch. Get Frewin here with whoever else can be spared,' Renouf said. He unbuckled his seatbelt and jumped out. Clarke did the same.

A man in a fluorescent jacket ran over.

'You can't leave that there,' he said, pointing in turn at the car and then Clarke and then back again at the car.

'Give him the keys,' Renouf shouted over his shoulder as he ran into the terminal. Christine scrambled out of the back and followed him into the building.

Clarke threw the keys at the yellow-jacketed man. 'Keep it safe,' he said, as he followed his colleagues through the open glass doors.

Ollie jumped up from his seat as he spotted Renouf, and then Christine, and shortly behind them a uniformed officer he didn't recognise.

He ran towards Christine. 'Dixon's gone through.'

'Did you see him?' Renouf asked.

'No, but –'

'Never mind,' Christine said, grabbing his hand. She dragged him back to the passport desk where the man on the phone was on hold, and holding up her pass, she took him straight through to baggage control.

'Bloody hell,' Renouf said. 'Clarke, stay here. There's a chance Dixon's still out here somewhere. Go upstairs and check the cafe.' He turned to the man at the desk. 'You. If you see a man called George Dixon, detain him.'

He ran through the door to the airside part of the building, where Christine and Ollie were standing on the opposite side of the metal detector, their arms outstretched as the guards patted them down.

Renouf held up his warrant card and stepped through to the join them, setting off the siren.

'I'm sorry, sir,' said the uniformed guard, looking up from the floor. He was patting Ollie's calves. 'You'll have to wait there.'

Renouf swore at the man, causing him to stand up, his full height barely bringing him up to Renouf's chest.

'I beg your pardon, sir.'

'Just do what you have to do and let me go through, will you,' Renouf said, stretching out his hands to either side.

'You two, wait there,' the officer said, stepping away from Ollie. 'I can't let you past those doors without airport security.'

He started to pat down Renouf, working his way along each arm and down his torso before sweeping his arms down both sides of each leg. A stout woman in a matching uniform came to join them, stepping out from behind a battered wooden door.

'Problem?' she asked, addressing the officer, who once again was back on his haunches, his hands working over Renouf's ankles.

'Anne,' Renouf said, recognising her from an island security meeting. 'Tell him, would you.'

'Marc.' She acknowledged, giving him a curt, businesslike smile.

'George Dixon...' – he pointed towards the apron – 'is on that plane.' He could hear the engines starting to roar as the pilot tested each one. 'If I don't stop it, he'll be back on the mainland before we've managed to question him.'

'Mmm-hmm,' she said, pursing her lips and nodding. 'And what would you need to question him about.'

'The murders of Rosalynd Holdbrook and Richelle Ibbott,' Christine said, stepping forward and offering her hand. 'I apologise for Mr Renouf. It's been a somewhat trying case, as you'd imagine.'

Renouf scowled, but Anne seemed more impressed by Christine.

'I see,' she said. Looking down at the officer on the floor, she asked, 'Any reason why he can't go through?'

'No, ma'am,' he replied, standing up and brushing his knees with his blue rubber gloves.

'Okay, then,' Anne began, but Renouf was already off.

He pushed his way through the waiting crowds to the open gate and the walkway along the apron.

*

The pilot was testing his systems, tilting the ailerons up and down, turning the seatbelt and no smoking signs on, revving the props and then letting them calm.

Dixon had settled into his seat. He'd loosened his laces and kicked off his shoes and clipped together his seatbelt. He dug out the Press from his holdall – the last edition he'd ever read – and quickly skimmed the front page. It looked to him like a filler: a not-so-much story about some wreckage found in the sea off Sark – a bell and some wood from a tug or a yacht.

He licked a finger and turned the page, and as he did so he looked out of the window. Oliver Carey was crossing the concrete runway, jogging behind two uniformed officers, one with a shock of red hair. Le P... Le P... he still couldn't remember her damned name. And before her... yes, he knew him. He'd seen him plenty of times on the news. Inspector Marc Renouf.

Dixon smiled, and slid himself down in his seat. He angled the paper towards the window, shielding himself from the outside world as the aircrew started their safety talk.

'That's a negative, Oscar niner four seven,' said the disembodied voice from the control tower. 'I have instructions to hold you at the stand.

Please power down and release your door. Over.'

The pilot of the Southampton flight cursed and turned to her first officer. 'What the hell now?' she asked.

A look of frustration came over her deputy's face. This was to be his first flight in control, and the morning had already felt like a long, unending drag. A further delay only prolonged the agony.

'You heard him,' the pilot told him. 'Power it down.'

She picked up the mic and confirmed the tower's instruction, then switched the circuit to speak to the cabin.

'I'm sorry, ladies and gentlemen. Seems we're going to be stuck here a little while longer. We're trying to ascertain what the delay might be and we'll let you know as soon as we hear. Chief purser, please report to the cockpit. Crew, release the doors.'

Back in the tower, the duty manager switched frequencies. 'Blue Islands, you are cleared to proceed to runway zero-niner. Wind is a steady four knots. Happy flying. Over.'

'Roger, tower. Zero-niner, pushing away,' the pilot acknowledged. 'Over and out.'

Renouf gathered round him the four available ground crew and set them about retrieving the aircraft steps. He caught up with Christine and Ollie just as the air stairs arrived, cresting the cab of a service truck.

The vehicle gave out a doleful beep, steady and solemn as it crept towards the aircraft. The driver looked up at the plane as Renouf ran around to the back of the truck and jumped on the still moving staircase.

'Le Page,' he shouted. 'Get over here.'

Christine ran towards him, turning briefly to see if Ollie was following. She'd dragged him through security, and though she knew he would want to be there - even if she hadn't - she also knew she'd feel responsible if anything were to happen to him. He might not have been there at all if her meddling with Amy Sloane hadn't got him suspended.

Renouf ran up to the top of the steps, arriving as the driver stood down on the brake. The staircase rocked back and forth for a second, and Renouf clung onto the handrail. As soon as it steadied he took the last step and banged the flat of his outstretched palm on the skin of the aircraft body.

A woman's face appeared at the small oval window, and a moment later he heard the clunk of the bolts receding into the door. One further turn and in it swung, revealing the galley beyond it.

'Police,' Renouf said, holding up his badge. 'She's with me.' He pointed at Christine, then turned his finger in Ollie's direction. 'He has no jurisdiction on this aircraft.'

He pushed past the stewardess with Christine close behind, but when Ollie made to follow them the stewardess stepped in front of him and folded her burly arms.

'I don't think so, sir,' she said.

Ollie pulled out his card, but she shook her head without reading it.

Christine and Renouf walked in reverse along the short central aisle of the craft, turning their heads as they passed each new row to look at the passengers' faces. Children and women, Renouf ignored. Anyone reading a book, he tapped on the shoulder to make them look up. Wherever a newspaper blocked someone's face, he pushed it down at the fold until he could see them clearly.

A member of aircrew came up behind him. 'Might I help you, sir, before we upset all the passengers?' His tone was mildly acerbic, and the look on his face suggested to Renouf that he considered him to be acting beyond his authority.

'And you are?'

'I'm the chief purser, sir,' the man replied, nodding down at his badge.

‘Malcolm,’ Christine said, leaning around Renouf to read the purser’s name. She put her hand on his shoulder and smiled. ‘Could you make an announcement? I’m sure these people would like to be on their way, and it really would be very helpful.’

The purser looked up at close to a hundred faces; most were unhappy, some looked scared. The rest were clearly bored. ‘I’ll need authority from the pilot.’

Renouf shook his head. ‘Sod this,’ he said, at last deciding he’d had enough of the courteous airside hierarchy. He turned around and addressed the rear of the craft. ‘My name is Inspector Marc Renouf of the States of Guernsey Police Force. This is Christine Le Page from our sister force on Jersey. We are looking for a passenger called George Dixon. Locals may know him from the radio. Visitors, you may not. You’re not missing a great deal.’

Christine raised her eyes, giving the purser a weak smile that she hoped he’d read as an apology.

‘Now I understand that most of you will be travelling in family groups, so you may think that this does not apply to you,’ Renouf continued. ‘However, we suspect that George Dixon will be travelling solo and I would therefore ask, if there is anyone in your row who you do not know – any man in his mid- to late-fifties – would you raise your hand. The sooner we are able to speak to Mr Dixon, the sooner you can be on your way.'

Four people raised their hands between where he stood and the back of the aircraft. Renouf could see without moving that Dixon wasn't in any of their rows.

He turned around and pushed his way past the purser, walking as far as the front of the plane and checking the men in each of the rows where someone had raised their hand. The final tally was twelve solo passengers, none of which was George Dixon.

Dixon put down the Press and slid the in-flight magazine out of the seat-back pocket. He turned to the back and checked the flight times to Alderney. Fifteen minutes. He looked at his watch. That would give him forty minutes to cross the island and rendezvous with the small boat to Dielette. From there he would strike out south-east and find himself a quiet bolt-hole in the Alps or the Pyrenees. He hadn't yet planned that far ahead.

He could feel the airframe tugging as the pilot ramped up the engines, and a moment later released the brakes and sent them bouncing along the runway. Past the parked-up aircraft, past the terminal, past the gold centre, and up into the cloudless sky. The force of the short, sharp take-off pushed him back into his seat. He leaned forward to take one last look at the island on which he'd once expected to live out his days, and as the tiny aircraft banked around the terminal building, he caught sight of two figures running out of a grounded flight to join a third on the mobile steps that led to the door in its tail.

They shielded their eyes to look up at his aircraft, and though he knew they couldn't possibly see him, Dixon couldn't help himself - he gave them a friendly wave.

Renouf ran back into the Southampton plane, and pushed past the purser, knocking the man into one of the rows of seats. He marched to the cockpit door, and finding no handle he banged on its surface and told a steward to open it.

'I can't, sir. It can only be opened from inside the flight deck,' the steward said, before adding - with a degree of sarcasm - 'security, sir.' He nodded down at the crest on Renouf's jacket pocket.

'Open up,' Renouf shouted, banging the door five times.

The purser recovered himself, and joining Renouf at the front of the craft, he picked up a phone set into the wall and pressed an orange button.

'It's the police,' he said. He paused while the pilot replied. 'Yes, he showed it at the door. We've not seen any ID from his companion, though.' He raised his eyebrows towards Christine who was standing once more in the aisle.

She dug a hand into a pocket and pulled out her fob, flipping it open to show her badge.

'Jersey,' the purser said into the phone.

Another pause, and then he put down the handset. A moment later the door unlatched, and the pilot pulled it open. The flight deck was cramped, and far too small for Renouf to enter with the aircrew already in place. He leaned through, steadying himself with one hand above him, pressing hard on the cockpit ceiling as he turned towards the first officer, assuming that he must be in charge on account of his gender. 'Get onto the tower. Get them to call up the passenger lists. I want to know if anyone called George Dixon is on that plane,' he said, pointing through the cockpit window at the rapidly diminishing flight turning north towards Alderney.

The first officer looked at the pilot.

The pilot looked at Renouf.

'On board this aircraft,' she said, 'you will address me. You will make requests through me, and you will remember your manners.'

Renouf turned and stared, tightening his jaw, keeping his eyes fixed on her the way he used to stare at Falla. But things were different here.

Who was this woman who didn't react? She looked at him, her eyes calm, her lips pressed together but certainly far from pursed, her brow soft and unlined; she seemed not to care that he was towering over her. She seemed to believe her badge outranked his.

'Oscar niner four seven,' said a small tinny voice. 'This is tower. Report, over.'

The first officer looked from his pilot towards Renouf and then back.

'Oscar niner four seven,' the voice repeated. 'Report your status, over.'

'Do we have an understanding, sir?' she asked.

Renouf relaxed his jaw. He sighed. 'I would be grateful if you would request from the tower any information they may have on a passenger called George Dixon who may be on that flight.' He nodded once more towards the small craft, before adding 'please' to his request.

'Do we have an understanding?' the pilot repeated.

Renouf paused, aware that Christine was close enough to have heard their whole conversation. He looked through the cockpit window. The

Alderney flight was turning again, correcting its course in advance of its short level cruise. It would start its descent in less than five minutes.

'We have an understanding,' Renouf said, nodding.

She released his gaze and turned towards her co-pilot, nodding almost imperceptibly.

The first officer touched a button and spoke into his microphone. 'Tower, this is oscar niner four seven. Request from States Police for details of a passenger on the Alderney flight, name of George Dixon, over.'

The tower confirmed the request, and then the controller put in the call. Renouf relaxed his grip, swinging back out to the passenger cabin and watching a clock in the cockpit slowly tick through the seconds. They seemed to pass far too slowly, the hand stumbling briefly before it crested each mark on the face. Christine sat down in an empty seat, lifting the armrest and swinging her legs across the aisle. Ollie felt in his pockets, hunting for his phone, until he caught his finger in a hole in the hip of his jeans. Then he remembered the crash. He remembered the sound of his phone as it skittered across the road, and he felt his heart surge for a moment. Freya would not be happy if he returned to the office without any pictures.

At last the answer came back. The tiny voice

leaked out once more from the padded foam headsets worn by the flight deck crew.

Dixon indeed had left the island and now, as Renouf had suspected, was well on his way to runway 14/32, the longer of Alderney's two grass strips while the asphalt one was closed for repairs.

'Roger, tower,' the first officer acknowledged. 'Message received and –'

Renouf leaned close to the officer's face – so close their cheeks were touching. 'Turn it around, and get that plane back on the ground,' he shouted, his voice carrying through the officer's mic. He'd got the answer he needed. He had no need for niceties now. 'Get it back here, and get it back now.'

The Sarnian, 8pm

Kira Spooner was not arrested, but it is understood she is helping the police with their enquiries. The BBC has tonight confirmed that she has been suspended on full pay, pending an internal inquiry into unauthorised payments made to contracted performers working for The Fleet. The Corporation has not yet confirmed whether the performer or performers in question include George Dixon.

Dixon was arrested upon his return to Guernsey Airport, after the Trislander flight he had boarded to

Alderney, from where it is understood he planned to travel on to mainland Europe, was instructed to turn around. He was attended by the Duty Advocate who declined to offer any comment on his client's behalf.

Ollie leaned back in his seat – his old, familiar, battered seat at The Sarnian – and cracked his knuckles as he read back his copy. It had now reached a little over four thousand words, broken down into sections to fill the first twelve pages of the next day's special edition.

He'd been gone for less than a day, but it still felt good to be back. His suspension had been abruptly cut short when Freya Carlisle had received a call from Amy Sloane asking what comment she'd like to make on Ollie's heroic contribution.

'To what?' Freya had asked.

'You don't know?'

'To. What?' Freya had asked again, clearly accentuating each word.

'Ah, but of course,' Amy had taunted 'Our dear Mr Carey is persona non grata. The Sarnian's very own Victor Hugo.'

'What is it you want, Miss Sloane? Money? Is that it? Is this your twisted way of chasing a commission?'

Amy laughed unconvincingly. 'A commission? From a dirty little rag like yours? No, my dear.

Sweet of you to suggest it, but no. All I want is a quote. Tell me, with Mr Carey playing so crucial a role in the apprehension, whether he'll be returning to the paper.'

'Enough of the riddles, Amy,' Freya said, trying hard to keep herself calm. 'Who's been apprehended?'

'You don't know?'

'Who?'

'Well, our killer. George Dixon.'

Freya threw down the phone and got up from her desk. 'Ella,' she called, before she'd even got to the door.

Ella looked up as Freya stepped out of the hive.

'Where's Carey?' she asked.

Ella looked down at the clock on her phone. 'Last I knew he was heading for the airport.'

Freya nodded. 'Get him back here now.'

It didn't occur to Freya Carlisle to ask how Amy had heard so quickly about George Dixon's arrest. She'd learned long ago that such a request always went unanswered, and so it was that only three people knew how the story had leaked: Amy herself, Christine Le Page, and Oliver Carey, who'd been sitting beside Christine in the airport terminal as she'd called through to Amy's office.

'Are you a gambling man?' she'd asked him.

'That rather depends on the odds.'

'How would you feel about a small wager,' she said. 'Ten pounds says you're back in gainful employment before the end of the day.'

They shook on it. Ollie was sure he would lose the bet, but was happy to pay her the stake in exchange for his job.

Speaking at a hastily convened briefing less than two hours after Dixon's arrest, Inspector Marc Renouf, who led the operation at Guernsey Airport that saw the suspect brought into custody, revealed that Dixon has been charged with two counts of pre-meditated murder – those of Richelle Ibbott, his partner, and Rosalynd Holdbrook, a retired producer who originally brought Dixon to the island to take a lead role in the BBC's ongoing radio drama, The Fleet.

He thanked Constables Clarke and Falla, the latter of whom regained consciousness in the Princess Elizabeth hospital shortly after the operation concluded, and acknowledged the role played by Christine Le Page of the Jersey Police Force, currently on secondment to Guernsey. Chief Constable Miles Bichard later announced that Le Page's posting to the force had been extended, at least until the case against Dixon has progressed through the courts. He was unable to give any indication how long this would take.

Ollie sensed that someone else had entered the

empty office, and turning around he found Ella Brouard reading the story over his shoulder.

'Didn't your mother tell you that was rude?' he asked.

Ella smiled. 'I can wait 'til it's printed, if you prefer.'

Ollie rolled out the seat beside him and patted the cushion. 'You know,' he said as she sat down. 'I never did get a chance to say thank you.'

'No,' she said, tracing her scarlet-tipped nail back and forth across his knee. 'That's not all, either.'

Ollie cocked his head and thought. He tried to recall their last conversation.

'Something about "when this is all over..."', Ella reminded him.

'Aah, yes.' He reached out and took her hand, in part because it was clear she wouldn't object, but just as much because she was starting to tickle him. He turned around and clicked Save, then closed the file on his screen. 'I guess that's finished.'

'And...'

'And...' Now that his access had been reinstated, he'd planned to spend the evening trawling the archive, digging up whatever he could on the boat that was wrecked on the cliffs around Sark. She squeezed his hand. It was just enough to convince him that the archives could wait. 'Do you have plans for dinner?' he asked.

'Yes,' she said, and she pecked him on the cheek. 'Where are we going?'

He watched as she walked across the office, the automatic lights turning on as she passed each sensor, and once she had disappeared around the corner he sent a quick text to Simon, warning him not to come to Portelet Harbour that night.

Portelet Harbour, 9.30pm

Christine Le Page stepped out from the trees at the back of the bay. She was just in front of the Lighthouse Keepers' Cottages, hidden by the small granite shed in which Remus Carey had stored his belongings.

She lifted the binoculars and looked across the beach; the view before her was clear, well lit by the generous moon. There seemed to be no one around. The beach was deserted, the kiosk was closed and only a handful of cars sat in the spaces outside the hotel. She focused on the boat for a while, watching something moving on deck. It was too small to be a person, unless they were laying and stretching their arms, but that would be... aah... it was a cat. She assumed it must have been Sampson.

Sure, at last, that she wouldn't be seen, she

dropped the glasses into her backpack, slipped her arm through the second strap and ran down the slipway and onto the beach.

The tide was starting to turn. Soon it would cover the sand and the rocks, and the only way she could reach the boat would be along the top of the harbour wall. That would be more comfortable than running across the wet sand – less messy, too – but the chances of being seen were much higher, and that was something she had to avoid at all costs.

She reached the boat in less than a minute and climbed up onto the deck. She rattled the wheelhouse door: it was locked. The windows were bolted from inside.

Carey, like his father, took his security seriously, and after a week of reading his notes, she'd expected nothing less. She'd come prepared.

She dipped back into her rucksack and took out a large evidence bag, complete with a zip-lock seal. It was just large enough for the thick wedge of pages she'd spent the last three hours redacting.

She slipped them inside and sealed the top, then weighing them down with a tin of varnish, she left them on the deck.

Portelet Harbour, 11.45pm

'It's fine,' Ollie said, leading Ella past the kiosk and on down the slipway as far as the beach. 'We'll sleep on the boat.'

The moon was high, and so was the tide. It wasn't long before midnight. Both had eaten and drunk too much for a pair of hacks rostered onto the early shift.

He bent down and picked her up, and carried her over the sand as far as the harbour wall. She laughed as she pictured him lifting her into the marital home.

She let her head fall backwards, and it felt as if the whole of her body was pouring out of her crown. The rushing sensation made her giggle, and as the stars danced above them, the giggle became a laugh until she was wriggling out of his arms, and Ollie had to lay her down for fear he was going to drop her.

He lay down beside her and they looked up together towards the stars, holding hands.

'I'm afraid it's single bunks,' he said.

She rolled herself over onto her elbow and kissed him with sandy lips.

'All the more cosy,' she said, and pushing herself onto her feet, she asked for permission to come aboard.

Ollie saluted. 'Permission granted.'

He followed her onto the harbour wall and helped her over the deck rail.

And then he caught sight of the folder, safely zipped up in the plastic wallet, the surface of which flashed amber and black, amber and black as the tilt of the boat caught the lights of Fort Grey.

He picked it up and reached for the lantern beside the wheelhouse door, and switching it on he read the unsigned note that Christine had slipped inside.

You might find this interesting. You might find it helpful. Whatever you do, don't try to find me. I'll give you more when I can, but this is all for now.

He slid the plastic zip to the end of the wallet and pulled out the scarlet folder. It was stuffed well beyond its capacity, and one of the seams was starting to tear. He opened the flap and his eye fell on three short words, the only ones on the whole of the page that hadn't been redacted: 'Remus', 'Carey' and 'Sark'.

'Are we going to find those bunks?' Ella asked, tugging her cardigan and wrapping it tighter around her.

'Sorry,' Ollie said, taking out his keys and unlocking the wheelhouse door. 'You go down. I'll be there in a moment.'

She stumbled down the steps, tripping on

the last two and letting herself fall towards the bottom bunk. She landed on its overstuffed mattress and fell asleep moments later.

Ollie sat down on the deck, the lantern before him, and started to leaf through the pages, stopping to read the ones that contained the most words, tracing maps with his fingers, and wondering over the missing words in the censored witness statements.

He turned the last page five hours later, lit by the first sun of dawn as it rose above the headland at Pleinmont. He knew, at last, what had led to his father's disappearance. It wasn't much more than a starting point - but a point, at least, from which to renew his search.

The Sarnian, Book 1
DEAD IN THE WATER

The author greatly appreciates you taking the time to read this work. Please consider leaving a review wherever you bought the book, or telling your friends or blog readers about The Sarnian.

Published by Ovingo Limited.

www.thesarnian.com

THE SARNIAN 2: Blowfish

Want to know what happened to Remus Carey? Find out in Blowfish, the second volume of the expanding Sarnian series.

Two years after his disappearance, agents at Interpol's global headquarters intercept a message bearing Remus Carey's codename. Christine Le Page is dispatched to find out whether he survived the events that led to his disappearance, and heads off on a race across Europe... at precisely the moment she's most needed at home.

For while Christine's past actions look set to put her in jeopardy, someone elsewhere on Guernsey is faced with the repercussions of a far more grievous transgression.

A fearsome storm has cracked open St Peter Port harbour, and exposed within its breakwater a body dressed in a Nazi uniform. While Ollie fights to be first to report who the body belonged to and how he died...

...the person who put it there is determined to do everything possible to make sure the story is never told.

Check out The Sarnian 2: Blowfish in your favourite online bookstore today!

Printed in Great Britain
by Amazon

58507595R00362